A CRUCIAL TASK . . .

The Red Prince met the cold eyes of Seif. "And you, my friend, have what is perhaps the most crucial task of all: the elimination of one man."

"That is all?" the killer asked flatly, rotating a shiny quarter from one massive hand to the other. "Who is it?"

"Alabaster."

Seif showed emotion for the first time. His round, bald head seemed to expand and swell. "That will not be easy. He hasn't been heard from in two years. He might be dead."

"I doubt it. What's the matter, my friend. Have you finally met your match in Alabaster?"

Seif smiled demonically. Deliberately, he brought the quarter he had been twirling up to eye level, placing it between both thumbs and index fingers. Without flinching, he began to twist it. The metal started to give, and in a few seconds, the quarter had been folded perfectly in half. His expression had not changed one bit throughout, the task apparently effortless.

"I did not mean to challenge your abilities," said the Red Prince.

THE SURVIVALIST SERIES
by Jerry Ahern

#1: TOTAL WAR   (960, $2.50)

The first in the shocking series that follows the unrelenting search for ex-CIA covert operations officer John Thomas Rourke to locate his missing famly—after the button is pressed, the missiles launched and the multimegaton bombs unleashed . . .

#2: THE NIGHTMARE BEGINS   (810, $2.50)

After WW III, the United States is just a memory. But ex-CIA covert operations officer Rourke hasn't forgotten his family. While hiding from the Soviet occupation forces, he adheres to his search!

#3: THE QUEST   (851, $2.50)

Not even a deadly game of intrigue within the Soviet High Command, the formation of the American "resistance" and a highly placed traitor in the new U.S. government can deter Rourke from continuing his desperate search for his family.

#4: THE DOOMSAYER   (893, $2.50)

The most massive earthquake in history is only hours away, and Communist-Cuban troops, Soviet-Cuban rivalry, and a traitor in the inner circle of U.S. II block Rourke's path. But he must go on—he is THE SURVIVALIST.

#5: THE WEB   (1145, $2.50)

Blizzards rage around Rourke as he picks up the trail of his family and is forced to take shelter in a strangely quiet Tennessee valley town. Things seem too normal here, as if no one has heard of the War; but the quiet isn't going to last for long!

Available wherever paperbacks are sold, or order direct from the Publisher. Send cover price plus 50¢ per copy for mailing and handling to Zebra Books, 475 Park Avenue South, New York, N.Y. 10016. DO NOT SEND CASH.

THE DOOMSDAY SPIRAL

JON LAND

ZEBRA BOOKS
KENSINGTON PUBLISHING CORP.

ZEBRA BOOKS

are published by

KENSINGTON PUBLISHING CORP.
475 Park Avenue South
New York, N.Y. 10016

Printed in the United States of America

For my grandparents, who always believed in me,
and
For Sensei, who taught me how to believe in myself

Special thanks to Dr. Morton Korn for his endless patience and knowledge

PROLOGUE

NEW YORK TIMES
TUESDAY, JANUARY 23, 1979

Reputed Planner of Munich Raid
Killed In Beirut

_____

BEIRUT, Jan. 22—The Palestinian guerilla leader who reputedly planned the attack on the Israeli Olympic team in Munich in 1972 was fatally wounded here today in the explosion of a remote control bomb.

Four bodyguards and five passers-by also died in the blast and several passers-by were wounded.

Wafa, the Palestinian news agency, blamed Israeli intelligence for the death of the security chief of the Al Fatah guerilla group, 38-year-old Ali Hassan Salameh, better known as Abu Hassan. The agency reported that the explosion was detonated by remote control. It said that a booby-trapped car parked a few yards from Abu Hassan's home was set off as he drove by.

High on Israeli Hit List

Abu Hassan headed Israel's list of most-wanted guerillas. The Israelis have said that, as head of the Black September guerilla group, he organized the operation resulting in the deaths of 11 members of the Israeli Olympic team in Munich. . . .

Vowing vengeance, Al Fatah said in a statement: "The murderers will not escape."

NEW YORK TIMES
WEDNESDAY, JANUARY 24, 1979

Israeli Officials Silent On Death of Guerilla But People Applaud

———————————————————

TEL AVIV, Jan 23—Newspaper and radio commentators here today applauded the assassination yesterday in Beirut of Ali Hassan Salameh, who under the name of Abu Hassan had been described as the planner of the massacre in 1972 of 11 members of the Israeli Olympic team in Munich.

Officials in Jerusalem refused to discuss Arab charges that yesterday's killing had been carried out by Israel. . . .

Mr. Salameh was said to have known that he was high on Israel's hit list of most-wanted guerillas; he reportedly changed homes, cars, and bodyguards constantly.

In the years after the Munich Olympics, several Palestinian guerillas in Europe, including some who were said to have been involved in the attack, were tracked down and killed. In some cases, they were killed by bombs set off by remote control—the same method by which Mr. Salameh was killed in Beirut. Israel has never taken the responsibility for any of the deaths.

PART ONE

ONE
Cairo, 1982

"Áhlan wi sáhlan! . . . Áhlan wi sáhlan!"

The tall man moved steadily through the Cairo Bazaar in the center of the still ancient part of the city. His pace was seasoned and sure, each step purposeful. The paved dirt that formed the street beneath him had been baked by the mid-afternoon Egyptian sun, so that it was dry and brittle and seemed to crack under his determined strut. His brow was soaked with sweat but he dared not wipe it, because he knew that the dark brown skin coloring might come off with the moisture that bonded it to his flesh.

Instead, his hands remained coiled by their sides, swaying to-and-fro in rhythm with his pace. Dressed in white tunic and cap, the tall man melded perfectly with those around him in the crowded square, lined on both sides with outdoor shops, the voices of their smiling proprietors booming boisterously above the rest of the unrestrained hubbub.

"Authentic Egyptian wares! Bargains today! . . . Bargains today!"

The words were repeated in four languages for the benefit of tourists. Other points were made in quieter fashion, sales soon to follow. Few left the square empty-handed.

But the tall man was interested in a different kind of merchandise. Fourteen children had been murdered. He was here to learn where the terrorist responsible could be found . . . one way or another.

The tall man picked up a churning sound to his rear, mixing with a slight but regular squeak. An alarm went off in his head. His defenses readied instinctively for attack. But the alarm was

11

false, the attack nonexistent. A boy passed harmlessly by on a bicycle, peddling barefoot, balancing a tray of rounded bread loaves on his head.

The man cringed. An empty feeling formed in the pit of his stomach. He had been only a few seconds and steps away from killing the boy. There had been a second of indecision, of doubt. His mind had been wandering, his thoughts on the past instead of the present.

How many streets like this had he walked down? How many countries had he entered under one name and departed under another? How many men had he killed?

The questions bothered the tall man, not because they lacked answers so much as he had raised them in the first place. After two years, he had hoped things would have returned to the way they once were. They hadn't. His eyes still saw two sides of a problem which could have only one. The icy coldness remained a state of mind instead of being. He would have to push for it now, push hard.

It was actually a long chain of events which led to the man leaving the Game twenty-six months before. But in looking back he remembered only one incident.

A bomb had gone off in a kibbutz, killing three and injuring a dozen. The man had followed the trail of the PLO culprit to a flophouse in Jerusalem. He kicked down a door, pistol in hand, and burst into a sixth floor room that stank of urine. In a corner chair sat a boy no more than fourteen, his face dimly illuminated by light spilling in the window.

"I've been waiting for you, Alabaster," the boy said.

The tall man studied the dark Arab features and black curls that swam across the young forehead. He raised the gun but could not fire it.

"What are you waiting for?" the boy asked.

Alabaster could not answer. Something in him was breaking. Or perhaps it had already broken. The pistol felt heavy and uncomfortable in his hand.

"Don't bother trying to interrogate me, I won't answer any

of your questions," the boy continued staunchly. "You can torture me all you want but I won't talk. *I won't talk!*"

"I didn't come here to ask questions."

"Of course not. The great Alabaster, the great hunter never has any questions to ask. He merely comes for the kill." The boy rose, pointing to the center of his sweat-soaked shirt. "Well, I'm ready to die. Go ahead, fire your gun. Gain your Jewish vengeance. Right here, in the heart." The boy was trembling now. "My life doesn't matter. You can't kill all of us. There will be more bombs. More of your people will die." Alabaster remained motionless. The boy again pointed at the center of his shirt. His trembling had increased. "Go ahead. Why waste any more of your precious time?"

"I won't kill you," the Israeli said. He lowered his Browning automatic pistol. "Get out of here. Go back to your people."

"No."

"I'm giving you your life. Get out of here before I change my mind."

"I want you to change it. I want you to kill me here and now."

Alabaster studied the youth before him. A boy turned into a monster by the world he had helped create. "You have not lived long enough to become a martyr."

"I was born a martyr, as all my people are thanks to yours." A pause. "I'll make you kill me! I'll make you!"

He lunged forward, waiting for the pistol to explode before him. It never did. Instead, Alabaster sidestepped his charge and tripped the boy up, sending him reeling face first onto the floor. He rose sobbing and rushed again. This time Alabaster twisted his shoulders and stepped into the center of the charge, using the boy's own momentum to send him into a headlong dive. The boy rose to his knees in an absurd position of prayer. He was breathing hard, shaking violently.

"Now get out of here," Alabaster said softly. "Go home."

"*No!*"

With an anguished scream, the boy rose to his feet and ran

for the window. Alabaster leaped to stop him but was too late. Glass exploded. There was one long hideous wail that stretched into oblivion as flesh and bone collided with concrete. Blood ran and pooled on the sidewalk.

Alabaster felt sick. The questioning had begun and continued for much of the past two years.

What the hell did it matter anyway?

Kill one and another took his place. The circle swirls unbroken, closing in. It was all pointless and futile. So Alabaster had left the Game, for good he thought, until he realized it was too much a part of him. He could turn his back on it but somehow the urge to twist his shoulders and glance behind him would always be there. He had stopped hating yet he had never stopped caring. That was the problem.

So when a terrorist bomb had blown up a school bus in Tel Aviv killing fourteen children, Alabaster decided it was time to return. He had learned from an informant in Beirut that Arab terrorist Abad Salim was the proprietor. And he had come to Cairo to find out Salim's hiding place from a second informant named Marabi. His sources told him Marabi could be trusted as much as any pigeon which still meant he could not be trusted at all.

Up ahead in the crowded square, Alabaster saw the rendezvous point. His sharp, unfeeling eyes scanned the area as he veered to his right in the direction of an alley. Licking the salt from his lips, he passed slowly into the shadows, at once missing the bright welcome sun above him.

His eyes quickly adjusted to the half-darkness, making out an Egyptian in a white suit and black turban wearing sunglasses before him. On either side of the Egyptian stood a man in an outdated brown leisure suit and white turban, the one on the right being significantly taller and broader than his counterpart. Alabaster did not recall their presence being mentioned as part of the bargain.

"You are Alabaster," said the Egyptian, removing his sunglasses and scrutinizing the man before him.

14

The Israeli had narrowed the gap between them to less than a yard. "And you are Marabi?"

"At your service." The Egyptian forced a slight bow. It was easy to hate Marabi which was good because Alabaster needed to hate now more than ever.

"It would seem so, considering how easy it was for me to set up this meeting."

The Egyptian allowed himself a bright smile. "I am told that when Alabaster wants something, making yourself scarce only delays the issue."

"My reputation precedes me."

"Indeed, as does your code name, which I assume it is. I'm interested in its origins. Did you choose 'Alabaster'?"

"For now, Marabi, the questions are mine. Where is Abad Salim?"

"Salim, Salim . . . Am I supposed to know this man?"

"Since he is a leading figure in Black September and you were once one of that organization's top operatives, I should hope so."

Marabi shrugged. "That was long ago, Alabaster. I have lost all contact with my former associates."

"Oh? Then you haven't been in Lebanon lately?"

"No."

"How strange. You were seen leaving a hotel there not three days ago with a number of your 'former associates'."

"I haven't been in Beirut in nearly a year."

"Who said the hotel was in Beirut?"

The Egyptian's dark skin whitened a bit. "All the same I cannot help you find this Salim. I don't even know what he looks like. It was so long ago. His name strikes only a vague chord in my memory." Marabi placed his sunglasses in his breast pocket. His English was virtually flawless and only slightly accented.

"Then let me refresh it," Alabaster said sharply. "In 1970, Yassir Arafat created what became known as the Special Operations Apparatus, *Jihaz al-Amaliyat al-Khassa:* Black

15

September, Marabi, also known as Al Fatah. The charge of the Apparatus was to undertake terrorist actions across the globe to gain attention for the cause of the PLO at the same time the PLO fought to gain credibility as a legitimate nation. Arafat's plan, simply stated, was to fuse two objectives into one and maintain the best of both worlds. Abad Salim became one of the original leaders of the Black September world, though I understand he has fallen out of favor recently." Alabaster's eyes moved from Marabi to his bodyguards. Their action would have to come soon.

"In the circles I travel in, Alabaster, you have always been known as somewhat of a legend," Marabi said coolly. "A bounty hunter who accepts no bounty. A master of disguise. A man whose true identity is not known even in the highest levels of the Mossad itself. A vigilante. . . . I have heard much rejoicing from my former associates since your sudden disappearance two years ago. These have been pleasant times for them indeed without you lurking around in the shadows."

"I'm sorry to spoil their fun."

"They always knew you'd come back. But I'm afraid you've picked the wrong time. Your trail has gone cold. I have heard of Abad Salim but don't recall ever meeting him. I have no idea where he is today."

"A week ago he was in Tel Aviv killing fourteen children and crippling twenty more."

"Ah yes, the bombing. Believe it or not, I was quite disgusted with that myself." Marabi tried to sigh and failed. "Believe me, if I knew anything I would tell you."

"Your intentions are meaningless to me. I want information."

"I can't provide it."

"You had better try."

"Toward what end?"

Alabaster nodded slowly, the traces of a smile flickering across his lips. "A rumor is circulating in Israel that you are and always have been a Mossad spy. Your 'former associates'

16

might not take kindly to you if that rumor were to, by chance, reach them. Cooperate with me and I'll make sure it's suppressed."

"And I am supposed to trust you?"

"You don't have a choice."

"Hah!" Marabi glanced at the bodyguards on either side of him. They stood silent and still, not seeming to blink. "You're speaking fairy tales, Alabaster. Nothing but fairy tales."

"People die in fairy tales, Marabi, often quite violently. Almost as violently as those children did in Tel Aviv. They cry out from their graves, begging for retribution against the man responsible for their murders. I hear those cries, Marabi. I hear them so clearly, I can't sleep. That is why I have returned. But you are going to help me rest easier. You are going to tell me where I can find Abad Salim."

"And what do you offer in return?"

"Your life."

The Egyptian's eyes flared with rage. He stepped back, swallowed by the frames of his bodyguards. "And how many other Palestinian lives have you taken? How many of those remote control devices have you planted? You want to wipe us out single-handedly, is that it? But you made one grave mistake when you dared assassinate the beloved Abu Hassan. That turned the fear we felt for you to hate. A price was put on your head, a hefty price. So you ran and hid but you finally came back as we always knew you would. It will give me great pleasure to claim the blood money, though the satisfaction of killing you will be payment in itself. Enjoy your last breath, Jew!"

The words were meant to distract Alabaster, to draw his eyes into a vengeful visual embrace with Marabi's so that when the Egyptian's bodyguards made their move, there would be no quick reaction to counter it.

But there was.

As the smaller man on the left drew his gun, Alabaster hurdled over the diving form of Marabi. In a blur, he had spun

17

quickly to his left, planting his right foot as a pivot point. The back of his right fist then shot out at the man holding the gun, crashing into the bridge of his nose and shattering bones upon impact. Blood poured in a steady stream from both nostrils. The gun fell from the man's hand as he brought his fingers up in a futile effort of comfort for his shattered face.

Almost simultaneously, Alabaster's left elbow had found its way into the larger man's solar plexus. But the blow was not so strong as it might have been and the large, well-muscled man merely recoiled backwards without doubling over. When the Israeli approached again, he saw a long shiny blade in his opponent's hand, glinting in the faint light of the alley. The man smiled, obviously confident of his prowess with the weapon. But Alabaster didn't notice the smile because he knew that looking at any one part of the body was an invitation to be tricked by false motion. He saw all of the man while seeing none of him.

So when the long blade shot out toward his stomach in a glistening blur, Alabaster was able to turn quickly and deflect the strike, grabbing the man's hand as it passed by. Reflexively, he then jerked the wrist in the opposite direction, pushing down with his right hand while twisting with his left. The large bodyguard was suddenly airborne, separated from the handle, crashing into the hard surface some five feet away. He tried to stagger back to his feet but Alabaster was quickly upon him with a vicious kick to the temple. The man slumped backwards with a gasp, eyes closing.

By this time, the smaller bodyguard, his sight clouded over by a painful mist, had begun to grope for the steel of the revolver on the dust-soaked ground beneath him, moving his hands about in desperate circles. Finally he had it in his grasp, or almost did, because before his fingers could close around the handle, a swift foot sliced through the air and swept the gun away from him. The bodyguard scrambled for it again, fighting to get back on his feet. He never did. Alabaster lashed out with a perfectly timed uppercut to the man's chin that lifted him off

18

the ground before tumbling him to the cool dirt of the alley. He landed unconscious with a sharp thud, blood still oozing from what was left of his nose.

Seeing this, Marabi began to crawl toward the alley's entrance. All at once, though, the tall man in the white tunic stood before him and blocked his path.

"Please! . . . Please!" Marabi's plea barely audible.

Without straining, Alabaster hoisted the Egyptian to his feet, gripping him by the lapels, and slammed him backwards against a wall. His strength seemed unreal.

"You ask me for pity, Marabi? After all this, you ask me for pity?"

The Egyptian was shaking with fear, breathing in rapid thrusts. "If I tell you what you want to know, will you still kill me?"

"If you don't, I most certainly will."

"I need more of an assurance than that."

"You won't get it." Alabaster tightened his grip across Marabi's chest, twisting the Egyptian's shirt across his windpipe. He continued to increase the pressure until Marabi's face turned scarlet red and then gradually eased off. "Now tell me where I can find Abad Salim or you will never talk again!"

The Egyptian swallowed a huge gulp of welcome air. "Haifa," he gasped. "Haifa . . ."

TWO
Providence, Rhode Island

The four men had arrived for the meeting separately to draw the least possible attention to themselves. Stealth had been their way of life for more years than they could remember, so entering an obscure American city without capturing unwanted eyes posed only a minor challenge for them. A greater challenge was presented by their own apprehension over why they had been called to America from their stations in Beirut and Amman. America was always declared off limits. Something had changed.

It was very strange indeed, considering they were all leading operatives of Black September.

Each had received his instructions only seventy-two hours in advance as a precaution. The current operation, they were told simply, required extraordinary security measures. They did not ask why and heartily obeyed their orders which had come direct from Arafat himself. Something big was up, of that they were certain. And now they sat in the living room section of a Biltmore Plaza Hotel suite eagerly waiting to find out exactly what.

The suite was one of the finest the hotel had to offer. The couch and easy chairs were covered in expensive red leather. The wall paintings were originals, not prints. The lamps were brass. The carpet was thick. The numerous tables were finely polished pine that showed not a scratch, as though they were made to gaze at and not use. The room belonged in a magazine, overdone in traditional Americana. The four Arabs were extremely uncomfortable.

No words were exchanged because there was nothing to say.

There were only questions none of them had the answers to.

The men tensed as they heard a key turn in the lock outside. Their fingers felt for the welcome steel of the revolvers each of them carried. The door swung open. A man entered smiling.

"Good afternoon, gentlemen. *Izzayy-ukum?*"

Four mouths dropped simultaneously. Four sets of eyes bulged for a double and then a triple take. They were looking at a ghost.

"*Subhan allah,*" muttered one of the four men.

The man who had entered pulled a leather armchair to the center of the room and maneuvered it so he was facing the other four. Again he smiled. He was a well-built man, taller than average. His thick black hair was combed straight back over his ears. His thick, even blacker mustache was perfectly groomed without a single hair out of place. Like the others in the room, he was wearing clothes suited for a typical Western business meeting. But unlike the others the garments seemed to fit his personality as well as his body. The angular features of his face were perfectly formed and accentuated, as though a master craftsman had chiselled them into place. He might have been a distinctly handsome individual, if it had not been for a series of lines under his eyes that betrayed a bitterness sharper than the teeth that appeared to spring from his mouth as he continued smiling.

Ali Hassan Salameh, alias Abu Hassan, known in many circles as the Red Prince, ran his tongue over his scarlet lips and sat down.

"It's good to see all of you again," he said warmly. "*Wahastu-ni w-allahi.*"

The four men seated before him did not respond. They were looking at a man who had been killed three-and-a-half years before on a street in Beirut. Slowly their expressions returned to normal, smiles of joy replacing masks of shock.

"Ali, is it you? Is it really you?" one asked.

Salameh chuckled. "I hope so, Mohammed, or else one of history's greatest deceptions has gone for nothing. By the way, do you have a match?"

"Yes, I, I think so." Mohammed reached his trembling fingers into his jacket pocket, emerging with a box of wooden matches.

"Thank you," said Salameh. He placed a long Turkish cigarette in his mouth and lit it. "But to provide me with matches is not the reason you have been called here today."

"Forgive me, Ali," said another man, Adman Tebara, "but, but Beirut . . ."

"It will all be explained in time, Adman," Salameh promised. "You must learn patience as I have. Let us say simply at this point that it was necessary for me to disappear for awhile in order to complete an operation ten years in the making, an operation so brilliantly conceived and foolproof that its upshot will be to destroy our greatest enemies and place us in a position of dominance not only in the Middle East, but in the rest of the world as well. And you four have been chosen to help me move it into the implimentation stage."

Salameh paused and took a long drag of his cigarette. Slowly he moved his eyes from one man before him to the next. As of today, they were the best Black September had to offer. Each of the four had been recruited for his specialty in the hope that the sum of their individual parts would exceed the whole in the current operation. There was Mohammed al-Kahir, who specialized in making seemingly impossible arrangements for apparently impossible plans. There was Hussein El Sayad, who had once been known as the most successful terrorist in the field before an Israeli machine gun stripped him of the use of his right arm. Crippled, he had moved mostly into the areas of propaganda and administration. There was Adman Tebara, a specialist in training terrorist forces and coordinating missions in the field. And finally there was Seif.

There was always Seif . . . the Butcher.

He was said to be the greatest and most feared killer in the world. Seif stood as near to seven feet as to six and carried over 400 pounds of rock-hard muscle on his frame. Each time he moved, a slight tearing sound sprang from his suit which struggled unsuccessfully today to contain his massive shoulders. His head was clean shaven and large. His features were lighter than most Arabs which made the scars that decorated his face all the more pronounced. His eyes were a ghostly shade of gray. One of his ears was missing a lobe.

The Red Prince smiled when his gaze found Seif who was twirling a quarter around in his massive hands with surprising dexterity. Yes, he was a good man. They were all good men.

"The *world*, Ali?" questioned Hussein El Sayad skeptically as he massaged his useless limb.

"Would I have done what I did for anything less?" Salameh shot back angered. "I couldn't even see my family, Hussein, because I knew the Israelis were watching them. You knew my wife and my sons. Weren't they beautiful boys? Do you know where I was when I found out that . . ." Salameh seemed to choke on the words. He swallowed hard and cleared his throat. "It does not matter. All that is in the past. We must concern ourselves now with the future."

"I didn't mean to hurt you," El Sayad offered.

"Hurt me? You really think you could hurt me any more than I have been hurt already? Do you know that sometimes I did not see the sun for weeks on end for fear that I would be recognized by the cursed Israelis before the preparations were complete? Do you know how hard it was for me to sacrifice the man who took my place that day in Beirut? He was my best friend, cursed with possessing an appearance similar enough to mine to fool the Israelis. But killing the man they thought was me was not enough for them or their American friends. No, they had . . ." Again the words seemed to jam in Salameh's throat. His fingers trembled. He tipped cigarette ashes onto the rug and forced himself calm.

Mohammed al-Kahir, the planner, tightened his stare. "We will all do whatever is necessary to help you gain your revenge."

"Ah, but Mohammed, it is not revenge I am after, only

justice. And not for myself, for my people—*our* people. We fight in the Mideast for a stretch of sand, a pool of water, an acre of farmland. Conceivably, we will eventually get what we want. But that is not enough; it never could be. Far more is required—the debts humanity owes us. But they are and always will be unwilling to pay as much as they must. Thus we will make them. The choice will be removed, the issue forced. The revolution will be expanded to include all those who presently denounce it. It is the will of Shaitan . . . the Shaitan Commandment."

The four men glanced at each other unsurely. The shock of seeing Salameh alive had now been totally superseded by the vast intent of his words.

"I don't think we understand, Ali," said Mohammed al-Kahir.

"You aren't meant to, at least not yet."

"Please do not skim over details on our behalf," snapped Hussein El Sayad.

Salameh shook more cigarette ashes onto the carpet. "Hussein, I had hoped our past conflicts would not linger."

"I only made a point."

"I assure you it is well-taken."

"I'm not interested in assurances, only results."

"And results you shall have in good time. . . . I chose you for this assignment. I can just as easily obtain a replacement."

"That won't be necessary."

The Red Prince smiled sinisterly. "See that it isn't." More ashes dropped to the rug beneath his chair. "Now, let's get back to business. I will begin by saying every bit of information in this operation will be given out strictly on a need-to-know basis. Therefore, to avoid any potential leakages, you will not be told everything today."

"Are you saying you don't trust us?" asked al-Kahir, somewhat perplexed.

"If that were so, I wouldn't have chosen you. No, it's not a matter of trust so much one of necessity. Leaks to the enemy have always been a problem for us. Not through you gentlemen, of course, but potentially through someone you are forced to take into your confidence along the line. Too many of our missions in the past have failed because our enemies knew just as much about them as we did. In this instance, if they know anything—anything at all—it will be too much. That explains why the city of Providence, Rhode Island was chosen as the site of this meeting. Boston, New York, and Washington are swarming with men who might recognize one of us. I need not tell you how badly the mission would be hurt if the Americans or the Israelis found out I was still alive. Accordingly, total secrecy must be maintained within certain limits."

"Limits?"

"Yes, you will be told everything you need to know at this time to get your particular phases of the Shaitan Commandment underway. At a later day in the near future, you will be told the rest."

"We would prefer to learn everything now," said El Sayad firmly.

"I believe you are speaking for yourself, Hussein, and I remind you of my previous warning," the Red Prince retorted, losing his patience. "You can be replaced. You are not indispensable to the success of this mission."

"If this mission were as important as you say, I would have thought Arafat would have been here himself."

Salameh's eyebrows fluttered. "Yassir wishes to maintain the low profile in such affairs he has so painstakingly developed in the past few years. He has placed me in full command, given me a free hand. And, Hussein, there is nothing stopping me from bringing that free hand down on anyone who stands in my way. Understood?"

El Sayad shrugged, glancing at his maimed arm.

"Good. To begin with, a bit of history is necessary, specifically of history pertaining to the Nazi movement of World War II. Two significant realizations emerged from

Hitler's Germany. The first was that the world would be far better off with all of its Jews forced into extinction. And the second, a realization which came too late for the Nazis, was that no worldwide revolution could succeed unless America was neutralized. You see, my friends, for years we have been fighting the wrong enemy—Israel. Our attentions should have been focused on the United States instead. Such is the basis of the Shaitan Commandment."

"To neutralize America?" asked al-Kahir.

The Red Prince shook his head and flicked more ashes into the air. "To destroy it."

Less than a mile away, Scott Krassner advanced the third roll of film through his new Minolta XG-7. His parents had bought it for him for his birthday after noticing how much the hobby had begun to interest him. Besides, at thirteen, he thought, a guy is ready for something other than a Kodak instamatic. So obsessed was he by this new pastime that Scott had signed up for a journalism course given at his private school to further expand it. In turn, this sun-drenched Thursday afternoon was being spent taking pictures to fulfill one of his assignments.

It was better when he took pictures just for fun. The assignment had been giving Scott trouble. It wasn't easy to fit pictures into what his teacher called "a particular motif" that was supposed to convey a certain message. If they were pretty to look at, wasn't that enough? He had already been granted one extension on the assignment and feared he might need another.

Scott moved to his right and readied the Minolta for another shot. He swung the long brown hair from his forehead, boyishly aware of his good looks. Sometimes those looks bothered him when he studied himself in the mirror. When he was younger, people often mistook him for a girl. But lately things had been looking better. The full-length mirror told him he was filling out in the right places. And friends of his parents had stopped asking him if he was Mrs. Krassner's daughter when he answered the phone. That was something anyway.

A soft spring breeze blew dust onto the camera lens and ruined the shot. Scott sighed. One thing he hated about April was the wind. What's more, he had been in this part of downtown Providence for almost ninety minutes now and was getting bored. But he still needed more pictures.

The boy stretched his arms, the camera suspended around his neck by a leather strap. He let it rest there while he tapped the back pocket of his tan corduroys to assure himself that the rolls of film already shot were firmly in place. Satisfied and brimming with confidence, he raised the Minolta to his brow and focused on the Hospital Trust Towers, the city's most picturesque building. The sun was in his eyes and felt warm on his face. He knew the angle was wrong for a picture but he snapped it anyway, eager to see the shutter close when he pressed down lightly on the button.

Still holding the camera to his eyes, Scott swung his head around in an ark. An endless succession of ladies lugging shopping bags passed through the lens into the viewfinder, convincing him that a change was sorely needed. His bike was safely chained-up on the outdoor Westminster Mall. He'd walk somewhere else for awhile. But where? . . .

The Biltmore Hotel, Scott thought. There were always interesting things happening at the Biltmore.

THREE

"The problem with the Movement as it stands today," Ali Hassan Salameh was saying, "is that we have become too complacent. We move on the Israelis and the Mossad retaliates. We expect it, they expect it. But for every one we kill, they kill ten. Our numbers dwindle while we accomplish basically nothing."

"Then what we need is another Munich," suggested Adman Tebara.

The Red Prince frowned. "Munich was a disaster in every sense of the word. What did it provide us with? A country of our own? International acceptance? Fear? Recognition? Anger? . . . As that mission's planner, I would venture to say that the final three were all we achieved in levels too low to matter. You see, the problem is that we have been fighting a revolution against the entire world, especially against the cursed democratic voice of America. It is time to stop fighting and coax America to join us."

"Join us? I don't understand," said Mohammed al-Kahir.

"You will. The issue we must face is that every move we make brings us head-on into the awesome expanse of American power. As long as this country exists in such total, untempered strength, our revolution—the Moslem revolution as a whole—is doomed to fail. Such is the problem. The solution is to destroy America as it is known today."

"Destroy America?" laughed Hussein El Sayad. "Hah! We'd have a better chance of parting the Red Sea."

The Red Prince's face remained wooden. "I don't think so. Understand, my friends, that I am actually talking about forcing America to destroy herself. I know that even the combined forces of all the Arab revolutionary republics could not cope with the vast power of the U.S. But there are now other means available to us."

"The Shaitan Commandment?"

"Exactly."

"Then why don't we simply use it against Israel?" posed El Sayad. "It would seem a more logical approach."

"Hardly," disagreed Salameh. "Launching this operation against Israel would subject us to retaliation by the U.S., just as anything we have done against Israel in the past has. Do you have any idea how many brilliant plans against the Jews have been scrapped out of fear of the Americans?" Salameh realized his cigarette was out and tapped the lingering ashes onto the carpet. "No, it is time to turn our attentions to a greater and more powerful enemy."

"Do you plan to tell us how?" probed El Sayad.

"I'm getting to that." The Red Prince tossed his extinguished cigarette onto the rug and removed another from his jacket, fingering but not lighting it. He leaned forward, pausing for effect. "Eight weeks from now, 175 of our agents will enter the United States from predetermined countries all over the world. Collectively these men and women make up the greatest attack force that has ever walked the earth. Their . . . training . . . has long been over and they will very likely never see more than a handful of each other again. But their presence in this country will pave the way for its ultimate destruction. Their actions will allow us to fulfill our destiny as a people. The revolution will explode. No area of the earth will be unaffected by the ramifications."

Hussein El Sayad shook his head cynically. "I hardly think that 175 men and women can do all that much for our revolution or our destiny."

"You are a well of ignorance, Hussein."

"All the same, Ali," began Mohammed al-Kahir, "it seems quite improbable. One hundred seventy-five people succeeding where millions through history have failed?"

"They must possess a great weapon," said the killer Seif in his deep voice, speaking for the first time, the quarter still moving adroitly from hand to hand through his fingers.

Salameh grinned. "Our friend Seif speaks the least but says the most of all of you. Indeed, they possess a great weapon."

"What is it? Nuclear, perhaps?" posed Adman Tebara.

"No."

"Warheads loaded with lethal biological toxins to be exploded over America's cities?"

"No."

"Deadly vials of poison to be released into her air or water, then?"

"Hardly."

"Are they merely an exceptionally well-trained force of terrorists?"

"They are far more than that. While the Shaitan force of 175 was being trained for its mission, you see, contacts were secured in sensitive areas all over the United States. As a result of these contacts, our agents have been placed proportionately and untraceably in these areas. The breakdown is as follows." Here the four men expected the Red Prince to extract a piece of paper. Instead, though, he spoke from memory, still fingering the unlit cigarette. "Fifteen of the agents have been placed on Capital Hill, 3 in White House related positions, 15 within the different media, 24 will maneuver within the armed forces, 10 will infiltrate Wall Street and other centers crucial to business. Then there are geographic distributions across the country itself: 11 in Los Angeles, 9 in Chicago and Houston; 7 in Boston, Miami and Philadelphia; 10 in New York, 17 in other selected major cities and the final 21 scattered strategically elsewhere."

"And they will carry out the plan from these positions?" From al-Kahir.

"Yes."

"And you are not going to tell us specifically how?" From

El Sayad.

"Not yet."

"Such conditions do not please me," pestered the cripple.

"They don't have to!" roared the Red Prince, his eyes on fire. "You joined the Movement of your own free will and it has been quite good for you as all of you have been for it," he said speaking to the four. "I urge you not to make waves. You have all been chosen for this mission because each is the best at what he does. If you fail to comply with your instructions, however, you will be branded a traitor and marked for execution." Three of the men gasped. Only Seif the Butcher remained expressionless. Salameh passed the unlit cigarette from one hand to the other, twirling it rhythmically.

"I can best answer your questions as follows," he resumed. "The actions of the 175 member Shaitan force will lead directly to the death of *a minimum of fifty percent* of America's population within three months after their entry. The country's government will tumble, her cities will be in riot, her armed forces and police will be decimated. She will be, for all intents and purposes, a country at war with herself. She will have joined our revolution. Or, at the very least, she will be powerless to stop it from succeeding." An uneasy silence filled the room. The unlit cigarette continued to turn in Salameh's hands. "And the greatest thing of all is that America will never know she has been attacked."

Al-Kahir tilted his head incredulously. "Half of her people will be dead and there will be no evidence of an attack?"

"The evidence will point to no one."

"Surely they will suspect."

"Perhaps but there will be no link to us or anyone else. None of the evidence will be overt. My friends, we are not talking about guns, or missiles, or bombs. We are talking about the most sophisticated weapon ever known to man."

"That will kill one hundred million people. . . ."

"Probably more."

"With no indication of attack?"

The Red Prince shook his head methodically, as though to prolong the motion. "None."

The room was again silent. The four Arabs stole glances at one another. Each felt something rising within him. Their hearts began to beat a little faster. The sweat beneath their arms turned cold. Salameh was describing the dawn of a new era which they had been selected to be a part of.

"What else do we need to know now?" asked Mohammed al-Kahir, speaking for all of them.

Salameh smiled. "Your specific roles in the Commandment. For example, you, Mohammed, will be responsible for making the necessary travel arrangements for the Shaitan force which I will go over in detail with you in private later." The Red Prince moved his eyes to Adman Tebara. "You, Adman, will be responsible for training an Al Fatah force of 1,000 to move in once our 175 agents have achieved their objective. It will be these 1,000 who insure that, unlike the Phoenix, America will not be able to rise from her own ashes." Salameh switched his stare to Hussein El Sayad. "Hussein, you will be charged with serving as the contact for the Shaitan force—the link between them and the rest of the Movement. Their reports will come into you on almost a daily basis. You will then draw certain conclusions from this information, based on material I will provide you with at a later time."

"A tedious job."

"But a most important one. And one that a man—how should I say it?—with your limitations is confined to doing." The ring of cruel condescension in Salameh's voice made El Sayad tremble with rage he was powerless to vent. "Agreed, Hussein?"

The cripple simply nodded, watching the unlit cigarette spin through his superior's hands.

The Red Prince met the cold eyes of Seif. "And you, my friend, have what is perhaps the most crucial task of all: the elimination of the only three men in the world we fear can offer a challenge to the success of the Commandment."

32

"That is all?" the killer asked flatly, rotating the shiny quarter from one massive hand to the other. His adroitness with the maneuver came as quite a shock to the others in the room.

"It is enough."

"That depends on who these men are."

"John Desmond, CIA Mideast operative working out of Clandestine Operations. David Rabanine, retired Mossad agent, but still that agency's greatest living expert on the Movement. Though still considered a threat, I am told he is hardly the man he once was. He lives in seclusion."

"I know," said Seif. "I killed his wife. That is what drove him there. He will offer no problem. Neither will Desmond. Who is the third?"

"Alabaster."

Seif showed emotion for the first time. His round, bald head seemed to swell and expand. "That will not be easy. Alabaster is elusive, like a slippery fish. He hasn't been heard from in two years. He might be dead."

"I doubt it. He is alive and will come back to haunt us unless we deal with him first. . . . What's the matter, my friend? Have you finally met your match in Alabaster?"

The killer grunted. "No man on earth is my match."

"Perhaps. But then again perhaps you are no longer the man you once were."

Seif smiled demonically, arching his eyebrows. Deliberately, he brought the quarter he had been twirling up to eye level, placing it between both thumbs and index fingers. Without flinching, he began to twist, the muscles rippling beneath his suit. The metal began to give, the effect mesmerizing. In seconds, the quarter had been folded perfectly in half right down the middle. Before the astonished eyes around him, the Butcher then tossed the coin into Salameh's lap. Seif's expression had not changed one bit throughout, the task apparently effortless.

"I did not mean to challenge your abilities," said the Red

33

Prince. But he did.

"No matter. I will find Alabaster and I will kill him. The challenge should prove interesting. I'm not used to challenges."

"I trust you will enjoy this one."

"There's one thing I don't understand about the operation," began al-Kahir. "Because no one has ever tried a plan such as Shaitan, utilizing the weapon we are about to, how can we be sure it will work?"

"A fair question," admitted Salameh, "and one that I am able to answer. We have arranged an experiment in America that will allow us to test the unknown factors of the Commandment in a practical situation. The experiment will begin within the next two weeks and will conclude in plenty of time for us to study the results and iron out any potential difficulties before the major force is scheduled to arrive."

"But an experiment of that magnitude will certainly make the Americans suspicious."

The Red Prince smiled in sinister confidence as he crushed his unlit Turkish cigarette and sprayed the remains on the carpet beneath him. "To use an American phrase, 'they will never know what hit them.'"

Scott Krassner had been right: The Biltmore Hotel was certainly a great place to take pictures. The outdoor glass elevator offered shots from several vantage points. And in front of the hotel, people were always coming or going, busy and determined in their motions, each with a unique expression on their face.

Scott didn't have a telephoto lens to go with his Minolta which forced him to take the shots from not more than fifteen feet away from the entrance where a doorman seemed expert at smiling and tipping his cap. The man was continually opening and closing doors, as well as slipping bills into his pocket. At first he had seemed to resent the boy's presence and appeared on the verge of asking him to leave. But now he welcomed Scott and his camera as relief from the routine of an otherwise mundane day. Besides, the boy wasn't bothering anyone by standing on the raised concrete island across the way that provides the Biltmore with a private drive freeing it from downtown traffic. And no one had complained yet.

Scott had finished one roll here already and was somewhere near the end of a second, making four in all for the day. It was getting late. He was worried about his bicycle. He wanted to go home. Just one more shot, he told himself. He would make it a good one. He pushed the long brown hair from his eyebrows and lifted the camera up to focus it. It was on the twenty-seventh frame.

Five men appeared in the viewfinder, superimposed behind the black crosshairs with a red dot in the middle. They didn't look like any men Scott had ever seen before, except in books. Their skin was dark and they looked a little scary; especially the big one with the bald head who might have passed for a giant Kojak if he hadn't been so ugly.

Without wasting any more time, Scott turned the focusing wheel until the picture was sharp and depressed the shutter button.

The man in the middle did not raise his arm quickly enough to block his face.

The clerk behind the counter of Colorlab Processing Studios had gray hair and tired blue eyes. He jotted some information down on an order blank and looked back at the boy in front of him.

"That's four rolls of color print film—36 exposures in each."

Scott Krassner smiled. "You won't ruin them on me, will you?"

"You take the pictures, son, and I'll develop them," the clerk said smoothly, looking out the window. He noticed a black, four-door Cadillac double-parked in front of the shop. He thought he knew every car in the neighborhood but he had never seen this one before.

"Everybody tells me Colorlab is the best," the boy said.

"They haven't steered you wrong." The clerk moved his eyes away from the black Caddy and back to the order form. "These will be ready Saturday morning, say around eleven."

"Sounds good." Scott reached into the right front pocket of his corduroys and pulled out a wad of singles. "How much?"

"Call it an even fourteen bucks. But you can pay when you pick them up."

Scott, though, wanted them to be sent directly to the home of his journalism teacher. That way she would have plenty of time to look the shots over before they discussed them. He was only thirteen but Scott still had a great sense of responsibility. His extension lasted only until next Thursday. Since Mrs. Kirkman had requested to see the pictures before he did anything with them, he could ill afford to waste any more time.

"Could you mail them?" he asked the clerk.

"Sure. What's your address?"

"Not to me, to somebody else."

"They're your pictures. Just tell me where you want them."

Scott recited his teacher's address. The clerk wrote it down. "Should have them Monday or Tuesday."

Scott thrust a pile of crumpled bills across the counter. "Thanks," he said, turning for the door. "See ya' later."

Scott climbed on top of his ten-speed and began to pedal away at the same time the clerk placed the film and voucher into a bin behind him.

He did not notice that the shiny black Cadillac had left its spot in front of the window.

His mind still on his pictures, Scott threaded his way through downtown traffic, reaching the base of College Hill. He downshifted to aid the steep climb and pushed his leg muscles toward pain as he began the ascent. He made it up with surprising ease and turned onto Waterman Street, a one-way road that runs all the way through the major East Side suburbs

36

of the city. The boy swung the bike onto the sidewalk. It was all downhill from here.

Scott was conscious of the camera suspended uneasily from his neck because it lifted up every time he went over a bump. He wondered what real photographers did to stop this from bothering them. But how many real photographers rode bicycles?

Scott glanced behind him as he halted the bike at a red light. A shiny black Cadillac was hanging back in traffic, its grill seeming to return his gaze. It looked familiar. He was sure he'd seen it before recently. Maybe he'd taken a picture of it.

Something gnawed at the insides of the boy's stomach. It was the same feeling he got when watching scary movies alone late at night.

But what did he have to be scared of now?

The ten-speed made its easy way down Blackstone Boulevard in the heart of Providence's richest residential section. The Boulevard is made up of a wide grassy knoll with a brown path worn down its middle by joggers and is bordered on either side by one-way streets moving in opposite directions. The houses that line both streets are masterpieces of staid construction, a pleasure to look at on a sunny spring day. This was the scenic route home and Scott often took it when he wasn't in a rush.

He was pedaling on the right-hand road, heading east, just another half mile or so away from his house which was good because his legs were tired and his eyes hurt from the sweat that dripped into them off the curled tips of his straight hair. His thigh muscles tightened and locked, begging for rest.

Behind the boy, a black Cadillac switched from the outside to the inside lane and began to slowly accelerate. It was nearly 750 yards to his rear on the long straight road, closing the gap deliberately. Suspicion had to be avoided. Escape insured. As for witnesses, well, people would not remember the details of something they had not expected to see.

Less than 300 yards now . . .

The droll monotone of an engine stuck in low gear and accelerating gradually caught Scott's ear. He turned slowly, careful to keep his balance on the bike. The sight made him shudder. The long black car he had spotted on Waterman Street was charging in line with him, its intent frighteningly obvious.

The boy moved his eyes back to the front and began to pedal furiously. His calf muscles spasmed, forcing him to cry out in agony as he began to churn his feet faster than he knew how. He thought about driving off into an adjacent yard but quickly saw this was impossible because a stone fence that surrounded a large cemetery cut off all means of entry, trapping him on the road.

Somebody help me! . . . Somebody help me! The plea formed but never uttered.

The driver of the Cadillac, knowing it had been spotted, forced the pedal to the floor and shoved the big car into overdrive. It shook under the pressure.

The roar of the engine was everywhere, drowning out all other sounds Scott might have been able to hear. The boy's eyes grasped onto the road before him, fearful of the sight turning to the rear would bring. But suddenly he realized he was pedaling in the Caddy's shadow, a dark expanse which stretched on, seeming to absorb him.

The big car lurched forward, its speed now near sixty, the sun bouncing off its silver grill and baking its black exterior. The driver spun the wheel quickly to the right, gripping it firmly with his sweat-soaked hands. The tires responded with a whine growing into a screech that might have been a growl. The Caddy lunged one final time, a hungry animal ready for the kill.

And then it was upon the boy.

FOUR
Crescent Falls, Wyoming

Mayor Jim Layton leaned forward with a sigh. "We've got to face the fact that the town's dying."

"Well, maybe it's just goin' through a re-ces-sion," suggested Sheriff Bugsy Tyler, running his fingers through his thick beard.

"I don't think so, Sheriff. I think we're in trouble. Big trouble. That's why I called this Monday morning meeting."

"Oh, I ain't disagreein' with you there, Jimbo. But we've faced some pretty bad times before and come out of them all right. Why's this one any different?"

"Because the railroad's moving out, Bugsy," said Dave Dean, a town councilman whose distinctly eastern sensibility had brought him into disfavor with some of the folks in Crescent Falls. "And we've been a railroad town ever since any of us can remember."

"Can't argue with you there," Bugsy conceded, settling his giant frame into the small chair woefully ill-equipped to support it.

Crescent Falls lies in the northeastern quarter of Wyoming near the junction of routes 59 and 387. A scant eighteen miles from the Belle Fouche River and a not so scant seventy-five from the city of Casper. It is a town detached from the mainstream of American and even Wyoming life, alone and isolated. There are times when six months will pass without a single stranger appearing. Everyone in town knows everybody else. The people like it that way.

Crescent Falls had been settled in the heyday of the railroad and had grown up with and around it. Nobody ever got rich in the town but the residents will tell you that nobody ever died poor either. The railroad had seen to that.

Until now.

Because the railroad was finally pulling up stakes and leaving the town it had built up from nothing. Without the money and jobs it now provided, there would be little left of Crescent Falls before all that long. Not that there was all that much to begin with. The total population of the town numbered somewhere around 142, although no one had really bothered to count heads lately which was the only way people in the town had ever taken a census. Say 140, give or take five. When the railroad left, though, it promised to take a good number, if not all, of those with it.

"Dave, are you sure we're not getting all bent out of shape for nothing?" asked Norm Shacklehorse, another town councilman who ran Crescent Fall's only bar and grill.

"If anything," Dean answered, "we're not getting bent out enough. Look at the figures." Dean glanced down at the paper before him on the hard oak conference table in the modest meeting house which doubled as social hall and movie theater on weekends. "The railroad employs 54 of our 74 working males. That accounts for one million dollars gross income a year. Take away that one million and you put a pretty big crack in our nest egg. Look, I *know*. I run the general store."

Sheriff Bugsy Tyler popped some Skoal chewing tobacco in his mouth, pulling a paper cup near him. He was a massive man, standing comfortably over six feet tall and weighing 350 once far more solid pounds. He had spent three years in the marine corps at one stage in his life after which he enjoyed a successful stint as a professional wrestler. That was followed by a brief career as a bounty hunter, an endeavor which failed because he was repeatedly unable to bring prisoners back in any condition to stand trial.

So he had ended up settling in Crescent Falls and running for sheriff five months later because he had nothing better to do. His platform was simple and, when asked to state it at a local town meeting prior to the election, Bugsy thrilled the audience by bending a steel bar with his bare hands. That was that. Crescent Falls was more than seventy miles away from the nearest Highway Patrol station, so a sheriff who could handle trouble on his own was welcomed with open arms. He won the election in a landslide and had run unopposed since, mainly because no one in town would dare take on an incumbent who regularly carried a drunk under each arm from the bar to the jail on Saturday nights. Not that Bugsy was a great politician. He didn't know the difference between a Democrat and a Republican. And the odds were no better than even that he'd be able to name the man elected president of the country the same day he won his first term as sheriff.

All the same, Bugsy was deceptively clever when it came to the performance of his job. There was the time, for instance, that a group of swindlers tried to con the people of Crescent Falls into buying thousands of acres of undeveloped land at rock-bottom prices. Only problem, Bugsy discovered, was that the land in question was situated in Grand Teton National Park. He had had a bad feeling about the whole thing right from the start. And Bugsy had learned over the years that if something felt wrong, it usually was.

It didn't bother Bugsy that the swindlers were part of a much larger syndicate operation straight out of the West Coast underworld. Nor did it faze him when three muscle-bound enforcers were sent to deal with the small town sheriff who had exposed the scam. The three men stepped off a passenger car one day and departed on a freight train the next sprawled out on shipping crates with enough bruises and broken bones to make their employer ask what rival family had been responsible for the assault.

"How's rubbers been sellin' lately?" Tyler asked Dave Dean.

"What the Christ does that have to do with anything?"

"Simple. When rubbers are sellin' well, people is happy. When they ain't sellin' so good, we got ourselves a real problem. Call me when they ain't." Bugsy smiled and spit some tobacco juice into the paper cup beneath him.

"I think what Dave's getting at, Sheriff," said Mayor Jim Layton, "is that next month at this time there might not be a whole helluva lot of men around to buy them. And they'd take the town's women folk with them."

"The point," Dean picked up, "is that the businesses in town depend on the money the railroad brings in. Take away the railroad and you take away the town's businesses. Then you haven't got much of a town."

"I don't think people are fixin' on leavin' so quick." Tyler spat again, this time almost missing his makeshift spittoon. "Folks has always stuck to Crescent Falls like flies to a pile of shit."

"And without the railroad, that metaphor becomes exceedingly accurate," said Dean grimly. "People won't have a choice *but* to move, Bugsy. Welfare sure won't pay the bills and the town hasn't got enough jobs to offer away from the tracks. They'll have to get out."

"Well, then I guess I won't have to go 'bout findin' myself a new deputy this summer." Tyler spat a third time, lodging a sizable portion of the thick juice on the rim of the cup.

"Is there anything we can do to keep the town from dying?" asked Norm Shacklehorse.

"How 'bout convincin' the railroad to stay put?" advised Tyler.

"Already tried that, Bugs," said Mayor Layton. "They won't hear of it. Say this freight line is just about all dried up. Say they got to move on to where things will suit them better."

"Which pretty much puts our coffin in the ground," lamented Shacklehorse.

"Not yet," said Layton. "And that's what this meeting's all about. There *is* some good news to go with the bad."

"'Bout time," said Bugsy, hitting the cup dead center this shot.

"Two weeks ago," the mayor resumed, "I received a very interesting request from what they call an oil exploration company. Seems that some scientists think that Crescent Falls might be sitting on an untapped lake of black gold."

"I'll be gawddamned . . ."

"So they want to come out with a small team of field men and do all sorts of experiments on the land. Actually, the team of men coming makes up the company. And, if it turns out they're right about the oil, they'll have an entire drilling team here come summer."

"And if they're wrong?" said Norm Shacklehorse.

"We'll sure in hell be no worse off than we are right now. And if they do find oil, the kind of rig they're talking about employs anywhere from 150-200 men. Now that doesn't mean that all of them would come from Crescent Falls. But some of them will. And more importantly somebody in town's got to own the land they'll be drilling on. Somebody, maybe a whole bunch of people, is gonna get rich. Think of it, Norm, with all that money around and new people rolling in from all over the country, think of how many hamburgers you'd be able to sell at the Bar & Grill. Christ, you might even be able to start charging more than thirty cents for a draft and get away with it."

Sheriff Tyler raised his huge, thick eyebrows. "Not on your life. Some things is sacred."

"And as for me," Dave Dean began, eyes glowing, "I probably won't have to close the radio shack section of my store. In fact, I might have to knock out a wall or two to expand my operation."

"Hell, maybe I could stay open till one AM every night of the week," beamed Norm Shacklehorse.

"Then how 'bout bringin' in some dancin' girls whose zippers go up and down more often than a busy elevator?" grinned Bugsy.

"Let's not get ahead of ourselves here," cautioned Mayor Layton, pushing his fingers through his thinning hair. "These oil exploration guys haven't even gotten to town yet. We still got no idea that there's really oil in our backyards."

"But if there is, Crescent Falls will become a boom town instead of a ghost town," reminded Dave Dean, making Mayor Layton feel very uncomfortable indeed. He'd been mayor of Crescent Falls for nearly fifteen years and realized for the first time that he might have to face an opponent in an election. Dave Dean, with his blond hair and pretty boy looks, was the kind of man who worried you that way.

"You know, Jimbo," began Bugsy Tyler, tugging at his beard, "there's one thing that bothers me 'bout all this."

"What's that, Bugs?"

"This oil exploration team—why'd it take them so long to decide there might be oil in Crescent Falls?"

"I don't know, I guess with the gas crunch and all, they're starting to look in areas they never have before because drilling might not've been profitable."

Tyler shrugged, not satisfied. "I got a bad feelin' about this."

"I don't see why."

"Because the whole thing don't wash no better than a whore with a crab-filled cunt."

Norm Shacklehorse cleared his throat uneasily. "When are the oil men supposed to get here?"

"They're due to arrive some time around the middle of this week—Wednesday, I think," Layton replied. "And it'll be up to us four to make sure they feel at home."

Bugsy was still tugging at his beard. He rose slowly, the small chair creaking from the strain. "Well, if you boys'll excuse me, I got to be goin'. Got an important case to follow up on this mornin'."

"What makes today different from all other days?" gibed Dave Dean.

"Well, seems that Billy-Jim Furman took Sandy-Lu Baker into a wheat field last night and got a little fresh. Took off the young woman's shirt and bra and went to work a suckin' on one of her boobs. I don't know, I guess he was a mite too eager or his teeth were a mite too sharp because he bit the nipple clean off."

"I'll be damned," said Mayor Layton.

"So will Billy-Jim, if old man Baker has anything to do with it."

FIVE

Leslie Kirkman, editor of the *Providence Journal's* Accent pages, entered the city's police department on Monday morning just as the meeting in Crescent Falls was breaking up. She was a warmly attractive woman with long brown hair slung neatly about her shoulders and dark eyes of the same radiant color. She wore a knee-length pleated skirt and a blouse that did barely enough to hide the firm lines of her breasts. Her skin was olive-colored, looking perpetually tanned, and her ivory teeth complimented it perfectly. Her features were stunningly sharp and sensuous. But her face was strangely long and drawn, as though something dark within was challenging the brightness without.

Leslie felt a chill run through her as she entered the anteroom and waited for a sergeant to "beep" open the electronic door. Coming down here to headquarters brought back the memories of her husband Roy's murder, and though she didn't hide from those memories she didn't like them forced on her either.

It was three years ago but sometimes it felt like three weeks. A drizzling spring evening. She and Roy were walking for some forgotten reason in downtown Providence. A man appeared before them, something shiny in his hand. Roy saw it in time to send Leslie reeling safely to the pavement. The action stunned and confused her but not so much as the flash at the end of the large barrel and roar that seemed to follow it.

Everything began to move in slow motion. Roy recoiling backwards, his chest a mass of scarlet, his face twisted in agony. The killer, features shrouded by darkness, turning the weapon toward her. Shouts from nearby bystanders forcing

45

the killer to turn and flee.

The police called it an assassination. Roy Kirkman, after all, was a leading criminal prosecutor, about to take a syndicate kingpin to trial. The press called it a vendetta against the new Attorney General's Crackdown on Crime program. The FBI called it a conspiracy.

Nobody bothered to call it a tragedy.

Then came the long hours in the police department pouring through huge volumes of mug books. The faces all looked the same to Leslie. One of them, detectives told her, might belong to Roy's killer. It was routine; everything was routine. Except her life.

Was this really happening? she remembered asking herself. Was Roy really . . . dead? She was a widow with a seven-year-old son born with a severe hearing impediment which was a polite way of saying he was half-deaf. The whole situation was comically obscene, a bizarre soap opera of a life being played out without benefit of commercials.

Roy had left a good deal of money in addition to a house in Providence's plush East Side. So Leslie could at least feel safe with the reassurance that she would always be provided for. But she didn't. It wasn't enough to sit home and wait for the weekly check to come from the bank. There had to be something more. She had graduated from Columbia with a journalism degree ten years before and one of Roy's friends helped her get a job with the *Providence Journal*. She had applied for a position on the news staff, ending up with a spot in the fashion department. And now three years later she had risen on her own to associate editor in charge of the paper's Accent pages.

The months had passed slowly at first, sleepless nights and dreary days. Soon, though, she adjusted to her new life and changed accordingly. So in all ways Leslie was not the same woman she had been three years before and in most she was better. She was stronger, able to cope with just about anything with an admirable degree of confidence. In the process she had

46

gained self-respect, self-understanding. And weren't things paying off because of it? Her son Jimmy was now doing remarkably well in the School for the Deaf. There was promise for more advancement in her job at the *Journal*. Suddenly she could see only ahead.

Until the call from a detective in Providence's homicide division had come early Sunday morning, asking her to come see him at eleven AM today. A buzz sounded and Leslie pushed open the electronic door and stepped into the past. All at once, she was able to see only behind again.

"Do you recognize any of the faces, Mrs. Kirkman?"

Sergeant Phil Scarpani's office was located on the third floor and Leslie had no trouble finding it. She remembered hearing Roy mention his name on several occasions. They had worked together on a number of cases and Roy, she recalled, was impressed by Scarpani's thoroughness but distressed by what he called an overactive imagination.

Scarpani's office was more of a box than a room with three desks squeezed into it, each with piles of paper littered on top. Wanted posters covered the walls and the paint was peeling in almost as many areas as it wasn't.

"Mrs. Kirkman?" Scarpani rose when he saw her enter.

"Yes."

The detective extended his hand. He had thick curly hair, save for a slight balding spot on his dome, and a dark shadow where his beard had been only three hours before. His face was hard and rectangular. His nose looked like a boxer's, as did his forearms revealed by rolled up sleeves. They seemed oversized with muscle. Scarpani, right down to the crumpled, poorly knotted tie, looked like a character from a gangster movie.

Leslie took his hand.

"It's nice to see you again, Mrs. Kirkman."

She sat down and smoothed out her green skirt. "Again?"

"We met briefly three years ago when . . ." Scarpani looked away. "Your husband was a great man, Mrs. Kirkman."

"He spoke similarly of you."

47

Scarpani's eyelids fluttered. "I doubt it. Roy always thought I read too much into crimes. Said I always saw deep-seated conspiracies and ulterior motives lurking in the shadows. In plain English, I was a pain in the ass to him. But let me tell you something about Roy. He was one of the few DAs who would put as much time and effort into fighting for a conviction as we would for an arrest. None of that fancy plea bargaining crap. He just plain worked his ass off. He was just too competent. That's why . . ."

Leslie spared him having to complete the thought. "But you didn't call me down here to talk about my husband."

"No, I didn't. But I'm afraid the reason I did call you is equally unpleasant." Scarpani's deep voice wavered a bit.

"I'm listening."

The sergeant reached into his desk and pulled out a scratch pad covered with doodling. He flipped to a blank page and picked up a pen.

"To begin with, Mrs. Kirkman, you teach a journalism course over at Moses Brown, right?"

Leslie nodded. "Yes." She had always wanted to be a teacher and had personally solicited the twelve to one daily class at the state's leading private school, refusing any pay whatsoever.

"Was a boy named Scott Krassner one of your students?"

"Yes." Leslie had read about the tragic hit-and-run accident that had claimed his life Thursday afternoon.

Scarpani jotted something down on the pad. "And he was assigned by you to hand in either a written or photo essay some time this week, is that right?"

"Actually last week." More jotting. "But Scott was having trouble so I agreed to give him some extra help."

Scarpani looked up. "In what form?"

"Well, he had just gotten a new camera and wanted to try a photo essay, but had no idea where to start. I told him we'd go over pictures he had taken on a certain theme at my house some evening and I'd help him get organized. . . . Sergeant, I'd like to know why you're asking me all this."

Scarpani took a deep breath. "Mrs. Kirkman, we—actually I—have reason to believe Scott Krassner was murdered."

"That's no surprise. Hit-and-run does qualify as . . ." The word "murder" remained wedged on her tongue. Roy's picture flashed through her mind.

"I'm not talking about ordinary hit-and-run, Mrs. Kirkman. I'm talking about premeditated murder."

"A thirteen-year-old boy? You can't be serious."

"But I am." Scarpani dropped his pen and placed his fingers on his temples. "I'll try to explain things from the beginning. I was assigned to the case as standard procedure and went into it expecting to find nothing. What I discovered, however, was too obvious to ignore."

"Go on."

"I want you to know first off that all the information I've gathered is circumstantial. I haven't even gone to my superiors with this yet. I've been a sergeant a long time, Mrs. Kirkman, maybe because I've got a tendency to see things that aren't always there. The men upstairs, they don't always want to listen to me, even when the proof I've got is pretty firm. And this time, individually what I've gathered doesn't mean much of anything. But put it all together and a very clear picture begins to emerge."

"I'd like you to draw it for me," Leslie said, suddenly intrigued.

"Number one, witnesses claim that the car that struck Scott Krassner was a black four door, late model luxury car; believed to be one of the General Motors variety, though it could have been a Lincoln. And some of these same witnesses claim that the car did not accidently swerve into Scott's bicycle—it purposely did."

"That's absurd. Witnesses, Sergeant, *can* be wrong."

"In fact, they usually are. But not so many about an event so out of the ordinary." Scarpani leaned forward. "When people see something surprising and unexpected take place, they usually remember only bits and pieces of it. Their imaginations

49

fill in the rest. So when a witness is relating a story of what he thinks he saw, you can never be sure of where to draw the line. All you can do is try to string together the truth by decifering what was said about a crime by the most people—the common denominators, in other words. And in the case of Scott Krassner, more than half the witnesses claim that the black sedan purposely accelerated and then swerved toward him."

"I see."

"That's just the beginning. One of the witnesses also claims that the black sedan ran over the boy a second time to make sure the job was finished."

Leslie shuddered. "I'm having trouble believing all this."

"So did I," Scarpani concurred, running his hands through his curly hair. "But you can't dismiss what people keep telling you again and again. Anyway, right from the start two things struck me as strange: First, that a car like the one described would be involved in a hit-and-run and second that the accident may not have been an accident at all. Most incidents of this sort happen when someone has had too much to drink and panics after losing control of the wheel. As far as I can tell, there is no evidence that the driver of the black sedan ever lost control of the car. If anything he knew exactly where he was going because there are no skid marks. Whoever was driving never put his foot on the brake." A pause. "Okay, now assuming the act was one of premeditated murder, I have to look for a motive. Why would the driver of a Cadillac or a Lincoln want to run over a boy? How well did you know Scott Krassner, Mrs. Kirkman?"

"Not very. There are twenty-six students in the journalism class and I'm only at the school between 11:45 and 1:15. There's not much time for individual contact. Why do you ask?"

Scarpani's stare hardened. "I spoke to his parents to find out if he was behaving strangely in any manner or if he had made any serious enemies. Routine, of course."

"Of course. And?"

"Not surprisingly, they reported nothing out of the ordinary. So then I've got to make myself look for something else. I asked them what he was doing in the time immediately preceding his death. They told me he was taking pictures. Downtown, they thought. That's what led me to you, Mrs. Kirkman. What kind of pictures would he have been taking?"

"People, places—that sort of thing."

"Nothing specific?"

"The assignment didn't call for it."

"No definite shooting area?"

"The choice was his. You'll have to excuse me, Sergeant. But I don't see what taking pictures has to do with all this."

Scarpani blew his nose into a wrinkled handkerchief. "The problem, Mrs. Kirkman, is that the camera we recovered had no film inside it and there were no rolls anywhere on the boy's person either, which means he must have dropped them off somewhere."

"So?"

"If I'm right about Scott Krassner being murdered, then the motive must lie somewhere between the time he left his house and the time he finished taking pictures downtown. It's quite possible that somewhere in that period he saw something he shouldn't have, maybe a person or a number of people who don't want to be recognized."

"And took a picture of them?" Scarpani nodded. "That seems like an unlikely motive for murder, Sergeant."

"All motives are unlikely, if you ask me. Some are just more unlikely than others."

"Then what you're saying is that the reason Scott was killed has something to do wtih the pictures he was taking."

"It seems too obvious a clue, doesn't it, Mrs. Kirkman? The best clues often are. Good detectives don't see what the ordinary man is unable to; they merely don't miss what the ordinary man usually does."

"Perhaps, though, the men in the car got the film after . . ."

Scarpani shook his head. "They didn't have time. Besides,

51

not one of our witnesses claims that any of the car's occupants ever got out, which means that the boy must have dropped the rolls off to be developed in which case they're at some processor's right now. . . . And I've got to find them."

The clerk behind the counter of Colorlab Processing Laboratories saw the two men climb out of the red Cutlass directly in front of the building. It had been a slow morning and the clerk welcomed any business as a relief to boredom and fatigue.

But the men who entered through the front door did not look like photographers, nor did they look like the kind the clerk enjoyed doing business with. Both were short and stocky with cold, deadpan eyes. One wore a gray rain hat. The other had thinning brown hair. It was the latter who placed both his hands on the counter, leaning toward the clerk. He smiled without showing any teeth.

"I'd like some information," he said.

"About film or processing?" the clerk asked tentatively.

"Neither. About one of your customers."

"Why?"

"It would be better for you to let us ask the questions."

"That kind of information is privileged. . . . Are you with the police?"

"No, but it would be in your best interests to give us some answers."

"As I said before, that information's privileged," the clerk persisted. "Perhaps something else . . ."

"No, I'm afraid nothing else'll do. I will ask you a question and you will answer it."

Brown Hair nodded at the man in the rain hat who took two steps forward so that his waist came into mild contact with the counter. He, too, placed his hands on the shiny surface, his fingers taut. His face was square, his nose pushed inwards as though it had been broken several times.

"I don't think so," the clerk said.

52

Brown Hair ignored his response. "Last Thursday after-noon, a boy brought a number of rolls of film in here to be developed. I want to know, very simply, what happened to them."

"I wasn't working on Thursday."

"You're a poor liar. Now tell us what happened to the film and don't wear my patience any more than you already have."

The clerk felt under the counter for the can of Mace he had permission to use in situations like this. "What'd you say the boy's name was?"

"I didn't. You're stalling. I suggest you stop. We want that film."

His hand was on the can now. "And I suggest you leave here right this second. My fellow workers will be returning from lunch any minute and one of them used to be a boxer. He'd make mincemeat out of you two."

"I repeat, you're a poor liar," said the man with thinning brown hair. "It's now eight minutes after twelve. Your friends will not be back until one and both of them are women. Now, for the last time, tell me what happened to the film."

"For the last time, that information is privileged."

The clerk had begun to move the can of Mace over the counter when he felt two powerful hands, belonging to the silent brute with the rain hat and twisted nose, grip his arms at the elbows and force his palms down hard on the counter. The can went flying through the air. Pain shot through the clerk's wrists. He couldn't feel his fingers.

"You have made it difficult for us. Therefore we are forced to make it difficult for you," said the man with brown hair.

The brute tightened his hold on the clerk's wrists, seeming almost to shut off the circulation of blood to his hands. Resistance was futile. The man was too strong. Meanwhile, the one with brown hair reached into his suit jacket and removed a small carpentry hammer.

"This is used to bang in undersized nails in fine woodworking," he said malevolently. "But it also does quite a

53

job when brought into contact with the small bones of the fingers, the ones that are almost impossible to set. The pain, I'm told, never really goes away. Somedays, when it rains, the fingers are useless. Understand?"

The clerk tried to swallow and found his throat muscles contracted in fear. "I'll tell you what you want to know."

The man with thinning brown hair shook his head. "Not good enough. You may lie. You must be taught a lesson."

With that, he brought the hammer down swiftly in a blur toward the clerk's pinky finger on his left hand. The pain forced the man's eyes to explode in their sockets. His scream would have been deafening, had not Brown Hair's other hand muffled it. The clerk felt his teeth tear into his tongue. Blood filled his mouth and filtered through his parched lips. The man directly before him was smiling, showing his teeth for the first time. The brute, meanwhile, remained silent and expressionless.

"Now, you can tell us what we want to know," said Brown Hair.

Leslie Kirkman picked her son Jimmy up outside the Rhode Island School for the Deaf at exactly two o'clock. He greeted her with a warm hug.

"How was your day?" she asked, careful to let him see her lips.

"Good," he replied in sign language.

Her eyes scolded him gently. "You know you're supposed to speak as much as possible."

The boy shrugged his shoulders and turned his face toward the breeze so that his dark brown hair was blown from his face. Although he was making great progress, he still did not speak very well and it embarrassed him. Since he was far more comfortable with sign language, he chose to rely on it instead of his broken speech as often as he could.

Leslie moved to face him and knelt down on the sidewalk, grasping the boy's shoulders. His hearing aids were invisible

54

from this angle. They could only be seen when looking at him from the side.

"There's nothing to worry about," she said softly. "It's just you and me. Don't be afraid to talk. You've got to practice to get better. That's why I don't want you using sign language when we're at home."

"I don't like that rule," the boy said, looking down at the cement.

Leslie smiled. "Then we can *talk* about changing it," she said after he had looked up again. The boy laughed awkwardly. "You can tell me why you don't like it on the way home but you'll have to speak because I have to keep my eyes on the road."

"You win," the boy muttered.

Fifteen minutes later, Leslie dropped Jimmy off at the local Jewish Community Center for a basketball game and then proceeded to her home just half a mile away on Intervale Road. She moved slowly up the front walk, pausing at the mailbox before entering the house. The small batch of letters and bills resisted her attempts to pry them out. Something was wedging them inside the small box. She reached her hand deeper into the unseen area, extracting a thick mailing envelope used for sending photographs.

A chill went up her spine. The photographs were from Scott Krassner!

In seconds, she was again behind the wheel of her silver Datsun sedan on route to the Providence Police Department and Sergeant Phil Scarpani.

She didn't have time to notice that a red Cutlass with two men inside had just pulled onto Intervale Road and was now behind her.

SIX

Night fell over London as CIA agent John Desmond crushed another cigar beneath his feet. His meeting with the Arab had been scheduled for seven o'clock. It was now nearly forty-five minutes past that.

Desmond was nervous.

The agent stepped into a nearby phone booth and searched through his pockets for the proper coin to insert. English currency always confused him; it was one of the reasons he hated London.

"The Golden Fleece," a female voice answered.

"This is Jason. It's cold outside."

"Wait, I'll get the Weatherman."

"Ask him to bring the latest report."

"Where might he reach you."

Desmond recited the number of the pay phone.

"Very well, sir, try to stay out of the rain."

The phone clicked off, only to ring twenty seconds later. Desmond picked it up clumsily, nearly dropping it.

"This is the Weatherman," a husky male voice said.

"It's colder than ever. Can you tell me why?"

"No. The forecast called for a warm night. No station has reported anything to the contrary. Would you like us to send you some extra clothing?"

"No, I think I can handle things on my own."

"We could bring you to a fire."

"Not necessary."

"It sounds like the weather had circled in around you. I'd like you to reconsider—for the sake of your grandfather."

"I can find my way out of the fog."

56

"Where can I reach you with an updated forecast?"

"By *my* fire."

Desmond hung up the phone and turned up his collar. It was indeed a raw night but his conversation had had nothing to do with the weather. He was supposed to meet with a PLO informant bringing information about an Al Fatah strike against Mubarek in Cairo. That was big news, certainly sufficient to draw him from the apartment that the Agency rented for him at nearly 200 pounds a month, though he was rarely there more than four weeks out of the year.

But for no good reason at all the Arab had not shown up or called. The street was all but deserted and fog was beginning to roll in. God, how he hated London.

More tonight than usual because something was wrong. If this meeting had been a trap, those who had set it would not have waited this long to spring it. They would not have allowed him to call in his status to the Weatherman. And if they had planned to kill him, they would have tried to already. Perhaps they had changed their minds.

Though they had good reason not to. After all, John Desmond was the CIA's number one field operative in Middle Eastern affairs. Some said he was the foremost expert on the PLO alive today. He had infiltrated it and built up a chain of informants on the inside and out. And these skills were buttressed by his expertise as a killer, although he much preferred the more subtle accomplishments of his work. For the past few months, it was said, Arafat and his leading subordinates couldn't take a shit without John Desmond knowing.

So when a most reliable source warned him of a coming strike against the Mubarek regime, Desmond was not surprised. But something seemed wrong, because word was out that several high ranking Black September operatives were in America. Desmond had just been about to begin investigating what the operatives were doing in the U.S. when word came in about the offensive aimed at Mubarek. Al Fatah seldom took on two major strikes at the same time and certainly not when one of them seemed to be aimed at America. The ramifications of the contradiction were clear: One of the stories was a decoy for the other.

But which was which?

And who was responsible?

Desmond would find out. Tonight the chain of his reach into the PLO had been broken. His contact had not shown up and had not bothered to call. In the underworld he moved in, a cardinal rule had been broken. The reason couldn't be anything so mundane as casual forgetfulness. It was almost definitely due instead to planned negligence.

Planned toward what end?

Desmond honed his senses even more than he had already. The walk back to his apartment suddenly seemed very long.

Desmond carefully inspected the door to his apartment. No attempt had been made to open it. Most agents usually secured either a piece of hair or scotch tape to the door and frame around it before leaving. Desmond always secured both as an added precaution and tonight both were in place. The only other means of entry was through a window that opened onto a small ledge. But only a skilled acrobat could scale the balconies necessary to reach it.

Desmond entered the living room, closing the door behind him. The shades were up, curtains undrawn just as he had left them, allowing lights from across the boulevard to force their way in and cast the room in murky radiance. Still scanning the area around him, the agent moved his hand to the light switch on the wall and flipped it.

Nothing happened.

There was a sound to his right in the far corner of the room. Soft. A sound most would not bother to hear. But Desmond heard.

Without pausing to think, he spun his left foot around his pivoted right, drawing his Walther in the direction of the corner the sound had come from. All this took no more than a second which must have been too long because before Desmond could move the trigger he felt something tear into his wrist and saw the gun go flying from his hand. He looked down, fighting to keep his calm, and saw the handle of a throwing knife protruding from his jacket, the blade deeply imbedded in the lower part of his forearm.

He spun quickly toward the wall, gasping in pain as he pulled the knife from his arm, intending to hurl it at whoever had hurled it at him as soon as his grip became firm.

His eyes now adjusted to the darkness, Desmond saw a large figure whirl toward him. He caught a glimpse of gray eyes and a bald head, realizing it was Seif the Butcher as he lashed the blade forward at the massive frame. But the killer grabbed the knife hand before it had extended fully and lifted his huge leg up in a vicious kick to Desmond's groin. The pain staggered the agent backwards. Blood raced down his wrist in steady rivulets to the Oriental rug below. The knife was gone, out of sight. The Butcher faced the CIA man head-on, five feet away smiling. Seif's fingers were open. He had no weapon. He was going to try and finish the agent with his hands.

Which meant that Desmond had a chance. Or, at least, thought he had.

His hand was useless, forcing him to use the blinding kicks that had earned him a black belt in Karate. He stepped forward with his left, planted it, and lifted his right in a swirling motion toward the Butcher's face. But Seif stepped into the circle and caught the leg, hurling Desmond against the wall. The agent's head rammed against the panelling. He was dazed. The pain was everywhere. The blood poured from the gaping wound in his wrist.

He realized at once that the Butcher's powerful hands were upon him, lifting him off the ground and then off his feet, gripping him in a bear hug so that his arms dangled over the large shoulders before him. He fought to expand his chest but felt his ribs begin to crack and his air escape him. With his last reserves of strength, Desmond boxed the killer's ears in an attempt to strip him of his equilibrium. The move had no effect.

The agent felt his arms fall, his air totally gone. With a final burst of strength, Seif crushed his spine like a discarded beer can and let the CIA man's lifeless body tumble freely to the bloodstained rug.

Desmond had been nothing but a plaything for him, an opponent who was no opponent at all.

It was time for the others.

Sergeant Phil Scarpani put another strip of tape across the envelope and handed it to the uniformed officer at the side of his desk.

"Make sure this gets to the FBI tonight, now if possible."

"The Providence office will be closed, Phil."

"Boston, then. Send it up by special messenger."

"Should I tell them what to do with it?"

"The instructions are inside, and I've already called the Boston office to alert them it might be coming."

"Anything else?"

"Make sure they know there'll be hell to pay if this package isn't in Washington by eight o'clock tomorrow morning."

"Sounds urgent."

"Yeah."

The uniformed officer left the office.

It was almost eight-thirty. Scarpani pulled his wrinkled handkerchief from his pocket and sneezed loudly into it. He had spent the last three hours studying the 144 pictures Scott Krassner had taken in the hours before he was killed. He couldn't be sure they held the answer to the boy's death because he didn't know what he was looking for. The shots were leisurely taken, obviously by an amateur since a good portion of them were blurred or were taken from the wrong angle. Most were of shoppers going about their busy way, oblivious to the presence of the camera.

One stood out—the twenty-seventh frame of the fourth roll.

The shot, one of the clearest of all, pictured five men; the one in the middle with his arm suspended between his chest and chin as though he were moving it to block his face. None of the men were smiling. Their look was hard and determined, their skin naturally dark. They looked suspicious, uncomfortable, men who blatantly stood out in a scene they had tried to become a part of. Foreigners.

Who were they?

Scarpani looked down one more time at the copy he had made of the shot of the five men standing outside the Biltmore. Still studying it, he picked up the phone and dialed Leslie Kirkman's number.

"Hello," she said. Scarpani could hear a television in the background.

"Mrs. Kirkman, this is Phil Scarpani."

"I've been waiting for your call. Any luck with the pictures?"

"I've sent them to the FBI. Hopefully they'll turn something up for us tomorrow." A pause. "Mrs. Kirkman, there's another problem that concerns you rather directly, you and your son."

Leslie's grip tightened around the receiver. "Me *and* my son?"

Scarpani sighed softly. "As soon as you brought the pictures down here, I sent a man over to Colorlab where they were developed. The lady behind the counter said the clerk who was supposed to be on duty had disappeared while she and someone else were at lunch. We checked his home address and found nothing."

"I don't see what this has to do with me."

"Maybe zilch. Maybe a lot. I mean he could have just skipped out for a drink and never came back. He might still be in the bar now. But the Colorlab people say that doesn't fit with this clerk's work habits at all."

"Perhaps they don't know him as well as they think."

"That's a possibility. But, Mrs. Kirkman, we've got to face the fact that a boy was killed over something in the pictures he took. Somebody must have wanted that film awful badly. And since they can't get it, the next best thing would be to eliminate anyone aware of its existence—the links in the chain. They know about the clerk and it's a good bet they know the film was sent to you."

"So you're saying my life's in danger."

"I'm saying it might be. I'd like to send over some protection but unfortunately what I've got so far wouldn't justify sending over a meter maid to my superiors. The next best thing would be for you to pack up and leave the city for awhile."

"And how long is that?"

"I don't know."

"That's the problem, Sergeant. Nobody's sure of anything yet, including you. All the evidence is circumstantial. You've got no motive and no suspects. But you still want me to pack up my life and leave. You want my son to miss school and me to miss work for how long? A day? A week? A month?"

"It was only a suggestion, Mrs. Kirkman. You're right, I don't know what we're dealing with here. But I do know it's a goddamn steamroller that'll crush anything or anybody in its path."

"If it exists . . . Sergeant, I'm not going to run away," Leslie said resolvedly. "I didn't run when my husband was murdered and I don't plan to now. I've got a stake in this too. Assuming your suspicions are correct, that boy was killed taking pictures for my class which means, one way or another, I had something to do with his death."

"Surely, you don't blame your—"

"Of course not. But I do bear some of the responsibility. If it hadn't been for me, Scott Krassner would still be alive. . . . I'd like to know who killed him and why."

"Even if finding out means putting your own life in danger?"

"As opposed to turning my back and hoping nobody sneaks up from behind for the next God knows how long, yes. Besides, if I ran it would be like admitting to these people that I know

62

something when you and I both know that I don't."

"I'll try to get you some protection."

"I've got a better idea. Let me come with you tomorrow. I could tell the paper I was working on a story, which in a way I am. That would keep you out of trouble with your superiors and provide me with the protection you're convinced I need."

Scarpani considered the proposal. Leslie Kirkman wasn't going to give in which meant this might be the only way he could be sure she'd be safe. "What about your son?" he asked.

"I'll drop him off at school and pick him up after. Security there is outstanding."

Scarpani wiped his nose and nodded to himself. "All right, Mrs. Kirkman, you've got yourself a deal. Be down here tomorrow morning at eight AM."

"See you then, Sergeant."

Leslie paused a second and then ascended the staircase, moving immediately for her bedroom. She opened the closet door and removed a small pine box with a key lock from the top shelf. Leaving it on the bed, she rummaged through a drawer in her night table until her hand emerged with a key. Seconds later the pine box was open.

A .357 magnum rested inside, its stainless steel glinting in the room's light. She reached down, feeling her heart beat faster, and lifted the revolver from its perch. It felt cold and slippery in her hand. The bittersweet scent of gun oil found her nostrils. She had never fired the pistol and wondered if she ever could.

"Mom . . ."

Jimmy's call, spoken from the doorway, startled her enough to make her lose her grip on the gun's handle. It dropped from her fingers and slid under the bed.

"Mom, is that a *real* gun?"

Leslie searched for an answer, while the two men in the red Cutlass waited outside her home uncomfortable in their anticipation.

SEVEN

Special agent Herb Weinberg of the FBI did not like Tuesday mornings any better than Monday mornings, or any other mornings for that matter. The black coffee was bitter, his head ached, and his department's budget wouldn't balance. Christ, why did everything have to balance in Washington when it didn't in Langley?

Once, a hundred years ago, Herb Weinberg had been a happy man. But then his son had been blown up by a landmine in 'Nam and more recently his wife's respiratory ailment had been diagnosed as lung cancer. She had had two operations already and a third was scheduled. There was a lot of pain and only a little hope. Weinberg was beginning to get used to the silent sleepless nights with a bottle of scotch as his bedside partner. But he would never get used to the loneliness.

There was a knock on the door.

"Come in, Connie."

A smartly dressed middle-aged woman entered. "How's the coffee?"

"Same as usual."

"That bad?"

"That bad. What's that you've got in your hand?" Weinberg asked, noticing a manilla envelope.

She placed it on his desk. "It just arrived express from Boston by way of Providence, Rhode Island. It's been marked priority by the Bureau office up there."

"Providence, Rhode Island? . . . Let me take a look."

Connie left the office, as the division chief in charge of Criminal Identification opened the envelope and withdrew its contents. Placing the color snapshots on his desk, he read

64

Sergeant Phil Scarpani's cover letter. Intrigued, he began to sort through the photos, giving few a second look until he came to the twenty-seventh frame of the fourth roll, the one Scarpani had said in the letter to look out for. Weinberg felt something stir in the empty stomach that was beginning to bulge over his belt. His thick graying hair seemed to stand on end. His worn, ashen features reddened.

"Oh my Christ . . ."

He stared at the snapshot a full sixty seconds longer before ringing Connie in the outer office. He was suddenly a nervous man.

"Yes, sir."

"Connie, get me the Director."

"He never gets in before nine."

"I know that. Find him, Connie, wherever he is. Is that understood?"

"Of course."

"And Connie?"

"Yes?"

"Make it fast."

"Have you ever seen these men before?" Sergeant Phil Scarpani asked, holding the snapshot before the eyes of the Biltmore Hotel doorman.

The tall, distinguished looking worker took it in his gloved hand and surveyed it carefully.

"Would it help if I told you this picture was taken Thursday afternoon here by a young boy?" Scarpani added.

"Oh yes, I remember the boy clearly. Good looking young lad. I wasn't really supposed to let him take pictures but there didn't seem to be any harm in it. Why? Has something happened to him?"

Scarpani ignored the question. "What about the men in the picture, do you remember them?"

"Only vaguely. I didn't see them arrive, just leave. They were picked up by a black Cadillac that had been parked right down there where that red Cutlass is now." The doorman pointed to a parking area twenty-five yards away.

"A black Cadillac?"

"Yes."

Scarpani glanced at Leslie Kirkman. Their eyes met, stares somber. The coincidence was too obvious to ignore.

"What else can you tell me?" Scarpani asked.

"Nothing really. Except that I did hear a bit of conversation between a couple of the men." The doorman handed the detective back the picture.

"What did they say?"

"That's just it. I couldn't make it out. It was some foreign language."

Scarpani thanked the doorman and escorted Leslie Kirkman inside the hotel. To bystanders, they might have looked like nothing more than a happy couple.

"Couldn't you have asked him about the Caddy's license number?" Leslie questioned as they passed through the large glass door.

"For what reason? Even if he remembered it, the number has definitely been changed by now. And that's assuming the car still exists. Considering what it was used for, it's a pretty safe bet that the Caddy's been reduced to a 2 X 3 cube in some junkyard. No sense asking any question when the answer can't help you."

Leslie nodded and followed Scarpani to the front desk where the detective showed his badge to the clerk on duty.

"Could I see you a minute please?"

"Sure, right this way," the clerk said, beckoning them toward a door leading into an office. His eyes were gleaming as though he welcomed the visit for whatever reason. He was a slight, unimpressive man wearing a brown uniform. Leslie and Scarpani moved through the door he had pointed out and then into a small, cluttered office. "Now what can I do for you?" the clerk asked.

"Were you on duty Thursday afternoon about three?"

"Most likely."

Scarpani handed him the snapshot. "Have you ever seen any of these men before?"

"No . . . I don't think so."

"We have strong reason to believe they were in the hotel Thursday afternoon."

"Well, unless they checked in then I probably wouldn't have seen them at all."

"And before then?"

"Not to my recollection. But someone in billing might remember something. I mean if they were guests here, they would have had to pay, right? . . . Do you mind if I take this picture up front to our cashiers?"

"Be my guest."

The clerk returned a few minutes later. "No luck," he reported. "No one remembers seeing any of these men."

"Does that mean they left Thursday without paying?"

"They could have prepaid their bill, but that's rather unusual."

"Which means it wouldn't be hard to track down all those who made such arrangements and checked out Thursday," Scarpani suggested.

"With our new computer system, not at all."

The clerk led them into a larger office containing a keyboard terminal attached to a display viewer. He sat down before it and pressed out a series of instructions. The machine responded in seconds.

"I'm sorry," the clerk said. "But no guests who had prepaid their bills checked out on Thursday."

"What about prepaid guests who are still here, or at least who are supposed to be?" Leslie Kirkman asked, stealing a look at Phil Scarpani as if to ask permission to speak after the fact. The detective smiled tightly and nodded at the clerk.

Again the small man pressed out a series of instructions. This time the machine spit out a more satisfactory answer. The clerk looked up from behind the display viewer.

"We have thirty-seven rooms presently occupied that have been prepaid," he said.

"How many of them are suites?" Scarpani asked, thinking that the five men would have needed a suite for whatever meeting had taken place.

The clerk checked the board. "Fifteen, I'm afraid. I know that doesn't narrow it down much but most of our prepaid customers do travel luxuriously."

Scarpani noticed that Leslie Kirkman had moved behind the clerk and was studying the screen before him. "Any way of checking to see if any of those suites are now vacant?" the detective asked.

"Certainly, but it will take a few minutes."

"That isn't necessary," said Leslie Kirkman, turning away from the white letters that seemed to dance on the blue screen.

"Why not?" Scarpani asked.

"Because our five friends who speak a foreign language must have a sense of humor. They reserved the suite in the name of Mote."

"So?"

"Mote is the Arabic word for death."

At that same time, a meeting was about to begin at the Central Intelligence Agency in Langley, Virginia in the office of the Director himself, Colonel Vernon P. Rossi.

Present in the room now, waiting for the Director's arrival, were Art Bartose, Deputy Director in charge of Operations (DDO); Bob Kincannon, Deputy Director in charge of Intelligence (DDI); and special agent Herb Weinberg of the FBI. All three men were, to say the least, jittery, though Weinberg was easily the most so because he had never been inside the Langley complex before and had always tended, like most others in the Bureau, to view the Agency as more foe than friend. The thought that the two could work together seemed as bizarre as it was ludicrous.

But they were about to.

And now Herb Weinberg wished his wife was home and healthy so he could fully concentrate on the meeting that was about to begin. He also wished he had worn a better suit. The vested gray one he had on was too tight, revealing too much of his protruding belly. He straightened his tie from his position in the third chair directly in front of the Director's desk. The office was uncommonly large but contained only one window in the rear that looked over a barbed wire fence and the woods beyond it. A couch rested against the back wall and several leather chairs surrounded the desk of the Director in a semicircle in the front. The carpet was thin and worn in several places by the tracks of Colonel Rossi's wheelchair.

The Director had been striken with polio shortly after the close of World War II while working for the intelligence forerunner of the CIA, the OSS. His legs had weakened and quickly became useless. His left arm and side had been slightly paralyzed. So he had gotten through the OSS by his wits, not his muscles. And those same wits had carried him through the various levels of the CIA, once it was created, until he finally achieved the position he had long cherished and had been unjustifiably denied him numerous times in the past.

Suddenly the office's only door swung electronically open and Weinberg watched Colonel Rossi wheel himself in.

"Good morning, gentlemen."

Weinberg rose with the other two men in the room, feeling a deep admiration for the man known affectionately as "the Colonel." His hair was a silvery shade of white, long and combed neatly from right to left except for a few knotted strands that fell over his forehead. His skin was bronze-colored, courtesy of a recent vacation in Miami, his first since taking over the Agency. He smiled and moved himself into position behind the large walnut desk.

"Gentlemen, I believe it's time we got started." His voice was deep but the words came out in a slight rasp. The paralysis, Weinberg had been told sometime before, had begun to effect his vocal cords. Most, in fact, said that Colonel Vernon Rossi was a dying man. "And the place to start is with the murder of John Desmond."

Bartose and Kincannon turned uneasily toward Weinberg. The Director sensed their displeasure. "Gentlemen," he said, "since my counterpart at the Bureau and I have already agreed that this is to be a joint venture, I'd suggest you end your squabbling and start cooperating with our friend from Washington."

Bartose still looked unhappy. "I believe this matter falls clearly within our jurisdiction."

"But the five terrorists were spotted *inside* the country," Weinberg reminded. "If anything, it's our jurisdiction plain and simple, an obvious *domestic* problem. Or so say my superiors."

"But you don't agree with them," advanced the Director.

Weinberg shook his head. "In Washington we tend to go about such matters with blinders on. Any terrorist group bigger than the Black Panthers is too big for us to handle alone."

"If your superiors knew you'd said that, I'd wager you'd be standing in an unemployment line this time tomorrow," quipped Rossi.

"Or worse."

The Director smiled. "You need us, Mr. Weinberg, and we need you. But I'm afraid even our combined resources may not be enough." Rossi pointed to his stomach. "I have a gut feeling about this right smack in my ulcers. It began as indigestion with the murder of John Desmond last night and escalated into heartburn when that snapshot of yours arrived this morning. Mr. Kincannon, will you please give us the details of Desmond's assassination."

Bob Kincannon adjusted his horn-rimmed glasses and opened a folder that had been sitting on his lap. He was a frail man with a gaunt face and short-cropped black hair. He had the look of nervous insignificance about him, never looking to be any more than the bureaucrat that he was. As Deputy Director

70

in charge of Intelligence, his primary role was to deal with all things administrative. He began to speak, glancing up from his notes.

"Yesterday evening, a meeting was set up by Desmond with one of his PLO sources for seven o'clock London time. The man, most reliable in the past, promised to deliver important information about a Black September offensive against the Mubarek government. The man never showed. It was obviously a red herring used to lure Desmond from his apartment. When he failed to report in at the specified nightly time, a team was sent to his building to investigate. They found him on the rug, his spine neatly snapped in two."

"Seif?"

"It appears likely. No other killer in our files could have penetrated an agent like Desmond's security and executed him in such a brutal manner. What's more, the fact that Seif is one of those present in Mr. Weinberg's snapshot seems to indicate a connection between Desmond's death and whatever is going on here."

Colonel Rossi turned toward Art Bartose, Deputy Director in charge of Operations. "Art, tell us what the murder of a leading deep-cover man like Desmond signifies."

Bartose leaned forward. He was a young looking fifty thanks to the thick dark hair that hung unkemptly over his forehead. He looked more like a college professor than a man in charge of one of the most sensitive departments in all of Langley. And, in point of fact, he had come to the Company by way of Princeton's political science department.

"Desmond was far and away our leading expert on Black September activities and had been ever since Munich," Bartose began. "If, then, Al Fatah was planning some sort of action against us with this country, his execution would be the first mandated step for success. And, by the same token, the murder of an agent of his stature can only mean that the terrorists are pulling out all the stops. Such things just aren't done any more. Al Fatah certainly knows they are subjecting

71

themselves to massive retaliation in the wake of such an action. But my guess is they don't care."

"From a practical standpoint, where does this death leave us?" Rossi asked.

Bartose sighed. "I'd like to say up the creek without a paddle, but I'm not even sure right now we've got a boat. Granted, we have Desmond's file but his mind and resources and contacts have died with him. The reach he had into the PLO provided us with the only real accurate information about Al Fatah we ever received; except from that obtained from the Israelis who are the only ones operating with any success and consistency in Beirut and Amman. In any case, the process of replacing him and setting up a new intelligence chain will undoubtedly be long, if it can be accomplished at all. And I doubt that Al Fatah, Black September or whatever you want to call them is worried in the least. Their timetable seems to be proceeding as planned."

"Timetable for what?" raised Weinberg.

"That's what we're being paid to find out," replied the Director. "And we had better start earning our salaries."

EIGHT

Colonel Rossi opened a desk drawer, exposing a panel of buttons. He pushed one and a map on the wall slid up to reveal a screen. He pushed another and the lights in the office were extinguished. He pushed a third and a picture taken four days before outside the Biltmore Hotel in Providence filled the screen, a bit blurred because it had been cropped to include only the upper bodies and faces of the five men.

"Go on, Art," he instructed.

Bartose rose and moved to the screen as though it were a blackboard. Placing a pair of glasses halfway up his nose, he began. "From left to right, here's who we're dealing with. . . ." The academic went through abbreviated versions of dossiers pertaining to Tebara, al-Kahir, El Sayad, and Seif from notes he had made earlier in the morning. "Of course, you've noticed that I skipped over the man in the middle. We all know who he is: Ali Hassan Salameh, alias Abu Hassan, known in Israel as the Red Prince. And he is still alive, although our Israeli friends assured us he was killed in Beirut more than three years ago. It is now clear that his apparent execution was a setup to rid him of the Israeli hunters who had been stalking him since Munich."

"But such an elaborate hoax?" posed Weinberg. "Isn't that going just a little too far to get some privacy?"

"Not when you consider the fact that his disappearance might have been called for by whatever offensive we are facing now. And not when you consider the personality of the man himself." Bartose looked at the Director. "If I may, sir . . ."

The Director hit two of the buttons in his drawer and beckoned Bartose on. The picture disappeared from the screen and the lights in the room came back on.

Bartose moved to his chair and lifted a folder from the briefcase that rested by its side. He opened it and strolled to the middle of the room with yellow legal pad in hand. Pushing his glasses back on his nose, he began to speak.

"Gentlemen, I believe it's imperative we know exactly how dangerous this man truly is." The academic cleared his throat and looked down briefly at the notes scribbled over the yellow pad. "We're dealing here with a striking paradox of a man whose compassion for killing is equalled only by his compassion for blended scotch whiskey. At times, he has seemed a reasonable sort seeking to find a peaceful end to the Palestinian problem. At others, far more frequently, he has been nothing less than a cold-blooded murderer who makes no secret of the fact that he enjoys taking lives.

"The first terrorist action he perpetrated, for example, took place in Jerusalem in 1968. He purchased a delivery van and drove it daily to a crowded market street filled with bottles of milk. The van and its contents became a routine sight in the square, so much so that the last day it was parked there nobody bothered to notice that the bottles were full of gasoline and were rigged to a fuse attached to dynamite. The truck exploded during the busiest time of the day, killing twelve people and wounding fifty-three more. And, as if that wasn't enough, Salameh held a press conference in Cairo soon after to take credit for the action personally. He smiled the whole time while cameras rolled and clicked, positively buoyant, making no effort to disguise his satisfaction with the results of the act.

"In the years he led Al Fatah, though, beginning in late 1970, his behavior became much more guarded. Public appearances were few and far between. He stayed on the move constantly, always changing bodyguards to avoid Israeli infiltration. But this clandestine existence did not interfere with his pursuit of an exquisite life of luxury. He slept with hundreds of women fit to be *Playboy* centerfolds in a score of cities all over the world. On some occasions he was known to tempt fate by frequenting great nightclubs and restaurants. Because of this thirst for the good life, Mossad officials gave Salameh the code name 'Red Prince' and used every effort at their disposal to eliminate him. Paradoxically, it was said he loved his wife and two young sons dearly and was deeply disappointed that his life on the run kept him away from them for such long periods at a time. After it was learned that he had planned Munich, he barely saw them at all because the Mossad increased its efforts ten-fold to kill him, to no avail I might add."

"And now we may be facing another Munich," offered Weinberg.

"Something on that scale seems likely," agreed Bartose. "Perhaps even more devastating because that's what Al Fatah needs to return attention to their existence and regain the strength within the PLO that they've lost."

"But why America?" Weinberg asked. "Why take the struggle out of the Mideast?"

"Because in the eyes of most Palestinians it already has been," answered the Director. "You can divide the extremist wing of the PLO into two distinct groups: one which believes they will never obtain their nation through diplomatic means, and one which opposes any negotiated settlement at all. And America, Mr. Weinberg, is caught right in the middle. The first group sees us as the barrier preventing them from achieving their nation and the second sees us as the main impetus behind the negotiations they loath. The logical strategy of either group, then, would be to aim their attack at us, the real country that stands in their way. Disgrace us in the eyes of the world . . . or worse. And it's the 'or worse' that worries me."

"There may well be another motive as well," picked up Bartose. "But . . ."

"But what, Mr. Bartose?"

Bartose leaned forward and adjusted his glasses. "Now I'm not a psychiatrist, Colonel Rossi, so I can't really talk about the affects of long-term isolation on a man. But the fact remains that for the past three-and-a-half years, it's very probable that Salameh never saw more than a handful of people directly associated with the scheme that's presently confronting us. That means even his wife and children were left to think he was dead, though he always knew someday he'd be able to return to them."

"I don't follow you," said Herb Weinberg.

"I do," muttered the Director gravely.

Bartose glanced at Rossi and then continued. "A little over a year ago, Salameh's wife and two sons—ages 15 and 12—came to America, supposedly as tourists. It doesn't really matter whether they really were or not because their stay and their lives were ended by a bomb tossed into the restaurant where they were having lunch. The story we gave out was that the bombing was the result of a city wide gang war. It wasn't."

"Oh my God . . ." Weinberg felt suddenly chilled. "But surely we, I mean you, didn't . . ."

"No, Mr. Weinberg," said Rossi, "we had nothing to do with it. But the Arabs thought we were responsible which means Salameh did as well. In other words, the terrorist action we may soon be facing is very likely the Red Prince's twisted version of revenge."

"And if he is truly mentally unbalanced," Bartose began, "then there is no limit to the harm he could cause because there would be no elements of conscience or morality around to inhibit him. There would only be a desire for revenge. Some say a terrorist is the worst kind of criminal. Others say a madman is. Well, gentlemen, we are dealing with a man who is a combination of both."

"A man about to launch a major offensive against us in the God knows how near future," added Rossi.

"What do the Israelis say?" asked Weinberg.

"All this comes as much as a surprise to them as it did to us," replied the Director. "And given the limited amount of time we may have, there would seem to be little chance of discovering exactly what the operation entails. Meanwhile, our best man

Desmond is dead and no one else seems to know anything that can help us. . . . We're in trouble, gentlemen. Our hourglass has cracked and the sand is running through twice as fast. We need help."

Kincannon smiled curtly. "Sir, I believe our intelligence capabilities are more than capable of defending our own security." He turned toward Weinberg. "Especially when one considers the cooperation we'll be receiving from our friends in Washington."

Rossi patted his stomach. "My ulcers disagree with you, Bob. First of all, we don't know what we're fighting. We don't know what the target is, or even if there is a specific target. All we are sure of is that five of Black September's top operatives were in America together at the same time. All we can do is guess, speculate as to why. We could put the computers on overtime on this one and all we'd do is overload the circuits. I repeat, we need help."

"From who?"

The Director turned to Bartose. "I asked Art that precise question three hours ago."

Bartose shook his thick hair from his forehead, reaching inside an envelope that had been sitting on his lap. "There are only two men in the world I believe can provide us with the immediate assistance we require." Bartose straightened his glasses and began to read from a typed sheet before him. "The first is David Rabanine, a retired Mossad agent. Though he is no longer active in the field, he is still considered Israel's foremost expert on PLO terrorist activities and is frequently called in to give consultation to Mossad operatives."

"I've heard his nerves were shot," said Kincannon.

"His dossier explains why," Bartose resumed. "He was born in 1940 in Munich, his parents fleeing to London to avoid Hitler, later emigrating to Palestine at the war's close. His father died in 1948 while fighting for the Haganah. His mother died of cancer in 1952. He was raised by his grandparents until he joined the armed services in 1956 by lying about his age and presenting falsified documents. He was recruited by the Mossad for intelligence work in 1960 and quickly became one of that organization's leading G-5 men."

"G-5?" From Weinberg.

"Our term for agents who are given more or less of a free hand. Rabanine was renowned as an expert in all matters pertaining to Arab terrorism and methods for counterattack. He is believed to have had an important hand in the theft of 200 tons of Uranium 'yellowcake' for use in Israel in 1968, as well as the theft of five gunboats from the Cherbourg Port of France in 1969. In 1970 he became head of a special task force that successfully penetrated several levels of the PLO. In 1971 he vetoed a plan to assassinate Yassir Arafat and had the decision blow up in his face with the Munich massacre. His wife of five years, Rivkah, was murdered in 1972 by a man believed to be Seif the Butcher in Hebron. Rabanine lives today with his thirteen-year-old son, Shaul, peacefully. A man old before his time, they say." Bartose hedged nervously. "But I suggest we contact him immediately."

"I don't see how a man old before his time can help us," Kincannon noted.

"He's all we have."

"You said there were two men."

"I hesitate to mention the second."

"Don't on my account."

Bartose looked to the Director. Rossi nodded. "The second is Alabaster," the academic said to his bureaucratic counterpart.

"Oh Christ."

Bartose swung back to the Director. "My thoughts exactly. Alabaster is undoubtedly the most deadly agent alive today, if he is still alive. No one is even sure of that. His identity is the best kept secret in Israel. Not even the highest ranking Mossad officials have ever met him."

"But you said he was an agent," reminded the man from the FBI.

"A poor choice of words on my part. If he is an agent, then the only organization he works for is his own. Alabaster is a vigilante. No one has ever assigned him to do anything. He does it all on his own. Planning, coordination, escape— everything. If he needs men, he recruits them. And the identities of the ones he chooses become just as secretive as his own. We don't even know what he looks like. There is no picture of him anywhere on file and no one has any idea how to contact him."

"He seems like the right man for this job," concluded Weinberg.

"But we have no way of telling him that there's a job to be done," Bartose resumed. "Alabaster comes out only after a crime against the state of Israel has been committed. For this reason, Arab terrorists fear him more than any other man. They hear him following after a bomb has gone off or a raid has been committed or hostages seized. Sometimes he's there. More times he's not. But the point has been made. Delays occur out of fear that Alabaster will appear to seek reprisal. Even the best in Al Fatah hesitate, perhaps even fail to carry out their assigned tasks. By merely existing, Alabaster accomplishes what he wants to. He's a kind of legend, a myth. Make no mistake about it, though, he's also a ruthless killer who plays by no rules other than those he makes up."

"And he may be dead."

"Or no longer alive. One in this case does not necessarily imply the other. However, it's worth noting that several sources in Israel say he hasn't been heard from in two years. Perhaps he retired."

Rossi shook his head. "He's not the type to take a gold watch and a pension."

"His past backs you up there, sir," Bartose agreed, again looking down at the sheet on his lap. "We can attribute a minimum of sixteen assassinations to Alabaster, five of which were directly tied in with the Munich massacre. This process culminated in 1979 when it is believed he organized the, ah, supposed execution of Ali Hassan Salameh in Beirut, acting even as the Mossad was setting up another attempt of their own. A white Volkswagen packed with 200 pounds of plastic explosives was blown up by remote control when Salameh's station wagon passed by it. . . . None of this, of course, has ever been confirmed by the Mossad. The Mossad never confirms anything, including the very existence of Alabaster. That's why I believe it's pointless for us to try to contact him."

"Seems to me like the very reason for the opposite," argued Weinberg.

"Indeed," concurred Colonel Rossi. "Indeed. . . . Bob," he said to Kincannon, "seal this thing up tight."

"Tight, sir?"

"As a drum." The Director turned toward Bartose. "In the meantime, Art, contact the Mossad and ask them to reach Rabanine for us. And find Alabaster. I don't care how, just do it."

Bartose shrugged. "By the time we reach him, it might be too late."

"If it isn't already."

NINE

Abad Salim was a happy man. The bomb he had planted in an Israeli school bus in Tel Aviv twelve days before had exploded before any of the children had gotten off. Fourteen had been killed.

Fourteen! . . . The number exceeded even his greatest expectations.

Next to killing Jews, Salim loved sweets best, especially chocolates. He was an obese man with a round balding head that seemed too small for his body and a chin that hung grotesquely toward his neck like a turkey's wattle. His stomach inevitably carried over the baggy pants he found himself forced to wear. But all of this did not deter Salim from eating small bits of candy whenever he was nervous; the more nervous, the more candy.

And tonight he had already consumed three boxes of French chocolates.

Because late tonight he was scheduled to make his escape from a dock in the port city of Haifa, located on the Mediterranean in the northern strip of Israel. He had hidden himself in the Zion Hotel on Baerwald Street eleven days before, as the police and Shabat officers searched everywhere. But his cover was good. They had not found him. And now he was going to escape.

Because he carried too much weight on his small frame, Salim's breathing was always hot and labored. He perspired heavily and was forever wiping his brow with a perpetually soiled handkerchief. On days he did not shower, no one would go near him because of the smell. This did not bother Salim in the least, though, because he didn't like people. His appearance was the kind no one ever took a second look at which meant he could come and go just about as he pleased even in Israel.

Which is what had allowed him to get in and out of Tel Aviv effortlessly and remain long enough to witness, actually *witness*, the masterful explosion of his bomb on the school bus. Salim remembered hearing the sound of the gears shifting into neutral in the moment before the blast. Windows shattered and steel bent as the machine came to its first stop. The bus spun violently and then crashed into the side of the building. Finally it keeled over and dropped to the ground like a dying animal to be engulfed by its own flames. It was all so gratifying for Salim. The dismembered limbs, the high-pitched screams of children. Watching the young Jewish blood stain the street with widening rivers of red.

He had been exceptionally happy that day.

But he wasn't any more because his room in the center of Haifa had come too much to resemble a prison. He had not left it once in the past eleven days except to get a newspaper in the lobby and even then he did his best to cover his bloated face from those who might recognize it.

All his meals had been delivered by room service. He slept uneasily, his dreams haunted by Alabaster coming for him with a knife that became a machine gun that turned into a powerful hand. Nor had Salim showered in all the time he had been here out of fear Alabaster would choose that time for an attack. Thus the room was filled with a putrid stench emenating from his ever perspiring body. He had grown used to it. As for others, well, they didn't belong in the room anyway.

He had just wedged an entire handful of chocolates into his mouth when he heard someone knocking at the door. It would be Daoud, the PLO's main man in Haifa—his contact. The man who had set up his escape. Uneasily, he swung the door open, relived to find the white-clad Daoud standing before him.

"It's good to see you, my friend." Salim smiled, displaying a nest of rotting teeth.

Daoud entered and closed the door quickly behind him,

bringing a sleeve up to his nose to hide the stench. "Spare me the false greetings, Abad. There is no time."

"You are always in a rush, my friend. Would you like some candy?"

"No. I'll leave you to stuff your face alone. We must hurry. The plans have been made. You leave Israel for Egypt in an hour."

"Last minute arrangements?"

"They were the only ones available. Haifa and the rest of the country are swarming with police. Pictures are being circulated. Yours is among them."

Salim swallowed hard. "Do they know it was me?"

"They know it might have been. And they are intensifying their search in this area."

"Then how can you get me out?"

"Do not fret, Abad, I have many contacts who after this is over will probably never want anything to do with me again, thanks to you. I have spent half this quarter's allotment securing safe transportation for you to Port Said. You are going by trawler. The captain is quite a businessman."

"Who is he?"

"His last name is Gibli, I don't know his first. He is an Israeli whose allegiance can be bought. He owns a forty-two foot trawler that has made several similar trips before."

"And his crew?"

"He uses none. I have two very well-regarded bodyguards prepared to make the trip with you. They will insure that nothing goes wrong."

"What happens when I reach Port Said?"

"Other arrangements have been made to get you to Cairo. The bodyguards know them."

"Does this Gibli check out?"

"As well as anyone who runs the sort of business he does. There are no assurances, Abad. But Gibli does have one major thing going for him."

"What's that?"

"A wooden leg. Doesn't make him much of a threat should he decide to turn against you at sea."

Salim popped another handful of candy into his mouth, talking with it jammed full, the words barely audible. "You have put me at ease, my friend. Someday I hope to be able to return the favor."

"Save the thanks. We must leave. There is little time."

Forty-five minutes later, Daoud's Citroen pulled up along a small, secluded dock in the Port Area of Haifa. He led Salim onto the dock toward the boat that would serve as his transport. Salim, a poor traveller under even the best conditions, shuddered at the sight. Gibli's trawler, tied haphazardly to the ancient decaying supports, seemed destined to sink with the first wave upon leaving port. Its wooden frame was weather-beaten and cracked in several areas above the surface. The letters of its name, *Carmelia*, were barely legible. Its deck was splintered and warped.

It was obvious to Abad Salim that no repairs had been made on the boat in many months. And when the captain named Gibli approached, flanked by the two PLO bodyguards, it was also obvious why. For he too was weather-beaten, his face a mass of cracks and creases courtesy of the hard sea air and spray. His uncombed long hair hung wildly over his ears and face. His eyes were dark, menacing, mad.

He moved slowly toward the two men now standing before him on the dock. His wooden right leg, extending from the knee down, clapped down hard on the decaying deck with each step, creating a strangely melodic beat not unlike a death march. Salim felt frightened as Gibli eyed him coldly.

"We cast off in five minutes—with or without passengers."

Salim turned away, not wishing to further meet his stare. The mad eyes shot through him like cold needles. Nervously, the Egyptian reached into the pocket of his wrinkled dark overcoat for some chocolates. The wrapper had come off and the pieces were sticking to the fabric. Salim stripped them off and forced them into his mouth, tugging at the lint with his tongue. He turned to Daoud.

"I am unhappy with this arrangement."

"Take it or leave it," said Daoud abruptly.

"This is not the way old friends should part."

Daoud, his white suit glistening with water tossed over the dock, ignored the words. "Your boat is leaving. I suggest you climb on it. *M'as-salémi.*"

"*M'as-salémi.*"

Salim took a deep breath and jumped onto the boat. His two bodyguards were immediately at his sides.

"Candy?" he offered. The men declined, locking their eyes on the broken man perched on the outdoor bridge eight feet above them. They had already searched the boat thoroughly and had found no weapons. Salim smiled confidently. Both bodyguards were large and heavily muscled, black turtlenecks slung tightly across their chests. There would be no trouble.

Salim heard the engine sputter and stall and the captain curse loudly, banging his wooden leg against the floor beneath it. Finally the ship came to reluctant life, seeming to fight against another voyage it knew its battered decks couldn't handle. Gibli cursed again and gassed the engine, spinning the wheel hard in order to steer the *Carmelia* out of its position in the dock. The sick boat ambled slowly, battling the water instead of flowing with it. The ship seemed to be in search of its own death, thirsting for the powerful current that would ultimately end its maritime misery. It rode the waves poorly, struggling for each inch in the black water below. The sea was choppy, the breeze cold and chilling. It was going to be a long trip.

Salim moved toward the stern and rested one foot on the gunwale, interlacing his arms to ward off the chill. His bodyguards stayed near the bow, one watching Gibli, the other surveying the sea for other vessels of which there were none. Salim's eyes, meanwhile, locked themselves on the city of Haifa, its gold lights lingering in the misty night but growing gradually obscure as the trawler continued to mark a slow path away from them.

Salim felt relaxed for the first time since the bombing.

That is until the trawler suddenly listed heavily to the right and tipped toward the sea, spilling him to the deck so that his head rammed the gunwale. Wood shattered. The dim light faded and then returned. The Egyptian's two bodyguards had fallen as well and would certainly question the captain about what had happened just as soon as they got back to their feet.

Dazed, his head aching, Salim pushed his obese body up, still facing the stern and Haifa's gleaming shores. As he turned slowly toward the bridge, massaging his head, he heard not the voices of his bodyguards but their screams blaring in the wake of two quick soft spurts from what he knew could only be an Israeli Uzi machine gun.

Salim gasped when he saw what was left of them.

The men's bodies were sprawled on either side of the deck, their faces arched forward in an open-eyed death grin, their chests a mass of torn flesh and blood. Salim raised his eyes and caught the figure of the captain, no longer standing on one good leg but on two, the wooden extension that had housed the Uzi standing erect by his side. He flexed the leg that had been hidden, trying to restore circulation to the cramped muscles. After a few seconds, still gripping the Uzi, he began to climb deliberately down the ladder, never taking his eyes away from the terrified face of Salim.

"*Alabaster! . . .*"

The captain had reached the deck now and was standing not six feet from the trembling terrorist.

"You remembered, Salim? How reassuring after all these years. I let you live then; it would appear I made a mistake." It had been Salim who three-and-a-half years before had provided Alabaster with the location of the Red Prince, allowing the Israeli to plan and carry out Salameh's execution. Alabaster hated the fat terrorist then and hated him more now. He had to fight back the urge to cut him in half with the Uzi as he stood.

That was too easy, too quick. In Salim's case, another method was called for.

"It wasn't me! . . . I swear it wasn't me!"

"What are you talking about, Salim?"

"The school bus! . . . I knew about it, yes, but it was the work of someone else. *I swear!*"

"And I am supposed to believe you, of course."

Alabaster took two large steps forward so that the tip of the small Uzi rested against the fat man's protruding belly. The Israeli's leg pulsated with pain, the muscles spasming in rebellion over being tied to his buttocks for the past two hours. It was an old trick, one that took years to perfect.

Alabaster had had many such years.

"If I had killed you four years ago," he resumed, "perhaps none of those schoolchildren would be dead today. I blame myself more than I blame you." Alabaster shoved the machine gun's barrel viciously into the large stomach before it. The Egyptian doubled over in pain, whimpering and fighting for breath. "You are like a sick dog, Salim. I look at killing you as a means to end your own misery as well as the misery you have caused the world."

Alabaster tossed the Uzi behind him and withdrew a long hunting knife from his belt. He reached his free hand down and lifted Salim to his feet effortlessly by the lapel. With that, the knife was against the terrorist's throat, its blade struggling to glisten in the murky light of the deck.

"Fourteen children are dead, Salim. I will slit your throat now thinking of them."

The terrorist's breaths came rapidly. He began to pant. His eyes blinked continuously, fighting not to look at the razor sharp knife poised at this neck.

"I have something to offer you in exchange for my life," he said brokenly.

"What?"

"Information."

"What makes you think I don't already know what you want

87

to tell me?"

"Because you couldn't. It's impossible."

"Nothing is impossible for Alabaster."

The terrorist shook his head, feeling the point of the blade prick his skin. "This time you are wrong. They have coordinated an operation without you knowing."

Salim felt the cold steel withdraw a bit from his neck. The Jew's eyes still shook him with their fierce intensity.

"In that case, Salim, I am listening."

"Will you give me my life?"

"If what you say is true, I will consider it."

"It is." The terrorist steadied himself. "An operation is about to be launched against America."

"What sort of operation?"

"I'm not sure. I have been excluded from the planning and learned of it only by chance. Total secrecy is being employed. I only know that the high command of the Movement is expecting the enemy to have severe numbers of casualties." Salim stopped, his breath echoing in the wind.

"Tell me more."

"It's all I know. Except for, except for . . ."

"Except for what?"

"A phrase, a German phrase somehow connected to the operation: *Der Teufels Befehl.*"

"Dare toy-fulls be-fail," the Israeli pronounced phonetically. "The Devil's Command?"

Salim nodded slightly. "An accurate translation."

"What does it mean for Black September?"

"A sort of . . . weapon."

"What sort of weapon?"

"A new and deadly one, capable of leaving drastic numbers dead."

"And that's all you can tell me about it?"

"Because it's all I know!"

"Unfortunately, that's not good enough. I will have to kill you."

"But I've told you *everything!*"

"Still not enough."

Salim's eyelids flickered. "There's something else you should know. Three-and-a-half years ago, our meeting, the Red Prince knew about it. He wanted you to know where to find him."

"You are wasting my time with lies, Salim."

"It's true. . . . *I swear!*"

"Then you set me up, all the more reason to kill you."

"*He* set me up. I only followed orders."

Silence enveloped the deck. Alabaster's eyes seemed unsure for the first time. "He wanted me to know about Beirut. . . . It makes no sense," he said more to himself than the terrorist.

"You must let me live," Salim pleaded. "I've told you something that will probably result in my death anyway."

"Perhaps," Alabaster said icily. "But if I don't kill you myself, word will circulate that Alabaster can be bargained with. I can't have that. Besides, there are fourteen children to think of."

"But you promis—"

The rest of the terrorist's words were lost in the night air as Alabaster jerked him around so his head was facing the stern and then pulled the knife violently in an upward thrust, watching the blood spurt out of the torn throat and surge onto the deck. A scream began in Salim's throat that became a gurgle before being stifled altogether by the dark red fluid that choked off his breath. He collapsed on the deck, his stare as twisted in death as it had been in life.

Alabaster sighed. He had enjoyed the action and this concerned him because it meant things were rapidly becoming as they had been before. Killing would once more become the dominant force in his life, an insatiable urge that rose within him and demanded to be satisfied. It wasn't that killing was a part of him, it was that he was a part of killing. And there was nothing he could do about it.

Carefully, Alabaster tossed the corpse over the side into the black water raging below which swallowed it up gratefully.

But the Israeli did not see it disappear because his mind was elsewhere. Salim's final words had been true; he could feel it in the terrorist's voice, which made one fact strikingly obvious:

The Red Prince had not died that day in Beirut!

It had all been a ruse, a clever scene played out for the world's benefit.

Salameh was alive.

Then why did he have to appear dead?

Der Teufels Befehl . . . The Devil's Command . . .

What did it mean?

What was the devastating weapon Salim had spoken of?

Alabaster would go to America. The answers would be there. And, in trying to find them, he would become again the man he had always been. Purpose had returned. He was needed now, he could feel it, more than he had ever been before. It was time to live once more the only way he knew how.

America . . .

PART TWO

TEN

There is a town in Israel that lies almost at the midpoint between Tel Aviv and Jerusalem. The town is best known for not being known at all. In fact, it has no name because it exists only in the minds of the Israeli officials who created it as a haven for recuperating or retired Mossad agents who have lived a great part of their lives on both sides of a gun and wish to live there no longer. Most will say that those who come to the town with no name do so to die.

But David Rabanine had come there to live. Or, at least, try to.

The murder of his wife eleven years before had faced him with a realization he could evade no more than he could a bullet: The great successes of his tenure in the field amounted to basically nothing. Actually less than nothing when you consider that the one life that had been taken from him far outweighed the lives he had taken from others.

There was no escaping that reality or the reality of his wife's death and Rabanine did not bother trying. Instead, he packed up his life in one large suitcase and took his two-year-old son Shaul to live in a restored house on one hundred acres of land supplied by the Mossad who always looked after their own.

But not their own's wives.

He was done. Finished. His skills and desire, David told his superiors, had eluded him. He was more than willing to offer advice and consultation when requested. But he could no longer deal in the circles of espionage. He could no longer fire a gun and preferred not to even hold one.

Rivkah was dead . . . because of him.

But he still had Shaul and that made life worth living. At

thirteen, the boy was everything Rabanine dreamed he would be. Tall and muscular for his age, Shaul had the body of an athlete and the face of an actor. It was soft, full and bronze-colored—the face of his mother—topped by long sandy-brown straight hair that stretched to his eyebrows and over his ears. His smile was his mother's as well; white, warm, disarming.

Shaul was Rabanine's reason to keep on living and to refuse any assignment the Mossage offered that might threaten the life they had built together. "I am retired," he told his former superiors again and again.

I am retired.

The land rover, being driven by one of the eleven men who watched over the estate and farmed some of the land, turned right onto a dirt road. Home was just up ahead. The rover hit a bump, sending David from the seat and into the air for a second. The driver apologized. The front gate of his property appeared fifty yards ahead.

The estate was surrounded by a six-foot high stone fence, as old as the town with no name itself. There was only one entrance and it was manned constantly by one of the workers. No one can get in or out without setting off an electronic alarm wired across the stone fence. If necessary, the guards' orders are to shoot intruders on sight. They are devoted men, committed to the man they have been charged with protecting. They are also superb soldiers. The estate is a fortress.

"Good to see you back, David," said the gate guard when the rover stopped to allow him to remove the heavy chain. Rabanine insisted that all of his men call him by his first name. "How was your trip?"

"Boring and tiring. I don't know which is the greater."

The guard smiled. Every time Rabanine returned from a conference at Mossad headquarters in Tel Aviv, he would ask him this same question and receive the same answer. He liked Rabanine immensely, as did all the other workers on the estate. David was an amiable man and a good-looking one as well. He was tall and might have been well-built, though it was hard to tell now because of the tired way he carried himself. His face was strong but weary, marked by deep creases and crevices of depression and fatigue. His eyes were deep but somehow empty, dull. His smile wide but much too rare.

As the rover pulled to a halt in the circular drive twenty-five yards in front of the large house, Rabanine saw Moshe moving toward him. Moshe was his most trusted ally, a huge hulk of a man whose strength in the mountains around the area was legendary. He had fought in all of Israel's wars, save for the first, and on three occasions he was known to have destroyed entire Arab regiments single-handedly. As usual, David saw that the giant, bearded Moshe was wearing a sleeveless shirt and sheepskin vest. As usual, David could feel that the immense power of the man was exceeded only by his gentleness. Rabanine loved to watch the giant teach Shaul the ways of the land. Peaceful ways.

"Good to see you," David said, firmly clasping the huge extended hand before him. Moshe squeezed gently. If sufficiently provoked, David reflected, the giant could probably break a man in two. "How have things been the last few days?"

"Good, thank God," Moshe replied. "All is well. Shaul is doing his lessons. He'll be out as soon as word of your arrival reaches him. He can't wait."

"Neither can I."

"How long has it been?"

"A week but it seems much longer. It always does." Rabanine noticed that Moshe was holding a large manilla envelope in his right hand.

"While you were away, this came for you from America. I wanted you to see it before Shaul comes out." Moshe handed the envelope to David. "It is a request for your services."

"Then you have opened it," said Rabanine, smiling.

"Don't I always," laughed Moshe, patting his massive chest. "If I didn't, the boy would. You wouldn't want that."

"No, I wouldn't."

David withdrew the contents of the envelope and began to read a page-long letter signed by Colonel Vernon P. Rossi, Director of the Central Intelligence Agency. His expression tightened as he lifted the letter up in order to see the 8 X 10 color picture that was clipped beneath it. The faces in the photo stared up at him. His mouth dropped. His face became pale and distant.

"Something is wrong, yes?" asked Moshe.

David didn't answer. His eyes were riveted on the five men in the picture, his mind moving backwards to capture lost moments.

"Something is wrong, yes?" the giant repeated.

"What? . . . Oh, I'm not sure. . . . I'm not sure."

Suddenly the doors to the great house flew open and Shaul ran down the steps smiling, dressed in blue jeans and work shirt. He ran forward and embraced David. Rabanine returned the hold briefly, placing the manilla envelope and its contents on the land rover's hood. Then the father moved the son away, still grasping his shoulders and smiled; the color back in his face.

"Good God, you seem to have grown in the week I've been gone. Keep going and you'll end up as big as Moshe."

"But not as clumsy, I hope," laughed the giant, again slapping his huge chest.

"I missed you," the boy said.

"When you were smaller, you always expected me to bring you a present from my trips."

"I still do."

"Oh?"

"A young girl, preferably French."

"Why French?"

"Because of those pants they wear in the magazines." Shaul smiled.

Rabanine turned toward Moshe. "I believe the boy is growing up."

"It happens to the best of us," the giant said wryly.

"Yes, we are all cursed."

"I don't consider those girls in the magazines a curse," Shaul said in mock argument.

"Wait a minute," said David. "What magazines are you . . . Oh, now I see. The magazines with the pictures."

The boy laughed, a bit embarrassed.

"Your time will come, Shaul. And you will live to regret it just like the rest of us."

"I hope I did not speed up the process by giving him the magazines," Moshe mumbled to David.

"I could get them in town anyway," proclaimed the boy. "Did you have a good time in the city?" he asked, eager to change the subject.

"As good as can be expected. Israeli girls are not as, ah, revealing as French ones are."

"Perhaps you will go to Paris someday."

"Perhaps I will take you with me."

"Really!"

"If you promise not to pinch anything that doesn't belong to you."

Moshe smiled. David was a different man when around Shaul. The boy seemed to recharge the vitality in him. Often when he returned from these trips, he would be depressed for days. Around Shaul, though, this depression was never obvious. Either it disappeared or was cleverly covered. Moshe was never sure which. Probably a combination of both.

"You better go inside and finish your lessons," David told his son.

"But a package came for you. I want to get it."

"Then go ahead."

The boy ran back toward the house.

"What package?" David asked Moshe.

"Just some of those agricultural books you ordered. I've opened it already, of course."

"Of course."

Rabanine picked up the photograph he had placed on the

97

hood of the land rover and began to study it again. His eyes were motionless, unblinking.

"They want your help, yes?"

"They seem to."

"Will you provide it?"

"I have no desire to open old wounds."

"But it is tempting, no?"

David nodded slowly. "I suppose."

"A chance to face old enemies. To achieve vengeance, a vengeance you thirst for in your soul."

"You know me too well."

"I am your friend. If you go to America, I will come with you, yes? I recognized the big, bald one in the picture as the man whose strength is said to know no equal. I have always wanted a chance to face him and prove this wrong."

David shook his head. "If I decided to go, Shaul would need you here with him. His safety must come first. Leave Seif to—" Something struck Rabanine. A detail, lost somewhere in the recent past. "Moshe, you said the books were agricultural. But the ones I ordered were not supposed to arrive for another two months."

"All the same, they are here."

"I guess they must have . . ." The giant watched David shudder and his face turn white with a fear he did not know his employer was capable of feeling. "Oh God . . . No! . . . *No!*"

Rabanine was running now, running for the huge oak door of the great house.

"Shaul! Shaul! . . . Don't touch the box!" His hand grasped the old knob, his insides a mesh of tightly gnarled wire. "Don't open that—"

David heard the blast at the very moment the door flew backwards, rocketing him from the porch. The ground below came up fast and hard and he felt himself land but was powerless to feel anything else. There was pain in his head and ribcage and warm blood was dripping from his arms that had cushioned the fall.

In the last seconds before consciousness slipped away from him, he knew he would live.

And he also knew that he did not want to.

At that moment halfway across the world, two men were sitting alone in a spacious office. One, a man with cold blue eyes, fidgeted before a massive desk. The other, a man with sizzling white hair, fidgeted behind it.

"So you see," said the man with cold eyes, "all our fears have been confirmed. The Arabs have suddenly emerged as the greatest threat to our destiny."

"Your destiny, not mine."

"Must we rehash old arguments?"

"Not if you leave right now."

The man with cold eyes tilted his head to one side. "You know I can't do that. We need you."

"There's nothing I can do."

"Isn't there? You're the only one left who knows enough to help us. Besides, you owe the organization quite a bit, all of this in fact," the man with cold eyes said, glancing around him. "We have come to collect."

The white haired man tightened his aged hands into fists. "We went our separate ways long ago."

"But they have crossed again." The man with cold eyes sighed. "At this moment one of our people is preparing an interesting report for the wire services about the true identity of a murderer who has thus far been able to escape punishment, a man who has risen to a position of great power and is known rightfully as a great humanitarian. He is waiting for a phone call before turning that report in. If I leave here now, I will make that phone call."

"And risk exposing yourself?"

"If the Arabs are successful, it won't matter."

The white haired man held back the rage that surged within him. "And how am I supposed to help you? Do you expect me to run from this office and stop the Arabs single-handed?"

"No, we will take care of that end. We merely will require your . . . expertise . . . in recouping what we've lost."

"It's been a long time."

"Not too long, I trust. Otherwise the papers will find themselves with an interesting story."

"And how do you expect to stop the Arabs?"

"Cerberus."

"A killer?"

"Not just a killer. Cerberus is a master of his work, probably the best of his kind in the world. He's been responsible for dealing with those who've come too close to us and our work for years. He has never failed and will not now. He'll be ordered to execute all those immediately responsible for implementation of the plan by the Arabs, as well as any others who get too close."

"And, of course, innocent people will die."

"If necessary."

"Isn't it always?" the white haired man challenged. "I don't suppose you'd be interested in hearing an alternative strategy."

"Not at this point. The decisions have already been made, the wheels set in motion."

"And me?"

The man with cold eyes chuckled. "We've paid our premiums. You, my friend, are our insurance policy."

Meanwhile, in Crescent Falls, Wyoming Sheriff Bugsy Tyler leaned his massive frame against the window of his office. 100 yards down the street at the railroad station he watched Dave Dean and Mayor Jim Layton shake hands with the five strangers who had just arrived to look for oil in the dying town. All five were dressed leisurely in polo shirts and slacks. None of them looked like the outdoor type.

The man who Bugsy guessed was the leader went through introductions and more handshakes were exchanged. Everyone was smiling.

Nervously, Tyler swirled a wad of tobacco juice around in his mouth and spit it into the garbage can beneath him. The hairs on the back of his neck were standing up. Something was wrong here. He had a feeling, just a feeling. . . .

Tyler then watched as six crates of heavy equipment were loaded into a pickup truck and station wagon. The strangers climbed inside one or the other and were gone.

Bugsy stepped out the office door into the cool spring air and sauntered slowly over toward the train station where freight manager Floyd Haskins was still standing in the street soaking up some early spring sun.

"How ya' doin' there, Floydy boy?"

Haskins turned quickly, startled. He was a medium sized man with a beer belly and grease coating both his hands and face.

"Oh, Sheriff, I didn't hear ya' coming."

"Yeah, I always had this problem 'bout bein' so light on my feet."

Haskins mopped his brow with a sleeve of his soiled work jacket. "So what do I owe the pleasure of this visit?"

"I want to talk to ya' 'bout those five guys who just arrived on the train."

"The oil men?"

Tyler spit onto the road beneath him. "Yeah." Here, he might have pulled out a notebook—if he had one. But Bugsy had given up carrying it a few years back when he realized he couldn't read his own writing.

"What do ya' want to know about them?"

"Anything strange, anything that stands out in your mind. Did one of 'em have tits? Did one of 'em have a glass eye? Did one of 'em play with his balls? Did one of 'em say something when they didn't think nobody was around when, of course, you was?" Indeed, Floyd Haskins was the biggest busybody in Crescent Falls.

"Not that I recall, Sheriff. But I was only around them the last half hour or so. You'd be better off askin' the conductor."

"He don't know shit and he wouldn't tell me if he did. Besides, Floyd buddy, I got a lot more faith in your word." Tyler slapped Haskins lightly on the back. Lightly because a normal slap for Bugsy was a severe jolt for the person it connected with. "I know you see things nobody else in this town does." Even if sometimes they're not there, Tyler thought to himself.

"Much obliged, Sheriff, much obliged. But it's like I said; there was nothing unusual about these guys. Nothing at all." Haskins fingered his chin. "Well, except . . ."

"'Cept what?" Tyler asked eagerly, moving closer.

"Their equipment. It was all crated up."

"How else was it supposed to get here?" Tyler felt a rush of disappointment surge through him. Again he released a wad of spittle, heavier this time.

"No, Sheriff, you don't understand. The crates were sent direct to Omaha by the manufacturer and then forwarded here on the same train as the oil men. They still had the manufacturer's labels on them. Hell, Sheriff, that means they ain't never been opened before."

Tyler raised his bushy eyebrows. "So these five oil experts came into town with a truckload of equipment that ain't never been used?"

Haskins nodded. "Yup. That's the size of it."

"Sounds kind of strange, don't it? You sure every crate had the labels still on 'em?"

"Absolutely." Haskins winked. "I took the liberty of checkin'. What's it mean, Sheriff?"

"That sometimes cellar rats give 'way their presence by leavin' turds out in the open."

"Huh?"

But Tyler had already turned and walked off.

ELEVEN

"Seif just called in from Jerusalem," said Mohammed al-Kahir, taking a seat along with the other two men in the small Boston restaurant.

"And what is the news?" asked the Red Prince, glancing around the virtually deserted dining room. Only two other tables were occupied.

"He isn't sure what to report. The bomb went off, but not as planned. We know for a fact that Rabanine's son was injured, perhaps killed. But the extent of Rabanine's injuries are not known at this time."

"But he will live."

"Unfortunately, yes. Should I have Seif make another attempt?"

"No, his efforts are needed elsewhere. We will coordinate something from this end. We have Rabanine's itinerary?"

"We will soon. But we are already certain he'll be coming into New York."

"Good. I'll contact our people there and have them handle things. That way, Seif can turn his attentions solely to Alabaster. After all, it is he who is the threat to us, not Rabanine."

"I'm not so sure we have to worry about Alabaster," said al-Kahir. "There are thousands of Western intelligence agents searching for him now. They have not a single clue where to look. It would seem that Alabaster does not want to be found. If he was going to pose a threat to us, he'd have surfaced already."

"All the same," Salameh persisted, "I want Seif there if he does surface."

"As you wish."

The Red Prince turned toward Hussein El Sayad. "And what is the news from Washington?"

El Sayad lifted his useless arm onto the table, aware that it had been dangling freely in the air. "Our source in the CIA says that the Agency has received the boy's pictures and has inspected them. They know we are in the country, but little else, and nothing apparently of the Shaitan Commandment."

"What actions have they taken?"

"None besides those we have already discussed. The Mossad has been contacted. A message was sent to David Rabanine. And everyone in Israel is trying to make contact with Alabaster."

"Since they are failing," Salameh noted, "I'd assume their current state is bordering on panic."

"It is. They know their nation's security is about to be threatened severely but they have no idea how."

"If it wasn't for the damned film, they wouldn't even suspect. That damned boy. . . ." The Red Prince pulled a slender cigarette from a pack that lay on the table. In seconds it was twirling through his fingers. "Hussein, is it true the boy was a Jew?"

El Sayad was taken slightly aback by the question. "We think so, yes. But, Ali, he was only a boy."

"So were my sons. Are they not dead as well?"

El Sayad said nothing.

Salameh switched the unlit cigarette from one hand to the other, splitting the filter in the process. "Now, Hussein, tell me of the men you sent to obtain the rolls of film so that they wouldn't fall into the wrong hands."

"Free-lancers," the cripple responded, aware he was being ridiculed for the choice. "They came reasonably well-recommended by the KGB. Unluckily, they didn't track the film down until it was already in the hands of a Providence policeman. They've been keeping close tabs on both the woman and the detective assigned to the case since."

104

"And?"

"They are getting nowhere."

"Are their deaths called for?"

"Not for the time being. It would lead to too many questions being asked and would create more problems than it would solve. The free lancers prefer to arrange a couple of convenient accidents. It will be better that way."

"We won't need these free lancers much longer anyway," said Mohammed al-Kahir. "Tebara's force should be ready before long."

"Ah yes, Tebara," said Salameh. "What's the latest news from him?"

"The recruiting process is going along smoothly. He should be able to start training the men and women within ten days."

"He will not have much time with them."

"He will have enough."

Salameh moved the cigarette from his left hand to his right, treating it like a baton. "What else do you have to report?"

Al-Kahir leaned forward. "All arrangements have been made for the Shaitan force of 175 to enter America on seventeen different airlines beginning seven weeks from today and ending seven weeks from tomorrow. They will be arriving from twenty-three different countries in no specific pattern, the idea being to make it impossible for Washington or Tel Aviv to find any link between them. They are just ordinary American tourists returning to their country after an extended vacation."

"Their papers have been put in order?"

"All but a few. The rest will be completed within three days."

The Red Prince nodded, allowing himself a small flash of a smile. "And what of the five men whose instructions differed from the rest?"

"By now, they have already reached the target area. I had them rendezvous in Omaha, Nebraska in order to allow them to arrive at the test site together. That way, we can be sure their cover has been and will be maintained. Their initial reports will be coming in within a few days. We should anticipate no problems."

"What of their weapons?" asked Hussein El Sayad, looking at the Red Prince. "You said the Shaitan force was going to be issued certain weapons."

"Not exactly," Salameh corrected. "In fact, I made mention of something else entirely—I said they *possessed* a weapon. It will come with them into the country."

"Past customs?"

"Past customs. Right, Mohammed?"

"I made their arrangements according to your specifications," reassured the planner.

"The customs officials will not know they are looking at the most deadly weapon ever conceived by man, if they even notice it at all," boasted Salameh.

"I think it's time you became more specific," nagged El Sayad.

"It is not the right moment."

"When will the right moment come?"

"Do not badger me, Hussein."

"I do not mean to," the cripple shot back, feeling bold. "But I must question the manner in which you are handling this operation."

"Question me and you question the Movement. . . . You know what that would mean, don't you, Hussein?"

"I was about to pose the very same problem to you. You say that Yassir has given you total control over the Commandment. I question whether he knows any more about it than we do."

"You are challenging me."

"Call it what you like."

"I do not enjoy being challenged."

"And I do not enjoy being humiliated." El Sayad looked at the gloved hand that sat motionless on the table. "I do not have the status in the Movement I had five years ago. But my word still carries quite a bit of weight with Arafat. . . . . I am thinking of contacting him." The cripple took a hefty gulp of air.

Salameh's expression wavered for the first time. "Then why not place the call from my room at the hotel? That way, both of us will be able to speak with him. I would suggest, though, that your interests would be better served if you merely followed through on the instructions I have given you. After all, a call to Yassir would signify an ultimatum to him: Either you or I must go. If you are correct in your suspicions, you will end up a hero. If you are wrong, you will end up a corpse."

El Sayad felt his momentary bravura vanish, replaced by a chill in his veins. His eyes left Salameh's and looked into the empty plate beneath him.

"I assume your lack of response means you have come to see things my way," the Red Prince continued. "Believe me, it is the best thing. Yassir authorizes every move I make. We are in constant touch. The operation is his as much as mine. Yet, Hussein, your words have provided me with an idea." Salameh turned back to al-Kahir. "Mohammed, we must assume the worst—that Alabaster will be found and that he will agree to help the Americans, in which case he might succeed in picking up our trail."

"So?"

"We must lay another trail along side it, one that will lead the great Israeli where we want him."

"I don't understand."

"You will."

At two PM sharp, Leslie Kirkman dialed the Providence police department and asked for Sergeant Phil Scarpani.

"Hello." A male voice had gotten on the line but it was not Scarpani's.

"I'm looking for Sergeant Scarpani," Leslie said anxiously.

"So am I, lady."

"Where is he?" she asked feeling her teeth rub against her lower lip.

"I wish I knew. He took off about noontime. Someone downstairs said he decided to take a vacation. He had a lot of weeks coming. Last minute plans, I guess."

"That can't be. You don't understand, we had an appointment at two o'clock."

"Hold on, ma'am," said the officer on the other end. "I'll check his calender. A brief pause and then he was back on. "Look, ah—"

"Leslie Kirkman."

"Look Mrs. Kirkman, the page for today has been ripped out. Phil must have spilled something on it. I guess you can consider the meeting cancelled."

"But he wouldn't do that!" Leslie lowered her voice. "It was a crucial meeting for both of us. We had something very important to discuss."

"More important for you than him, it seems. Is there anything I can do for you?"

"I don't know."

"Phil and I, Mrs. Kirkman, we go back a long way. Just tell me how I can help you."

"Get me a meeting with our superior and tell him it's urgent," Leslie said firmly. She needed help. Phil was gone, certainly not of his own will which meant they had him.

"When?"

"Now."

The office was little bigger than a closet but neat and in a policeman's sense, Leslie guessed, plush.

"I'm Lieutenant John Lucas," said a round-shouldered, balding man as he rose from behind a desk that was fashioned from imitation wood.

Leslie took his hand and then seated herself in the black vinyl chair in front of his desk. "You're Sergeant Scarpani's superior, I presume."

"Yes, and you're the woman who claims she had vital business to talk over with him," Lucas said coldly. His dome was totally bald and he had nothing but stubble on either side of his head for hair. He wore a white, wrinkled shirt and thick blue tie complete with J.C. Penny clip. He stank of cheap after-shave lotion.

Leslie nodded. "I want to know what happened to Sergeant Scarpani."

"He went on vacation, effective this noontime. He had quite a bit of time built-up and he's been putting in a lot of extra hours lately."

"We had an appointment he wouldn't have broken . . . unless he was forced to," Leslie said already sure she had come to the wrong place for help.

Lucas chuckled snidely. "I assure you, Mrs. Kirkman, no one forced Phil to break any appointment. I'm sure he did so on his own. Obviously, he didn't share your enthusiasm for the topic of this appointment you claim existed. Maybe you just got your days mixed-up."

"The only thing mixed-up around here are the people who are doing a pretty poor job of hiding something," Leslie charged. "Lieutenant, I happen to be a reporter for the *Journal* and you can bet I'm going to find out what that 'something' is with or without your help."

Lucas whitened a bit. "Why don't you let me try to help? Tell me why you and Scarpani had that appointment scheduled."

"You're not going to like this. . . ." Leslie told him everything; beginning with Scott Krassner's murder, Scarpani's suspicions, the hotel, the refusal of the FBI to identify the five men in the picture. "I hope you understand that was a capsulized version," she said at the end.

"It's quite a story, all the same."

"So now you know everything that's happened and I'd like to know what you plan to do about it."

Lucas waved a hand before him. "Now hold on just a minute. All I know is everything you *say* has happened. But there's no one and nothing to back up your rather incredible tale."

109

"Phil would but he's—"

"—on vacation," Lucas completed.

"Bullshit! What have you done with him, Lieutenant? If you really are a lieutenant, that is. How are you connected in all this?"

"I resent that, Mrs.—"

"And I resent your damned patronizing attitude. Your act of innocence isn't working. You know more about all this than I do. You just won't admit it."

Lucas' eyes flared. "The only thing I'll admit is that your story is so full of discrepancies that even the *National Enquirer* wouldn't buy it. First off, you say that Sergeant Scarpani began a homicide investigation into the accidental death of a boy named Scott Krassner. But his signed report—that's *signed* report, Mrs. Kirkman—reads negligent homicide caused by hit-and-run. You also say that this boy was killed because he took a series of pictures he shouldn't have—four rolls to be exact which were later forwarded to the FBI in Washington. But we have no voucher and there's no record of the film ever being sent."

Was Lucas really saying this? "The negatives!" Leslie screamed, lifting herself from the daze the lieutenant's words had lulled her into. "Phil put them in his drawer. He told me!"

Lucas picked up the phone and dialed one number. "Yeah, Steve, you wanna check Scarpani's desk for some color negatives." A pause. "Not there? Okay, thanks." Lucas turned back to Leslie. "No negatives, Mrs. Kirkman."

Leslie shook her head, her fiery rage unable to dim her reason. "If the pictures never existed, how did you know the negatives were color?"

Lucas licked his lips. "Look, Mrs. Kirkman, you come in here with some whale ass story and expect me to believe it with absolutely no substantiating proof at all. I'm just trying to help."

"Or go through the motions."

"Call it what you want but I'm a busy man. I can't spend

110

time with every crackpot who comes into my office."

"You have plenty of time for yourself." Leslie watched Lucas' features explode. She spoke again before he had a chance to. "And what about the terrorists, Lieutenant? Are you going to ignore them too? Or maybe you're working for them."

"Ah yes, these child-murdering terrorists of yours. And Arabs no less. Probably the top of the line sent over to shock the world by doing some dastardly deed in Providence, Rhode Island. Not exactly a great city to gain international exposure, wouldn't you say?"

"Which is exactly why they chose it."

"And registered under the name of 'Mote' at the Biltmore which just happens to be the Arabic word for death?"

"That's right, Lieutenant."

"So our terrorist friends decided to give themselves away."

"They had no way of knowing we'd be onto them."

"But they killed a young boy to make sure we got a big lead."

"He took their picture. They couldn't chance being recognized. They panicked."

Lucas was nodding sarcastically. "Now I get it. Five international terrorists come to Providence to plan some murderous strike and panic when a thirteen-year-old boy snaps their picture. That makes as much sense as anything else you've said." Lucas thrust an accusing finger forward. "Look, Mrs. Kirkman, I'm going to prove to you once and for all that your terrorist story is a lot of crap. Then you are going to leave this office and never return and feel very lucky that I don't find some reason to put you away in a padded room for awhile." Lucas picked up the phone before him. Leslie watched him dial a number. "Hello, Biltmore, this is Lieutenant John Lucas from the Providence Police Department. I'd like the reservations manager please."

Leslie's eyes met the lieutenant's. The seething grasp held.

"Yeah, Henry," Lucas resumed, "I wonder if you could tell me if you had a reservation in the name of Mote any time in the

111

past month. . . . Sure, I'll wait." The seconds stretched into a few long minutes. "I see. Thanks a lot, Henry."

Lucas hung up the phone and brought his eyes up to meet Leslie's again. Triumph shone in them. "Henry Platt, the reservations manager over at the Biltmore, says that no room or suite has been booked in the name of Mote since the hotel opened."

Something sunk in Leslie's stomach. This couldn't be happening. It wasn't real.

"He's lying," she muttered.

"Somebody is," said Lucas.

TWELVE

"You are a lucky man, David. By some miracle your son escaped serious injury. A few cuts, contusions. A concussion. But nothing that won't heal. I'll send him to a hospital in Tel Aviv for some tests as soon as he is ready to travel."

The village doctor's words comforted Rabanine only slightly as the TWA 747 made its descent into Kennedy Airport. The bomb had been an extremely intricate device, equipped with a motion sensor set off by a timer. The explosives, a powerful plastic type, and the electronic heart of the bomb were located in the bottom book in the large box; a book that had only the fringes of pages, the centers having been cut out to allow for placement of the device. It had been rigged to go off the first time that this book was removed.

Whoever put the package together knew that the bottom book would not be touched until Rabanine returned home. Which meant that he knew Rabanine's schedule. Which meant he had penetrated Mossad security. Which was not good at all. Shaul was alive now only because he had not touched the books. The bomb had been activated when the boy accidently dropped the box down the stairs in his eagerness to bring it out to his father.

". . . There will be no scars. Everything will be as it was. . . ."

That is where you are wrong, Doctor, David thought as he felt the landing gear of the large jet lower in preparation for the final descent. Because for the first time the violence of his life as an agent had reached his son. David had come to the town with no name to escape it. But the violence had stalked him doggedly, refusing to leave him alone.

He could run and hide no more. His wife had been murdered

and now his son had nearly joined her. It was time to confront the men in the photograph.

The giant Moshe had begged for a chance to go with him. But David politely refused. "Someone has to stay with Shaul," he remembered saying. "It must be you, Moshe. He is all I have left. You must stay by his side always and protect him from the evil that pervades my life."

The giant had shrugged his massive shoulders. "I will do as you say."

"I will be in touch."

The 747 came to a halt in front of the TWA terminal building. People were already moving quickly toward the exits. It had been a long flight, leaving from Tel Aviv at 7:10 Thursday morning and arriving at Kennedy at 1:55 in the afternoon with a stopover and plane change in Paris. But the time sequence is confusing because of the loss of seven hours when one travels so far west. The travellers were anxious and weary. They had begun the journey smiling. They disembarked with sighs of relief.

David followed the flow of traffic into the TWA building where he was suddenly surrounded by a sea of faces. Any one of them might have been marking his movements, preparing to strike. If so, he would be ready.

His travel bag slung over his shoulder, David made his way to an escalator in search of a more secure place from which to make the call to Washington. The flight he was booked on to the Capital was not scheduled to leave for another hour. There was time to kill. He was worried.

Behind him on the escalator, a New York state trooper put on a pair of dark sunglasses and began to slowly snake his way through the people who moved aside only after seeing his uniform. His methodical pace was designed to attract no attention to himself even when he was upon the man he sought, now ten steps ahead.

"Excuse me. . . . Excuse me. . . ."

The officer continued his mild surge until David's travel bag

114

came clearly into view. He was five steps away. The escalator would reach the next floor in a matter of seconds. The moment had arrived. In the confusion that comes when people force their way off at the end of the ride up, he would make his escape. The closeness of the gun to the target's body would muffle the shot well-enough amidst the bustling crowd in the jammed terminal. A man would fall over, the victim of a heart attack. Few would bother to notice. Still fewer would bother to stop. People were like that. Thankfully. He had been in a dozen other situations similar to this and they had never disappointed him.

The man drew his long-barrelled revolver and held it hidden by his side, invisible to those around him on the up-escalator as well as to those passing next to him on the down. Slowly, he ascended three more steps and raised the gun forward so that it was almost level with the target's spine. A quick shot and then he would disappear.

Six inches from the jacket now. Five . . . four . . . The man cradled the trigger, preparing to pull.

Before the revolver had reached a point three inches from its target, though, Rabanine spun quickly, grasping his shoulder bag and whirling it backwards in the same motion. The hard leather struck the man in the state trooper's uniform square in the right side of the face, dazing him.

His eyes clouded, his senses—sharp as they were—escaped him. He tried to raise the gun again, ready to shoot, but realized it had slipped from his fingers or had been taken from them.

Then, as he stooped down dizzily to probe for it in the mass of feet below, he felt something crash into his chin with sufficient impact to send him flying over the safety rail on the up-escalator into the people fighting for space on the down. They whined in discomfort as much as shock and collectively tried to help the unconscious officer in sunglasses back to his feet.

Rabanine had seen him well before reaching the escalator. Their eyes met and something about the would-be officer's

115

activated his defenses, telling him the man was not what he appeared to be. David had then waited until the last possible second before executing his counterattack, knowing that the killer would have timed his shot to coincide with the escalator's arrival on the next floor. It was the way such things were done.

Aware of his motions and the motions of those around him, the Israeli tread a deliberate path to a series of phones laid out in a circle in the middle of the terminal floor. He chose one that allowed him an optimum view of his surroundings and dialed the number of the Agency scrambler. A male voice, slightly garbled by distance and device, answered.

"This is Rabanine. I'm on my way in."

David hung up the phone and was gone.

At that moment, Leslie Kirkman was standing before the desk of *Providence Journal* managing editor Peter McSorely. He read her story quickly, appearing only to scan it when his trained eyes actually picked up every word. He finished the 1,500 word piece in just over three minutes.

"Right now, Lez, the only place I might be able to print this story is on the cartoon page," he said, handing it across the desk. McSorely was an average sized, slightly overweight man with a near crew cut who always carried a pack of cigarettes in his shirt pocket.

"Why?" Leslie asked.

"Because it reads more like a short story or movie treatment. Little boys being run over by bad men in big cars. Disappearing people. Conspiracies. Cover-ups. Corrupt cops. You've got all the ingredients of a first-rate paperback. But a page-one story? Be reasonable, Lez. Stick to the Accent pages."

"Don't bullshit me, Pete. If they've gotten to you, I want to know."

"If *who's* gotten to me?"

"That's what I'm trying to find out."

"I got that impression from reading your story."

Leslie sighed and sat down in the chair four feet in front of McSorely's desk. "Well, what can I do to make it publishable?"

"Take it to the *National Star*."

"Pete . . ."

"Okay, I guess quotes from some of the other people involved would be helpful."

"The only other person involved was Sergeant Scarpani and he disappeared."

"But what about the people at the Biltmore? The doorman, maybe, or the room clerk you and Scarpani talked to. If what you say is true . . ." He silenced her coming outburst with a raised palm. ". . . then somebody will remember something. And talk to this Krassner boy's parents, talk to his teachers, talk to anybody. Just get me something solid to put into print."

"Then you . . . believe me?"

"Lez, I've known you for three years and your husband for almost ten before that. You're integrity is unimpeachable, even if your imagination is somewhat vivid. After reading your story, I'm convinced you might be somewhat prone to exaggeration. But you sure as hell didn't make all this up for my benefit. The problem isn't in the pieces but in the way you've put them together. So to answer your question, yes I believe you when you say that something's going on here. But you've got to get me some proof if we're gonna expose it to our readers."

Leslie found herself smiling widely. "Pete, I don't know what to say."

"Say nothing. You're on company time. Just get to work finding me some answers."

For the first time in three years, Leslie really felt like a journalist right down to the black notebook and three pens. She picked Jimmy up at three o'clock and dropped him at a friend's house after informing the friend's mother to please not let him out of her sight. She was beginning to let herself worry, to feel truly endangered for the first time. All links to

117

the five men in the picture were being severed. People were disappearing, lying, covering up. If the terrorists were responsible for it all, murder seemed as likely an option as any. They had already killed a young boy. What was there to stop them from killing a widow or that widow's son?

The chill returned to Leslie's spine, the feeling now familiar but never welcome. She thought of running away, of packing up and taking Jimmy far away. But what would that accomplish? When you ran away in fear, you kept running always yet you could never really hide. Every stranger was an enemy. Every room a prison. It was no way to live. She had to stay and fight in her own way. If her story ran, people would have to take notice. The lies would stop, or at least be clearly separated from the emerging truth. People would demand answers.

She arrived at the Biltmore, her resolve firmer than ever, and walked across the street toward the doorman whose back was turned to her.

"Excuse me," Leslie said, tapping him on the shoulder. The man turned. It wasn't the same doorman that Scarpani had interrogated just days before. Somehow this didn't surprise her.

"Oh, I'm sorry. I was looking for the doorman who usually works this shift," she explained.

"That would be Randall, ma'am. I'm afraid he's taken ill."

"Rather sudden, it seems."

"I wouldn't know, ma'am. I'm merely filling in. They called me this morning. I usually work the night shift. I'll have to pull double duty until they find a replacement or Randall comes back."

"I wouldn't count on that happening too soon," Leslie said, already moving for the hotel entrance. Twenty yards away, two men had emerged from a red Cutlass and were following in her tracks.

Inside she approached the front desk. What was the clerk's name who had helped her and Scarpani on Tuesday? She searched her memory. He was wearing a black nameplate on his lapel. What was it? . . . Debons, that was it, Frank Debons. She was at the front desk now, a new strategy in mind.

"Hello, my name's Leslie Kirkman," she said to a pretty female clerk, not thinking to use a name other than her own. "Mr. Frank Debons was supposed to leave an envelope here for me before he left today."

"One minute and I'll check." The pretty clerk disappeared briefly. "I'm sorry. There's nothing on his desk. But he left very quickly this morning. Sickness in the family, I'm told."

"Oh, I see. Thanks anyway."

Leslie moved into the center of the lobby and considered how this affected the bizarre game she had been drawn into. Two more links had been cut. Someone was out to destroy the chain. The thought made her shudder inwardly. How long could it be before they came for her? She would have to expose them in print before they had the chance. And she would have to act fast; time was running out.

But who else could help her add credence to the absurd story McSorely had rejected? Who else might have had some contact with the five men in the picture? She pondered the question. In front of her, a janitor was emptying ashtrays. Something clicked in her head, something she hadn't thought of before. Not the *men* but the *room*. Room 710! . . . Leslie rushed to the elevator.

All of these motions were observed by two men seated comfortably in the hotel lobby. The one with thinning brown hair rose and moved to a pay phone while the other, a brutish looking one with a twisted nose, scarred face and gray rain hat, continued to look on as the elevator doors closed. His expressionless features were indicative of a slow mind that was more than compensated for by the raw power of his compact body. A small smile crept across his face as he recalled how he had strangled the clerk from the photo lab three days before.

The small smile grew larger when he considered the fact that he might be called upon to repeat the task very soon.

119

Meanwhile, on the seventh floor, it did not take Leslie very long to locate the maid's office. Five women, all in white uniforms, were gathered inside smoking cigarettes. She had just caught them before they left the building.

"Is one of you responsible for suite 710?" she asked nervously.

A dark haired maid with heavy bags under her eyes stepped forward. "Who's asking?" she said, pushing a wad of chewing gum to the rear of her mouth.

Leslie moved forward and flashed her press card. "I'd like to ask you a few questions."

The maid chuckled as her fellows looked on. She glanced at them and winked. Her jaw flapped rhythmically as she continued to chew. "You'll have to show me more than that if you want answers." Leslie handed her a ten dollar bill. The maid stuffed it in the breast pocket of her uniform. "I'm all ears."

"Did you notice anything strange about suite 710 in the last week or so?"

"Most of the time, I didn't notice nothing. I guess you could call that strange, if you know what I mean."

"Why?"

"Because it was on my list as occupied. But every day I went in it was the same. Nobody was occupying it, if you know what I mean."

"Did you report that?"

"Yeah, once. Then I figured why bother. Whoever reserved the room was paying for it so they had the right to do as they pleased. Some high-class hooker with thousand dollar tricks, maybe. There was just one day the suite seemed to have been used, and then it was only the living room section."

Leslie felt her eyes broaden. Her heart skipped a beat. "And you cleaned it, of course."

"Sure, but there wasn't all that much to clean. I guess somebody was using that room for something they didn't want the hotel to know about, if you know what I mean." The maid

120

flashed a knowing grin.

"What did you find?"

"I don't follow your drift."

"When you cleaned the suite that one day."

The maid was still chewing. "Not all that much really, except these funny cigarettes. Not joints, I know what they look like. All I found was tobacco and part of the filter. The tobacco was darker than any I had seen before and it smelled funny. At first I thought it might have been a cigar. But then I found the filter. It had funny writing on it."

Leslie wrote down a few Arabic letters on a page in her black notebook. "Did the writing look anything like this?"

The maid took the book. "Yeah, sort of. You know, scriggly lines that didn't make no sense."

Leslie took the notebook back. "And that was the only day you found anything in the room?"

"That's right."

"And you didn't, by chance, happen to see any of the people who were inside?"

"Nope. I find it a lot easier to mind my own business. I'll tell you one thing, though. They didn't leave no tip."

"Thanks for your help."

Leslie left the small room and hurried to the elevator. Arabic writing on the cigarettes meant they had been bought directly in a Mideastern country, presumably by one of the five men in the picture. It was a small shred of proof, another strand to weave into the complex mesh of whatever was going on.

She breathed deeply as the compartment began to head down. It was almost time to rewrite the story.

In the lobby, the two men watched her emerge from the elevator and followed her out the building.

Their orders would be coming soon.

"Eastern Airlines announces the departure of Flight 672 to Washington, D.C. now boarding at Gate 17."

David Rabanine rose from his carefully selected seat against

121

the wall in the terminal waiting area and began to move with the other passengers toward the gate where a stewardess on either side was prepared to take his ticket. He wouldn't feel safe until the plane left the ground and even then the enemy could still reach him, though with a drastically reduced field of alternatives. He would not eat or drink anything on the plane. Nor would he sleep. The men of Al Fatah knew where he was. They would act again soon. Again he would be ready.

As Rabanine made his way onto the 727, a tall, broad shouldered man entered a phone booth in clear view of the boarding gate. His hair was blond and wavy, his cheekbones set high in a finely sculptured face dominated by a pair of sizzling blue eyes that reflected light like mirrors. His body was firm and trim, the build of an athlete, with tautly coiled muscles. The man grasped the receiver tightly in his left hand and pressed it against his ear. The call was going through to a party six thousand miles away.

"Hello," came the voice of his superior.

"The days are long," the man said.

"But the nights are short," his superior completed. "What is your message?"

"Rabanine is on his way to Washington. The Arabs failed to eliminate him just as we expected, bunglers that they are."

"You will follow him, of course."

"I will be on the same plane."

"He might see you."

"I doubt it." The man's voice was drenched in confidence. "I could take him out on the flight if you wish."

"And make his son an orphan? How dreadful of you . . ."

The man did not laugh. He disliked his superior's attempts at humor. In fact, he loathed any attempts at humor by anyone at all. It was a waste of time. "Can I take that as a no?"

His superior cleared his throat. "There is no reason yet. He might lead us to some of the men we want more."

"Alabaster?"

"And others perhaps." A pause. "You are our best man.

Much is riding on your mission."

"I won't fail. All those who stand in our way will be killed."

"Our destiny is at stake."

"It will be fulfilled."

The man with the sizzling blue eyes switched the receiver from his right hand to his left and then replaced it on the hook. Systematically, he then moved the edges of his thumbs across the tips of his fingers. They were his instruments, his tools, and had to be treated accordingly. They brought him pleasure by causing others pain.

Between kills he kept them sharp by playing the piano for hours each day. He was quite a virtuoso the people who thought they knew him said. The man didn't care. The ivory keys meant nothing to him. Only the thoughts of death that dominated his mind as he played mattered. How much he enjoyed feeling his victims squirm as he choked them, or watching blood erupt from their bodies, or twisting a sharp knife so deep into them that the life literally poured out as they gurgled and their eyes lost all color. One way was very much like another. A corpse was always a corpse.

Cerberus had arrived in America.

THIRTEEN

The early Friday morning sun struck Washington, D.C. with its warm rays, as Oman Abbu-Taabes strolled slowly down Constitution Avenue approaching the vast grounds of the Washington Monument. Abbu-Taabes was a ranking attaché with the Libyan embassy and was known as a man with many friends in many places. Over the years, the short stocky diplomat had cultivated the skill of listening into a fine art. Words and phrases, obscure and meaningless to others, made sense to him. Abbu-Taabes put inconsequential statements together in his computerlike mind to form sums of information not even suggested by the individual component parts.

And Abbu-Taabes was also a man with a conscience. His country was the Arab Libya but he had not been home in nearly seven years and had no desire whatsoever to return. His values and, more importantly, his life style had been utterly westernized. Even his politics and international sympathies had been singed by a small fire of democracy. He was, for example, a quietly firm supporter of Israel. In short, Oman considered himself to be an American; if not in heart, at least in mind.

Which is why he had agreed to the meeting that was about to take place. The diplomat continued to walk, once in awhile popping a peanut into his mouth from a small bag obtained from a street vendor outside the embassy. He had been circling the area for nearly twenty minutes, making sure that no one was in the vicinity who didn't seem to belong.

Satisfied that he had waited long enough, the diplomat moved off the sidewalk onto the neatly landscaped grounds that enclosed the Monument. A bench lay in the center, a wino

124

presently passed out on top of it. The man wore a torn brown overcoat and old gray hat tipped low over his forehead. His mouth hung open and his face was coated with the stubble of a good week's beard growth. Oman could smell the alcohol on him as he approached closer, finally taking a seat at the opposite end of the bench and dedicating himself to finishing off the last of his nuts.

"Aren't you going to offer an old friend a peanut?" The voice came from the wino but its depth and clarity did not fit the face it sprang out of. He had heard it before. Years ago.

The diplomat smiled. His tremendous memory had pinpointed the exact time and place. "I had expected a more extravagant entrance."

"These are hard times." The wino tipped back his hat a bit and slid nearer to Abbu-Taabes. "With inflation and all."

Oman nodded, flashing another smile. "It's good to see you again, Alabaster. How long has it been?"

"Nearly six years."

"God, how time passes. I'd say you haven't changed a bit but the last time we met I believe you were made out as a cocktail waitress."

"And I believe you were trying to pick me up."

"As you said, these are hard times." The diplomat's expression tensed. "I didn't expect to see you in America."

"Something has come up."

"So I've heard."

"What can you tell me?"

"Very little . . . and that frightens me."

"How?"

"Well, in most instances—more accurately all—our friends in the PLO have more to say than anyone is willing to listen to. But this time is an exception. No one is talking because no one knows anything. Al Fatah needs a dramatic event to regain their stature. It appears that event may be in the offing."

"Would it help if I told you the Red Prince was behind it?"

"But you yourself killed him more than three years ago."

125

"Somehow I failed. It was a setup. The world was supposed to believe him dead, perhaps so he could work on this latest operation without fear of Israeli pursuit."

"Of course!" The diplomat struck himself weakly in the side of the head. "I should've realized it myself. It explains so much." His features lost some of their sharpness. Uncertainty floundered in his eyes. "But it also might very well confirm my suspicions about the potential of the plan. Black September has never gone to such lengths before, even with Munich."

"What have you learned?"

"Much that points in the direction of a coming assault of major proportions on America but nothing that offers any firm proof. First off, there is a death list containing three names: John Desmond, a CIA man—" Abbu-Taabes watched Alabaster arch his eyebrows. "You know him?"

"I *knew* him. He's dead, murdered in London this past Monday."

"Then we can only hope that a similar fate does not await the other two men on the list because David Rabanine is one and you, my friend, are the third. You know Rabanine?"

"Vaguely. I've heard much about his past but little about his present. I've only met him once but he didn't know it was me."

"I'm not surprised. In any case, besides the death list there is a small rumor floating around about a terrorist force soon to enter America. But its objective and tactics are totally unknown."

"How big is the force?"

"I've heard estimates ranging from fifty to five hundred. Whatever the number is, though, people high in the Al Fatah command are confident of the force's ability to cause irreparable damage to this country. But no one—no matter how high-up—seems to have any idea of the means through which this is to be accomplished."

"Another source alluded to a new kind of weapon."

"If so, I am unaware of its existence."

Alabaster remembered the phrase Abad Salim had used to

describe the coming assault. "Oman, have you ever heard of *der Teufels Befehl?* It's German for the Devil's Command."

Abbu-Taabes shook his head slowly. "No, I don't think so. . . . But wait, months ago, at a gathering of influential Arab countrymen, I overheard another phrase mentioned that was something like that. What was it? . . ." The diplomat lowered his head and rubbed his temples, twisting his features into a contemplative mask. "Ah, I have it: the Shaitan Commandment."

Alabaster nodded, considering the words. "Shaitan is Arabic for Satan. . . . The Devil's Command becomes the Shaitan Commandment. It makes sense."

"None that I can see. What does a phrase out of Germany's past have to do with a phrase out of the modern day Middle East?"

"Something, Oman. . . . Something."

Mohammed al-Kahir found the Red Prince standing by the sun-drenched window, unlit cigarette in hand, later Friday morning.

"Ali, the two men from Providence have called in. There are new developments."

Salameh turned slowly and faced the planner. "I'm listening."

"I'm afraid that woman in Providence must be dealt with. She's making things difficult for us. The free lancers called in yesterday to report this and just a few minutes ago to confirm it. She's asking questions, following-up leads. Sooner or later someone might believe her. What's more, she works for a newspaper. From that position, she might be able to do us some fair degree of harm."

The Red Prince smiled. "We can't allow that, Mohammed, can we?" Al-Kahir shook his head. "In that case, tell the men in Providence to eliminate her from the scene."

Al-Kahir moved for the door.

"And, Mohammed?"

"Yes, Ali?"

"Tell them to make it painful."

At that moment in Langley, Virginia, David Rabanine arrived at CIA headquarters for his meeting with Colonel Vernon Rossi. Immediately he was ushered through the white, maze-like corridors in the huge complex of interconnected buildings that somehow led to the Director's outer office where a receptionist greeted him.

"Mr. Rabanine is here, sir," she said into an intercom.

Rabanine heard a buzzer and saw a door with no visible knob swing open. He entered the large, plush office of the Director. Present in the room and in the same chairs as Monday were Bob Kincannon, Art Bartose and Herb Weinberg. Once again, Colonel Rossi's wheelchair was situated behind his desk.

"Sit down, David," said Rossi, beckoning with his good hand to a chair that had been placed between Weinberg's and Bartose's so that he would be facing the Colonel head-on. "Let me introduce you around. . . ."

"I wish we could've met under better circumstances," Rabanine said after the introductions were finished.

"We're glad you could make it, David. We know you're not active in the field any longer," said Bob Kincannon tersely.

"I prefer to call it voluntary retirement, Mr. Kincannon. The situation forced me to reconsider my decision for the time being."

"Quite a coincidence, wouldn't you say?" challenged Art Bartose.

"That depends on what you mean."

"Let's not mince words. Your wife was murdered eleven years ago by Seif the Butcher, whose face coincidently appears in the photograph sent to you by us."

"Are you implying something, Mr. Bartose?"

"I'm merely suggesting you may have done the right thing for the wrong reason. There's no place on this side of the Atlantic for quests of vengeance." Bartose turned to Rossi.

"And I think it's only fair that we inform Mr. Rabanine that we see his role as primarily an advisory one and that we don't feel the time is right for him to enter the field again with so much at stake."

"You question my abilities?" posed David.

"I wonder what's left of them."

"Your point is well-taken, Mr. Bartose."

"My point is that we have yet to find the man we really need. I am speaking of Alabaster. We were hoping you might know a way to contact him."

"You've obviously failed in your attempts. What makes you think I could fare better?"

"Because you're Israeli."

"What makes you think he is? The truth is that no one is sure about anything pertaining to Alabaster. People say he is the deadliest man alive, yet they aren't even sure he is still alive. Is there a place on this side of the Atlantic for such a man?"

Bartose cleared his throat, face reddening.

"Don't get me wrong, Mr. Bartose," David went on. "I believe what you said makes a great deal of sense. It's only natural to assume that my sole reason for accepting an assignment after all these years—and from a foreign country yet—was to get a shot at Seif. I'd be a liar and a fool to suggest otherwise. Of course, I would like to meet up with the Butcher. We have a debt to settle between us. But you can all rest assured that my personal grudges will not get in the way of my professional performance." A pause. "Speaking of which, I would appreciate being brought up to date on what has been learned since you contacted me."

The Director leaned back in his wheelchair. A section of his silvery hair fell to his forehead. As he spoke, his gravel voice seemed bathed in defeat. "David, many in the world will tell you that the Agency is the finest intelligence gathering unit on the globe, your Mossad not withstanding. In this case, though, we have been frustrated at every turn in finding leads. John

Desmond is dead, his contacts—severed. None of the efforts of our other Mideastern operatives and deep cover people have turned up anything. We captured three top Black September agents who had been under surveillance by both us and the Mossad for almost a year. And we blew the cover of some of our best placed agents to detain them. . . . They knew nothing, David. Even the latest truth serum, the most potent ever by far, failed to reveal anything because the two men and one woman had nothing to reveal. In short, we are at a dead end, no further along than we were four days ago. It embarrasses me to admit that."

"It shouldn't. Black September has been planning this operation for at least five years, probably more. They've got quite a head start on us."

"We don't need consolation at this point. We need a new strategy that will allow us to determine what the hell these Arab bastards are up to. If it weren't for this damn iron box I'm stuck in, I'd go back into the field myself and you can bet your ass I'd find some answers." Anxiety laced Rossi's voice, the crevices of his tired face standing out more than ever. He fought off a coughing spasm and continued. "Do you have any suggestions, David?"

"The Arabs' plot seems to defy counter strategy. Keep in mind, sir, that it does not appear that Al Fatah is planning to make a threat. It's not going to be a 'give us this or we'll do that' situation. And in most cases—Entebbe, for example—a strategy cannot be generated until the threat has been made and the enemy has put all the cards on top of the table. Right now, I'm afraid, the Red Prince holds all the cards and hasn't even bothered to tell us the game he's playing."

"But you can bet it will be by his rules."

"And if we are going to win, we have to change them to suit our needs. But the Arabs have a tremendous advantage, Colonel Rossi. They are after nothing outside of inflicting a major wound on this country. There will be no ultimatum issued, no either/or confrontation. We either play their game when we find out what it is or we make them play ours."

"The latter is obviously preferable."

"And it seems equally obvious that we aren't going to learn anything about their operation through normal channels. A cloak of secrecy has been placed over it like none I've ever seen before. Accordingly, I recommend that you allow me to handpick a network of experts to match the ones Al Fatah has assembled. All the people I have in mind are present in your files. They are the best available. I know," David said reflectively. "I've worked with them before."

"This is not the time for a reunion," howled Bartose. "You are asking us to trust you with the safety of our nation. You want to return to your glory days in the field at the expense of the United States of America. That will be Alabaster's job, after we find him."

"You never will."

"Why?"

David's expression was forged in stone. "Because, gentlemen, I am Alabaster."

FOURTEEN

"You . . . *Alabaster?*"

It was nearly a minute before the shock of the men gathered in Colonel Rossi's office abated. Their mouths had dropped seemingly on cue, eyes bulging and eyebrows raised. Only the Director's countenance had remained unchanged; cool and detached, studying the speaker with no small degree of admiration.

"If you would allow a compliment," Rossi said finally, breaking the silence, "I think it was a positively brilliant idea."

"Logical perhaps but not brilliant," David disagreed. "What better way to take on terrorists than to create a myth, a legend, who stalks them always? A myth who in himself has no identity, no existence. A myth who seems to appear and disappear out of thin air at will."

"And you constructed the myth following the murder of your wife in 1972."

"Not exactly. I first used Alabaster in 1969, as I'm sure you know, following a terrorist raid on an El-Al jet in Paris. We knew the identities of the terrorists and were prepared to take retaliatory action. But a snag developed over them being granted clemency by the damned French government in exchange for future considerations by the PLO. Even the Mossad must obey certain channels and Israel at that time was trying to reestablish relations with France. The retaliation was delayed, some of us feared indefinitely. Sure, we could hit Palestinian bases in Jordan as a vendetta but that would leave the true culprits free to walk the streets again. I couldn't stomach that. So I decided to act on my own. I created an avenging vigilante, leaked his existence in the right places, and killed the terrorists myself; after which, the vigilante disappeared, never I thought to be heard from again."

"Then the creation of Alabaster was not planned as a long-range affair?"

"Hardly. He had served his purpose and I was done with him. But reaction from the Arab terrorist community and emerging Black September leadership was staggering. They sent their best agents all over Europe and the Mideast searching for Alabaster. They were obsessed by him, frightened for their very lives. So I elected to keep Alabaster alive."

"How did you come by that name?" asked Herb Weinberg.

"Alabaster itself is a hard, bonded marble compound used in ceramics and generally considered to be one of the strongest elements available. But at the same time it possesses a translucent quality that allows light to pass through it. When the light is right, it makes one think he is looking at something that isn't really there. A phantom."

"That makes sense, considering your penchant for disguise," noted Colonel Rossi.

"Disguise became mandated once I decided to become Alabaster on a more regular basis. My wife had been murdered and my nerves, as David Rabanine, were truly shot. I no longer could handle the day-to-day pressures and hassles of the field. It wasn't the work so much as the obligations to report and make account. I began my career at a time when Mossad agents killed often and spoke little. There were never any questions, so we didn't bother with answers. When things became more moderate, then, I used the opportunity to retire and live with my son. But I also thirsted for revenge against the planners of Munich and killers of innocent Israelis all over the world. Accordingly, from time to time I took to the field as Alabaster to track down and execute those responsible for terrorist acts against the state of Israel. After I had accomplished what I set out to, I'd return to my home as though nothing had happened."

"Almost like Jekyll and Hyde."

"An accurate analogy because over the years more and more I found Alabaster taking on a personality of his own, separate and distinct from my own. He would say things I never would, take chances I could never consider, kill in manners so violent and vicious that they would turn my stomach later. I had created a personality so strong that even I came to be taken in by it. He was his man, I was mine."

"But surely someone high-up in the Mossad suspected the truth?" posed Bob Kincannon.

"If they did, they never let on to anyone else. There were certain inconsistencies, such as physical examinations I passed with flying colors while the psychological ones still marked me as a nervous wreck. But what reason did the Mossad have to uncover the true identity of Alabaster? He was a one man death squad who saved them much time, trouble and money."

"And where did Alabaster get *his* money?" asked Bartose.

"An account was set up in Geneva. Money was deposited there regularly by a Mossad official who had no reason to ask questions. He knew where the money was going."

"Then you had help. There must have been others."

"Indeed, four to be exact. All experts in tracking down those who do not wish to be and extracting information that is otherwise impossible to obtain. I last worked with them in January of 1979 in Beirut. We had tracked the Red Prince there and, we thought, successfully eliminated him. In fact, though, we had been made unwitting participants in a bizarre hoax. The Red Prince wanted the world to think him dead. What better way to accomplish this then to have himself apparently killed by the great Alabaster?" David paused uneasily. "And now he has surfaced again because he no longer has a reason to stay underground. He has accomplished what he wanted to. The plan we are facing now is obviously many years in the making and he has come here to set in motion. I believe the operation has been coded 'the Shaitan Commandment' . . ."

David went on to explain his meeting with Oman Abbu-

Taabes, the diplomat from the Libyan embassy, stressing the fact that the terrorist force soon to be entering America numbered probably no more than 200 and was linked somehow to a new and deadly weapon.

"That seems hard to believe," grumbled Art Bartose. "A plot five or more years in the making that utilizes only 200 agents and a mysterious new weapon?"

"It does sound rather absurd," concurred Bob Kincannon.

"Its potential success may well lie in its absurdity."

"Do you have any idea what actions the force will take once it reaches America?" Colonel Rossi asked.

"Conceivably, their mission will be to infiltrate key areas in American government and proceed to engineer mass assassinations at a specified time."

"Impossible," scoffed Bartose.

"On the contrary, not possible enough. To start with, mass assassinations do not take more than five years to plan and, more importantly, if they were carried out America's angered retaliation would destroy the PLO at any cost. Therefore, I believe whatever we are dealing with is of a far greater magnitude and destructive potential, something they do not think we will recover sufficiently from to mount a significant retaliation."

"They'd have to wipe out the whole country to achieve that," Kincannon derided.

Rabanine said nothing.

"In which case," Kincannon went on wryly, "their weapon would have to be something straight from the future."

"More likely the past."

"The past?" quizzed Rossi.

David nodded and explained Abad Salim's mention of *der Teufels Befehl*, the Devil's Command.

"But what does an obscure German phrase from an unknown period have to do with what we're facing here and now?" asked Bob Kincannon, already worried about the expense tracking it down would cause.

135

"Maybe everything. What the Devil's Command was in Germany, I think, explains what the Shaitan Commandment will be in America."

"Not a bad thesis at all," Rossi began, "when you consider that it is common knowledge that Hitler pondered several plans meant to neutralize America once the war was over to insure him of total world domination. Whether, though, any of these ever left the embryonic stage is doubtful. . . ."

"But," broke in David, "what if the basis of the plan has been rediscovered by Black September? What if the terrorists under the guidance of the Red Prince have taken *der Teufels Befehl* and made it operational?"

"I do not choose to think of the ramifications," said the Director, his gravel voice breaking for the first time. "We'll run a check on the phrase. Handle it, Bob."

"But we have no idea what period of Germany history the phrase originates from," protested Kincannon.

"The computers might."

"In the meantime," said David, "I would like to study every bit of information you have accumulated since Monday."

"That amounts to quite a volume and much of it is meaningless."

"From now on everything must be viewed under a microscope. We can't afford to miss any clues." David checked his watch. "Let's meet again in three hours after which I shall begin to contact the four members of my task force . . . with your permission, of course."

"It's been a long time since you've worked together, David," Colonel Rossi warned.

"They will still be the best."

"And what about you?" pressed Bartose. "Our files say Alabaster hasn't been heard from in two years."

Rabanine's eyebrows flickered. "I felt at that time my services were no longer required."

"But you changed your mind."

"Do you blame me?"

"I only wonder what a two year layoff might do to a man even of Alabaster's . . . skills."

"We'll find out soon enough."

"Leslie, could I see you in my office for a minute?"

Something in managing editor Peter McSorely's voice worried her, something about the tone. She tried to dismiss it.

"Sure, Pete. I'll be right there."

It was almost four o'clock on a rainy Providence afternoon. Leslie had spent half the night rewriting her story. She had pieced together the facts she had and blended them professionally with the overriding, though unsubstantiated, suggestions. The result was a competent enough bit of investigative journalism that was still sorely lacking in corraborating quotes and evidence.

Leslie arrived in McSorely's office to find the editor staring blankly at the wall before him.

"Is something wrong, Pete?"

His eyes stayed on the wall. "There's a problem with the story."

"It isn't going to run in tomorrow morning's edition?" she managed, fearing the answer. The published article was going to be her savior, was going to turn hunters into hunted.

"It isn't going to run at all."

Leslie felt suddenly heavy. "But you liked it," she pleaded. "You said—"

McSorely cut her off, waving his hand as he spoke again. "It wasn't my decision."

"You're the goddamn managing editor."

"But I don't own the paper."

"Then the owners killed it."

"I'm not sure."

"How can you not be sure?" Leslie demanded.

McSorely looked at her for the first time. "Look, Les, I'm going to level with you. Somebody important wants that story dead and buried. This is a first class sham. I've seen it before and I'm sure I'll see it again."

"You . . . you could have done something."

"No, I'm afraid I couldn't."

"Then I will! . . . I'll go and see the bastards responsible for this!" Leslie moved for the door.

McSorely caught her by the shoulders. Fear swam in his eyes.

"Listen to me, Les, I don't know what's going on but you can be damned sure that storming into the publisher's office won't get you anything but a pink slip. You stumbled onto something that must belong in an important closet somewhere and important people are obviously trying to get it back inside. Now I'm going to give you some advice and please, for the love of God, take it: Go home, pack a suitcase for you and your kid and get the hell out of Providence as fast as you can."

"I didn't run away when Roy was murdered and I don't plan on running now."

"Don't confuse pride with common sense, Les. You can't fight something you can't see. I'll cover for you here at the paper. Call it a vacation with pay. Just leave the city and get in touch with me the moment you get settled."

"You sound very eager to get rid of me," she said, realizing at once her tone had conveyed suspicion. God, she thought, if I can't trust Pete, who can I trust?

"I just don't want anything to happen to you," the editor said. "I promise to keep following this thing up on this end. I'll ask some innocent questions. I've still got a few contacts lying around here and there."

"But you don't want me around to help."

McSorely sighed. "Both of us are in over our heads, Les, but that doesn't mean we both have to drown."

The ten minute drive back to her house seemed to stretch for hours, as Leslie screeched down the city's streets and around or over curbs. One thought filled her mind: her son, Jimmy. He was supposed to have been picked up by Mrs. Rosenberg today, whose son also attended the School for the Deaf. In all the excitement over her story, Leslie had neglected to change the arrangements. And now she was frightened that . . .

The thought made her shudder. But Jimmy would be all right. Claire Rosenberg would have picked him up. He might be home already.

But he wasn't.

"Clair, this is Leslie Kirkman," she said to Mrs. Rosenberg, the receiver trembling in her hand. "I was wondering if Jimmy was s-s-s-still over there."

There was a pause on the other end before Clair Rosenberg responded. "I thought you picked Jimmy up." Leslie's heart sank. "I mean when he didn't come out with Brett, I just assumed . . . and, well, I asked Brett but he said he hadn't seen Jimmy since lunch. So I . . ."

The rest of the words were lost somewhere in Leslie's tortured consciousness. The receiver dropped from her hand and struck the floor. She tried to stem her trembling and failed. Her worst fears had been confirmed. They had Jimmy and it was because of her. They had already killed one boy. It would mean little to kill another.

Leslie wanted to cry but couldn't. She felt herself slipping away into conscious shock but fought hard to bring her mind back to reality. She had to function. But why bother? What was there she could do? They had her son and she was helpless. It was as grotesquely simple as that.

Her mind conjured up a picture of the men in the picture, the men who had killed Scott Krassner, standing before Jimmy asking questions. The boy would be nervous. He would forget to read lips. The men would think he was being uncooperative. They would . . .

Oh God!

Wasn't there anything she could do?

Yes! Yes!

Feeling a lukewarm wave of resolve rush through her, Leslie knelt down and replaced the receiver on its hook, pausing only long enough for the dial tone to return. She would call the police, the FBI, the National Guard—everyone until someone would listen and come to help her. Since Roy's death, never had she felt so alone and helpless. She had spent three years trying to convince herself she was strong only to find out she was weak after all. She had let herself down and she had let her son down. Never in the past forty-eight hours had the danger she might have been exposing him to entered her mind. She had been too busy trying to prove something. Well, she had failed and miserably. But maybe it wasn't too late.

She lifted the receiver and brought it back to her ear. The dial tone was gone. There was no sound at all.

"No! . . . No!"

She pressed buttons repeatedly, searching for the missing sound. But it was gone . . . like Jimmy.

She pressed and pressed and pressed until finally she lifted the phone and flung it across the room. Bells echoed and fluttered into silence.

She realized she was moving about the room in a circle, the motion stopped only when she saw a red Cutlass parked across the street from the house. A man with thinning brown hair was getting back into it. She thought she saw him smile at her.

Leslie felt herself slump against a wall and wondered if the madness would overcome her before the men who had Jimmy did.

Three hours after the first meeting in Langley, Virginia had ended, David Rabanine sat down in his same chair in the Director's office. The other principals were already seated.

"Did you find the volume satisfying, David?" Colonel Rossi asked. The Director's expression was dominated by bags that lay large and dark beneath his eyes. He coughed loudly, excusing himself.

"Confusing would be more like it," David replied. "What

about *der Teufels Befehl?*"

"Nothing. The computer drew a complete blank. There is no record on any of our history tapes of the Devil's Command. We're cross-checking now. Anything else?"

"I might want to question the Providence police detective responsible for forwarding the pictures to Washington."

"That won't be hard," said Bob Kincannon. "He's being kept under wraps in a safe house not more than an hour from here."

"I assume similar accommodations have been arranged for the woman I read about," Rabanine said. Kincannon made no response. "Mr. Kincannon?"

"No, they haven't," the bureaucrat said flatly.

The Director leaned swiftly forward. A grimace stretched across his face, evidence that the sudden motion pained him. "What are you talking about? I gave orders that anyone with knowledge should be quietly removed and the whole matter sealed up tight."

"It was sealed," defended Kincannon. "I just felt that it would be superfluous to our interests to remove the woman once her story had been suppressed. Her son would have had to be taken care of as well and we do have the taxpayers' money to think about."

"You mean you left this woman *alone* up there?" Rabanine asked incredulously.

"You're a damn fool, Kincannon," charged Colonel Rossi.

Rabanine had already stood up and was moving for the knobless white door.

"Where are you going?" the Director asked.

"Providence."

"What about contacting your task force?"

"It'll wait. Now open this door before Mr. Kincannon's blasted taxpayers have to pay for a new one."

At five o'clock that evening in Crescent Falls, Wyoming,

141

Mayor Jim Layton held his water glass triumphantly before him.

"Gentlemen," he saluted, "a toast to the rebirth of our town."

"Don't you think that's a bit premature?" asked Norm Shacklehorse from across the table in his Bar & Grill.

"Maybe it is, maybe it isn't. The point is that we've got a chance which we didn't before."

"Jimbo, does that mean you're fixin' to spring for this here dinner?" asked Bugsy Tyler, looking very uncomfortable in the too small sheriff's uniform he usually wore only on the Fourth of July. Both the top and bottom two buttons had to be left undone to prevent the shirt from ripping. "Don't mind tellin' ya' that I'm as hungry as a whore workin' a double shift."

"Bugsy, if things go as I expect they will, we'll all be eating steak every night for the rest of our lives," said Dave Dean.

"I'm only interested in gettin' me some tonight," Tyler muttered.

"You're that sure?" Marge Kitter asked Dean. She was a council member who owned and ran the town's only gas station. Marge had not been present at the first meeting because Abel Towe's wife was having a baby. Marge was also the town's midwife.

"Let's say I got a feeling," responded Dean.

"And I got me a pain in my stomach," said Tyler. "Christ, Norm, I hope becomin' rich makes you do somethin' about the service in this place because it stinks to hell right now."

"Just eat another roll, Sheriff," suggested the mayor.

"Already ate seven. My stomach's askin' for that big, thick steak right now."

"So has everybody met our five friends?" Dean asked.

Marge Kitter shook her head. "Been too busy over at the station. Lots of repair work, you know. Seems like people are gearin' up to travel in case these guys don't find what they're looking for. I'll try to make some time tomorrow to catch up with them. Maybe around noon."

The mayor shook his head. "Don't bother, Marge, they'll be working in the fields by then. Doing what they call 'preliminary exploration.' I've seen their equipment. It's really something."

"Nice and shiny, I'll bet," said Bugsy Tyler. Layton eyed him quizzically.

"You know," began Dave Dean, "since they got in here day before yesterday, they haven't even been able to say hello because they've been so busy."

"Where'd they start working?" asked Norm Shacklehorse.

"Told me the old Simpson place. Said the soil samples from that part of town had proven to have some of the best potential. They been there all day today and most of yesterday."

"I saw them when they got back an hour ago," said Bugsy, fighting a temptation to pop some chew into his mouth. "Which reminds me of a question I wanted to ask. How well do you know these five guys?"

Mayor Layton and Dave Dean looked at each other. It was Dean who spoke. "How well could we know them, Bugsy? I mean they haven't even been in town three days yet."

"So you never had no contact with any of the five before?"

"No. Why?"

Tyler ignored Dean's question and asked another of his own. "What company you say these guys worked for?"

"They don't really work for a single company, Sheriff," said Jim Layton. "They're free lance sort of."

"What the hell's that mean?"

"They work in the field and sell their discoveries to the highest bidder. With the price of oil what it is now, I'm sure they do quite well for themselves."

"I ain't interested in how much they got stored in their pocketbooks, or which hand they wipe their asses with, or how often they play with themselves. I just never heard of no free lance oil exploration team before."

"You're not exactly an avid reader of the *New York Times*,

Bugsy," laughed Dave Dean.

"No, the *Crescent Falls Gazette* gives me all the news I need. But I got one helluva nose that tells me these guys may not be what they say they are. Like I said before, I saw them come back from the Simpson place just an hour ago. Their shoes was all full of dark brown mud."

"So?"

"Well, there ain't no dirt by that color on the Simpson spread. I know 'cause I helped old J.T. haul some cows out of the mud when we had that downpour in the fall. The dirt's all red, almost like clay."

"I don't see that the color of dirt on their shoes means very much," said Mayor Layton.

"It means they might not have gone to the Simpson place like they said they had. Maybe they don't even know where the Simpson place is. Maybe they don't care."

"Sheriff, you been watchin' too much TV lately," said Dave Dean, momentarily lapsing into the Wyoming accent he tried so hard to suppress. "These five men are the best thing that's happened to Crescent Falls in a hundred years. What's the goddamn difference whether they went to the Simpson place or not?"

"First of all," Tyler shot back, "my old tee-vee don't pick up no channels no more. And the goddamn difference is that they said they was goin' somewhere where they didn't go."

"Maybe they changed their shoes somewhere along the line."

Bugsy shook his massive head. "Uh-uh."

Jim Layton leaned forward and tightened the droopy features of his face into a scowl. "Sheriff, these men deserve a hero's welcome from this town and I just happen to be planning a ceremony for next week when they're all gonna be made honorary citizens of Crescent Falls. Now don't you go shootin' your mouth off about this dirt crap. You blow this for us and someone else will be wearin' your badge come next election."

Tyler gave in to temptation and popped a clump of Skoal between his cheek and gum. "Oh, I'm gonna be real quiet about this for sure. It don't make too much noise to get the names of these five guys from Sally Black's boardinghouse and run a check on them, a real *quiet* check. . . . Yeah, I'm gonna be as quiet as a hard-on in a rubber factory."

FIFTEEN

Night fell over Providence. It had rained for most of the early evening hours and now, although the storm was over, it had left behind a murky mist over the city. In front of Leslie Kirkman's house, the mist was broken only by two streetlights that spilled their rays through the blackness.

Inside, Leslie sat motionless on a chair. They had Jimmy and it was her fault. Outside two men were waiting in a red Cutlass. Certainly, they knew she wouldn't try to escape without first hearing something about her son. And even if she could escape, where would she go? Who would listen to her? She thought of managing editor Peter McSorely but quickly realized she could not bear to have anything happen to him as well because of her. She was in this alone.

Suddenly she heard the back door slam and felt herself rise involuntarily from the chair and crash backwards into the wall near the living room window, paralyzed with fear. Beneath her tight green corduroys, her legs shook and her bladder weakened.

She had no weapon. Roy's magnum was upstairs. She hadn't even considered its use since coming home. After all, how could it help her get Jimmy back? It didn't matter. They had him and now they were in the house soon to take her. But the feet that stepped lightly across the linoleum floor, squeaking and making no effort to silence themselves, were not the feet of a man.

"Hi, mom."

It was Jimmy, moving down the hallway that led from the kitchen to the living room. *Thank God!* . . . She ran to her son and embraced him, feeling tears swell in her eyes and roll down

146

her cheeks.

"Where have you been?" she asked, careful to insure he could see her lips.

"At Kurt's house."

"But you were supposed to go home with the Rosenbergs."

Jimmy lowered his eyes. "I couldn't find Brett after school so I wasn't sure what to do. Then I got a ride from Kurt. I've been at his house; then his father got home and brought me back here. I asked his mother to call you but the line was busy. . . . Is anything wrong?" the boy asked, suddenly resisting Leslie's grasp, fear forming in his face.

"What makes you ask?"

"I thought I saw a man in our backyard when I came in."

Leslie's mouth dropped. The reality of the situation returned to her. She couldn't let Jimmy see her fear.

"Why'd you come in the back?" she asked.

"I always do, you know that."

Leslie moved her hands from Jimmy's shoulders, aware that she was trembling, her mind fighting to find a way out.

"Mom, are you all right?"

She grasped her son's arms firmly. "Listen to me, we've got to get out of here. Somehow we've got to get out of here."

"Why? I, I don't un-understand."

"Just trust me. Everything will be all right."

Stealing a glance at the red Cutlass parked across the street, Leslie took Jimmy's hand and led him up the stairs. There had never been a kidnapping. The men outside were here to do far more than just watch her. But what were they waiting for? The almost total blackness of the house's second floor gave her the answer: They were waiting for it to get dark before they made their strike.

Leslie switched on the light at the head of the staircase and turned back to Jimmy. She had an idea.

"I want you to go into your room and put on the darkest clothes you have."

"Why?" the boy asked nervously, his eyes beginning to fill

with tears.

"I'll tell you soon. Now just do as I say." The boy hesitated. "Please, Jimmy, *hurry!*"

There was desperation in her voice but no anger. The boy had to be saved and this was the only way she could see to save him. He turned and ran into his room sobbing. Leslie wanted to follow him, wanted to embrace him and soothe away his fear. She had to keep herself strong, though. She entered her bedroom and went immediately to the closet. With trembling fingers, she removed the pine lockbox and put it on the bed. The shades in the room were down, casting it with a shadowy luminance in the dim light. Leslie removed the single key from her night table and opened the box.

The .357 magnum looked up at her, seeming to smile. She lifted it out and tried to balance its awkward weight in her hand. The trembling became worse. Her fingers wouldn't close around its grip and trigger. The steel felt cold and clammy in her hands. The gun was slippery. The scent of oil and grease soaked her nostrils.

She fought to steady herself, filling her mind with thoughts of her son. Any minute now the men would rush the house. She would fight them, knowing she couldn't win and that her own death was a virtual certainty. Perhaps, though, she could hold them off long enough to enable Jimmy to make an escape through one of the second story windows. It was not a sacrifice but an obligation. And in the hopeful scenario running through her mind, Jimmy might even escape and bring help back fast enough to save her as well. But he was not an athletic boy; asthma had seen to that. And the prospects of him maneuvering successfully on the roof before jumping to the grass below were not favorable, though they were the only prospects she had.

Feeling her fingers relax a bit, Leslie reached into the bottom drawer of the night table that had been Roy's and removed a box of cartridges. She opened the magnum's chamber just as Roy had shown her and began to ease them into place. Six in all.

One of the bullets jammed in the small hole, pinching her skin. Blinded by the sudden pain, Leslie pulled her finger away in a rush, sending the bullet flying across the room. In the next room, she could hear Jimmy rummaging furiously around.

Finally all the cartridges were in place. She snapped the cylinder back in its slot and made sure it was tight by spinning it, just like she had seen Roy do on several occasions. Or had she seen that in the movies?

More scampering from Jimmy's room.

Nervously, Leslie stuffed a handful of bullets into the back pocket of her corduroys and ran her left hand down the barrel of the magnum. It felt chilly and unfamiliar. She lifted the gun up to face level and pawed the trigger lightly. The magnum was heavy and uncomfortable to her touch, in her mind poorly balanced. Beneath her cream blouse, she felt cold beads of perspiration dripping from her underarms.

"Mom, is that gun loaded?" Jimmy stood in the doorway, dressed in a black polo shirt and very dark blue jeans. The shirt was barely tucked in, the fly only halfway zipped. It was as though he had forgotten how to dress himself.

She moved closer to him. "Jimmy, you've got to pay attention to what I'm going to say and do everything I tell you, all right?"

The boy hadn't listened or read her lips. His eyes remained locked on the magnum. "What are you going to do with the gun?"

"Use it to frighten away some people." It was time to tell the boy part of the truth. Leslie knelt down, resting the gun on the floor, grasping her son's shoulders tightly. "Listen, there are men out there in the yard who want to hurt us."

"Hurt . . . *us?*" The boy's words were nearly swallowed by sudden terror.

"But we're not going to let them. They don't know how strong we are."

"Are we going to fight them?"

149

"We're going to try," Leslie said, surprised by the coolness of her facade. To steady her own fear, she needed only to see her son's. "And each of us has a special job to do. I'm going to go downstairs and keep them out, while you are going to climb out one of the upstairs windows and run to one of the neighbor's houses and tell them what's happening and to get help."

"I want to stay with you," the boy whined.

"I need you to do this for me."

"But I'll be scared on the roof. I've never had to go on it before. I might fall." The boy collapsed forward, throwing himself upon his mother. "Please don't make me. I might start wheezing and lose my breath. I don't want to go. I want to stay here. I can help you. I'll do anything you say."

Leslie pulled the boy closer to keep him from seeing her tears. She couldn't get the vision of Jimmy falling off a slippery, wet roof out of her mind. When fleeing one danger, you often encounter an even greater one. Such might be the case here.

"All right, Jimmy. You'll stay with me. But you've got to do everything I say."

The boy remained silent. His sobs had given way to full tears that tread a constant path down his red-stained cheeks. Leslie held onto him tightly, hoping their embrace would somehow shut the rest of the world out.

Outside, however, Leslie knew men were waiting to kill her and that the madness would begin any second.

Leslie had turned all the lights inside the house off, leaving only the outside ones on. She wanted to see who she was dealing with and hoped at the same time that they would not be able to see her in the darkened interior.

She had hidden Jimmy in the back of the kitchen closet where he promised to stay silently . . . no matter what. And now she was crouched down uncomfortably on the throw rug, facing the front door with the pistol clutched unsteadily in her

150

hands, her back supported by the couch.

She stroked the gun's barrel with her free hand, trying to familiarize herself with its presence. She *had* to feel at ease with the weapon. It was the only thing that stood between her and . . . She buried the thought deep in her mind.

Leslie stroked the trigger. Could she pull it?

Yes! Yes!

She had to be able to aim at a chest or head and fire. Squeeze, don't pull, Roy had told her. Squeeze . . .

But what if she couldn't?

All at once, the doorbell began to ring almost continuously. Someone was pounding on the door in harmony with the chimes. And then a voice came, loud and frantic.

"Mrs. Kirkman! Mrs. Kirkman! Are you all right? I'm from the police. I've come to help you. Lieutenant Lucas followed up on your story after your editor called him. He found you were telling the truth."

"Go away!"

"He sent me over. I just saw two men get out of a car across the street. I think there are more in back of the house. What's going on? Let me in."

"Go away!"

"I've come here to help you. *Please let me in!*"

"Go away!" Leslie screamed again. "I know what's going on. You work for the same people that killed Scott Krassner. But you'll find me a lot harder to murder than a boy." Inside her chest, Leslie's heart seemed to be exploding. Her resolve strengthened with each flailing word. Adrenalin surged through her body. Now she was trembling with anger and rage more than fear. "I've got a gun and I'll use it if you don't leave—all of you. Believe me, I know how!" As though she were trying to convince herself.

The ringing and the pounding both finally stopped. The man outside began to speak quietly, his tone sedate and conciliatory. "Mrs. Kirkman, you're hysterical. You don't know what you're saying. Let me in. We'll talk about it. There are men in the neighborhood who want to hurt you. You need help. I can supply it. You can't beat them alone." He slapped the door several times with his open hand.

"Go away! . . . Do you hear me? . . . *Go away!*"

"I want to help you."

"You want to kill me!"

"No, I swear. I'm not one of them. I'm really a cop. Open the door a crack; let me show you my badge. You've got to believe me. You're not alone. I've been—" Leslie heard the man gasp. "Please, Mrs. Kirkman, open the door. I just saw a shadow under the street lamp. They're across the street. I can't see them now. They're hiding. I'm a sitting duck out here. *For God's sake, open the door!*"

Leslie knew she was weakening, starting to believe the words because she wanted to. The story seemed logical in its desperation. If this man was not a cop, why would he have bothered to go through such an elaborate deception? And if he was a cop, and she didn't let him in, his death would be on her conscience.

She would go to the door. But she wasn't going to open it until she got a good look at the man on the other side and the badge he promised to produce. She released the slight pressure she had on the trigger and began to prop herself up. The muscles in her legs had spasmed and, as she began to rise, she was forced to sit quickly down again to relieve the pain.

It was that motion that saved her life. The series of sounds was rapid, seeming to come at once. A soft spit, glass shattering, and the explosion of plaster behind her in the wall. The gun had been fired at the precise moment her body had reached the pencil-thin beam of light that came from the window.

The window!

Leslie spun quickly toward it, her finger poised uneasily on the trigger. A body stood against the glass on the outside, peering in, confident of its safety. Without thinking, Leslie swung the pistol upwards in the shadow's direction and

152

depressed the trigger.

Once . . . twice . . .

The blasts stung her ears and the kickback flung her back toward the couch, nearly spilling her over it. More glass shattered. The hot, acrid smell of cordite filled Leslie's nostrils and made her think of firecrackers. The barrel of the magnum was hot and smoking.

The power of the gun surprised her and in that newfound power lay a semblance of security and confidence. There was a chance at least, whereas before there had been none.

Her shots had been wild but near misses nonetheless. The point had been made: She was not about to submit. She was an opponent. The men outside had a fight on their hands. Knowing this, maybe they would leave. Or perhaps a neighbor would hear the shots and call the police.

Leslie gripped the magnum tightly, suddenly sure of her grasp. The first shots had taught her that she could fire the gun. The next ones would prove she could aim it. She would pull the trigger and the men would die. It seemed so simple. . . .

The house was bathed in silence inside and out, as though it too was frightened. Jimmy's soft whimpering came and went in her ears, breaking the soundless monotony. She thought of telling him to stay quieter. But the time it took to do so would provide her assailants with the advantage, and that could not be allowed. She held the pistol tighter still, shifting her gaze around the room from window to window to door.

Glass exploded somewhere upstairs. Leslie began to move for the steps. But wait . . . Without a ladder, no one could have gotten up there. It was a trick, a distraction. She would not let herself be fooled. Her breathing was hard and deep, her finger a coiled spring on the trigger. She swallowed, gulping down a hot burst of breath.

Her ears detected a sound, distinct and shattering. She turned to her left, away from the stairs. The lock portion of the front door had exploded, allowing it to swing open held closed only by the chain. A hand appeared and then an arm inside,

153

probing for the chain lock in order to unfasten it. Finally the fingers found their target. Leslie raised the gun, aimed briefly, and fired.

A wailing scream erupted. Blood ran from the man's arm as it withdrew itself, hanging limp. Leslie ran forward and threw herself at the entrance, sealing the door closed, her back hard against the wood. Entry would again be denied. The hinge caught but only for a second as a body crashed from the outside against the battered oak. Leslie was thrown forward off balance, slipping on the rug. She steadied herself and fired at the door. Twice she pulled the trigger. Splinters of wood flew everywhere from two pale, jagged holes amidst the brown door. The smell of cordite was stronger now, burning her nostrils. The blazing barrel boiled the skin near it. But the men had stopped their surge. The door swung forward, stopped again by the safety chain.

Leslie's eyes swept the room, her finger taut on the trigger. They were pounding at the door again. But a sudden sound to her left made her spin, the gun swinging in her hands. A man, dark in the shadows of the misty night, had propped himself up on the sill of the room's far window to the right of the rolltop desk. A pistol stretched in his hand, steel shining against the pane. Leslie hesitated but just for a second. She fired at the instant the man had planned to. The bullet struck him square in the center of the chest. A stream of blood erupted on the fragmented glass. The man screamed and fell backwards, landing with a thud on the ground beneath him.

Mesmerized by her own action, Leslie approached slowly, her pistol flexed and ready before her as both guide and probe. Perhaps she expected the man to still be alive and to leap at her when she leaned near the window. In her tortured consciousness, the idea that even this could be a trick was not too far remote. Her eyes, though, revealed otherwise. The man lay sprawled on his back, body twisted and torn, eyes empty and staring at nothing. Blood painted his midsection in a bizarre impressionistic design.

Leslie suddenly felt dazed, queasy; her iron resolve at once tempered by the reality of violent death around her. The gun shook in her hands. She wanted to drop it, felt she should. She needed to vomit or faint. She had just killed somebody . . .

She leaned over slightly and fought to keep her hands away from her face. Slowly, she backed away from the window. Sweat dripped into her eyes. Her blouse was soaked through with icy perspiration. She was shaking.

The front door exploded inward again. She felt herself run toward it and raise the gun not to fire but to strike. The chain finally gave, the door swinging totally free. An arm appeared and then another. The body began to show itself. Blindly she struck at it again and again, screaming, unaware of whether or not she was making contact with flesh. Suddenly a desperate plea reached her ravaged ears; penetrating even her own wails.

"Mom, help! . . . Help!"

Jimmy! . . .

Leslie bolted down the small hallway toward the kitchen. The magnum levelled by her side. Her eyes blazing with fury. She reached the hard tile floor in time to see a brutish looking man with a twisted nose and gray rain hat dragging her son toward the back door.

"Stop!" she screamed, showing the magnum.

The brute's eyes narrowed when he saw the gun. His grip on Jimmy loosened and the boy pulled free, recoiling with his back pressed against the refrigerator, his face a mask of terror. Leslie steadied the gun and fired, eager to welcome the hot blast that would tear into the brute's body.

Nothing . . .

Again she depressed the trigger. Still nothing. The gun was empty!

Without hesitation, she lifted the weapon over her head and brought it down in the direction of the brute's skull. He raised his right arm in time to deflect it, so the steel only grazed his shoulder, barely fazing him.

Leslie was moving forward to strike another blow when she

felt something strike her sharply in the back of the neck. She staggered, her balance gone. There was another strike, sharper and more painful to the area behind her lungs. Her legs buckled, the gun dropped from her fingers.

"No! . . . No!"

She was conscious of Jimmy's cries but only for a second. Her legs had already betrayed her when the third impact came and her world seemed to end. Something sharp had seemed to violate her, sapping her strength and life. There was a spasm in her bowels and an explosion of colors in her mind. Her eyes stayed open but light failed to reach them. She was falling . . . falling; the pain in her back replaced by a spreading numbness that was everywhere. The floor came up fast but she did not feel its impact upon her shattered body.

There was only air and darkness.

Darkness and air.

SIXTEEN

Brown Hair was staring down at her when she awoke. He slapped her hard in the face.

"It's about time," he said. "We were starting to get worried."

She was alive; that was something anyway. But for how much longer?

Leslie moved her head slowly and felt the pain that stretched up her spine into her neck and skull. She tried to move her arms but realized they had been strapped behind her. She was tied into the recliner, her arms stretched to the maximum and laced to the rear of the chair to insure she could not move without tearing her own muscles. The recliner had been pushed outwards so that it angled slightly. Its hidden leg rest had been extended from the bottom. Leslie's legs were wedged between the chair's arms and the rest's sides, tied tightly to prevent even the slightest squirming. She was slumped down, her head pressed on the recliner's top, her position a cramped sort of obscene spread eagle.

Brown Hair peered down at her with his cold eyes. His face, she saw, was a mess of small scars and beard stubble. His build was stocky, though not as stocky as his brutish counterpart who held Jimmy in the corner of the living room, a knife pressed against the soft flesh of his neck. Leslie could see the boy was motionless. His jeans were soaked through with urine released by the fear and trauma that had stripped him of conscious thought.

"You killed one of our friends, miss, and wounded another. You have to pay for that." Brown Hair smiled demonically, his eyes shining. "Yes, you have to pay, miss. Don't bother screaming or I'll have Earl cut out your tongue."

"Surely, you're not going to kill a boy! . . ." Leslie glanced at her helpless son. *"You can't!"*

"Orders are orders, miss. We can and we have to. A pity isn't it, miss?" Brown Hair asked, feigning compassion. He watched her eyes scan the room. "No one can help you, miss. We have a man at both the back door and the front."

Fear raged inside Leslie's tortured, trembling body as she fought to grapple with the inevitability of her death. Her chest sagged as her breaths came in rapid heaves. Brown Hair seemed to enjoy the hideous motion her breasts made. Wasn't there something she could do? Something she could say?

"I have money, jewelry. Take it all. I'll show you where it is. But please . . . leave my son a-a-alive. I won't talk; I promise I won't."

"Surely, miss, you're not forgetting about the dead body outside or the broken glass or the cracked door. There will be many questions." Brown Hair grinned. "You *will* talk, miss. So we have to kill you and your son. And, as for giving me something to change my mind, well, you have only one thing I want and I plan to take that anyway." Brown Hair licked his lips, undressing her with his eyes, intent obvious.

"Just don't hurt the boy! . . . Do anything you want to me but just leave him alive."

"We will do anything we want to you whether we leave him alive or not. But there's no sense in having him grow up an orphan now is there, miss?"

Leslie saw the brute named Earl press the knife harder against Jimmy's throat, breaking the skin and drawing a few specs of blood. The boy tensed.

"I'm afraid that Earl prefers boys to women," Brown Hair resumed. "He usually makes it quite ugly for them before he's finished. But I promise to kill you before Earl gets started with him. That's the least I can do." Brown Hair paused and ran his eyes over her body again. "I think we'll show the boy a little something before Earl has his fun."

158

With that, Brown Hair reached toward Leslie's shirt and ripped it from her chest along with the bra beneath it, exposing her large breasts and firm nipples that seemed to dance atop the quivering mounds of flesh. Then his hand was on her belt, unbuckling and tearing it away. He unzipped the green corduroys and pulled them past her hips. He ran his tongue across his lips when the sight was revealed.

"Bring the boy closer where he can get a better view," Brown Hair instructed and Earl obliged, dragging Jimmy forward in line with the chair, the blade still against his jugular. The boy didn't even bother to try looking away. His face was expressionless, a mask of silent despair.

Leslie realized Brown Hair's eyes were locked on her breasts and vulva. "Perhaps the boy will enjoy this, miss." His hands were on his belt now, slowly undoing it, fingers reaching for the zipper. "He will watch me fuck you and then Earl will have some fun with him."

Leslie wanted to scream but found her throat clogged. She opened her mouth but no sound emerged. It was over, escape impossible. Brown Hair held his grotesque organ erect in his hand. He stepped nearer, preparing to mount her.

Just then, out of the corner of her eye, Leslie saw a figure moving down the hallway, dragging itself along by using the wall for support. The figure wore a jacket bloodied in the arm. This was the man she had shot when he tried to break through the door. Now, though, he seemed to be wounded somewhere else as well, for Leslie saw a large splotch of red widening on his white shirt. His head hung down, his face indistinguishable in the darkened hall. A pistol, a big one, was gripped loosely in his right hand, looking like it was on the edge of falling to the floor.

"Frank, what happened?" Brown Hair asked, sticking his penis back in his pants. "What's wrong out there?"

Frank's motion had stopped. He stood silent and still, held up by the wall in the half-light.

"Earl, help him. Get him over to the couch."

Earl the brute tossed Jimmy aside like a discarded toy. The

boy's body toppled to the rug.

"Hurry up, Earl," Brown Hair said, pulling his zipper up. "I think he's—"

Before Earl could move any further and before Brown Hair could complete his sentence, the slumped body sprang from the wall with lightning quickness, raised the large gun, and steadied his right hand with his left. Two flashes blazed in the darkness.

The first bullet caught the brute Earl in the center of the forehead. A massive explosion of scarlet erupted outward. Flesh and brains splattered against the wall.

The second bullet tore into the left side of Brown Hair's chest as he moved away from the recliner, trying to reach for the gun in his jacket. It lodged in his heart, the blood being pumped by the vessel at that moment spurting out everywhere. Brown Hair clutched the wounded area for only a second and then keeled over, falling face down.

Seconds later Leslie sensed the presence of an immensely strong man above her, a man who not long before had seemed a corpse himself needing a wall for support. The blood on him, she realized, was not his own. Words and thoughts stampeded through her mind as he untied her. But only one phrase, a question, emerged from her trembling lips.

"Who are you?"

The man paused before responding, as if unsure of the answer.

"My name is David. . . . David Rabanine."

He told her everything on the drive to Boston's Logan Airport, at least everything that pertained to her. Leslie listened carefully, half not believing what she heard. It seemed too fantastic. And yet it had happened—*was happening*. They stopped only once; in a cheap, all-night store to get David a change of shirt, his now being bloodstained.

"Then Scott Krassner *was* killed because of the pictures he took," Leslie reflected when he had completed his story.

David nodded. "The men of Al Fatah couldn't take the chance that someone—anyone—might recognize them, especially the one called the Red Prince. They thought that killing that boy would sever any link his camera held to them. But it ended up doing the opposite. Had they left him alive, it's doubtful anything would have come of it. Washington would still be in the dark."

"And that's where we're going?"

"To what's known as a 'safe house' where your safety will be insured by the government. We're taking you out of circulation for awhile until this matter is resolved. You'll stay at the Ambassador Hotel until something more fitting can be arranged."

"It would seem that such arrangements should've been made earlier," Leslie said bitterly.

"The whole matter was closed up tight. The CIA just neglected to include you in the seal."

"How thoughtful of them. . . . I hope such mistakes aren't common."

"In American intelligence, they're a way of life."

"Then the lives of other innocent people have also been jeopardized."

"Or lost."

"Like mine would've been if you hadn't shown up when you did." A pause. "I hope the man guarding the front door didn't mind you borrowing some of his blood."

"He no longer had any use for it once I had finished with him. I threw on his jacket over my bloodstained shirt to give the impression that I—he—had been shot again. I wanted to lure the big one away from your son."

"Then you knew what was happening."

"I looked in the window."

"But the men didn't see you."

"I didn't let them. A man can make himself virtually invisible if he knows how."

"You sound like this sort of thing is nothing new for you.

161

Killing, I mean."

David's fingers tightened around the steering wheel. "I'm a professional, part of me is anyway. Certain skills are often necessary to survive."

Leslie studied his dark features and sharply angled face. "You're not American, are you?"

"No, I'm Israeli."

"You work for the government there?"

"I work for myself. Sometimes our interests overlap."

Leslie hesitated. "You mentioned they killed your wife. When?" she asked gently.

"Eleven years ago in the city of Hebron. She stopped at a roadblock. It was a trap."

"Meant for you?"

"No. They knew I was in Tel Aviv at the time. But they also knew that her life was more important to me than my own. They wanted to cause me eternal pain, not quick death. They also, though, wanted me out of the way. So on the same day my wife was murdered, they placed a fake bomb in my son's crib."

"Why would they do such a thing?"

"Because they knew if they had murdered him, I'd have killed every last one of them—or at least tried. The fake bomb was meant to show me what the ramifications of vengeance would be, how they could strike at my son any time they wished."

"What's his name?"

"Shaul. He's a little older than . . ."

"Jimmy," Leslie completed, stealing a glance at the boy sleeping peacefully in the back. "And thanks to you he's still alive."

"Thanks to me, Shaul was almost killed three days ago in an explosion. Only a miracle saved him. But there'll be other attempts unless I find those responsible."

Leslie sighed. "I killed a man tonight, David. And what scares me most about it is that I'm certain I could do it again. I'd *like* to do it again if the victim was another of the men who

162

plant bombs in babies' cribs."

"You must not feel that way."

"Why? You've killed many times."

"Not me, another part of me. A part that surfaces when I need it . . . and sometimes when I don't. A part that sometimes I thirst to be rid of and other times wonder if I could live without."

"You're confusing me."

"I don't mean to. It's just that it's very hard to explain."

"Don't bother trying." She placed her hand on his shoulder, feeling it tense beneath her touch. Unsure, she pulled the hand away. "We're much alike," she managed. "You—"

He turned quickly toward her with eyes blazing, the fire in them deep and consuming. "Don't say that! . . . Don't ever say that again!"

"David, I—"

But he was faraway so she shifted her gaze back to the front, staring out the windshield before her into the dark misty night; its blackness unbroken. The road ahead seeming to lead nowhere and anywhere at the same time.

Leslie closed her eyes and tried to force herself to sleep.

In the lobby of the Ambassador Hotel more than three hours later, Cerberus watched the man and woman enter the elevator. His face seldom showed emotion. At this moment, though, he could not stop his masklike features from squinting in astonishment.

He was certain now and in that certainty lay the logic of the action he would undertake.

He had been in Washington for thirty-six of the most revealing hours of his life. Cerberus had worked all over the world, always well and often superbly. But nothing before had ever compared to this. Nothing.

He had followed Rabanine and found . . .

It couldn't be . . . and yet it was.

. . . he was trailing Alabaster. But sources had to be checked, confirmation sought. Cerberus never made a report until he was certain. His organization's people in Washington quickly supplied him with the bits of information needed to confirm his suspicions. It was incredible.

Rabanine was Alabaster and Alabaster was Rabanine.

Cerberus was in the phone booth now, hoping he'd have no trouble convincing his superior of what he found so difficult to convince himself.

"Hello."

"The days are long."

"But the nights are short. What is your message?"

Cerberus took a deep breath, his sizzling blue eyes gleaming off the naked steel around him. "I hope you are sitting down . . ."

SEVENTEEN

"Fools!" screamed Ali Hassan Salameh. "Utter fools! . . . Hussein, the responsibility for this disaster must be shouldered by you."

"That is unfair," protested El Sayad. "You gave me orders. I relayed them. Alabaster was just too good for the men I hired."

"The Kirkman woman killed one of the men you hired."

"And Alabaster killed three. Only one escaped with his life."

"Who must be killed anyway."

"Already taken care of," said Mohammed al-Kahir.

The Red Prince jammed a Turkish cigarette into his mouth, started to light it and then stopped. He moved slowly toward the window of his room in the Regency Hotel on Park Avenue in New York City. His eyes locked themselves on the morning traffic below as he began to speak in a faraway tone.

"He has us on the run. We keep moving from hotel to hotel and state to state out of fear that the great Alabaster will track us down."

"Or the great Rabanine," al-Kahir reminded.

"Ah yes, they are one in the same. Well some good can come of that anyway: when we kill one, we will at least not have to worry about the other. If only Seif had not failed . . ."

"But the fact remains that he did," charged El Sayad, rubbing his useless arm as if to restore life in it. He was seated on the couch in the living room section of the suite. "And Alabaster is alive and in America, no doubt beginning to put together our plan."

"Impossible! How could he?" The Red Prince pulled the cigarette violently from his mouth and began to scratch at the filter with his thumb. "There have been no leaks. No one who might have talked knows enough to hurt us. How can Alabaster possibly realize the truth about Shaitan?"

"He has ways."

"Not enough."

"I disagree," argued El Sayad beligerently. "By your own admission, the Shaitan Commandment can succeed only under the auspices of total secrecy. When the Americans begin to die, however that is to be accomplished, no link can exist that might lead them back to us. But, Ali, that link *already exists*."

The Red Prince smiled, twirling the long cigarette smoothly through his fingers. "I smoke these," he said gazing at it, "because I can't stand the American variety. Everything in this country reeks of profit and control, including cigarettes. They are smaller and made with less of a cruder grade of tobacco. Yet the cigarette companies get rich off them because the Americans know no different and keep on buying. They blandly accept whatever is thrust upon them by the damned capitalists while we suffer. It's time to teach them something other than benign acceptance. It's time we made them learn the kind of suffering we have learned."

"I don't wish to make a political issue out of this," said El Sayad. "I merely suggest that we at least postpone the operation until Alabaster can be dealt with."

"Postponed? Because of one man?"

"Alabaster is no ordinary man. He knows something is going on. He will track you down and kill you and your death will forever end the possibility that the Shaitan force will succeed in its mission. I beg you, Ali, to reconsider your position."

"There's nothing to reconsider. Alabaster will not find me."

"Others have had similar statements written as their epitaph."

The Red Prince broke his cigarette in two and let one half fall to the rug. "You're trying my patience, Hussein, and you're not being faithful to the Movement by jeopardizing the success of this operation."

"On the contrary, I am trying to insure that success." The

cripple paused, glancing up at Salameh who was now standing over him, not more than a yard away. "Others will agree with me."

"Arafat?"

"At least those close to him."

"They are fools like you."

"Like me, they believe that this operation will be detrimental to the long-term concerns of our nation. How can you expect the world to recognize us as a sovereign state when we behave like a bunch of children, upset over the quality of cigarettes? Like me, I'm sure they will see that the Shaitan Commandment ought to be aban—" El Sayad cut off his words in mid-sentence. He had said too much, revealed what he had sworn to himself he wouldn't.

The Red Prince smiled down at him, spinning half the unlit cigarette in his hands. "So, Hussein, the truth comes out at last. You are a moderate after all. You would seek to establish our nation on the floor of the UN. You would have the great nations of the world sit in judgment of our requests, while we dress well and wash our faces and act like civilized men so that maybe we will win a cursed strip of forgotten land near the Jews who must always be our enemies. You aim your sights low. It is the world we must have and the Shaitan Commandment can give it to us."

"In the end it will also destroy us."

"It will destroy only America."

"Just as the beginning," El Sayad persisted. "No weapon as great as the one you have spoken of can be used only once. It'll be used again and again against any who dare oppose *you* not *us.*"

"I think you should reconsider this path, Hussein. It is not yet too late."

"I'm afraid it is . . . for both of us. I must remain faithful to my ideals."

"Your ideals are as crippled as your body!"

"Perhaps but they are ideals all the same."

"My people are everywhere. They will stop you from reaching Arafat. You will be dead before you set foot on Arab soil." Salameh watched El Sayad make his way for the door. "I will make sure that—"

But the door to the suite had closed. El Sayad was gone.

Indecision swept through the Red Prince, the feeling foreign and unwelcome. A trusted man had turned on him and was now committed to destroying what he had created.

"Why do you not go with him, Mohammed?" Salameh asked the other man in the room.

Al-Kahir smiled. "There is a game psychologists play in which they stick a mouse in a maze and place a piece of cheese at the finish. Then they watch, taking notes on their clipboards, as the mouse fights its way through the cramped corridors, past the dead ends, maybe reaching its daily meal. If it fails, it does not eat that day which is, of course, part of the test used to develop conditioning." A pause. "I am sick of being the mouse, Ali. I want to be the man holding the clipboard."

Salameh's features relaxed. "Then tell me how things are proceeding at the test site." He sat down and reached into his jacket for another cigarette.

"The men are in place," al-Kahir reported. "In a matter of days they will infiltrate the final phase of the experiment. No difficulties are expected, though we must realize that the smaller ratio will allow for a slightly higher death count. But the indications should prove fairly accurate nonetheless."

"Have you worked out their escape routes?"

"Yes, and the men are well aware of everything they must do to insure a smooth flight from the town. If all goes according to plan, the others will join them in America beginning precisely three weeks after the expected conclusion of the experiment; plenty of time for us to fully analyze the results."

"El Sayad's behavior today proved I was right in taking you into my confidence first. You haven't really told me yet what you think of our weapon."

"You were right: It is the most sophisticated one ever conceived by man . . . and the most deadly. I can't believe we came up with it first."

"Fate was on our side. Now tell me of the false trail I asked you to construct for Alabaster's benefit."

"It has been laid out just as you requested. Not extensively, mind you, but it should buy us the time we need."

"That is all it's supposed to do for now." The Red Prince smiled broadly. "You have done your job well, Mohammed. You will be one who goes far. You have a great future in the Movement."

"I am concerned now with the present. Hussein worries me . . . He seems bent on preventing Shaitan from running its course. He—" Al-Kahir hesitated, unrest rising in his eyes. "He might choose to seek out others with . . . similar interests."

"I'm counting on the fact that he does exactly that."

Stanislaw Kowalski stared blankly with his good eye at the huge pile of exams he had just collected from his engineering class. In a capsulized sense, they summed up his life as it was now at the University of Warsaw. A neatly compacted life in which his past was stored away in the vast pockets of his memory.

So much had happened. So much had changed.

Kowalski was a Pole who had hated Hitler from the beginning. When the nightmare began, he became the leader of an underground movement designed to provide Jews with safe passage out of the country. Once he had been caught, and for his refusal to tell the Gestapo anything other than that which they already knew, a hot poker was jammed into his left eye.

Thirsting for revenge, Kowalski branched out into a new area. His father had been a demolitions expert in World War I and had taught his son everything he knew prior to his death in 1938. Stanislaw decided to put the knowledge to good use. In the months following his run-in with the Gestapo, he made himself an expert in every field of explosives and electronics as they pertained to warfare, eventually becoming one of the great underground resistance fighters against the Nazis, carrying his personal war all over Europe. In the process he became a sort of legend. No one was feared and hated more by the Nazis, it was said, than the man who wore a black patch over his left eye.

After the war, Sanislaw's life slowed down. He moved to Palestine in 1947 and became a member of the Haganah and later the Mossad in its formative years. Though he was not a Jew, Kowalski was known as a man who'd fought for the Jews in Poland. And he was also a man who considered the Jews his people, not by birth but by choice.

Then one day in 1972 a call had come from a stranger with a deep voice asking to meet him. The man recognized his expertise and offered him a place in the most elite force in the country. A force sanctioned by and answerable to no one.

They had met and worked together several times in the next seven years. Stanislaw's role primarily was to design powerful explosive devices that would fit in unusual places prior to detonation, usually by remote control. In the receiver of a phone, for instance, or the fender of a Volkswagen.

But one day the calls stopped, his expertise obviously no longer required. He returned to Warsaw to teach electronics and engineering at the University. Doctors told him to make the best of the next few years ahead; his sight was failing in his remaining eye.

Kowalski was so caught up in his thoughts that he almost failed to notice that the phone was ringing. He picked up the receiver.

"Hello?"

"Quoth the Raven, 'Nevermore.'"

The deep voice from his past had returned. The lost years swirled and became one. All that had been was again.

"'Nevermore,'" Stanis repeated, the blood pumping, his body charged.

170

"Five PM Sunday. Ambassador Hotel in Washington, D.C. Room 1227."

The phone clicked off.

Dalia Herzog rested comfortably on the standard issue army cot. It had been a long day of training and she was thoroughly exhausted, considering a shower but lacking the strength to force herself into the stall. Her powerful, well-muscled legs throbbed more than usual. And why shouldn't they? After all, today she was one day older than she had been yesterday. And at thirty-five, every day counted in her profession.

Dalia Herzog's profession was chief of training for the female members of Israel's armed forces. A country charged with constantly fighting for its life doesn't allow sexual biases to interfere with a strong defense system. Women must be counted on as well as men. And Dalia was counted on to train them for a war she prayed would never come.

But she was getting too old for the day-to-day rigors of her position and wondered if the time had come to retire to the kibbutz she had always dreamed of.

Perhaps that would make her happy. She was not happy now because she had been cast into the role of a teacher when she was nothing else but a soldier. Ten years ago she was regarded as one of Israel's best anti-terrorist commandoes. Her exploits were well known in all circles of the military. But a year ago they had thought her past her prime and had reassigned her. Because she was a woman. . . . *The bastards!*

Dalia massaged her aching legs through the khaki-colored pants, running her hands curiously close to her vulva. She was still quite attractive, thanks mostly to a firm and well formed body. Her hair was dark brown and femininely short, her features dark and radiant and breasts large—too large for her own tastes.

Thoughts of the one man she had ever really loved consumed her as her fingers crept even closer to the softness beneath her zipper. The man, though, had never returned her love because

171

he hadn't seemed capable of it. She had tried to coax him but never with any success. Theirs, she resolved, was a business arrangement. Specifically, her job was to discreetly recruit and lead the best commandoes available in certain situations where the man required backup or advance forces. She never argued. She believed fully in what he was doing, though his motivations were never made known to her.

Then he had stopped calling. And around that very time she had stopped living.

The phone began to ring on the desk. Headquarters often called at this time of day and Dalia wondered if she should simply let this call go unanswered. No. She never had before; it just wasn't her way. Fighting against her own muscles, Dalia propped herself up from the cot and moved to the phone, scooping up the receiver in a slightly angered flurry.

"This is Herzog."

"Quoth the Raven, 'Nevermore.'"

The man had returned. The past and the present had merged to form the future.

"'Nevermore,'" she repeated, the ache gone from her muscles.

"Five PM Sunday. Ambassador Hotel in Washington, D.C. Room 1227."

The phone clicked off.

"There's a call for you on line one, Mr. Ben-David."

"I'll take it in my office, Sarah."

Isser Ben-David, a short man with a large round face, looked every bit the Bank of Israel manager that he was. Specifically, his role was to coordinate the various international branches that the bank maintained in cities all over the globe and this role he played very well.

But the real reason why he maintained this position— actually why the Mossad maintained it for him—was that it provided Ben-David with the ideal cover with which to coordinate the operations he was assigned to from one end of the earth to the next. Isser was known in intelligence circles as a "feasibility expert" which is to say that he had a knack for establishing the right way to get the right people in and out of the right place at the right time. When the Mossad wanted Adolph Eichmann, they came to Ben-David. When the government wanted the missile boats from the French port of Cherbourg, they came to Ben-David. When the Defense Department wanted to obtain the latest war plane in the Soviet arsenal, they came to Ben-David.

Over the years there had been few failures and many successes. Now, though, Isser Ben-David was a tired man of near sixty years. His quick mind had slowed drastically as of late and he found himself wondering whether he should refuse the Mossad the next time the organization called. He wondered if this was them on the phone right now.

"Yes, Mr. Ben-David speaking."

"Quoth the Raven, 'Nevermore.'"

It was a voice he never thought he'd hear again. Years before he had coordinated a series of operations for the man on the other end. His mind picked up its pace of old, beginning to work out contingencies for a plan that did not yet exist. Acceptance was mandated, refusal out of the question.

"'Nevermore,'" he repeated.

Every afternoon at one o'clock on the Rue Plaisir in the center of Paris, a pay phone rings. And every afternoon a man in a white suit picks it up after the third ring.

His name is Jacques Chevallier and he serves as a sort of broker, buying information from one party and selling it to another. In cities all over the world, people—important people—who want to learn something unattainable through normal channels seek out the man in the white suit. His sources extend everywhere, existing without the slightest factor of randomness. Instead, Chevallier's men in the field make up an immense network of fact finders, specifically of facts thought to be out of the reach of any other than those

173

with whom they had originated.

The Frenchman's organization exists on a par with a good number of official intelligence units all over the world. Many of these often come to him for help. They pay very well and are seldom disappointed.

Through the years, Chevallier's reputation has been virtually unflawed. He never promises what he cannot deliver or fails to deliver on what he promises. All the same, he is also a man of conscience and morality. Not anyone can become his client and most who request information are denied a contract. Few had the number of the Paris phone that was manned twenty-four hours a day.

Chevallier is conservative in his politics and immensely loyal to the democratic nations of the world. For this reason, the height of his career—a pinnacle he might strive for but never reach again—had come during a seven year stretch in which he worked regularly for the only client he had ever truly respected. A man who sought information for justice rather than blackmail, subversion, or exposure. A man who needed Chevallier's vast underground network to help him track down some of the most murderous individuals in the world.

The phone in the booth was ringing. One . . . two . . . three. The man in the white suit picked it up.

"Bonjour."

"Quoth the Raven, 'Nevermore.'"

The receiver nearly fell from Chevallier's hand. The man had returned, his voice unchanged in its surety; his purpose, the Frenchman knew, unchanged as well.

"'Nevermore,'" he repeated, already considering a replacement for himself in the phone booth in the days ahead.

PART THREE

EIGHTEEN

The old desk chair squealed in protest, as Bugsy Tyler leaned comfortably backwards.

"Yeah, information, I'd be much obliged if you could get me the number of the Wyoming Department of Natural Resources located in Cheyenne." Tyler lifted a pen from the desk before him and was in the process of searching for a piece of paper when the operator recited the seven digits. "Could I have that again, ma'am? . . . Thank-ya." He scribbled the number onto the desk's decaying wood surface. "Have a nice day now."

It was blazing hot outside, far above normal for spring, and Bugsy felt the sweat dripping down his temples only to be swallowed by the thick black beard that gave his face what he liked to call character. He was always uncomfortable in the small confines of his office, especially on hot days like this when the poorly insulated building became an oven without an OFF switch.

Slowly, Tyler tilted his massive frame forward and dialed the number he had traced into his desk's dusty finish, hoping the office would be open even though it was Saturday.

"State Department of Natural Resources," a soft male voice announced.

"Yeah, who am I speaking to?"

"Dr. Paul Glover."

"Well, Doc, could you please put someone on the line who can talk to me about how much oil there is in Wyoming."

"I'd be more than happy to myself. . . . At least I think I would."

"I thought you said you was a doctor."

"Yes, a doctor of geology."

"Well, what the hell do ya' do, perform half-assed examinations on rocks?" Tyler laughed heartily.

"Something like that," the geologist said unsurely. "Now, do you mind telling me exactly what it is you do and want?"

"No sweat, Doc. My name is Sheriff James T. Tyler—T is for Thomas—and I'm chief law enforcement official here in Crescent Falls. You can call me Bugsy. And I'm calling 'cause I got this here problem you might be able to help me with."

"Well, Sheriff Tyler—"

"Bugsy."

"Well, Bugsy, I'm always happy to cooperate with the law in any way I can."

"Glad to hear that, Doc, glad to hear that. What I got, see, is a couple of questions."

"I hope I can supply a couple of answers."

"Me too." Tyler swung his eyes about the room, passing the door to Crecent Fall's two jail cells and the entrance to a small room in the rear with a cot that he often slept on when he was too tired or drunk to walk home. The walls of his office were barren save for a collection of wanted posters portraying criminals long since captured or killed. Bugsy was unimpressed by the urgency of such matters. "What I want to know, Doc," he continued, "is whether there's any oil up here in Crescent Falls?"

"Where exactly are you located?"

"A stone's throw away from the Belle Fouche River goin' south."

"Hold on just a minute, Sheriff, I'll get my records."

Bugsy decided to take immediate advantage of the pause by reaching into his pocket for the container of Skoal. Wedging the receiver between his ear and shoulder, he popped it open and shoved a large pinch into his mouth, sliding a dented metal trash can over just as Glover came back on the line.

"Sheriff?"

"Still here. Just enjoyin' a chew. And I told ya' to call me Bugsy."

"Bugsy, I did the final report on that area myself so I'm sure it's accurate. What you've got to understand first of all is that people are just beginning to realize there's oil in Wyoming because of the new seismology equipment they've got that's able to measure shock waves under the ground. Oil fields, you see, are full of what we call sedimentary rock. So what we always did until a few years ago was study shock wave rebounds looking for a sedimentary pattern as opposed to the pattern given off by certain nonoil-bearing metamorphic rock. In many parts of Wyoming, though, we've recently found that there's actually metamorphic rock on top and sedimentary underneath, thanks to this new equipment. That explains why oil rigs are just starting to get set up in selected areas of the state, but not necessarily yours. You said you're located just south of the Belle Fouche, right?"

"Unless the town moved while you was talkin'."

"In that case, Sheriff, I can say without doubt that the rock under the countryside around your town is metamorphic through and through. There's no trace of sedimentary structure anywhere to be found."

Bugsy nearly swallowed his tobacco and leaned forward so fast that the chair almost cracked under the strain. "Does that mean we got no more oil in this town than a whore's got morals?"

"Absolutely."

The Sheriff did not bother to keep his smile down. "Well, Jesus H. Christ . . ."

It was nearly eight-thirty Saturday night when the phone by David's bed began to ring. The sudden noise made him jump wildly from his half-sleep, his body a mass of tension.

"Hello," he said clearing his throat.

"I am looking for Alabaster." It was the voice of Oman Abbu-Taabes, the diplomatic attaché from the Libyan embassy.

"You've found him, Oman."

"Then the room number you gave me was your own."

"One of my own. I have five that I am continually in and out of. The switchboard has graciously arranged to put all the rooms on the same line."

"Thanks to your friends in Langley, no doubt."

"Of course. But why have you contacted me? Your own personal security precautions would seem to make such a call impossible."

"I made an exception. But I must talk fast. I am speaking from a pay phone down the road from the embassy but even it may have been tampered with. Something important has come up. There is a man in my rooms at the embassy right now who wishes to speak to you. I believe you know him. His name is Hussein El Sayad."

"Good God." Alabaster's ears were struck by mention of one of the men from the picture. "Has he turned?"

"Not exactly. Against Black September—yes. Against the PLO—no."

"A strange dichotomy."

"He is a strange man."

"Who wishes to speak to me?"

"Yes."

"What about?"

"The Shaitan Commandment."

Blood rushed to Alabaster's head. "How much does he know?"

"That he will tell only you. In return, he asks only that you arrange safe passage for him out of this country."

"It makes no sense."

"I did not say that it did. I am just an intermediary. My reputation, I'm afraid, spreads further than I had expected. I might need your help myself someday soon."

"It's yours for the asking, Oman. But what of this meeting?"

"Twenty minutes from now in Fort Dupont Park. Tardiness by a single minute on your part will be justification on his for terminating the rendezvous."

"But that's not enough time. I have to call for backup. This could be a trap. Logically, it *should* be."

"I have arranged many such meetings before, my friend. Some of them have been traps, most have not been. In all cases, I have known which was which. This one, I would swear, is not. El Sayad is scared. He is running away from something that is bound to catch up with him. He needs the help of Alabaster to escape."

"You trust him, I trust you; the rendezvous takes place."

"The progression seems logical."

"Except, Oman, that I have stayed alive these many years by trusting no one. You are asking me to make a rather severe exception."

"No more severe than the one I am making by calling you now from a phone that is very likely tapped by every embassy in the city. And if that is so, I will most certainly become the victim of a mysterious ailment that forces an abrupt return to my home country or the bottom of the Potomac—whichever proves more convenient."

Alabaster quickly considered the options, reducing them in five seconds to only one. "I will meet him in twenty minutes."

"Nineteen now. In Fort Dupont Park. Be on time or he will not appear. And leave your friends from the CIA behind or he will take his chances at escape without your help. How will he find you?"

"I will find him. Tell him not to worry, Oman. All his conditions will be met. Give him my word."

"I will. Until later, then."

"Good-bye, Oman."

Alabaster hung up the receiver. He trusted Abbu-Taabes enough to know that El Sayad had not set a trap. And even if he had, the bait was almost too much to refuse: the Shaitan Commandment. He could not risk giving up a chance to learn its meaning, its purpose.

But there was so little time. Certainly not enough to call Colonel Rossi for support. Besides, the Director would not warm up to the idea of a potential shoot-out in Fort Dupont

Park. It was a domestic matter, which meant the FBI would be called in. Channels had to be crossed, delays inevitable. And delays with only eighteen minutes left before the meeting could not be tolerated. The rendezvous *had* to take place.

Still, Alabaster could not go alone. He needed a driver at the very least. There was only one other person, though, available for such a task on such short notice. He had sought a reason for seeing her again all day; now he had it.

Leslie Kirkman.

Leslie pulled the black Cougar that the CIA had placed in the parking garage for David the day before, into a space on Capitol Street on the northern border of Fort Dupont Park. She turned toward the man sitting beside her, a man whose appearance had changed almost totally during the seven minute ride.

His curly brown hair was now matted down and combed backwards. He had placed makeup all over his face to whiten his features. His suit was old, cheap but well-pressed. He had the look, she lamented, of a corpse on route to burial.

"You look like death warmed a little bit over," she told him.

"That's the way a blind man on a dark night like this is supposed to look," he responded, placing a rumpled black hat over his head and tilting it toward his eyebrows.

"A blind man?"

"Yes." He put on his sunglasses.

"And with those over your eyes, how can you expect to recognize a trap if there is one?"

"If you see a trap, you're undoubtedly already caught in it. You have to feel it first, sense that everything is not as it should be. You don't stay alive in this business very long by trusting your eyes. They can deceive you. Killers count on it."

"I still don't like it. You should have called the CIA."

"I called you instead."

"And what exactly am I supposed to do?"

"Watch the street for suspicious movements: a car that goes

182

too slow or stops too suddenly, people gathering together. And watch the action inside the park. If you feel I'm in danger signal me by blowing the horn. And don't stop until I'm back in the car."

"But this is only one of four roads bordering the park. What about the others?"

"This is the only one we have to concern ourselves with. It offers by far the quickest access to the freeway and men who deal in murder think of escape above all else."

Rabanine opened the Cougar's door and took one last look at the woman in the driver's seat. Her brown hair hung lusciously behind her shoulders. The soft light of the interior revealed the smooth texture of her face, now taut with worry.

"Be careful, David. Please be careful."

He turned away from Leslie's impassioned gaze without speaking and closed the door. Slowly he walked off, the brown cane marking the path before him, seeming to show him the way.

Hussein El Sayad stood in the middle of the park in an open grove that lacked any semblance of cover outside of a few large trees. It was the most likely place for a trap to be set and thus the least likely where it would be. The Arab anxiously checked his watch, noting that in thirty seconds Alabaster would be officially late. And since there was no one in sight other than a blind man trudging erratically through the park, the meeting must certainly be considered off.

But wait. The blind man was now walking directly at him. El Sayad tensed, his dead arm tingling with the phantom spasm of muscles that no longer operated. The blind man was closing in on him with each step. A yard away he leaned over to tie his shoe.

"Hello, El Sayad. Your conditions have been met. Here are the materials and arrangements for your escape." Alabaster rose and handed the Arab a thick white envelope.

El Sayad took it in his good hand and tucked it nervously

into his jacket. "They know I'm here."

"Soon you'll be free of Salameh's people."

"Only temporarily."

"Will you return to Arafat?"

"I'd be killed by the Red Prince's people if I ever set foot in the Mideast again."

El Sayad watched Alabaster raise his head suddenly, removing his sunglasses and placing them in the pocket of his white suit.

"Then we had better conclude our business fast," he said. "Tell me about the Shaitan Commandment."

"Don't get the wrong idea about this meeting, Alabaster. You are my sworn enemy, an enemy of all those who seek to found a Palestinian state. You are really not much different than the Red Prince. You're both killers devoted to your beliefs, willing to die for them."

"But something must separate us or you wouldn't have turned and certainly you wouldn't have contacted me."

"I have not turned!" El Sayad's eyeballs bulged, the lids flickering madly. "If anything, it's the Red Prince who has turned. He is fighting a war of the past, still living in the time of Munich. He doesn't realize that people and countries have changed. It's a new age. There are costs of terrorism and we have all paid the price." Here the Arab glanced at the black glove on the hand he couldn't feel. "We have accomplished nothing, gone nowhere, and found ourselves struggling for our lives instead of fighting for our homeland. We *are* a people of ideals, Alabaster. The Red Prince, though, has allowed his ideals to become tarnished. He must be stopped."

"The Shaitan Commandment must be stopped."

"They are one in the same. One does not exist without the other."

"For now I am concerned only with Shaitan. A pattern is developing. I will ask you questions to help fill it in. It will be the quickest way, avoiding repetition of that which I already know."

"Whatever you say."

"I am aware of a small force that will be entering America in the near future and of their connection to a new type of weapon. How many does the force number?"

"One hundred seventy-five in the primary body and five serving as advance."

"Advance?"

"A test is being conducted to gauge how effective the weapon truly will be. Since the plan has never been tried before, no one knows for sure what to expect."

"How is the effectiveness of the test to be measured?"

"By numbers dead thanks to this new weapon, or weapons system, that I was never made privy to. So I have no real idea of the means, only of the ramifications should those means prove successful. The Red Prince estimates that fifty percent of America's current population will be dead within three months after the primary force arrives in seven weeks. A *minimum* of fifty percent."

The words struck Alabaster like a blast of cold wind. "Fifty percent? . . . Impossible!"

"I believe the next few months will prove differently. This operation has been in the works since Munich. The Red Prince has made it his life."

"But what of the weapon? You must have some idea what it is?"

"I know only what Salameh says it isn't. It is not nuclear nor is it biological warfare—at least not in the traditional senses. Both are too overt. The great beauty of the Commandment was to have been that no one would realize an attack was taking place."

"But one hundred million people are supposed to die. Surely it will be obvious that some sort of aggressive action has occurred."

"Even if it was, it wouldn't matter because by then, according to the design of the plan, the government and all supportive services will have been destroyed. Chaos will reign

185

and feed off itself until this presently great nation will no longer be a nation at all. I have also been told that the weapon is to be carried into the country on the persons of our 175 agents."

"Tell me more about them."

"Most have been placed proportionately in the most sensitive areas of this country: government, armed forces, business, media. Others have been scattered in major cities and hubs."

"A quick-strike concept?"

"Of sorts, I suppose."

"Surely, though, it—"

Alabaster broke off his sentence. He sensed something, cold and evil, in the western sector of the park. Instinctively, he stepped back a few paces so that his body was shielded by a large tree.

El Sayad's eyes exploded with fear. "What's wrong?"

"Keep quiet and don't move."

A horn began to blast on Capitol Street, blowing in short quick spurts. Leslie! She had seen something. But what? Alabaster scanned the area around him. Nothing. The dim park lighting obscured his vision.

"What's wrong?" El Sayad repeated, his face contorted in panic.

Alabaster continued to search the area with his eyes, still behind the tree. "Quiet!" he ordered. "Move slowly toward me, out of the open."

Instead of obeying, however, the Arab began to back uneasily away.

"It's a trap! That's a signal! . . . You set me up! You set me up!" El Sayad moved back still more, trembling.

"Don't be a fool. I didn't set you up. I had no reason to. Al Fatah is out there, not—"

But the Arab was already scampering toward the trees twenty-five yards away, his pace slowed by the dead arm by his side. His eyes glanced back over his shoulder at the man he was fleeing.

"Stop! Stop!"

Against his own judgment, Alabaster had begun to move toward El Sayad when the first spurt of fire erupted. It was smooth and rhythmical, the mark of an M-16. As El Sayad disappeared into the grove of trees, the bullets tore through the air, slicing into the dirt and stitching a path around the now exposed Alabaster. Only fortune saved him from being torn in two by the powerful shells.

Alabaster dived to the ground, rolling back toward the tree that had been his cover. The M-16's fury was coming straight at him, the bullets sending dirt and pebbles flying against his body. He reached into his belt and withdrew the Beretta M-84, his favorite handgun. But the Beretta had limitations and long-range was one of them. Its sleek design and fourteen shot clip made it a worthy defensive weapon, though its effectiveness was lost at distances exceeding seventy-five yards.

Nevertheless, Alabaster poked his arm and head out and fired a series of rounds in the direction of the M-16. It was token resistance, meant to worry the killer, not neutralize him. The police would be arriving in minutes. The man in the trees 150 yards away could not hold his position much longer. But the Israeli wanted him to try in the hope he might be able to somehow capture him.

Alabaster's second emergence from behind his position of cover was greeted with another spurt from the M-16, this time more accurate. Hot dirt flew into his eyes, blinding him. He felt something sting his wrist and realized that the Beretta had been sent flying from his hand into the open area. He rolled backwards behind the tree again, his right arm a mass of agony that was hot and icy at the same time. He felt blood running down his arm from his injured shoulder. The bullet had grazed him. There had been no penetration. There was pain, however, and temporary uselessness.

Gripping his injured shoulder, Alabaster again poked his head out from behind the tree, this time on the other side. In the far-off distance, he saw the barrel of the M-16 reflecting the spill of streetlights. But the barrel was being lifted away, the gun no longer pointed in his direction. There was a man, a large man, his features indistinct in the darkness. The man was retreating, moving farther into the light. Escaping.

Alabaster was on his feet now, moving for the Beretta, picking it up with his left hand and running for the street in the direction the killer had taken off in. The man worked for Al Fatah, a *living* link. Alabaster would catch him and force him to reveal the position of the Red Prince. If the man could not tell him that, at least he would tell him something.

The gun was held tightly in the Israeli's palm, his finger a claw on the trigger. Alabaster could shoot with either hand, though he preferred the right one which dangled useless by his side, the pain only hot now. He was running with all the speed he could muster. He crashed into a tree, its branches scratching his face. He had lost sight of the killer and was now following strictly on instinct. The road appeared up ahead.

He followed it while keeping his feet churning on grass to maintain cover and silence. An almost open grove came up fast, perfect for an ambush. Alabaster didn't hesitate for a second. He entered the grove at top speed, darting sideways between an irregular series of wide bushes. Fifteen yards away, he recognized the sound of rapid footsteps that seemed to be moving away from and toward him at the same time. Another branch scraped his face and he nearly tripped on an exposed root. Still he kept going toward the footsteps.

Something was wrong. . . .

The next few moments were as confusing as any Alabaster could remember. The muted sound of two soft spits sent him diving to the ground, just as the grass was about to change to asphalt. A gun equipped with silencer had been fired. But at whom? Certainly not him, the noise wasn't loud enough. Who, then? He had begun to rise in slow, careful motion when a car door slammed nearby. An engine revved. Tires screeched. Someone was escaping. The killer?

Alabaster spurted forward, from one tree to another for cover. Ten feet away a shape lay sprawled on the ground in the darkness. He approached leery of a trap but relaxed a bit when he saw an M-16 lying by the shape's side. Two bullets had been fired into the body. Both direct hits. One in the head, one in the chest. Enough of the man's features remained for Alabaster to know he was an Arab. An Al Fatah American operative, he guessed. The man who had tried to kill him and El Sayad.

But the man was dead . . .

He had brought his left hand up to comfort his wounded shoulder, when a sudden screech forced him to ready the Beretta again. A black car had come to a squealing halt five feet before him. A black Cougar. The passenger door swung open.

"David, get in! Please get in!"

Leslie's command lifted him from the daze that had overtaken him. Reality returned in a dim blur, slowly sharpening into focus. He settled into the seat.

"Get the hell out of here!"

"The days are long."

"But the nights are short. What is your message?"

"The Arabs failed again tonight."

"Did you rectify their mistake?"

Cerberus hesitated before responding. "I had planned to but circumstances forced me to kill the terrorist instead."

"Circumstances?"

"He ran right into my path."

"Witnesses?"

"None."

"His backup?"

"Will believe Alabaster was responsible."

"And you will finish with Alabaster tomorrow."

"Yes, tomorrow."

189

NINETEEN

Leslie placed the strip of white adhesive tape over the gauze bandage, attaching it to the skin below Rabanine's minor shoulder wound.

"You're lucky, David," she said. "It's only a scratch. But when I saw the blood, I feared the worst."

Rabanine was seated in the easy chair of his hotel room for the night. He was uneasily aware that Leslie's large breasts hung at eye level, stirring feelings in him long dormant. He fought them down, turning his stare away.

"You must be a brave man," Leslie said smiling, backing away to inspect her handiwork. "You didn't flinch once when I poured too much alcohol on the wound."

"In my profession, one has to get used to pain."

"But you *do* feel," Leslie said unevenly.

"Yes, I do feel." He paused, returning her smile. "And you are a most efficient nurse."

"I've taken a few first aid courses over the years."

"My luck."

"*My* pleasure."

He stared deeply into her eyes. "You helped me back there at the park. I want to thank you."

"Who did I help, David? You or that other part of you?"

"Sometimes we merge into one. You helped a combination."

"It was a trap, wasn't it?"

"Yes, but El Sayad had nothing to do with setting it. He had no idea what was going on. The men he had run out on had been following him all day. They let him get as far as he did because they hoped he would have tried to meet with me—Alabaster, that is—which would have given them an excellent opportunity to finally be rid of me. But I sensed something and

190

moved behind a tree just in time, out of the line of fire."

"Not far out of it. The bullets must have missed you by only inches."

"If that . . ."

"Something else is bothering you."

He looked at her, his eyes confused. "Someone killed the man sent by Al Fatah, the one who shot at me."

"One of the CIA's people perhaps."

"They knew nothing of the meeting."

"Then someone else must be looking out for your safety."

"I don't believe in guardian angels. Whoever it was was there for a specific reason."

"Coincidence?"

"I don't believe in coincidences of this sort either. There's something I'm missing in all this, a part I haven't considered or have overlooked."

Leslie moved forward, placing her hands on his shoulders and massaging them. Her grip was unusually strong for a woman, though soft at the same time. David flinched beneath her touch.

"You're tense," she told him.

"It's been a long night." He allowed himself a sigh. "Are you enjoying your stay in the hotel?"

"As much as can be expected. How much longer do you think we'll be here?"

"It's a better spot for you than a safe house because there's so much activity. So I'd say until all this is over."

"What about the detective who helped me in Providence?"

"He's back on the job."

"And my house?"

"It's being repaired, the tab to be picked up by the U.S. government. When you get back, it'll be as good as new. All traces of what happened last night will be gone. You'll be free to forget."

"Will I?"

"To try, at least."

"Like you have tried? But you've never forgotten. You carry

191

what they did to you like a chain on your leg. Is that my future, David?"

He turned toward her, taking her hands in his and squeezing them gently; the gesture uncomfortable in its distantness.

"Your future will be what *you* make it," he said softly. "I have made mine what it is, for better or worse. . . . They killed my wife. I can never forget that."

"You can't know that until you try."

"I have no desire to."

"What would you say if I told you I would like to sleep with you tonight?"

"I'd question your taste."

"I assure you it's quite good."

"Then I'd wonder about your judgment." David fought to maintain a cool exterior while inside his emotions were blazing.

"The past three years have made it very strong."

"Not this time."

David eyed her wordlessly. She had just articulated the central conflict of his life. It was hard to admit the truth to himself, even harder to accept it hinted at by someone else. The simple fact, though, was that he liked his life the way it was. He enjoyed killing. The act gave him a sense of self-esteem, of being worthy to live in the violent world he had helped make. Two years ago, he had thought he was finished, thought his nerve was gone. Maybe it was. He still, however, enjoyed slipping into the guise of Alabaster. He saw himself as the exterminator of human rodents who lurked in alleys and bars plotting terrorist attacks on unsuspecting innocents. He had once believed that part of him to be dead. But the past ten days had shown him it was still thriving. He had slit Abad Salim's throat without pause or compunction. And he guessed there might even have been a twinkle in his eyes when he drew the blade against the fat terrorist's jugular.

Now, though, his penchant for avenging the deaths of innocent people had an opponent. At this moment, he was struck by an urge to approach and embrace Leslie, draw her in

192

close to him. Feel her warmth and strength against him. How long had it been since someone had stood by him, knowing what to say and when to say it as well as when to say nothing? Too long. Long enough . . .

No! No!

Women were a weakness to be used by enemies to mangle and twist like insignificant voodoo dolls. What you did to the doll happened to the woman of whom it was a likeness. Only Rivkah had been a living person cut down by Seif the Butcher's hands. And when she had died, a part of him had died too. But that part had been replaced by another: the cool, calculating ability to kill without remorse. To do anything necessary to protect the state of Israel, the only thing he had left to believe in.

But suddenly there was Leslie Kirkman, here to show him that the original part was not dead at all, only suspended in time and space. It thrived and grew in him, grasping for his thoughts and emotions; its tentacles reaching, probing. That grip had to be resisted, the feelings denounced.

"You'll find that I don't give up easily," Leslie was saying.

"I'm glad to hear that," David responded, though he wasn't sure why.

"I want you to explain what happened last night." Colonel Rossi's harsh tone jarred David from his early morning complacency. The Director had wasted no time in getting to the point.

David tightened his grip on the receiver. "I wasn't aware I had anything to explain."

"It is not customary for my men to engage in shoot-outs in public parks."

"I am not one of your men, Colonel Rossi."

"You are in America on my authority which makes me answerable for your actions. And believe me, there have been a lot of questions this morning. For instance, why didn't you inform us of the meeting?"

"There wasn't time. I couldn't risk jeopardizing a chance to

193

meet with someone inside Al Fatah."

"I hope the meeting proved enlightening."

"I suppose you could call it that."

"In any case, after your call last night, we took care of the body. The Washington police were most cooperative; they usually are. We're running a check on the dead man right now."

"There was someone else in the park."

"I read the report. It was very vague on that aspect."

"I was as specific as I could be. I never saw him. I only heard his gun."

"You think he was there to protect you?"

"I think he was there to kill me, if the man from Black September had failed. The Arab must have gotten in his way somehow."

"This complicates matters."

"Considerably," agreed David.

It was eleven AM when David finished a light breakfast in the hotel coffee shop. The four members of his task force would begin arriving just past noon and he wanted to be ready to greet them. He wondered how much they had changed, how much he had. He would find out soon enough.

Rabanine stepped into the elevator and pushed 12. The doors had begun to close when a bellhop dressed in the standard blue uniform of the Ambassador forced his way in.

"Just made it," he said, as the elevator began to move. They were alone inside the compartment.

David's reply was a perfunctory smile. Something bothered him about the man, a vague sense of familiarity. He moved and looked like an athlete, the uniform a poor fit over his broad shoulders. His red cap only partially covered the wavy blond hair that made his steely blue eyes even more sizzling.

The eyes! He had seen this man before . . .

The moment of revelation was obscured by the sound of the elevator grinding to a halt. The machine floundered, seeming to die, its lights flickering for a second before fading into

194

blackness broken only by the glow of a red emergency button.

All at once, the blackness was pierced by something silvery and metallic swirling downward in the direction of David's chest. Rabanine sidestepped the cylindrical blur, watching it pass by him as he grabbed the arm it was attached to.

Something, a knee he guessed, crashed into his midsection and the scent of expensive after-shave lotion became heavy in his nostrils. Still gripping the knife arm with his wind escaping, David lashed out with a snap kick at the shape before him. Impact came somewhere on the target's leg, forcing him off balance for a second which was long enough for David to shoot his free hand forward in the direction of what he thought would be the man's groin.

But Cerberus deflected the blow and rammed his elbow into David's solar plexus stunning him. The Israeli felt the knife hand pull from his grasp, aware that the weapon was again free to slash down at him. Still fighting for breath, he heard the blade whistle at him and dodged to the right at the exact moment it would have pierced his body. The knife swung overhead once more and this time David avoided it by recoiling backwards against the back of the compartment, searching for a fix on his assailant's position.

The man had obviously used darkness as a stratagem before. But more than likely his previous kills had been quick, accomplished with one thrust. Which meant that an awkward balance now existed in the blackened compartment, now inundated with the sweet smell of after-shave.

There was a sound to his right, a foot planting itself, and David spun agilely into the center of the compartment. He thought of drawing his Beretta but dismissed the idea knowing that the motion would provide his assailant with the second required to complete the kill. Instead he held his ground and saw the blade slash toward him in a darkened blur. He blocked the strike with his left arm extended like steel. In less time than it takes to blink, his right fingers had reached under and wrapped themselves around his assailant's hand, twisting it violently until ligaments and tendons snapped.

Cerberus screamed in pain. The knife went flying. Coiling his body like a snake, David was behind him now, his arm locked around the man's neck in a grip that would allow him to snap it with only a slight twist of his shoulders.

Just then, the elevator's engine began to whine. The lights came back on. The machine was moving again. Rabanine felt his own breath on the back of the assailant's head. The after-shave soaked his nostrils.

"Make one move and I'll kill you, understand?" David warned, wrenching his grip.

The man grunted an acknowledgement.

The doors slid open on the twelfth floor and Rabanine led his prisoner into the first open door he saw, a linen closet. He hurled him inside hard against a large metal support and drew his Beretta. Towels tumbled from their racks. David slammed the door.

"Sit down," he said, motioning with the pistol to a single steel chair in the corner of the cramped room.

Cerberus moved cautiously toward it, his eyes never leaving their violent embrace with Rabanine's.

"You know who I am, don't you?" Cerberus asked, sitting down.

David moved to within five feet of him. "Yes, as well as who you work for. I expect you to fill in the rest."

"So the great Alabaster does not know everything."

"Not yet."

"You will learn no more at my expense."

"Then I will kill you."

"You will anyway."

"Just as you would have killed me in the elevator. I assume you had a man in the control room responsible for turning the power off and then on again after a specified period of time."

"Assume what you wish," Cerberus said indignantly, his sizzling blue eyes measuring his chances for a successful leap at his captor.

David raised the gun so it was in line with the forehead in

front of it. "You are not being very cooperative."

"Then go on and kill me, Jew. It doesn't matter. Others will follow."

"I want to know what stake your people hold in this."

"Stake? . . . You speak like it was a card game. Believe me, it is much more. The Arabs have stumbled on something that belongs to us. We plan on taking it back."

"You have failed in your mission. Your superiors will not like that."

"They will understand. Someone will be sent to replace me."

"Tell me what it is the Arabs have stumbled upon."

"Isn't it obvious?"

"The Shaitan Commandment?"

Cerberus' expression remained unchanged. "They will die for it."

"Not by your hand."

"Someone else's, then. Their passing is a foregone conclusion, as is yours, Alabaster. We are marshalling forces all over the world." Cerberus' eyes left David's briefly. Sensing his intent, the Israeli tightened his grip on the Beretta.

"Strangely, we seem to be fighting the same enemy," said Rabanine ironically.

"Only for the time being."

"You killed that man in the park last night."

"I was planning to kill you. An unfortunate stroke of fate placed him between us." Cerberus tensed his muscles, preparing for one final attempt to complete his mission. "He, like all the Arabs, was an amateur without pride or training. An easy opponent to overcome. You will find us much harder to deal with, Alabaster. We are professionals. Something has been taken from us and we intend to take it back."

"You are living in the past."

"On the contrary, I am contemplating the future."

The man lunged.

Alabaster pulled the Beretta's trigger.

197

TWENTY

"The man you killed was travelling under the name of Sam Caudill, a foreign investments counselor," said Colonel Vernon Rossi, as David wheeled him down the carpeted hall of the Ambassador's twelfth floor five hours later.

"I hope you're not disappointed that I pulled the trigger without calling you."

The Director turned and looked up at David, smiling tightly. "You could have at least checked in before you loaded the gun." The smile vanished. "But I seriously wish you could have taken him alive."

"It wouldn't have mattered."

"We could have questioned him."

"He wouldn't have talked."

"At least we might have learned the identity of his accomplice."

"Who was very probably on his way out of the country at the very instant I was putting a bullet through Mr. Caudill's brain."

Rossi swung his head back to the front. "You seem to understand these men quite well."

"It was an established methodology."

"And the man travelling as Caudill, you knew him too?"

"Only by the reputation he had gained in several European cities."

"An assassin?"

"More of a watchdog."

"You seem fairly well acquainted with him."

"As well as the people he works for, Colonel Rossi. The problem is that I can't make myself believe it."

"I'm an old man, David. I can't stand being kept in suspense."

"You'll have to until later."

"Later?"

"The meeting."

Room 1227 was the only one of David's five hotel rooms equipped with a living room area complete with couch, easy chairs and bar. By five PM, the four people reached by Alabaster's code phrase were present inside along with Colonel Rossi, his wheelchair placed inconspicuously in the room's far right corner.

David had met all four at various times during the afternoon. With Stanislaw Kowalski, Isser Ben-David, and Jacques Chevallier, the reunion had been pleasant; signalling a return to old times and purpose. But for the fourth, Dalia Herzog, those old times brought back with them memories of her frustrated love. Their meeting after so long had been strained, laced by understatement and coated by frivolity.

But now, as Alabaster entered the living room of his suite, dressed leisurely in blue slacks and red short sleeve shirt that revealed his well-muscled arms, the personal was discarded and the professional rooted clearly in its place.

". . . And may I present Colonel Vernon Rossi, Director of the Central Intelligence Agency whose vast resources have been made available to us during the course of this operation," David said, concluding whatever introductory remarks he felt were necessary. In the corner of the room, Rossi nodded, his face deeply flushed. "And now let's get to the reason why I summoned you here today. . . ."

He told them everything that was presently known about the Shaitan Commandment from who was behind it to its sinister purpose. Scott Krassner's picture and death. The murder of Desmond. The attempts on his life. His meetings with Abbu-Taabes and El Sayad. So many variables adding up to form an impossible scheme. All he left out, much to the dismay of

Colonel Rossi, was the incident from that morning.

". . . The Red Prince, then, is alive. We last met together over three years ago to plan his death in Beirut. But we were tricked. And it is now clear that the Shaitan Commandment is the reason why. Still standing, David turned toward Stanislaw Kowalski. "Stanis, you are an expert on arms and electronics. Tell us what this new catastrophic weapon might be."

Kowalski leaned forward in his chair, rolling up the sleeves of his brown tweed jacket to expose sinewy forearms. He was a heavyset man whose black eye patch gave his face a sinister look, though anyone who looked closely could see the compassionate lines etched permanently over his expression.

"Well, David," he began, "you have already said that El Sayad ruled our nuclear arms and biological warfare—the two most likely choices. That does not leave us with very much."

"Obviously."

"And you also say that El Sayad told you that the weapon is small enough to be carried on the persons of the 175 Al Fatah agents. I suggest, then, that each might conceivably be bringing in a small part of a much larger, deadly mechanism to be assembled once all the agents have reached America. This, of course, means that something prevents them from bringing the weapon into the country in one piece."

"But if the mechanism is not nuclear, what might it be?" David questioned.

"I don't know. It must be something we have never dealt with before. Perhaps something on the ion or antimatter principle."

"In that case," resumed David, "let us turn to Isser Ben-David, Israel's greatest planner. Isser, if you were in charge of this Al Fatah strike, what course would you be proceeding on, given all the variables?"

"To begin with, I agree with Stanislaw completely," said Ben-David, his large round face full of vitality and belying his age. He was dressed impeccably in a pinstripe suit complete with carnation he had purchased from a vendor outside the hotel. "I would think first of what I couldn't do and work from there." Ben-David removed a pipe from one jacket pocket and began to carefully pack it with tobacco from a pouch stored in another. "Poisoning the food supply is a possibility, or better yet the water. That would explain the purpose of these 175 agents entering the country. Perhaps they are bringing with them vials of a liquid that will be dumped into the water supply in all major cities across the country. That would explain the purpose of this test you speak of, David. They want to check the potency of the contaminant, make sure that it'll work on a large scale."

"Sounds logical," said Rabanine.

"But do such poisons exist?" asked Jacques Chevallier, dressed in one of the elegantly tailored white suits that had long been his trademark.

"Yes, but there are discrepancies," replied Stanislaw Kowalski. "A botulinus toxin, for example, exists that is potent enough to poison all of New York City's water supply, rendering it fatal in more than fifty percent of all cases if drank, if only three ounces were poured into the reservoir system. The problem here is that David tells us we are dealing with a time sequence of somewhere around three months. With any powerful contaminant, the effects would show up much quicker than that. In fact, the system would probably be shut down before the poison was able to reach a majority of the people."

"How so?"

"The water you drink today and probably tomorrow comes from purifying plants, not the reservoir itself. Thus, once the effects begin to appear in low-lying areas, the faucets in the rest would be shut off. And even if they weren't, 175 people are hardly enough to reach all the major water supply systems in this country at the same time—something that would be mandated for success in such a plan."

"I think we must look in another direction," said Jacques Chevallier, stroking his mustache, his English broken slightly

201

by a thick French accent. He was a diminutive man with soft features. His skin was flawless, his coiffure styled so that every single hair was just where it should have been. *"Certainement,* the idea of poisoning the water supply does not account for why so much of the invading force has been placed in sensitive areas crucial to the day-to-day managing of this country. That fact seems to suggest something else entirely. Indeed, I would propose that this part of the Shaitan strategy is aimed at crippling those areas that would be needed most in the event of a disaster, serving to sever America's body from her brain. The problem will be bad enough, but take away those charged with finding a solution and . . ." Chevallier's shrug completed the thought.

"Which leads me to my personal theory," broke in Ben-David, still with the pipe not lit. "We must keep in mind, friends, that every plot has two sides: that which is and that which appears to be. In other words, I believe this business about wiping out half of the U.S.'s population is meant as a distraction, a brilliant piece of disinformation supposed to draw our attention away from the true essence of Shaitan."

"Which is?"

"Mass assassinations of government leaders to be carried out at predetermined times by this 175 member Black September force."

"The Red Prince didn't have to disappear for four years to plan mass assassinations," argued Rabanine.

"He probably disappeared for another reason entirely. If nothing else, David, it got you off his back, didn't it?" When Rabanine didn't answer, Ben-David continued. "The mass assassination plan could have come later and, make no mistake about it, such a plot *would* take years of preparation. Contacts would have to be attained. Positions secured."

"That's just it," said Rabanine. "Too many people would have had to have been involved. Someone, somewhere, would have talked. Our channels would not all be so dry."

"The very reason why I am inclined to agree with a portion

of what Jacques said," noted Stanislaw Kowalski. "I believe we should focus more on the strategic proportioning of these 175 agents. Why has Al Fatah placed so many of them in centers crucial to the smooth functioning of this country? What can they achieve in the White House, on Capital Hill, on Wall Street?" He paused, as though waiting for the answer. "I believe we are looking for the wrong kind of weapon. I believe that the terrorists may have come up with a complicated plan to subvert the economic and political mainstreams of the United States that somehow deals with infiltration by this Shaitan force."

"And what about the 100 million Americans who are supposed to die?" reminded Isser Ben-David. "Are they all going to kill themselves when the stock market plunges fifty points?"

"Was it ever said that the terrorists were going to be *directly* responsible for their deaths?"

"Mere semantics."

"Hardly. The possibility must be considered that the Shaitan force's actions will *lead* to the deaths, not *cause* them. Perhaps they are going to cause another depression, or invest billions in commodities to destroy the market, or maybe they plan to start a race war. Or perhaps a combination of all three. The problem is that this plan has been in the works for so long that there is no limit to what the Arabs think they can accomplish. The possibilities are endless, going all the way to a genuine revolution. The seeds of discontent are strongly present in America. Only the leadership of a few great men would be necessary for them to sprout." Kowalski leaned back, satisfied with his own explanation.

"Your theory is excellent," David complimented, "except for the fact that we know an experiment is or soon will be underway to test the effectiveness of the Shaitan Commandment. If the means of attack are truly economic or political, the purpose of such a test would seem to be superfluous."

Kowalski shrugged. "Perhaps."

Dalia Herzog cleared her throat, as if to remind the men in the room that she was there, readying them for a female opinion. She was dressed, as always, in pants. Today those pants were white and stylish, worn below a green blouse that could not stop her large breasts from swimming freely. There had been several rumors over the years pertaining to Dalia sleeping with attractive women from her training groups but nothing concrete to substantiate them. That is, no complaints.

"Gentlemen," she began, feeling comfortable in a room of men because as a soldier it was men with whom she'd spent most of her life, often as the single woman, "I'm a soldier and I speak from a soldier's frame of reference. If I had a troop of 175 to train as I wished for four or more years, they'd end up more machines than men. Their actions would be programmed. They'd be masters in every field of guerilla warfare. They'd be capable of disrupting an entire nation with well-timed assassinations and general terrorism. Look at the Red Brigades in Italy and multiply their effect 100-fold. A bomb there, a machine gunning here; the numbers add up."

"But not to one hundred million, Dalia," David interjected somberly. "And that's the number we're talking about."

"If we still believe that to be true," said Ben-David, finally lighting his pipe as surely as he did everything else.

"For now we must assume that it's true," Rabanine resumed. "We have no choice. There's something all of us are forgetting: We weren't supposed to know anything of this plan. We're aware of its existence only because of a young boy with a camera. Counting on him to snap a picture at a precise time was no way to begin a disinformation strategy."

"He could've been a plant," theorized Ben-David.

"You're giving the men of Al Fatah credit for more intelligence than they possess."

"The very existence of Shaitan indicates otherwise."

Jacques Chevallier began to stroke his mustache again, the sign that his thought processes were at work. *"Mes amis,* this leads my humble French mind to deduce that whatever Shaitan is, it *still* can be stopped."

"Of course it can," concurred Isser Ben-David without lifting the pipe from his mouth. He continued to puff away. "After all, the entire plot revolves around these 175 operatives entering the country. Stop the operatives and you stop the plan no matter what it turns out to be."

David smiled. "It seems we may have been proceeding on the wrong track. We have been focusing our attention on discovering what Shaitan is when we should have been seeking means to prevent entrance into the country by the agents charged with perpetrating it."

"What is the time scheme again?" asked Ben-David.

"The operation, according to El Sayad, is scheduled to begin within the next seven weeks."

"In that case," reasoned Dalia Herzog, uncrossing her legs, "the matter could be resolved by ending foreign flights into the U.S. around that point until we are able to take more permanent action."

Rabanine turned to the Director of the CIA. "Colonel Rossi?"

"For how long, Miss Herzog?" Rossi asked her. "For how long would you restrict us from allowing flights *and* boats in? A week? A month? A year, perhaps? And what do you say when people ask you why? What answer can you give without causing a panic? . . . No, I'm afraid that's not the answer but I believe we're on the right track."

"So do I," agreed Ben-David, finally taking the pipe from his mouth and handling it gingerly. "What we must do is somehow discover who the 175 agents are before they enter the country."

"Impossible!" exclaimed Dalia Herzog.

"Highly improbable, yes, but not impossible. The realm of possibility I have learned over the years is little more than a state of mind." Isser returned the pipe to his mouth and began at once to puff away furiously. "It will not be easy but it *can* be done."

"How?" David posed.

"I will need access to passenger reservation lists on all flights scheduled to arrive in major American cities from abroad beginning let's say six weeks from now."

"Colonel Rossi?" David turned to the Director.

"The airlines will be mad as hell but they'll come up with the lists. The American ones won't have a choice. The foreign ones might cause us some headaches."

"The foreign lines are the most important."

"We have agents who should be able to obtain the lists."

"If I may interrupt for a moment," said Chevallier, again stroking his mustache. "I believe my sources might be able to aid us in this regard."

"How so?"

"My people are placed everywhere in the world. The nature of their business requires that they travel often and come into contact with individuals who specialize in making difficult arrangements for people who want to go where they shouldn't. We must assume that the 175 agents we are speaking of will be coming in from countries all over the world. But since we can also assume that one man—Mohammed al-Kahir—has been responsible for coordinating their itineraries, it is probable that only a handful of intermediaries have been used to obtain the necessary papers and reservations. If my people were able to track these intermediaries down, we would find out quickly who we are dealing with, or at the very least, know when they will be arriving. *Oui?*"

"It will be hard, Jacques," warned Rabanine. "There are thousands of such intermediaries the world over."

"But only a few al-Kahir has used in the past. Men like him seldom vary their patterns. It is the Arab mind." Here the Frenchman twirled his finger about his ear, returning it quickly to his mustache. *"C'est fou."*

"There is another way we can go about this as well," began Ben-David, pipe in hand. "El Sayad said a test was going to be conducted by an advance team of five agents. David, what did

206

you say his words were?"

"That 'since it's never been tried before, no one knows what to expect.'"

"Which similarly means there must be a notable lag between the conclusion of the test and the entry of the principal force. In effect, Al Fatah will be supplying us the major clue we need to uncover their secret. We only have to learn where this test is being or has been conducted in time to make it matter."

"And we can do that," picked up David, "by checking every single report that comes into America's various investigative agencies concerning anything out of the ordinary."

"Don't limit yourself," Isser advised. "What we're looking for may be so obvious that we can't see it. We must consider everything."

"That would be a monumental task," said the Director sullenly.

"An important one all the same. Find the test site and you insure that the rest of this country will not become guinea pigs for Shaitan."

"How can it be handled, Colonel?" David asked.

"Well, the FBI is tied into every law enforcement agency in the country. I suppose they could gather the information, the problem is sorting it." The Director held his eyes closed for a drawn out moment. "We're not sure whether we're looking for a needle in a haystack or the haystack itself."

"I suggest you look for both, sir," said Ben-David sharply. "This is *your* country."

Rossi's face reddened with mild anger. "Let's understand ourselves very clearly. You are all here as much for your sakes and the sakes of your own countries, as for ours. If America tumbles under a big push from the PLO, I'm afraid the rest of the free world would be bound to fall with us. If our economy collapses, havoc will occur in business centers all across the globe. Why I'd wager that with us not around to pick up the pieces of this constantly breaking world, anarchy on a global scale would occur within . . . *Oh my God.* . . ." The Director lowered his head, his features ashen, struck by the enormity of what he had been saying.

Rabanine nodded slowly. "That's the idea, Colonel. America was not chosen randomly because of its politics. Certainly that figured into the choice but more important was the fact that you exist as the economic and political hub of the world. The dollar is still the international exchange unit. The President remains the most powerful man in the world." A pause. "Which is why we have another important task facing us." He turned toward Chevallier. "Jacques, there is a German phrase, *der Teufels Befehl*. I want you to circulate it; learn its meaning, its origin."

"D'accord." The Frenchman jotted the phrase down in a small notebook, pronouncing it softly to himself.

"Isser," David went on, "you know Wiesenthal, correct?"

"We worked closely together on the Eichmann kidnapping."

"Then contact him. The phrase should be somewhere in his files."

"Why is it important?"

"Because it will tell us what the Shaitan Commandment is."

"David, don't you think you're making too much of this phrase business?" the Director criticized. "We're not even sure it comes from the World War II period."

"Yes, we are." Rabanine's eyes glared into Rossi's. "The man I killed this morning was named Klaus Krieger."

"A German?"

"Not just. In Europe he was known as the Watchdog of ODESSA, code name Cerberus. . . . Krieger was a Nazi."

TWENTY-ONE

The hot sun was bouncing off the freshly paved surface of Main Street in Crescent Falls, as Bugsy Tyler made his way toward the Bar & Grill. It was one in the afternoon and the street was deserted. But Bugsy wouldn't have noticed passersby anyway because for the first time since being elected sheriff he was going to really exercise his powers of office. In preparation, he had put on a brand new uniform but already three buttons had popped, unable to stand the strain placed on them by his huge frame.

The hell with it, Tyler thought. He tore open the collar, sending the shirt's remaining buttons falling to the pavement below. He entered the Bar & Grill with the top of the uniform hanging over his belt, a white t-shirt clinging to the skin beneath it. It was oppressively hot and humid for spring. Past eighty already today and still climbing. People were saying it was the hottest spell ever for this time of year. The summer promised to be a scorcher.

The dining room was empty save for five men seated at a table in the middle. Bugsy had watched them come in fifteen minutes before and had tried to time his arrival to coincide with the arrival of their lunch. People always talked more while they ate. Seeing the men were still in the middle of a pitcher of beer, Tyler knew this part of his strategy had gone for nothing, though the overall plan need not be affected.

"Afternoon, fellas. Mind if I pull up a chair?"

Without waiting for a reply, Bugsy pulled a chair away from another table and turned it backwards so that the back rested against the table the five men occupied. Two of them shifted their positions uneasily to make room. Tyler sat down, his arms crossed in front of him around the chair's back, confident he could move fast if he had to.

"You must be Sheriff Tyler," said the man Bugsy remembered was the leader.

"Better known as Bugsy. And who might you be?"

"Lou Marshall." Marshall extended his hand across the table, smiling.

"Pleased to make your acquaintance," the sheriff said, rising slightly out of his chair to take it. "I'd like to meet these other guys too."

Marshall looked uncomfortable. "Yes, of course. Let me introduce you. This is Bob Tucker . . ." The leader waited for Tyler to shake Tucker's hand before proceeding. "This is Bill Kendrick. . . . This is John Hopkeith. . . . And this is Roy Rickers."

"Nice to know ya'," Tyler said, extending his hand for the fifth time.

"And nice to know you, Sheriff," said Marshall. "This is a fine town you've got here. A little hot, though."

"Yup. That it is, that it is. . . . Mind if I chew?"

"What? Oh no, of course not."

"Thank-ya'." Tyler reached into his pocket and withdrew his can of Skoal, popping a huge mound into his mouth. He reached to his rear for an empty glass on another table and placed it in front of him. "At least this stuff don't cause cancer." The sheriff leaned further forward with a smile that revealed at least part of the huge brown wad wedged between his cheek and gum. "How you fellas makin' out in your search for oil?"

"Surprisingly well, Sheriff. Far better, in fact, than we had expected," beamed Marshall. "There's oil in this town all right. Oh, it's way down deep in what we call the third underlayer. But with the new equipment those riggers have, they should be able to have it spurting up in no time."

Tyler spit some tobacco juice into the glass beneath him. He grinned briefly. "That's mighty interestin', Mista Marshall, mighty interestin'. It's also a mite funny, 'cause I put in a call the other day to the Department of Natural Resources in Cheyenne. And you know what they told me? They told me that it was impossible for oil to be here under this land. Somethin' to do with rock formations under the soil."

Marshall laughed loudly. The four others forced themselves to join. "You must have talked to some college boy on vacation, Sheriff, because our equipment tells us there's enough crude in Crescent Falls to take a good measure of the oil business away from those damned Arabs. The resources department was probably basing their information on studies conducted twenty years ago. A bit outdated, wouldn't you say?"

"Hell, yeah. I mean you guys seem to know what you're talkin' 'bout and everythin'. And you sure got yourselves enough equipment to back you up, though I ain't seen most of it yet. I guess you all been at this quite awhile."

"Between us, we have seventy years experience in the field," Marshall boasted.

"Seventy years," repeated Tyler, shooting a wad of spittle dead center into the glass. "That sure is a long time, Mista Marshall. But somethin' else then becomes funny. I shook all of your hands when I came in and didn't feel one callus on any of them. Sounds kind of strange that men with a combined total of seventy years in the field wouldn't have one callus between them."

"It's not all fieldwork," Marshall explained. "In reality, most of it takes place behind a desk with a slide rule and a compass. We've got to know more about computers than we do about shovels."

"Is that a fact? Dave Dean told me you guys were just about the best around. Must have worked for all the major oil companies."

"We've been associated with Shell, Texaco, Mobile, Exxon, and many others."

"Then how come none of their personnel departments has

ever heard of ya'? Wasn't just an oversight either because they gave me numbers of the five leadin' oil exploration companies in the country and not one of them had ever heard of any of ya' either. I think we got ourselves a problem here, fellas. What did that guy say in that Paul Newman movie? . . . Oh yeah, 'What we got here is a failure to communicate.'"

Marshall's face whitened. "There must be some mistake."

"And you made it, buddy boy, you and all your friends here. Now, I don't know what you're up to here but it don't seem logical that men who got no calluses on their hands would be looking for oil in a town that ain't got none, saying they work for oil companies that ain't never heard of 'em. You brought a lot of fancy machines with ya', though I don't rightly know what you been doin' with them in these last few days, considerin' they're all brand new. Fact is, fellas, I don't think you know how to use your equipment any better than a twelve-year-old virgin knows how to use hers."

Marshall rose, his clenched fists resting on the table below him. "Sheriff, I assure you that you're making a mistake. We're here to see if a rigging team should be sent to Crescent Falls, and if we decide it should, all the inhabitants of the town are going to find themselves very rich. Right now our prognosis is favorable. But we can pack up and leave just as quickly as we came before our work is finished. And if we go, we'd take the economy of your town with us."

"You'd give up your commissions just 'cause of little ol' me? How downright unselfish."

Marshall almost smiled, his eyes meeting Tyler's. "Be reasonable, Sheriff. Let's just forget this whole afternoon ever happened."

Tyler spat again, the wad landing on the tablecloth. "You can forget 'bout it if you want but I think I'm goin' to keep it in mind. Matter of fact, I'm runnin' a check on you five guys right now with the FBI in Washington to find out who the hell ya' really are." The men on either side of Marshall began to rise slowly, hands flexed at their hips. "I wouldn't do that if I was you, fellas," Tyler warned coolly. "I used to be a wrestler, pretty damn good one 'till I tore up my knee. They used to have me fight three and four guys at one time. Always used to win. Then again, I never tried five."

Bugsy remained motionless in his chair, as though unaware of the imposing threat. He swung two fingers inside his mouth and emerged with a brown clump of moist tobacco between them, wiping it off on the rim of the glass. The men in front of him had sat down again, their faces blank but seething. The wad of Skoal was crawling down the side of the glass. Tyler stood up.

"Well, fellas, if you'll excuse me I got some work to do." Slowly he backed away toward the door, stopping halfway between it and the table. "Now if I was you fellas, I'd be strongly considerin' stickin' your pricks in the butt of some other town, 'cause if you try to here I'll make sure you lose the balls that go with 'em. . . . Have a nice day now."

With that, Tyler turned and ambled through the door.

"I'm still not sure of the Nazi connection," Dalia Herzog said after their orders had been taken for lunch on Monday afternoon.

David took a sip from his water glass. "The Shaitan Commandment must have originally been some sort of plan developed by the Nazis in the closing years of the war. Another of their great uncompleted projects, under the title of *der Teufels Befehl*. The idea was probably going to be to use it to secure the Third Reich or as a basis for founding the Fourth. Somehow, though, Al Fatah and the Red Prince stumbled upon it and destroyed the scenario."

"And the Nazis want it back," concluded Dalia. Besides her and David, Stanislaw and Isser were seated at the round table. One place was empty, Chevallier having been called to the phone. "But that doesn't explain the presence of Cerberus and his attempt to kill you."

"Doesn't it?" posed Rabanine. "The existence of ODESSA

revolves around protecting Nazi war criminals from capture in order that they may emerge again as leaders of the Fourth Reich. Krieger, Cerberus that is, was known all over Europe as the watchdog who would eliminate all those who came too close to exposing the important Nazis the organization placed much emphasis on keeping safe and happy."

"Then what was he doing in America?"

"Somehow ODESSA must have learned that *der Teufels Befehl* had fallen into Arab hands. Cerberus was dispatched to kill all those who had activated it as the Shaitan Commandment. The Nazi goal at that juncture was to eliminate all traces of Shaitan so that their master plan would be able to continue unscathed. That meant killing me as well as the Arabs, who he never got to."

"This all sounds so foolish," said Stanislaw Kowalski. "The Nazis are old men now. They are no threat to us."

"That is not, though, how they perceive themselves. What's more, worsening economic conditions in Europe have brought the neo-Nazi movement into the limelight again. Suddenly many of Hitler's basic principles are beginning to make sense to a lot of people. The membership is growing with a significant chapter sprouting in the United States. They'll never be able to organize on a global level and will remain splintered and mutually exclusive clubs more than anything else. But ODESSA remains a threat to us. They have an army of killers who will follow in Cerberus' place. They will attempt to thwart us from stopping Shaitan so they can stop it themselves, thereby assuring it will succeed.

"A most gruesome scenario, David," lamented Isser Ben-David.

"Which is why we must learn the meaning of the original Devil's Command. It's our only lead to determining what Shaitan is."

"So now we must fight the Arabs while the Nazis fight us."

David nodded, about to speak when the white suited Jacques Chevallier returned to the table with a cautious smile on his lips.

"I think I have something," the Frenchman said. "It came in from a source in Cairo not an hour ago. A noted informant has information to sell to the highest bidder. He claims to have knowledge of a plot aimed at a major power that promises to send shock waves throughout the entire world."

"Shaitan?"

"He does not mention it by name, only insinuation."

"How much will the whole story cost us?"

"One hundred thousand American dollars should suffice, to be paid upon contact. He is known in our circles only as 'Squid' because he seems to bear allegiance only to the nation that pays him best. He has proved exceptionally reliable in the past."

"In short, the ideal man for Al Fatah to use if they wanted to bait a trap," Kowalski said conclusively.

Rabanine considered his friend's words. "But he must know something, or at least think he does."

"The Squid is very good at what he does," noted Chevallier. "He would not risk his own life foolishly; the life span in his business is short enough as it is. I believe he has something worthwhile to offer us."

"Then we must agree to his terms," said David.

"He will choose the place, we the time," Chevallier reported.

"Of course," snickered Dalia. "That way he will have the opportunity to have others on the premises around him."

"So will we," reassured David. "I don't plan to walk into a trap without people capable of springing me out of it."

"Then you'll make contact yourself?" Kowalski posed.

"Did you expect anything different?"

"No, and I'm sure Al Fatah didn't either."

David ignored the warning. "Jacques, the Squid will choose a location in Egypt, correct?"

"He always has in the past."

"Dalia, how are we fixed for support in Cairo at this time?"

Herzog shrugged, her large eyes a bit sullen. "Since the treaty, there has been little reason to maintain any major clandestine unit in Egypt and I doubt that the Mossad would

215

risk endangering relations by sending one in so suddenly. We do have a small force placed in Fayoum on a bank of the Nile. They are a kind of safety valve should things ever heat up again, their covers deep. Many are women and teenagers but they are very good. I trained some myself."

"Do you have clearance to lead them?"

"I can obtain it from Tel Aviv." She paused. "But David, I'm not sure even the Mossad will approve of exposing them and destroying their covers. It is a tremendous risk to mobilize such a well-hidden force under such short notice."

"We must meet with the Squid as soon as possible, though. There are no other alternatives. . . . Alabaster has done much for the Mossad over the years. It is time for them to return the favor."

"You think they will agree?"

"I can't see them refusing, not under the circumstances."

"Then I should contact the Squid, *mon ami?*" From Chevallier.

"Tell him his terms have been met and that we request that the meeting take place no later than Wednesday night."

"That doesn't leave us much time," cautioned Dalia.

"We don't have much left."

"One hundred thousand dollars? That's quite a bit of money, David, and in cash yet." Displeasure was mildly evident in the gravel voice of Colonel Rossi.

"It's a small price to pay for the information this man might possess."

"'Might possess?' I believe we're taking an unnecessary risk to obtain something that this informant quite probably won't have."

"We're running out of alternatives, Colonel Rossi. The risk is a necessary one. I must meet with the Squid and learn what he has to say, trap or not. Be assured that precautions will be taken."

"I could have a team of agents meet you in Cairo," Rossi offered.

David shook his head. "No good. The Squid would learn of their presence and cancel the meeting. The Mossad has a small force stationed in Fayoum. I'll use them as support."

The Director let out a sigh that grew into a frown. "They got Desmond, David. He was very good."

"Seif got Desmond and Desmond wasn't as good as Alabaster."

"No, not as good as Alabaster." Rossi depressed the first button on his intercom, leaning forward to speak into it. "Mr. Kincannon, draw $100,000 in cash—twenties and fifties—and pack it in a black attaché case." Rossi paused and smiled at Rabanine. "File it under miscellaneous expenses."

David placed the black case on his bed. Before him alongside each other sat Isser Ben-David and Stanislaw Kowalski. Jacques Chevallier stood by the phone, as though he expected it to ring. Dalia Herzog was by the window.

"All is set," said the Frenchman. "I have spoken personally with the Squid and am satisfied that he believes the information he's selling is of the utmost quality. He has chosen Luxor for the rendezvous point, specifically the Temple of Amon-Ra. I left the specific time up in the air, although he seems eager to get it over with as soon as possible. He seems nervous, a sign in this business that one wants to part quickly with the product in his possession. I have a number for you to call upon reaching the airport in Cairo. The final arrangements can be made then."

Rabanine looked at Herzog. "Dalia?"

"I have prepared the security arrangements with Isser. Luxor is located approximately 425 kilometers from our base in Fayoum. The two of us are booked on a flight to Cairo leaving Washington at nine PM tonight and arriving in Egypt at six PM tomorrow, Cairo time. We'll then be driven by one of my soldiers to Fayoum where we'll meet up with the troop and spend the night on the bank of the Nile. We must allow for five hours of travel by truck on Egyptian roads to reach Luxor by nightfall the next day. I will have an advance team stationed all day at the temple to watch for possible unwanted appearances by any Al Fatah operatives. They would not, I think, go into an operation blindly."

"Neither will we," reassured David.

Early that evening, an FBI agent was busy sorting out a mound of case reports and vouchers for information. As a member of Herb Weinberg's special task force formed only forty-eight hours before, his job was simple. All he had to do was sift through the mass of reports that lay beneath the florescent lamp on his desk in an otherwise darkened office and determine which ones represented something out of the ordinary, a break with the mundane.

The agent was doing his job well.

Before him on the desk, slightly to his right, sat two distinct piles of papers and folders. One, quite larger than the second, contained reports he felt called for no further attention. The other somewhat smaller one, meanwhile, was composed of scraps of material he felt should be passed on to Weinberg himself which he would indicate by jotting the letters "HW" in the upper left-hand corner.

He was tired and his eyes were failing him, spots dancing in the bright beams on his desk, when he came across a tracer that had arrived in Washington a few days earlier. Its origins surprised him: small towns seldom called on the services of the Bureau and almost never contacted Washington directly. And obviously whoever had sent this request was unfamiliar with proper procedure or felt that the exception superseded the rule. He began to read the yet unfilled request for information sent by telegram out loud to relieve the boredom and fatigue that forced his eyelids down in the dimness of the room.

"From Sheriff James Tyler; Crescent Falls, Wyoming. Please run an identification check on the following persons . . ."

Even before finishing it, the agent reached for his pen and printed "HW" in the top left-hand corner.

TWENTY-TWO

Dalia Herzog inspected herself in the port bathroom of the 747. Moving closer to the mirror, she began to study her face. There was strain and hardness carved permanently on her expression, features that overcame whatever tenderness that might have once existed.

The rumor in camp that always spread quickly among the new recruits was to beware of Commander Herzog. Watch her hands reaching for your breasts or buttocks and never return her smile. To do so was to pave the way for an invitation to her bed. But the rumor wasn't true . . . at least not totally.

She *had* made love to women, more times than she had to men. She did so out of physical need, however, not emotional desire. Was it so bad to feel wanted? Not to be rejected?

She was still young, reasonably anyway. But what did she have?

Nothing except David. . . . There would always be David. She dreamed often of him coming to her at night, taking her as she wanted to take him. Strangely, in these dreams the act of love was never consummated. Only that which led up to it. And then reality would always return as a spoiler. Dreams were so short.

Dalia checked herself one final time in the mirror, aware that someone was pounding on the lavatory door. Her brown slacks showed off the firm, strong lines of her lower body in addition to her powerful thighs. Certainly she didn't look thirty-five.

But was David looking?

When she returned to her seat, she found him checking to make sure the black attaché case was still secure beneath the seat.

"I dozed for quite awhile," he said.

"You needed it. The next few days will be long ones." She paused. "David, does it bother you to entrust your life to a woman?"

He looked at her quizzically. "What do you mean?"

"You're about to embark on a sensitive mission in which your life will almost surely be threatened. Are you concerned over the fact that a woman will be leading the force charged with protecting you?"

He smiled faintly. "Not when the woman is better at what she does than any man I know. No man can match your experience. I have seen your work in the field. Your orders are never hesitant. No speck of doubt ever enters your voice. You have escaped from situations even the best man would have been killed in. If my life was on the line, there's no one I would feel safer with by my side than you." He took her hand. "Something disturbs you."

"Just nerves."

"No, something else. A person has feelings that are like colors in their distinctness. I see a color in you other than nervousness."

"Perhaps your eyes deceive you," she lied.

"Perhaps." David persisted no further. Her silence and her eyes spoke for her, telling him things he did not want to hear.

"Hello," a metallic voice said, as David shifted the receiver from his left ear to his right, clutching the case tightly in his free hand.

"I am looking for the Squid. I have a package for him."

"Its contents?"

"A present from the Frenchman."

"The color of his suits?"

"White, of course."

"In that case you are talking to the Squid now," the voice said indifferently. "And who are you?"

220

"Alabaster."

"That is impossible."

"Why?"

"Because Alabaster does not deal in information, he deals in death."

"Sometimes the two are interchangeable, especially in the case of the Shaitan Commandment. I presume your information pertains to this?"

"It does."

"How much do you know?"

"Everything."

"I find that hard to believe. No one else seems to know anything at all."

"No one else is the Squid. I came upon my name for a reason, just as you did yours."

"I hope so, Squid, because I've killed people for lies of far less significance."

"I am aware of that and look forward to meeting . . . the great Alabaster," the Squid said snidely. "At the Temple of Amon-Ra in Luxor. The time is up to you."

"Tomorrow evening, Wednesday, at ten o'clock. Bring the information."

"Bring the money."

The phone rang off.

Immediately upon receiving a dial tone again, David reached the foreign operator and asked for a number in Israel.

"Hello." The voice of Moshe.

"Moshe, it's David. How is everything?"

"Fine, my friend. The Mossad sent nine more guards down yesterday as a safety precaution. They all check out. Shaul is very well protected."

"He needs no one other than you."

"You don't forget yourself, I hope."

A pause.

"So do I."

"Things are going well, David, yes?"

"As well as they might be. Progress is being made. How is Shaul?"

"Making a fool of the doctors who said his injuries would be a month in healing. You should see him. . . . You are coming home soon, yes?"

"I hope so."

"Would you like to speak to the boy?"

"No, not now. I don't want to upset him."

The giant sighed. "You sound upset yourself."

"Just tired."

"Two years is a long time to be away from one's work, my friend, no matter how good you are at that work. Perhaps you should reconsider what you are about to do."

"I already have. There's no alternative."

"I was afraid you might say that."

"Because I must kill again?"

"Because you want to." Moshe took a deep breath. "Killing is more than your business, my friend, you have made it your life. You will go on and on until every Arab terrorist in the world has been silenced and then you will find other enemies to spend your time chasing because you live your life in pursuit of justice. But someday a man will track you down just as you have tracked down hundreds. Sooner or later you will meet a man just as quick and as smart as you who will put a bullet in the back of your head. There's not much justice in that."

"What would you have me do?"

"Come home before that man finds you."

"You are worried for my safety?"

"I am worried for your son. He is growing up. He cannot be fooled much longer. Soon the truth will have to be made known to him and it may . . . hurt."

"Take care of him, Moshe," David said distantly. "Whatever happens, take care of him."

"*Shalom*, my friend."

The drive to Fayoum was a quiet one, neither David nor

Dalia speaking much except for him to brief her on his call to the Squid and the final arrangements for the meeting.

"Why ten o'clock at night?" she asked.

"Because there are two many people around the Temple when it's light and the darkness of very late night would make us susceptible to attack from virtually every angle."

"I'll arrange for the advance team as soon as we reach the base."

"Base?"

"A makeshift one set up on the bank of the Nile. My people have been contacted. They will all be there by the time we arrive."

The ninety minute drive brought them to a lavishly green embankment overlooking the world's greatest river. Wide bushes blew steadily in the soft breeze, watched over by tall palm trees that stretched like giant umbrellas over the horizon. Tents, well camouflaged to blend with the area, lay scattered everywhere. The driver pulled the Renault to a stop between two large green trucks. David and Dalia stepped out, surrounded immediately by the troops that had been gathering here over the past five hours.

"Good to see you again, Dalia," said a well-built man with thick black hair and mustache as he emerged from the group. "I trust you had a safe trip."

"Very." Dalia moved forward to greet him. "Daniel, I want you to meet David Rabanine."

The man named Daniel smiled broadly and extended his hand. "So you're the man responsible for us being called into action. It's a great chance we have taken, leaving the lives we've built here painstakingly for years so suddenly. People will talk. We might never be able to return. But I, for one, don't care. I am a soldier. It's been some time since I've seen anything but maneuvers. I welcome the chance to see action again."

David gripped his extended hand. "I'm glad to hear that but it's my hope that we see no action at all."

Daniel eyed David closely. "Rabanine, Rabanine," he said softly to himself. "I've heard of you. . . . A top Mossad agent who retired some years ago."

"I was forced back into action by the present predicament."

"So I'm told. My name's Daniel Kaim. I was once called captain. But that was long ago."

"Not too long, it seems."

For the first time, David glanced at the other people gathered around him. About five of the thirty or so faces belonged to women. Another ten belonged to boys no older than twenty. Their expressions were full and bright, barren of cynacism or wear. Rabanine guessed they had never seen action before. The remaining fifteen, though, were a different story. They were all hard, seasoned men who had fought many battles and won most of them. They represented an insurance policy Israel kept tucked away in Egypt for situations like this one. Accordingly, there was no bitterness in their stares, only precisioned certainty and somber rejoice over returning to the lives they had chosen long ago. The garb of all thirty members of the force was combat green, casting them into the scene as though they had sprouted up from the fertile ground below.

Daniel Kaim stepped forward and took Dalia's hands, kissing her lightly on the cheek. "I officially turn command over to you." Kaim stepped back and saluted pretentiously.

Smiling, Dalia returned the salute. "Then before the power goes to my head, David and I better brief you on tomorrow's schedule. . . ."

"Cerberus failed. He was killed in Washington two days ago by Alabaster," said the gray haired man with cold eyes.

The white haired man smiled from behind his desk. "You've come all the way here to tell me that?"

"And more. The Americans have linked the Shaitan Commandment to us. I'm afraid things are not looking very good at all."

"And what happened to the army of devoted men willing to give their lives to our—your—cause, Hans?"

Hans bit his lip before responding. "There are simply too many who know, too many who would have to be killed. It's not worth it. We'd only draw more attention to ourselves than has been already."

"Come now, Hans, can't all those brilliant minds at ODESSA figure out a way to cut off the major links at least? Or are they too busy searching for their names in history books?"

"The links are no longer our major problem. We have strong reason to believe that the Arabs are going to be successful enough with their operation to ravage the entire world."

"Then why have you bothered to come back to me?"

"We need your help. We must learn how to stop the Commandment."

"I thought I was just your insurance policy."

Hans grimaced.

"You will do things my way without argument or question?"

Hans nodded.

"And when this is over, if it ever is, you will leave me to reconcile my past—and my future—alone?"

Hans nodded again, swallowing hard. "You spoke last week of an alternative strategy."

"I did, didn't I?"

TWENTY-THREE

"What the hell are you doing, Sheriff?"

Mayor Jim Layton's demand was preceded by his stormy entrance into Bugsy Tyler's office with Dave Dean by his side. Tyler, sitting comfortably behind his desk, did not have to ask the mayor to explain himself.

"My job, Jimbo," Bugsy said simply, his expression unwavering.

Layton's thighs brushed up against the front of the desk. He was trembling with rage. Dave Dean stood off to the right a bit, his features screwed up into an angered stare.

"Does your job include harassing men who are trying to do something good for this town?" the mayor asked harshly.

"Why? Ya' know any?"

Layton's lips puckered. "Don't get smart with me, Bugsy. We been friends a long time. But lately I just haven't been able to figure out your behavior."

"I guess Lou Marshall's been in for a visit."

"With a list of complaints against you longer than a cow's tongue."

"Did he mention anythin' 'bout his calluses?"

"His wha— . . . What the hell are you talking about?"

"Ask him."

"I'm asking you."

"But you're not listening, Jimbo," Tyler said, still sedate.

"No, Bugsy, you're the one who's not listening," Layton accused, thrusting a finger menacingly forward. "I'm telling you that these guys are working their butts off trying to discover the black ooze that just might keep this town going. And it isn't making their job any easier to have a lamebrain sheriff jumping on their backs like a frigging dog in heat, badgering them with questions and accusations that just plain aren't called for."

"So what do you want me to do?"

"I want you to lay off them."

"Lay off? You want *me* to lay off? . . ." Tyler rose slowly from his chair, resting his massive hands on the desk top. "Now hold it just a gawddamned minute there, Jimbo. It seems you and your silent partner here are a little mixed up when it comes to duties in this shithole of a town your five oil buddies are makin' such a streamline effort to save." Tyler stuck his finger into the center of his badge. "My duties as sheriff include investigatin' any person or persons actin' suspiciously. And Marshall and his pals fit into that category just as tight as a ten-incher in a whore's ass."

"Bullshit," muttered Dave Dean, looking away.

Tyler swung his eyes toward him. "That might well be what they're diggin' for, Dave, 'cause it sure ain't oil."

"Bugsy, will you just *try* to be reasonable," pleaded the mayor.

"Jimbo, these guys's story stinks more than an old whore's breath."

"Prove it," challenged Dave Dean.

"To begin with, there ain't no oil in this town," Tyler shot back. "A guy at the Resources Department told me the rocks is all wrong."

"An opinion."

"A fact, gawddamnit!"

Layton shook his head. "Marshall says there's no way anyone can know whether there's oil here or not until they do some exploratory digging which is what he and his boys are doing now."

"Then why hasn't anybody in the oil industry ever heard of 'em, huh? Answer me that, Jimbo." Tyler thrust his index finger in the mayor's direction.

"Marshall explained that to me, too. Said that he and his

boys work kind of on the sly. They undercut prices and get paid under the table."

"You know how it is in these big industries, Bugsy," said Dave Dean, forcing a smile.

"No, I don't. All I know is how it is in Crescent Falls. And right now I know these five candy-assed sweet-talkers has got you and the rest of this town brainwashed. Christ, they come into Crescent Falls with dollar bills rollin' out of their pockets and you start followin' 'em like they're the fuckin' pied piper. Your fuckin' noses are so brown that you can't see past the end of 'em. I guess that's the problem."

Bugsy reached into his pocket for his Skoal and pried the can open. Finding it empty, he tossed the tin angrily against the wall, obliterating the head of a Utah prison escapee who had been caught six months before. Layton and Dean skipped backwards upon impact.

"Why, Bugsy? Why would they con us?" the Mayor asked, worried that the next thing thrown would be a punch at his face—a blow from which he might never recover.

"What would they have to gain, Sheriff?" From Dean.

Tyler steadied his temper and sat back down. "I don't know, not yet anyway."

"I mean it's not like we're paying them anything," Dean reminded in his best rendition of an Eastern accent. "If they don't find oil, they go hungry."

"We both do," added Layton.

"Doesn't it bother you guys none when they got answers for everything?" Tyler asked.

"Not when you already asked them the questions."

"They didn't give me the same answers."

"You didn't give them a chance."

"Like you boys ain't givin' me one?" Tyler tilted his eyebrows upward.

Dean and Layton glanced at each other. "Look, Bugsy," consoled the mayor, "Sunday afternoon these guys plan to issue their preliminary report before the entire town in the meeting hall. Yesterday Marshall hinted to me that it just might be promising." Layton tried to look the sheriff sternly in the eyes but failed. "Now," he resumed, "I don't want you to do anything else to upset them before then, nothing that might jeopardize the results of the work these guys are doing."

"What do ya' expect me to do, drink all the oil they're so cocksure is under our houses?"

"You know what I mean."

"I'll tell ya' somethin' else I know. By Sunday, the FBI's report on your five friends should be here, providin' those cunt lips in Washington take the sticks out of their asses. Then you fellas will have your proof."

There was a brief pause before Mayor Layton spoke again. "Or we'll have your job, Sheriff."

The Temple of Amon-Ra lies at the figurative beginning of the city of Luxor overlooking the Nile. The structure, striking in its antiquity, is equally striking in its size and design. It stands as a monument to the reigns of some of Egypt's great pharaos, allowing modern day man a taste of the symmetrical aestheticism of his ancestors.

The mazelike complex of buildings that links the past with the present can be entered only from the north side into the Courtyard of Ramses II through a passageway adorned with sculptures of scenes from the battle of Dadech. The entire Courtyard is watched over by massive statues staring eternally down at visitors from their perch between columns. At the end of the Courtyard there is a long corridor hemmed in on both sides by two rows of immense columns in the colonnade of Amenophis III.

The corridors in the Temple of Amon-Ra stretch forever, reaching dustily for the past and grasping it. There is only a small semblance of a roof, meaning that visitors are exposed to most of the elements even when inside. The stages of the Temple lie at different levels, some higher or lower than others. The sight is awesome in its mysticism and chilling in its vastness.

The sun had already set when two trucks of mundane green design pulled onto the road before the grass courtyard that sits in front of the Temple in a checkerboard pattern lined by wide sidewalks. Other than these vehicles the area was deserted. The drivers parked them on the edge of the courtyard. Two men and one woman climbed out of the lead truck. One of the men, dressed as a civilian, held a black case in his right hand.

"We're right on schedule," David announced.

"At this point," agreed Dalia, checking her watch. She looked away. "The men I placed inside the Temple will have spotted us. They should appear shortly to give their report."

As she finished, a man cloaked as an Egyptian guide moved out from the foreground of the Temple and approached them.

"Good to see you, Yakov," Dalia greeted. "What kind of day has it been?"

"Hot." The man wiped his brow with the sleeve of his tunic. "Over a hundred. But there is nothing to report concerning suspicious strangers lingering about. No Al Fatah operative has been here today."

"You sound very sure," said Rabanine.

"It is my business to be sure. Who am I addressing?"

"David Rabanine."

"Of the Mossad? . . . Forgive me, sir. I'm sorry. I did not mean to be rude. It's just that it's been a long day."

"It will be a longer night, if your information proves wrong. Is there anyone inside the Temple now?"

"One man. He arrived five minutes before you. He is worried, obviously frightened of something. I believe he is the man you seek."

"I hope so. No one else, then?"

"Besides my men who will now be dismissed, no. We have watched every inch of the Temple's area all day. No one has been here whose motives seemed questionable. And no one who entered failed to depart."

"It's a large area to speak so decidedly of."

230

"We are large men, sir. We know this meeting must be crucial to the security of Israel. I assure you, no mistakes have been made."

"I believe you." Alabaster turned to Dalia. "I'm going in."

"You will have nothing but the light of the moon to guide you."

"That's all I need."

"You will be too susceptible to an ambush."

"Your man says no one other than the Squid is inside. I have nothing to fear."

"All the same," said Dalia, her tone totally professional. "I must insist that you wait for me to deploy the troops in the area. We must prepare ourselves."

Alabaster studied Herzog, a striking paradox of a woman whose dark, feminine features did not seem to jibe with the khaki uniform and gun belt she wore around her waist.

"And," she continued, "I will bring up your rear once you enter the Temple." She clutched the Garilla machine gun swung behind her shoulder.

"Your presence might bother the Squid."

"He will never know I am there."

David smiled. "Very well, then."

Dalia nodded to Daniel Kaim who whistled loudly. In seconds both trucks had been emptied of all thirty occupants, leaving only the drivers inside to pull the vehicles out of sight. All the soldiers' faces were staunch and sure, perspiring from heat but showing not a trace of fear. Each of them wore a gun belt similar to Dalia's and held either an Israeli Garilla or Uzi machine gun in their hands. Kaim faced them as they stood in a line, studying their expressions. So many were no more than children fighting a war their fathers had determined for them. These adolescent faces were the only ones that showed any hint of emotion, that of eagerness tempered enough by training. Hopefully enough.

"You know your positions as instructed last night. Get to them now," Kaim ordered.

231

Acting as one, the troop deployed itself across the area in front of the Temple and to its sides, finding cover in the shadows; some disappearing behind a stone fence that surrounds the complex. The Temple entrance was in plain sight of all, though none of the soldiers was closer than eight feet to it. Their position was defensive, meant to keep people out.

Kaim glanced around him, studying the area. "They are good soldiers, Dalia. They have learned their lessons well."

"Still, we must hope they will not have to rely on them any further tonight." She turned toward David. "You aren't going in unarmed, are you?"

"Hardly." He pulled up his shirt and faced away, revealing an empty leather holster hanging between his shoulder blades. "Hand me the Uzi by my attaché case."

Dalia obliged and watched Rabanine fit the weapon snugly into the holster, pulling his bulky shirt down over it and tucking the shirt into his slacks. He picked up the black case beneath him.

"I'm going in."

"I'll be right behind you," reassured Dalia.

Alabaster entered the eerie darkness of the ancient Temple. The smell was rustic and dry, the air laced with a mustiness that had the feel of death. He passed a series of skyscraping columns, his movements watched by stone eyes that had been fixed in their positions centuries before. Dust flew into his nose and mouth, courtesy of the soft breeze which blew over the Nile into the blackness of the night broken only by the moon. The hard dirt floor beneath Alabaster creaked under each step, as though the Temple were protesting his presence as a threat to its sanctity.

The Squid was nowhere in sight but then nothing was. He had heard of the man before. He was the type who would prefer to make contact first, always suspecting that things were not as they were supposed to be. A man does not live long in his business by taking chances.

Alabaster trained his senses to the rear, his eyes moving from side to side at the huge structures that guided his way. The darkness was greater here, a slight roof blocking out the rays of the moon. His eyes fought to adjust, his feet choosing their way more discreetly, still once in awhile striking a rock beneath them. He had been aware of Dalia's presence behind him about fifty yards the whole way. But suddenly he felt another presence much closer. It was moving beyond the column of statues, using them for cover. But it was narrowing the gap, approaching slowly.

The darkness was almost total now, the blackest area in the entire Courtyard of Ramses II upon him. Silently, without varying his pace, Alabaster turned to his right and moved toward a column, circling around it. A glimmer of steel facing the position he had left caught his eye and he shot his hand swiftly toward it, snatching a wrist and grasping it like a vice before the holder of the gun was aware that anything had happened.

"Who, who's that?" the metallic voice of the Squid stammered. The sweaty smell of fear lingered in the air around him.

"It is Alabaster, Squid, and I do not like having guns pointed at me."

"I was merely taking precautions until I was sure it was you. I see you have taken precautions as well."

Alabaster released the Squid's wrist and tightened his grip on the handle of the black case. His other hand now held the Squid's pistol, wet with perspiration.

"They are here for your protection as well as mine," Alabaster said tersely.

The Squid compressed his features into a scornful mask. "I don't think you trust me."

"I trust no one, especially those with connections in Al Fatah."

"I do *not* work for them!"

"You move in their circles. It's almost the same thing."

233

"Can I have my gun back?"

Alabaster paused before answering. "You don't wish to shoot me, do you Squid?"

"I'd be dead before I pulled the trigger. I have heard much about you, Alabaster. I will not try anything. . . . You have the money?"

Alabaster's eyes had finally adjusted to the darkness. The figure of a short, nondescript man in dark sports jacket worn over an even darker shirt came into view. The face was extraordinarily pale for a man of Arab nature.

"Yes, I have the money. And it will be yours as soon as you pass on the information I have purchased."

"Not here," the Squid said nervously. "We will go to a place where there is more light: the Colonnade of Amenophis III. I must check the money."

He began to move to the right when he felt Alabaster's powerful hand choke off his progress by grasping his arm.

"You're hurting me," the Squid squealed.

Alabaster continued to squeeze. "We will go straight ahead."

"But there is a shortcut." Alabaster tightened his grip. "As you wish."

They walked toward a higher level of the Temple filled with row after row of monumental statues, some cracked and broken by the winds of the ages or, in some cases, vandals. They were out of the blackness now, moving into an area reasonably well lit by moon rays. They proceeded down a less narrow corridor between stone pillars thirty feet high with the remains of what had once been the floor of another level propped upon them. The two men were hemmed in.

"Here," said Alabaster.

"But we have only the columns for protection. They could strike at us at any time."

"Who could strike at us, Squid? Al Fatah?"

"I did not say that!"

"You meant it. Perhaps you made a deal with them as well."

"No! . . . I swear! . . . No!"

"Then you should have nothing to fear."

"In my business there is always something to fear." The Squid sat down on the base of one of the pillars. "Let me see the money."

Alabaster opened the case and handed it to him. The Arab checked it briefly in the naked light, his eyes bulging for a moment before he closed it again and placed it near him.

"That was fast."

The Squid rose back to his feet. "I have no need to count it, Alabaster. One hundred thousand dollars is not really a lot of money for men such as yourself. You would not have taken a chance at cheating me and not receiving the information I possess which, I think, is considerably more valuable than any sum either of us could muster in a hundred years."

"Very astute of you."

"The Frenchman would not do business with me if I was not astute."

"What do you know of the Shaitan Commandment?" Alabaster asked, delaying the issue no longer. Behind him, he sensed that Dalia had stopped moving and had stationed herself twenty yards away from him.

"I am told it will destroy America and I believe it," the Squid replied.

"How?"

"A fascinating means really. You are aware of the American dependence on nuclear power, of course."

"Yes."

"And of the general instability of these nuclear plants?"

"Certainly."

"Then tell me, Alabaster, what would happen if ten of these plants, all located in the most densely populated areas of the United States, were to be sabotaged and forced into what is called a meltdown?"

Alabaster felt suddenly chilled. "The winds would carry the contamination hundreds of miles away, poisoning the food and

235

water in addition to people who lived in the wind's path. And, since so many plants would be involved in such densely populated areas, few would be able to escape the radiation and its affects. Panic would result. Disaster. Death."

"Exactly. A very thorough analysis," complimented the Squid. "And there would be a lot of death, because the wind and clouds would spread the radioactive poison to untold millions hundreds and hundreds of miles away from the nuclear accidents themselves. Within three months, more than half of America's population will have been contaminated, dead or soon to be."

"You sound like an expert."

"I am only repeating what I have heard from experts."

"And you say Al Fatah is planning to sabotage ten of these plants?"

"Maybe more. I have heard as low as six, as high as fifteen. All strategically located near major cities that would have no hope to evacuate in time, so I am told."

"Where?"

"The Hudson facility in New York, the Santa Monica facility outside of Los Angeles . . ." The Squid went on to name five other plants and their locations. "These are the only ones I am sure of. I could guess at the others but then I'm sure you could too just as accurately." He seemed relaxed now, filling his eyes with the sight of the case resting at his feet.

"And the 175 agents I have heard about who will be entering the country soon. They will be responsible for the sabotage?"

The Squid nodded. "In small groups, I am told. They have been training for years in the design of nuclear reactors and have learned where the most sensitive places are to plant explosives."

"But these plants have automatic shutdown devices in the event of an explosion."

"Those devices, however, can be circumvented by someone who knows how. I am told it is a relatively simple process."

236

"They would have needed detailed plans of the plants' design."

"And they have had those plans for years, since the very time Shaitan was conceived. Obtaining them, in fact, was the catalyst for the whole operation."

"How will the 175 execute their missions?"

"I am told a few of them have been placed in sensitive areas within the plants themselves. Security perhaps. Maybe even the control room. At the proper time, they will make arrangements for the rest of their team to join them. I am told tours have been conveniently arranged on the day Shaitan is to be implemented. The sabotage will be carried out by people in these groups with help from their fellows working in the plants. And that, as they say, will be that."

Alabaster thought for one moment and then another. "This contradicts information I had gained previously," he said, thinking of the strategic displacement of the Shaitan force.

"Then your previous information was wrong."

"I must find out who these 175 agents are."

The Squid waved a hand in front of his pale, empty face. "I can't help you there, Alabaster. I have not been told their identities."

"Then how did you come by this information?"

"From a man very close to Arafat himself, some say his homosexual lover." The Squid allowed himself a grin.

"You trust him?"

"Implicitly. He has supplied me with information before."

"How many times?"

"Four. Five. What does it matter?"

Alabaster pressed on. The Squid's story hadn't felt right from the beginning. Now he knew why. "The answer to that doesn't concern you. When did this man first tell you of Shaitan?" he demanded.

"I don't remember precisely, but it was recent. Within the past week, I think. I don't understand the line of this—"

Alabaster ended the sentence by placing his hand over the Squid's mouth. "Don't speak or move," he whispered. The Israeli had heard a rock move, striking another as if it had been kicked accidently. There was a presence. He could feel it lurking in the darkness beyond the columns.

"Hand me your pistol," Alabaster commanded softly, taking his hand away from the Squid's mouth.

"Why?"

"Don't ask questions. Just do as I say if you want to live. We have company."

The Squid handed the small automatic, a lady's .22, over. His fingers were trembling madly, facial features even more pale than usual.

"Don't move," Alabaster warned, taking the weapon, his eyes locked on the black area beyond the statues that enclosed the two men. "Remain just as you are."

In the darkness, Alabaster caught sight of a lone figure, not really a figure so much as a flash of movement. A change in the level of darkness as though someone dressed in black was slicing through it, closing in. The man was exceptionally well-trained. Only a rock in his path had given away his approach. And then only because his quarry was Alabaster. Dalia's man reported that all who had entered the Temple today had left it which meant the man had been inside since yesterday. Only one school of killers would use such a sabotage, a school based in Japan. The man in the darkness was a Ninja and Alabaster had heard it said often that the only time you saw a Ninja was right before he killed you.

The Squid began to move suddenly away, back toward the Courtyard of Ramses II. "I won't let you gamble with my life, Alabaster. I'm leaving. I've got to get out of here!"

"Don't give away that we know—"

The Israeli's whispered words were cut short by a sound in the breeze, a whirling noise that surged through the silence. Aware that his presence was now forfeit, the man in the darkness had made the first move but directed it at the wrong

238

party. The knife wedged itself firmly between the Squid's shoulder blades, forcing his body to convulse and his mouth to hang widely open for a scream that was buried by death. He fell forward in a heap, the knife's handle still protruding from his back.

Alabaster dived behind the base of the column the dead man had once been sitting on, raising the automatic. In the darkness beyond him, the Ninja—if he was a Ninja—was moving forward, dodging behind columns to obscure his approach. But there was a pattern to the erraticness and, not wanting to waste time, Alabaster fired into that pattern as the figure darted from one massive pedestal to the next. Three bullets rocketed outward, each striking the black-clothed figure in the chest. A high-pitched scream erupted. The figure in black was a woman. It made sense. Most agents would not expect an assassin to be female. They could look directly at her and not see her. So it might well have been.

As Alabaster reached to the holster strapped to his back for the Uzi, he heard the rapid pounding of Dalia's feet making their way toward him.

"What happened?" she screamed, her Garilla levelled before her, probing for a target. Her eyes found the Squid's body.

"I killed an attacker who killed the Squid."

"But my men—"

"The attacker was a woman and an exceptionally well-trained one at that. She'd been here since yesterday, perhaps even the day before."

"Then we're safe now."

"I don't think so. We've got to warn the others."

Alabaster's eyes swung furiously around him, the Uzi cocked and ready. The woman who had killed the Squid was not alone. She was part of a force that would surely rush the Temple if she failed. And since she had no doubt expected to complete her mission without the use of bullets, that failure had been signalled by *his* gunshots. The force would be on their

239

way in now, an alternative plan put into effect.

"Let's get out of here!" Alabaster commanded.

They had begun to move back down the corridor when flashing lights appeared above them over the Temple in the black night. A swirling sound, hard and regular, reached their ears evolving from a soft sputter to a loud blast.

"Oh God," Dalia muttered. "It's a helicopter!"

In the absurdity of that notion, there was sense. Alabaster had expected everything and anything but an offensive mounted within one of the holiest sanctums in all of Egypt. It seemed unthinkable for Arabs to desecrate their own tradition, to bloody a pillar of their own history. These, though, were not Arabs.

They were the men of Al Fatah.

Alabaster and Dalia, stopped in their tracks, watched the machine whirl overhead and then heard the machine gun spitting fire at their troops by the entrance. At the same time, a parade of sedans pulled up on roads bordering the east and west sides of the Temple. Their well-armed occupants climbed out quickly and moved toward the areas of the massive structure that lacked openings, where all progress was stopped by mammoth bricks laid centuries before.

A few of the Arabs, carrying high-powered automatic rifles, sped to concealed positions in sight and range of the Temple entrance, thereby cutting off the Israelis' movement while the chopper readied for another pass. Alone the threat posed by either the snipers or the helicopter could have been circumvented. But together the obstacle they presented was insurmountable. The soldiers were trapped, powerless to enter the Temple without being mowed down. Alabaster and Dalia were alone.

"They're going to kill my men!" Dalia screamed. She began to move toward the corridor, stopped only by Alabaster's powerful hand upon her shoulder. "Don't try to stop me, David. There are women and boys back there. I'm responsible for them. I must go back."

240

"There's nothing you can do to help them, not now."

The helicopter's lights flashed over them again. It was cutting a circular route through the sky, spilling down a sea of bullets each time it passed over the Temple's entrance in the vicinity where most of Daniel Kaim's troops were deployed. Most, the seasoned professionals, had the sense to force their bodies low to the ground and stay under as much cover as possible. But the younger ones, mesmerized by the whirling machine, had risen to fight it with rifles that were little more than toys in comparison. The helicopter's 50-caliber machine gun chopped them down on the second pass, spraying their young blood into the sacred ground beneath them. Others tried to reach the entrance when the copter swirled away. The sniper's bullets, though, caught them in the back before they even made it to the steps.

Alabaster pulled Dalia toward him, shaking her at the shoulders. "Listen to me! Listen to me!"

"I've got to save those troops!"

"There's a way we can. But I need your help. We've got to act quickly. The helicopter's only a distraction. They want me—us now. We *can* stop them, though."

"How?"

Alabaster searched the huge columns above him, swinging his eyes about. "Let me have one of your grenades."

She obliged unquestioningly, pulling the one grenade from her belt and handing it to him. Alabaster wedged it in one of his back pockets, well aware that the pressure on the firing mechanism was already too great. He placed his Uzi on the ground beneath him, ready to explain his plan to Dalia.

And then the explosions came.

241

TWENTY-FOUR

The echoes of the blasts stung Alabaster's ears. They had been set off 150 yards away on both the east and west sides of the Temple. The message was clear: Enemy troops were foraging their way toward their location through gaping holes in the once solid structure.

"They're destroying the Temple!" Dalia exclaimed.

"The Temple doesn't matter," Alabaster told her. "Our lives do."

"And the lives of my troops."

"We can save them. But you've got to help me."

"Just tell me what to do."

"How long before the terrorists reach us?"

"The terrain in the areas they are coming from isn't meant to be walked through. There are no corridors. They'll have to climb and push their way."

"How long?"

"Ten minutes, if we're lucky."

"We can't count on luck. . . . You've got to cover me." His eyes were focused above him.

"Cover you? . . . Why?"

"Because I'm going to knock out that helicopter. I've got to. It's the only chance we've got. Right now, Kaim's men can't budge without being cut down by it or the snipers. And the Arabs who just blasted their way into the Temple will be heading toward them just as soon as they've dealt with us. But if I can destroy the helicopter, our forces will have freedom of movement. They'll be able to save themselves . . . and us."

"But *a helicopter?* You can't. You haven't got the firepower."

"I've got a grenade. It's all I need. . . . Cover me."

Dalia smiled uneasily. "Be careful."

Alabaster stepped up on the base of a statue whose head had been severed years before. The statue was enclosed by a column on either side with a sort of pedestal on top, sufficient in size to hold the frame of a man.

"What are you going to try?" Dalia asked him.

Alabaster lifted his right foot up so it was braced on the statue's arm. "The helicopter sweeps right over here on its way to and from the entrance. I'm going to throw the grenade inside it while it passes overhead."

"They'll shoot you down before you get the chance," she pleaded.

"Maybe."

Alabaster reached his right hand up and found the headless statue's shoulder, gripping it with all his might. His left foot steadied his motion on the stone man's left arm as he pulled his right foot up even with the pectoral muscle so that his body was actually horizontal, seeming to defy gravity.

Pulling hard with his right arm, the sinewy muscles rippling with strain, he hoisted his body upward so his left foot reached the statue's shoulder. He wavered for a second, thinking that a fall now would surely set off the grenade in his pocket, before finding the strength to lift his right leg up to the stone shoulders and finally pulling the rest of his body up to where the head had once been.

He sat for a second in a squatting position, strengthening his balance, aware that this part of the climb had taken all the force he could muster and knowing that the next part would take even more. Slowly he began to stand, maintaining his equilibrium, until the pedestal was just a yard or so beneath his grasp. He took a deep breath and leaped gracefully toward the target, just making it. His fingers dug in hard to keep him from slipping back down.

His timing, perfect in respect to the leap, had been off in another, for the helicopter was moving for another strike and was almost above him now. He held his breath, felt his heart exploding in his chest, and wondered whether someone in the chopper might see him. Its lights flashed overhead, blinding him. But it kept moving. Alabaster's feet dangled in the dusty air. If he pulled himself up now, he would betray his position and the copter's gun would shoot him dead. He had no choice but to stay just where he was until the flashing lights had totally passed his line of vision.

The pain in his hands which now supported his entire weight, though, was staggering. He had gripped the rock formation above him so hard with the initial grasp that now the tips of his fingers and his palms were bleeding. The pain didn't bother him but with pain often came numbness and with numbness came the loss of feeling which would strip him of his grip and send him plunging downward to the dirt floor below.

Alabaster heard the now familiar spray of bullets and knew the helicopter was over the entrance again. Wasting no time, he hoisted with all his strength and lifted his body slowly upward using only the muscles of his hands and then his forearms.

"Hurry, David! Hurry!"

Dalia Herzog's voice made him accelerate his motion just a bit. A moment later his stomach had cleared the plane of the hard stone surface. Another moment and he had reached the top, propped on his knees, and removed the grenade from his pocket.

Alabaster watched the bright red sparks fly in succession as the helicopter spit out another chain of bullets toward the men clutching the ground, near the entrance, for their lives. He wondered how many were left. Kaim was a good man. There would be some, enough. Alabaster then saw the progression of flying sparks cease. The chopper turned itself in midair and began to head toward him, almost right on with the pedestal. A bull charging for the matador in the center of the ring.

Fifty yards away . . .

He pressed his body further down against the cold gray stone. Concealment was necessary until the last possible second.

Thirty yards away and closing . . . The swirling monster was still moving head-on with him. It buckled, as though unsure of its motion, the pilot having caught sight of the man lying flat on the pedestal. The machine's front light sliced through the darkness, illuminating the path to its prey. The chopper clawed the air, a bull clawing dirt, and flew forward; its gun spewing pellets of death.

The angle of the fire, though, was wrong. And, as he clutched the grenade tighter, Alabaster thought he could see the figure of a man fighting to change the position of the 50-caliber machine gun in the copter's rear to aim it toward him. He was used to firing from a stable position, not a moving one. The alteration confused him. Each time he made a correction in the angle, another one was already necessary.

Nevertheless, Alabaster heard the bullets under the revised line of fire whisk by his ear, estimating that a few had missed him by not more than an inch. Chunks of rock spit up around him, covering his body with dust.

Then the whirling machine was coming straight over him, the angle of the 50-caliber off again, the pilot jockeying for position. It was time. Alabaster pulled the pin.

Eight seconds . . . seven . . . six . . .

He rose to a cramped squat, hurling the grenade up for the cockpit at the precise moment the chopper roared over him. The Israeli had practiced this toss from a thousand different angles over the years. The practice had paid off.

Four seconds . . . three . . .

The grenade landed between the two seats in the machine's forward section, wedging itself in tight. It was too late before the men inside realized what had happened.

Two seconds . . . one . . .

The helicopter exploded in a furious orange blast, spraying metallic embers everywhere in the moonlit sky. Its forward momentum carried it on through the air, the remains of its propeller tilted toward the earth and swooning down. The machine landed in a nest of thick trees just beyond the east flank of the Temple, fire sprouting up almost on contact. One final explosion sent the flames reaching higher for the black sky, smoke billowing into a gray umbrella over the scene.

Alabaster moved slowly off the pedestal and began his descent back to the ground, retracing the same path he had taken when climbing up.

"You did it, David! You did it!" Dalia applauded as he reached the floor.

Meanwhile, shots echoed through the long corridors of the Temple. Kaim's men were taking on the snipers. The firing was constant.

"I only bought us some time," Alabaster said. "But I didn't buy us our lives, not yet. How long has it been since I climbed to the pedestal?"

"Eight minutes or so."

"Then the terrorists who blew their way into the Temple will be upon us any second."

"With the chopper down, though, Kaim's troops will be able to help."

More shooting from the entrance area, showing no sign of letup.

"Only we don't know how many troops he has left," David reminded. "Chances are not very many and it will take those time to subdue the snipers."

"Then we'll fight the bastards ourselves." Dalia closed her fingers around the Garilla, an Israeli version of the M-16, that rested in her sure hands. "We can do it, David. We've done it before. It will be like old times."

Alabaster almost smiled. "Better." He lifted his Uzi from the base of the pedestal.

In the darkness twenty yards to his left, Alabaster heard the thrashing of feet over stone. There were anywhere between twelve and fifteen men, he guessed, moving methodically. He turned toward Dalia. Their eyes met. He nodded; she smiled.

They stood within the stone structure, their bodies squeezed between the statue and columns on either side of it. Alabaster could now hear enemy troops approaching to his right as well, lagging a bit behind the ones on the other side but similar in number, making somewhere around twenty-five in all. There was little time left and Kaim's men were still engaged in battle at the front of the Temple, though the firing had declined markedly.

"Now!" Alabaster screamed.

As though by rehearsal, he and Dalia spun away from the stone pillars simultaneously, he to the right and she to the left. Their guns began to crackle and pop, sending a steady stream of bullets toward the killers who were now only fifteen or twenty feet away. The move took the terrorists by surprise, the front line on both sides falling immediately under the assault. The rest, around seventeen, dived for cover and returned the fire accordingly.

Alabaster felt the heat of the Uzi blaze in his hands, its barrel seeming to melt under the strain. He paused for a second, bending down behind cover and shifting his position to allow a better shot at some of the concealed enemies to his right. They were in the Uzi's sights, their eyes finding its holder too late to return the fire that poured into them and rocketed their bodies backwards.

Dalia, meanwhile, had ducked behind one of the columns and slumped downward, baiting a trap, knowing that enough of the terrorists on her side would use the opportunity to try and better their positions and close the gap further. As they did, however, Dalia rolled from her hiding place, stomach on the hard ground, the Garilla blasting promised death forward at the now panicked shapes searching futilely for cover. She pulled the trigger and held it. The power of the gun tore their bodies from the ground, hurling them into the air before dumping them down.

She had begun to rise, searching for the pillar again, when something hot ripped into her right shoulder. She felt the fiery slivers of pain jabbing into her and knew by the warm blood that had already reached her elbow that she had been wounded badly. But to comfort the damaged area or to even look at it was to create a moment of hesitation in which she would surely be killed. She couldn't give up. The Garilla continued to spit red at the end of its barrel. The terrorists returned it, sending chips of the stone column spurting everywhere as Dalia sprung behind it.

At this time Alabaster, sensing indecision on the part of the terrorists before him, ran forward within their line of fire, diving to the ground and rolling toward them. The men, unnerved by the sudden offensive, fired randomly, their shots going well wide of the mark. Their fingers did not stay on the triggers long, though, because Alabaster took three of them out with a quick spurt and forced another five onto a desperate defensive from which only wild shots emerged.

But one of the stray bullets found its way into the side of Dalia Herzog's thigh. The pain and shock of the entry forced her leg to buckle and her balance to waver. At almost this same moment, her Garilla exhausted its bullets and she tossed it aside, knowing there was no time to reload. She was drawing her pistol when her wounded leg gave out and she felt herself tumble to the ground.

Before she met the dusty surface, her eyes met those of an Arab woman, approximately her own size and age. Their stares locked for an eternal second. Then Dalia caught a fleeting glimpse of steel flashing before her and saw the eruption of red at the end of the barrel before the machine gun's bullets tore into her midsection. The quick spurt of fire stood her up for a second before she collapsed forward, clutching her stomach with scarlet-soaked hands. A scream began but was muted by the blood that filled her mouth and throat so that only the beginning of a word emerged before there was a sudden spasm and then nothing.

"Dav—"

Alabaster heard the scream and turned to his rear. The sight of Dalia's body slumped against a column charged him with a hate and anger he had not felt in years and had wondered if he would ever feel again. A bullet sped forward and grazed his head. Whatever sensation this caused, however, was overcome by the wrath that raged within him, a wrath born in helplessness and reared in despair. His eyes furious, Alabaster fired four rounds at the female terrorist standing near Dalia's body, diving forward as his finger met the trigger. The bullets splattered the woman's brains on the stone behind her. The Israeli then spun back to his right, preparing for a last, desperate act of vengeance.

Because he was going to die, the great Alabaster was finally unable to meet the challenge presented by his enemies. He knew that much and accepted it. But he also knew that he was going to take plenty of them with him. He began to fire the few remaining bullets in his Uzi randomly in all directions, his bearings lost and control gone.

At the moment the now confident Arabs began to close for the kill, though, other shots cut off their approach. Captain Daniel Kaim and the remainder of his troops roared into the scene, their eyes blazing almost as much as the barrels of their guns. They cut down the terrorists just as they stood. Those Arabs who turned and tried to run were shot in the back without any twinge of compunction. The Israeli soldiers had seen too much to concern themselves with anything so insignificant as conscience or compassion. This was their revenge and they exercised it to the fullest. Holding their triggers until the clips were exhausted. Firing at enemies long past dead.

Alabaster stood almost in the center of the fray that had raged around him, dazed by the suddenness of the action and by the graze near his temple. Daniel Kaim stood by his side.

"David, are you all right? I think we better get you to a

doctor." His eyes swept the area around him. "And we'd better move fast."

But the words never reached Alabaster's consciousness. He rushed over to the column where Dalia Herzog lay slumped, the flow of blood from the gaping holes in what had once been her stomach finally stopped. Her large eyes were open and motionless, seeming to stare down at the legs contained beneath the red-soaked khaki uniform.

Alabaster closed the eyes and embraced her, drawing Dalia's body toward his until he could feel the cooling blood that had given her life spill onto him.

"Oh God," he muttered softly, near tears.

Daniel Kaim knelt down and separated him from the corpse. "We've got to get out of here. People will be coming. There'll be questions we can't answer. They will be looking for someone to pin the blame on. We can't let it be us."

Alabaster rose cautiously to his feet, dimly aware that his head felt like it was rupturing from the inside. Within him, a strength greater than any he had ever felt surged and grew, thirsting to burst out. He could taste Dalia's blood on his lips and smell its acrid aroma on his body. It charged him more, sending a flurry of thoughts rampaging through his mind that somehow jelled into a coherent pattern: Before Rabanine had been substance and Alabaster merely shadow. But now things had become twisted and turned. Shadow was substance and substance was shadow. The two men had become one, that one's purpose clearly defined and firmly rooted. The reality of the resolve was strengthened all the more by the necessity of it.

The animals of Al Fatah had killed and killed and killed again.

And now Alabaster would kill and kill and kill again, as many times as he had to, until the day when the animals would walk the earth no longer.

It was the only way.

TWENTY-FIVE

Daniel Kaim drove David to Cairo where he checked into the Carlton Hotel under the false name on his passport. Little conversation had been exchanged on the trip, there being little to say. Of the thirty Israeli soldiers, only eighteen had lived through the battle at the Temple. The ability of these survivors to remain calm in the face of almost certain death is what had allowed Rabanine to escape with his life.

His battle would continue.

"I want to go on with you, David," Kaim had said before the two men parted. "I owe these bastards something."

"You are needed more in Israel."

"That is not much consolation."

"It's the best I can offer. Your troops behaved admirably last night because they were well led. Although they have been scattered along the Nile, your leadership helped them respond like a fighting unit with many years together in the field."

"Twelve of them are dead."

"And eighteen are alive. It's not a bad ratio, all things considered."

Kaim stared deeply into David's eyes. "You can be a very cold man."

"It's a tool. I use it like any other."

"How is the wound in your head?"

"As the doctor you provided said, it's only a scratch. Another inch and I'd have come to Cairo in a box," Rabanine reflected, rubbing his fingers over the small bandage near his temple. "You've heard nothing from the Luxor police?"

"No, and ironically the terrorists actually helped us in that respect by raiding the police station and neutralizing all men and equipment before launching their attack on the Temple. It would have been very embarrassing for Israeli troops, placed clandestinely in Egypt, to be saddled with the blame for the destruction of an ancient relic."

"I see your point."

Kaim checked his watch. "I must be going. I want to be with my troops. We'll all be leaving Egypt within thirty-six hours. Do me one favor, though."

"Anything."

"Kill the bastards, David, *all of them!*"

"Dalia . . . *dead?* Oh God . . ."

On the other end of the transatlantic line, Rabanine felt the shock in Stanislaw Kowalski's voice.

"You'll tell the others, Stanis, all right?"

"What? . . . Oh, yes . . . yes. I'll tell them. I just can't believe it. We hadn't seen each other for so long. But the past week brought it all back to me. All of us had been so close before that we never really parted. But now Dalia is dead. . . . I just can't believe it," Stanislaw said softly, stroking his black eye patch as he always did when nervous. "Something was gained from all of this at least, I hope."

"Not enough to justify her death."

"Of that, I am certain. But *something*, at least."

"We only know another thing that Shaitan isn't. The Squid told me that the Commandment is a plan to sabotage a series of nuclear power plants in heavily populated areas all across America, sending radioactive gases into the air and contaminating untold millions."

"The Squid lied?"

"He was used as a clever decoy to draw our attention away from the truth."

"How can you be sure?"

"I'll tell you later. First, I'd like to know if there's anything new on your end."

Kowalski sighed. "Nothing much, I'm afraid. Chevallier has

learned that the travel people al-Kahir usually employs have all strangely disappeared and Isser is having no luck in trying to determine who the 175 agents are. There are just too many possibilities. More than a quarter of a million people will be flying into the United States during the few days in question. We just don't have enough time to check them all,"

"Has anything turned up at the FBI that might tie in with the experiment?"

"Since we have no idea what to look for, it may have. But we haven't seen it."

"And *der Teufels Befehl?*"

"No one Jacques has contacted has any information on it at all. Isser is waiting now for a return call from Wiesenthal; I believe he is our last hope. I'm beginning to think that the Nazis never heard of the phrase themselves."

"They've heard of it, you can rest assured of that."

A pause.

"David, you must tell me why you so quickly dismiss the possibility that what the Squid said about the nuclear power plants was true."

"He was obviously a plant, sent to tell me things meant only to confuse matters further."

"That doesn't mean his words would have all been lies, especially considering that the terrorists never expected you to live to report any of it. It sounds to me like a logical, if not brilliant, plan."

"There's a problem."

"What?"

"The Squid said Al Fatah had detailed designs of the plants in question in their possession and that obtaining these plans nearly ten years ago had been the impetus for Shaitan in the first place."

"So?"

"Four of the seven he mentioned had not even been conceived ten years ago."

*   *   *

Herb Weinberg shifted his position in the chair, seeking comfort but finding none. The pile of papers that cluttered the desk before him was so massive that no matter how long he worked at reducing it, the pile seemed to retain all of its original size. In fact, thanks to the efforts of his overly efficient secretary who had delivered additional material as it arrived in his office, the pile had actually grown. He had worked the last forty-eight hours straight probing through the reports forwarded to him by subordinates in search of one that would send the proper chill up his spine.

Weinberg had lost count of the number of cups of black coffee he had downed, his tongue numb from being burned too often. But he did know that when this was over he would never drink another cup again. Besides, he felt lousy. His wife was back in the hospital probably never to come out again. He knew he should be by her bedside, even though there was nothing he could do. Instead he was here and there was still nothing he could do.

Weinberg took a deep breath and reached for a telegram that had emerged on top of the stack. Somewhere in this mess, he thought dryly, was a tie and yesterday's underwear. He'd give himself ten more minutes and then take a shower. Maybe five.

The telegram contained an urgent request from a small town sheriff in Crescent Falls, Wyoming for information on five men. Whatever subordinate had forwarded the telegram was right; this was certainly out of the realm of the ordinary. But did it pertain to the security of the nation? That was something else again.

Weinberg took one more look at the cable and then tossed it into his discard file which was nothing more than an overstuffed wastebasket.

He'd take that shower now.

"Isser," Rabanine said into the pay phone, covering his free ear to shut out the noise around him. "It's David. I'm calling from Paris. I have a two hour layover here. Can you hear me all right?"

"Yes and I have news, good news."

"What did you say, Isser?" David pressed the receiver closer against his ear so that the plastic seemed an extension of his flesh.

"I said I have *good news.*"

"I could use some."

"Wiesenthal came through. He has traced that phrase of yours—*der Teufels Befehl,* the Devil's Command."

David dug his fingers into the receiver. "What does it mean?"

"To begin with, it took Simon hours to track it down because the phrase was even more obscure than any of us had thought. It was cross-filed under the name of an old blind Jew living right here in Georgetown, a survivor of Auschwitz."

"But what does it *mean?*" Rabanine asked exasperatingly.

"The man's card does not explain the meaning of the phrase. The card only lists the Nazi who originated and was responsible for it."

"Who, Isser? Who?"

"The Angel of Death, David . . . Josef Mengele."

PART FOUR

TWENTY-SIX

Sunday evening at nine o'clock, David rang the bell on the right side of a two-family brownstone at the corner of 38th and Dudley streets in Georgetown. The small exclusive suburb is usually reserved for politicians and dignitaries living within the hub of Washington life. This section, though, is populated mostly by college students and, to a far lesser degree, by old people.

Rabanine had spent the entire plane ride back to America thinking of Dr. Josef Mengele. His exploits in the Auschwitz concentration camp were engrained in the mind of every Jew who grew up in the years following the Holocaust. David remembered virtually nothing about this period, save for the frantic days when his father successfully engineered his family's escape to London.

But he did know about the hideous medical experiments the Angel of Death had performed in quest of Hitler's master race. Twins were his most recurrent fetish, Jewish and otherwise. What accounted for slight differences in their structural makeup? Mengele had killed thousands trying to answer that question through crude genetic research.

And now Rabanine was about to meet with a man named Hyman Wasserman in an attempt to answer another: What did the Angel of Death have to do with the Shaitan Commandment?

In David's early years with the Mossad, several teams of agents had been sent into the steaming jungles of Paraguay in search of the man who had also supervised the selections for the gas chambers. The idea was never to set up an Eichmann-like kidnapping of Mengele; the idea was simply to execute him. But he proved to be too well-guarded. Although one team was able to penetrate his security, none of its members were ever heard from again. Such was the way of the Angel of Death.

The man who responded to the doorbell, meanwhile, was nothing like David had expected. He had led himself to believe that Hyman Wasserman would be a decrepit, battered old man. Yes, Wasserman was old but there was nothing decrepit or battered about him.

"Mr. Wasserman, I'm David Rabanine from the Israeli embassy. I believe you're expecting me."

"Yes, Mr. Rabanine, please come in." The blind man beckoned him in with an outstretched open palm. Wasserman was a tall, thin man who stood proud and erect in the doorway. His hair was silvery white, neatly combed and showing no signs of baldness. The old man's face was creased with wrinkles and small scars but the features remained alert. David guessed the eyes would have been too had they not been covered by dark glasses.

"This way, please," Wasserman instructed.

Rabanine walked slowly behind the blind man who held a cane before him, though he didn't seem to need it in the familiar surroundings. The two men entered a living room, Wasserman leading David to a couch. Rabanine sat down. The blind man stood over him.

"It's good to have company once in a while," Wasserman said. "I have so few guests these days. That is why I live in the middle of so many young people who go to the University. It makes me feel more alive. My friends are all . . . Ah, you don't want to hear about my problems and I haven't even shaken your hand yet." Wasserman extended a surly arm. David took the hand, finding the old man's grip surprisingly firm. "I sense that I surprise you."

"I had expected someone different."

"Someone ruined by the years instead of merely beaten by them?"

"Something like that."

Wasserman felt his way backwards, seating himself in a worn-out easy chair. "I feel something else from you as well," he said. The cane rested gingerly in his right hand.

"What's that?"

"It's in your grip. You are a man of tremendous strength and power. The touch of your hand, though, also tells me you're a very gentle man with many calluses to show for years harder than he would like me to know. . . . The hand I shook was not the hand of a diplomat."

David arched his eyebrows. "A feeble lie. I apologize for it, Mr. Wasserman."

"Call me Hyman and don't worry. I'm sure you didn't announce your true profession for fear that it would frighten me. But you are an Israeli, I can tell that from your voice. Do you work for Wiesenthal?"

"What makes you ask?"

"Why else would a man as strong as you travel across the world to speak with a dying man, if not to question to him one more time about the Nazis—one Nazi in particular?"

"You're only half right, Mr. Wasserman. I *am* here to inquire about a certain Nazi but I don't work for Wiesenthal."

"Who then?"

"The Mossad," David replied, not wishing to be more specific.

The old man's face brightened. "I am honored by your presence. I've heard much about your organization, about what it has done to safeguard the interests of our country. Someday I would travel to Israel but money is, well . . ." Wasserman sighed. "So your visit concerns a certain Nazi I have firsthand knowledge of?"

"It concerns Josef Mengele," David told him. Wasserman cringed at mention of the name. "I didn't mean to startle you," David apologized.

Wasserman waved him off. "It doesn't matter. The years don't erase the pain, they only make it a bit more tolerable. Only death can end the memories and now my death is

261

approaching. I have told the story many times. I can tell it once more. Yes, I knew the Angel of Death, better than any Jew still alive today. You've heard of Mengele's attempts to turn brown-eyed Jews into blue-eyed Aryans?"

"Of course. He sent untold thousands of children to their deaths that way. Twins, I think."

"Not just children, David, and not just twins. I was just over thirty at the time. They chose me because I was the strongest new arrival in the camp. Does that surprise you, looking at me now, to think that I was once young and powerful and fit?"

"Not in the least."

"It is strange, is it not?" the old man resumed after a barely perceptible pause, "that I don't know whether to take issue with you because I have not seen myself in nearly forty-two years and thus have no idea what I look like now and have forgotten what I used to look like anyway."

"You looked strong then. . . . You look strong now."

The old man smiled faintly, gripped his cane about the handle, and began tapping it lightly on the hard wood floor in rhythm with his words. "You make me feel good, David. But, achh, I am babbling again. To get back to the subject at hand, I was escorted to Mengele's private laboratory where he examined me very closely everywhere. He seemed pleased, as though I was what he had been searching for. All I needed, he told me, was blond hair and blue eyes and I could pass as an Aryan. All his experiments had failed with children. He wanted to try them on adults. I was one of those he selected—the chosen. *Der Ausgewählter,* he called me." Wasserman paused and leaned back in his chair, still tapping the cane. "It was a simple matter, the doctor explained, of altering the genetic structure. A few injections, that was all. I remember a long needle coming toward my left eye. The pain was unreal when it entered, forcing me to pass out because, of course, I hadn't been given any anesthesia. While I was unconscious, he gave me another shot in my right eye."

tap . . . tap . . . tap . . .

"But you survived." Rabanine had to force the words out.

tap . . . tap . . . tap . . .

"The camp population felt sorry for me, even the Germans. I was branded with the mark of one of Mengele's misfits and treated almost like a leper. The guards avoided me. My fellow prisoners tossed me scraps of food. Yes, I survived. . . . The good doctor, the Angel of Death, kept me out of the ovens. He seemed convinced that the transformation of my features would begin eventually. I was *der Ausgewählter*, after all. Mengele gave me more shots, an average of one every two or three weeks. The pain alone would have killed me had it not been for . . ."

"For what?"

"Not what, who: Dr. Walter Schmidt, one of Mengele's assistants. The other, a doctor named Johann Gessler, was as cruel as Mengele himself, maybe even crueler. But Schmidt sympathized with the condemned of Auschwitz. For reasons he never explained, he stole us extra food and when I began to return regularly for injections he gave me a local anesthetic, each time at the risk of his own life. Oh, there was still pain, a great deal in fact. But thanks to Schmidt, I survived. Five times I came down with infections—twice with staph and three times with dysentery. And each time Schmidt treated me late at night with antibiotics meant for the Germans. I've often wondered why. . . . But you haven't come here to hear about me. It's your turn to speak."

tap . . . tap . . . tap . . .

Rabanine breathed deeply. "It's difficult to explain. The obsession for world domination didn't die with the Nazis. It still burns in the hearts of enough madmen to threaten all our lives. One of these madmen has resurrected a scheme born in Nazi Germany to destroy America, thereby crippling the entire world and paving the way for global revolution."

"This man is a member of Al Fatah?"

"He is the leader."

"And what link does his plan have with the Angel of Death?"

"The operation has been named the Shaitan Commandment. In Nazi Germany I believe Mengele gave birth to a similar, if not identical, plan known as *der Teufels Befehl*—the Devil's Command."

The old man's face whitened until it almost matched the color of his hair. The tapping of his cane ceased for a stretched out moment before beginning again. But something had changed. The precise rhythm was gone, the movements out of sync.

"It can't be . . . It can't be . . ." The words barely emerging from Wasserman's mouth.

"Then you've heard the phrase before."

tap, tap . . . tap . . .

"Many times, David, more than I care to remember." The smooth flow of Wasserman's thoughts was gone. Mention of the phrase had struck a dormant chord in him that stripped his features of their vitality. He looked suddenly much older and broken, like the man David had expected to see when he rang the doorbell. "I hope you are wrong in your theory, David. For the sake of all that is holy, I hope you are wrong."

"Why?"

"Because the Devil's Command was the talk of Auschwitz for the last few months before the liberators stormed over the hills. For awhile, none of us believed it. We merely assumed it was just another of the mad Angel of Death's rantings. It had to be . . ."

"But what was it?"

"It was hell, David, a living hell for everyone in the world not of the Aryan race. How is your knowledge of European history?"

"Good enough, I suppose."

"Then surely you are familiar with the effects of the Black Death . . ."

Five hours before, the residents of Crescent Falls had gathered in the town hall for a special Sunday meeting. The auditorium was built to hold only 110 people comfortably, so the 130 now present had to squeeze themselves in. A few moved to the back for refuge but found this no better than the front. It was hot and hard to breathe. Around eighty outside, a shade over ninety in.

"Ladies and gentlemen," Mayor Layton began into the microphone, although the system hadn't worked for over a year, "if you could all quiet down a bit, I'll get this meeting over with as soon as I can." The voice level lowered to a murmer and then extinguished completely. "Now, I'm not sure how many of you have had the opportunity to meet our five friends from the oil industry." Here, Layton turned his outstretched hand in the direction of the five men seated with him on the stage. "For those of you who haven't," he resumed, "at this time I'd like to introduce you to Lou Marshall, the team's leader."

More muttering, gradually replaced by sporadic applause as Marshall stepped up to the podium and addressed the crowd.

"First, I want to thank you all for being so hospitable. You've really made the five of us feel at home and we appreciate that very much." More applause, less sporadic. "I'm not much of a speaker, so I'll come right to the point. Crescent Falls is sitting on a river of oil that promises to make a good number of you folks very rich."

There was a moment of total, exasperated silence that gave way to shouting, stamping, and clapping. On the podium, Marshall smiled, waiting for it to die down on its own before he continued.

"I don't want to get your hopes up falsely, because it's going to take awhile. But it is going to happen. You can rest assured of that."

Thunderous applause shook the room, followed by a standing ovation for the speaker. Humbly, Marshall waved to the crowd and sat back down with his four fellows, turning the podium back over to Mayor Layton who saw in Marshall another man with political aspirations. Needless to say, the mayor was worried.

"It's hot and we all want to celebrate," Layton said. "So if you'll leave here and go across the street to the Bar & Grill, you will find refreshments courtesy of our own councilman Norm Shacklehorse. It'll give you all a chance to meet the five men who are going to make our town rich."

The five men seated behind the mayor smiled to themselves and then to each other. That morning, each had taken a needle out of a small black case and injected a colorless fluid into their bloodstreams. Each man possessed a vial full of the serum but had been instructed to take only ten CCs for the final dosage. They were then supposed to stay in the town for another ten days, at least, to chart the results.

Thanks to Bugsy Tyler, though, they didn't have ten days. The sheriff was onto them and Marshall knew it. Tyler didn't know everything but he knew enough to make the next ten days very unpleasant indeed. So Marshall and his men had decided to change the rules of the game a bit. Instead of 10 CCs, each had taken 15. For them the difference would be miniscule, although it would probably speed things up a bit in Crescent Falls meaning they could get out of the town earlier with Tyler silenced forever.

Marshall thought about calling the phone number he had and relating the problem. But he was afraid that his team would be recalled and another test set up. He didn't want that. Too many years had been spent waiting for this day. So he had made the decision on his own, fully confident it was the correct strategy for the time.

Everything was going as planned. The reception would provide the five strangers with an ideal setting to begin spreading the infection they now carried on their breaths. Accordingly, as Lou Marshall moved down the center aisle of the auditorium and pumped more hands than he had ever seen before, he didn't bother to keep his smile down.

Because the town of Crescent Falls was not going to get rich. It was going to die.

Finally Marshall saw Bugsy Tyler a few steps ahead of him. The Sheriff had been standing menacingly in the rear of the hall the whole time, leaning his monster frame against the door and conspicuously failing to applaud when the rest of those present had. As the leader of the five men approached the sheriff now, he saw that Tyler's huge mouth had cracked into a half smile. Bugsy took two steps to the right and blocked Marshall's path, shooting a wad of tobacco juice onto the floor.

"It won't be long now," he said.

"No," Marshall agreed. "It won't."

The mention of the phrase "Black Death" had made Rabanine shudder.

"Surely the Devil's Command has nothing to do with the plague," he said, fearing the answer.

tap . . . tap . . . tap . . .

"No," the old man responded. "It was nothing so crass, nothing so simple. I was in the lab one day when Mengele was speaking of it to one of his assistants. Hitler had ordered the doctor to come up with a means to destroy any country from the inside that opposed the Fatherland once the war was won. The Führer wanted more than the H-bomb, you see. He didn't trust rockets or missiles. He wanted the ultimate weapon that no country could formulate a defense against. He wanted a weapon that would enable a small force of men to wield the power of a vast army that could render any nation that opposed the Nazi empire or its ideals helpless. No, more than helpless—dead."

"Through a disease?"

"Of sorts."

"I don't understand."

tap . . . tap . . . tap . . .

"Mengele did, David. Did you really think that all his experiments with genetics went for nothing? They didn't, I can assure you of that. The Angel of Death searched for the means to create a disease that would work on the genetics of the body, its DNA—the very life force that keeps us going. I'm not a doctor, David, so my understanding is that of a layman. I know only that Mengele was trying to find an organism capable of

267

wiping out at least half a civilization in a phenomenally short period of time."

"And did he succeed?"

The old man shook his head. His lips quivered. "The reports that liberation was coming soon forced him to flee the camp before his experiments got very far underway. He escaped, leaving himself to worry about saving his own life instead of taking millions of others. To my knowledge, the organism was never created at Auschwitz. I cannot speak for what has happened since. Tell me, though, do you think Mengele is now working with the Arabs?"

tap . . . tap . . . tap . . .

"No. Our information leads us to believe that Al Fatah has merely picked up where the Angel of Death left off." A thought struck David. "But what about his assistants?"

"Schmidt was shot during liberation of the camp while trying to help us. Gessler escaped some days before, to where I don't know."

"Would he have known enough to complete Mengele's work?"

"He'd be the only man left alive who would."

"Then I have to find him." David rose slowly.

"You're going now," Wasserman said, following David's lead. "Perhaps you'll come and see me another day."

David fumbled for words. "I wish there was something I could do in the meantime, some way I could thank you."

"There's no need. I have all I require. This house was purchased for me by a fund established for concentration camp survivors. I have a small pension. My dreams might never come true but I still have the dreams."

"And the nightmares. . . . I know how painful it is for you to remember; I know how you must feel."

The old man shook his head. "No, David, you don't. And God help us all if you ever do."

Rabanine knew something was wrong as soon as he reached

the Cougar parked across the street from Wasserman's brownstone. In deliberate fashion he scanned the area but found nothing. The street was empty in darkness.

David moved to the front of the Cougar and checked the two pieces of scotch tape he had placed on the hood before leaving his hotel, one of which was affixed to the catch underneath. Both were present, as was the one strung across his door. No one had tampered with the car. But he wasn't relieved. He sensed the presence of someone behind him. His hand felt instinctively for the Beretta holstered near his armpit. His other hand jammed the key into the door and began to turn. He was baiting a trap.

"I wouldn't do that if I were you," came a voice from behind in German dominated English. "The Arabs booby-trapped your automobile while you were inside. Please, *Herr* Rabanine, I beg you to believe me for both our sakes. And you don't need your gun. I mean you no harm."

Before the voice had finished its words, David had spun to the rear, drawing the Beretta and readying to fire. A man who might have been a twin of Cerberus, except he was smaller and less broad, stood before him with his arms raised straight in the air.

"As I said, *Herr* Rabanine, I mean you no harm."

David studied the German's calm features and relaxed his trigger finger. "How do you know the Arabs booby-trapped my car?"

"Because I have been watching you and, accordingly, them all day."

"You're lucky neither of us killed you."

"A corpse would have been unable to deliver the message I have for you."

"Message?"

"*Ja.*" The speaker stepped forward, lowering his arms slowly. "Dr. Walter Schmidt requests the pleasure of your company . . ."

TWENTY-SEVEN

"A meeting with a dead man?"

"Apparently, Colonel Rossi, Dr. Walter Schmidt is alive and well and living in Switzerland."

"Or so said that mystery man in Georgetown. Our files state conclusively that Schmidt died just as Wasserman told you he did."

David rose from his chair. "You know better than I how many Nazis faked their own deaths to make establishing new lives easier and that mystery man in Georgetown saved me from that poisonous gas cannister under my car."

Rossi rocked himself forward in the wheelchair and then back again. "What happens after you reach Geneva?"

"I'm to be met at the airport."

"That's all?"

"That's all I was told. Schmidt must be taking an awful chance by meeting with me. I assume he wants to keep my presence as secret as possible."

"Assumptions, David, get men killed."

"Not as quickly as the Shaitan disease will unless we do something."

"So you're going to throw yourself into the hands of a Nazi in a country where we have practically no influence at all. . . ."

"A *former* Nazi and I don't see another alternative. Colonel Rossi, somehow these 175 Al Fatah agents about to enter America are the carriers of a disease at least as deadly as the bubonic plague. How, though, can a person be a carrier of a deadly disease and not die of it himself? An organism like this isn't something you can turn on and off. Yet somehow Al Fatah has come up with a way of spreading the disease in one country

270

without infecting others."

"A means of isolating it inside our borders?"

"It would seem so."

Rossi gave a beaten sigh. "There must be something I can do at this end while you're gone."

"There is. We've known for some time that an experiment was underway to gauge the effectiveness of the Commandment. But we weren't sure what this test entailed. It's safe now to assume that a city or town somewhere in this nation is being used as a guinea pig. Somewhere an entire community has been infected by the organism which means that in a matter of weeks a minimum of half this community will be dead with the effects beginning to show up considerably before that." David paused. "We've got to find that community. Remember, Colonel, at the very worst a good portion of the town will still be alive. If our scientists can find out what allowed the body mechanisms of the survivors to fight off the infection, we'll be on our way to finding an antidote or a vaccine."

Rossi looked up and then down again. "I'd better bring the Center for Disease Control in on this. Anything else?"

"Two things, the first a matter of minor inconvenience. I would like you to have $100,000 placed in a savings account under the name of Hyman Wasserman and the passbook delivered to his home no later than tomorrow."

"That's a lot of money."

"Call it my fee for this assignment and file it under . . . miscellaneous expenses."

"Touché. And the second thing?"

David took a deep breath. "A bit more serious, I'm afraid. The terrorists have known my every move since the time I first arrived in Washington. They've always been one step ahead of me right up to the gas cannister under my car tonight."

The Director felt something heavy move in his stomach. "I don't like what you're implying."

"Neither do I, but we've got to face the facts. Somewhere

271

along the line there's been a leak."

Monday morning at eleven o'clock, the man who called himself Lou Marshall woke up congested and nauseous. During the preparations, he and the others had been warned to expect to feel some of the symptoms of the sickness once the final dosage had been administered. But Marshall had been given no reason to expect them to be so severe as they were now. He rose from the bed and moved toward the window, opening the blinds in his boarding-house room and looking out over a sunny day in Crescent Falls, Wyoming.

Something was wrong.

Marshall saw nothing, heard nothing, because there was no one around. None of the businesses on Main Street had opened. The flag in front of the school had not been raised. Marshall knew Crescent Falls well enough to realize that this was always a busy time of day for the town folk who were early risers and usually hit their daily stride around this hour. Certainly the outcome of the infection could not have struck so suddenly, so totally. It was impossible, as though everyone in Crescent Falls had just forgotten to wake up and get the week started. It couldn't be.

Or could it . . . ?

Marshall sneezed loudly. Again. And again. Without warning, a spasm overtook him and loud eruptions in his chest kept coming and coming, making it impossible for him to catch his breath. Finally the spasms stopped, leaving him face down on the end of the unmade bed, his face flushed and his head on fire.

There was a tremendous pressure in his throat, as if the walls of skin were closing in on the passage, making it gradually harder for him to breathe or swallow. He rose, massaging the glands under his chin that had blown up like balloons. He began to feel dizzy. The room spun crazily around him.

This wasn't supposed to happen. . . .

The plan had called for the five men to begin sending their reports of the infection's effects today. He was to make contact as soon as possible. Nothing in the plan, though, said he was supposed to feel the symptoms so strongly himself. Had they tricked him?

He fought a stumbling way into the bathroom and splashed his face with water. Then, as he stood leaning over the sink, he felt vomit rise in his throat and pour onto the white porcelain beneath him. The violence of the contraction forced his eyes to close and, for a second, he felt better; the effects seeming to have passed.

But then he looked down.

Blood was moving down the sides of the sink in a steady flow—*his* blood, blood he had just spit up in his vomit. He screamed at the top of his lungs, aware now that no one could hear him, feeling more blood-soaked vomit rising in his throat. This time he fought it down and ran from the room, colliding with the door and wall outside it. The world appeared to be standing on edge.

Marshall followed the path of the wall he had fallen against down the corridor until he reached the first room occupied by one of his four fellows.

"Help, John! . . . Help!" But his cries were no more audible than his soft, desperate poundings on the door.

His hand finally located the knob and he turned it, falling into the room, his body an inferno. A pungent smell penetrated the congestion of his nostrils. It was everywhere, a putrid stench like nothing he had ever smelled before. Then he saw the man named John lying faceup in bed, his eyes open and bulging, his body and the sheets around it layered with blood-soaked vomit. He had died in his sleep, a few convulsions probably having woken him for just a second before the end came.

Marshall fought his way back into the corridor. It was clear now; something *had* gone wrong. Those sent to infect the town had become infected themselves. The years had not been

273

enough, the fifty shots insufficient. And the town itself seemed . . . dead.

It couldn't be!

Marshall's final rational thought was to reach a phone and call the number he had been given. There was still a chance in his tortured mind that he could live, that the disease would spare him as it had no one else. There was a pay phone near the staircase. He began to crawl toward it, his body shaking volcanically, his eyes closed to block out the dizziness.

A few feet further, however, and Marshall's forward motion was stopped by a wave of rumbling in his stomach. His body began to heave and twitch, forcing him to rise involuntarily from the floor, his eyeballs exploding from their sockets. The last sensation he had was a massive eruption in his chest. He felt the vomit flowing up his throat without end and saw the first wave pour freely in a stream from his mouth.

His eyeballs then locked as they were, seeing only darkness. Marshall collapsed downward, the thing that had been his body writhing spasmatically in the throes of death before it passed into a wretched, black abyss.

And then there was nothing.

Leslie Kirkman watched as David stood sullenly by the window of his hotel room. She sat on a chair in silence, hoping some words would force their way forward and that she would know how to say them. She had realized that she loved this enigma of a man who seemed incapable of returning that love. He was a mass of confused complexities and tightly strung wire, his conflicting emotions like electrical impulses always on the verge of short-circuiting.

"Did you love her, David?" she asked suddenly, at once wishing she hadn't.

"Who?" he shot back, as though angered over being lifted from his trance.

"The woman I heard was killed in Luxor."

"What does it matter?" he asked harshly, his eyes cold.

274

"Because if you did, it would explain why you are acting like you are."

"It explains nothing. I am acting the way I am because of what I am. It has nothing to do with anything so trite as being hurt. I feel nothing. Not anymore."

"I don't believe that."

"I don't give a damn what you believe." David moved away from the window and faced Leslie, unsure of the feelings that raged within him. "I didn't invite you down here, nor did I ask for your counselling. Who are you to tell me what I feel and don't feel?"

"Someone who has been through what you have."

"How can you say that? Do you know how much death I've seen in my life? How many do you think died in the Temple battle alone? Come on, how many do you think?"

Leslie remained silent.

"I'll answer the question myself. Say around forty; it's a nice round number, though it could have been a few more or a few less. But what do a few lives matter anyway? It doesn't bother me anymore because what happened in Luxor made me see clearly that I *am* death, walking death."

"Don't talk like that!" Leslie pleaded.

"Like what? Does the man I really am frighten you? Terrify you? Do you want me to slip a mask over my head and become someone else for your benefit?"

"Before you left for Egypt, you were someone else." She moved uneasily closer to him. "Don't you see, David. You can't live with killing no matter how much you'd like to. So you've created Alabaster to live with it for you. That way you can keep on being the man you really are at least most of the time. It's always *his* finger on the trigger, not yours."

"Either way, the murderers of Al Fatah die and they will continue to die."

"And what will that accomplish? Others will merely take their place, pick up right where they leave off."

"Then those will be killed as well."

"Perhaps you are no better than they are."

"I never claimed I was but that changes nothing. We are a people surrounded on all sides by enemies while possessing extraordinarily few friends. We fight for our lives, our survival, because we cherish those lives and that survival *as a people* more than anything else. I don't think you can relate to that. I don't think you truly understand the complexities of the problems we face. Someone you loved was taken from you three years ago. One person, one tragedy. We have known thousands, millions, and will certainly know more."

"What makes you think one death is any easier to cope with than one hundred, one thousand, or one million?"

"Why don't you ask the survivors of the death camps?"

"I'm not so sure their answer would be the same as yours. . . . You'd rather have me be like you I suppose: Denouncing the value of life to make death easier to handle and accept. You run and hide behind the shadow of Alabaster, a robot you've created to justify the path Rabanine has chosen. But that path doesn't go anywhere, David. You're only running from yourself."

"And after those who murder children . . . or doesn't that count in your book of morals?"

Leslie closed her eyes briefly. "Sometimes you and the way you talk revolts me as much as that does."

David's expression became totally blank. "You think you know everything, but there's still one small thing you're not aware of—not that it matters. Because of the way the Arabs disposed of my wife's body eleven years ago, I didn't find out she had been murdered until the fake bomb was discovered in my son's crib. The explosives were real enough; they just weren't wired to a firing device. Do you know what the fuse holding them together was made of?"

"How could I?"

"Yes, how could you? . . . It was made up of strands of my wife's hair. They had scalped her, Leslie, and she was still alive when they did it. . . . Does that revolt you as much as I do?"

*　　*　　*

The Red Prince looked out the window of the isolated house in North Conway, New Hampshire.

"I'm worried Mohammed. Why haven't the men from the town called in?"

"They're only four hours overdue. A change in schedule perhaps."

"Not without informing us. The men know they must call in. The fact that they haven't can only mean problems have come up."

"There is no problem that could possibly deter them at this point, Ali. As you described yourself, the experiment was a mere formality. We knew it would achieve the results we wanted."

The Red Prince folded his arms and sat down. His strong features had lost their sharpness. A haggard look of frustration painted the nervous lines of his face.

"We must hope so, Mohammed, because Alabaster is still alive."

"How he escaped our assaults in Luxor and Georgetown is beyond me."

"But the fact remains he did and now we must come up with another way of eliminating him."

"I disagree, Ali. Instead I think we should plan *around* him, forget he even exists."

"Impossible! He is everywhere!"

"The Shaitan force will begin arriving in America barely six weeks from now," al-Kahir reminded. "There's nothing even Alabaster can do to stop that. And our source in the CIA tells us that the Agency isn't even close to learning the identities of the carriers."

"I am more worried about Alabaster."

"And I repeat there is nothing any one man can do to stop us now. We can't kill Alabaster. We must resign ourselves to that fact. The false trail we laid through the Squid led him right into our trap in Luxor and yet he still lives. The man has no weaknesses, no flaws. Leave him alone, Ali."

The Red Prince smiled sinisterly. "Ah, but he does have one flaw and I understand it better than anyone. I should have seen it before. . . . We've been proceeding on the wrong track, employing the wrong strategy all this time. It's time to forge a new one."

"You have a plan?"

The Red Prince nodded. "Get Seif in here. I need his specialized services. . . ." A glimmer filled Salameh's eyes. "The Butcher is going to lead a mission that will result in the destruction of the great Alabaster."

TWENTY-EIGHT

Twenty-four hours later, across the world in the town with no name, Shaul Rabanine looked up from his magazine.

"Moshe, when do you think my father will come home?"

The giant had heard the question a hundred times before. He smiled warmly from his perch behind a large oak desk where he was making out the latest security report. "What's the matter? All of a sudden I am not good enough company for you?"

"I just miss him, that's all."

"He will be back, as always, when his work is finished. I think it will be soon."

"Is his work . . . dangerous?"

Moshe shrugged. He hated lying to the boy. It was time for him to learn the truth but it would have to come from David. "It is work he is very good at and feels he must do," he said simply.

"But for a long time he didn't do it anymore. Why is he again?"

"Because there is a need."

"You still haven't told me if his work is dangerous."

The giant rose from his chair and laughed heartily, smacking his huge chest like a gorilla. "Ah, Shaul, you are growing too smart for me." He moved closer and threw his arm around the boy's shoulder. "Before I know it you will be going into town with the men on Saturday nights, no?"

Shaul smiled. He loved Moshe almost as much as he loved his father. The big man had a way of making him feel good when he was lonely and he had found himself lonely more often as of late. Something was pounding inside him demanding to be let out. It made him feel different, funny. He had always been happy in the small, secluded town but in the past few months he had done a lot of thinking about what it would be like to live somewhere else and be around more people his own age. Now there were only three boys and two girls in the small school he attended. They were all his friends but they were not enough.

"You know, boy," Moshe told him, squeezing his shoulder in a massive hand, "I think you and I should take a trip into the mountains soon. It is a beautiful time of year. The seasons are changing. Animals will be everywhere. I will teach you how to approach very close without frightening them, yes?"

"You still haven't answered my question," Shaul persisted, his brown eyes widening.

"I used to always be able to make you forget it. You are getting too old to ignore, no? But not old enough to understand, not yet. I won't lie to you, I won't—"

Moshe's sentence was cut short by the sound of a high-pitched alarm that stung his eardrums. The warm smile vanished from his lips. His features became stonelike. His heart began to beat faster.

"Is it a drill, Moshe? . . . It's a drill, isn't it?" Shaul asked; his voice hesitant, fearful.

The giant didn't have to answer. Shots and explosions began to sound everywhere. Automatic weapons spurted fire, stopped, and then started again. Orders were given, warnings shouted. Men screamed.

Moshe glanced down grimly at the terrified boy beneath him, now on his feet. For years he had prayed this wouldn't happen and for years he had prepared for it. He knew immediately that the estate had been raided by a huge party of men possessing infinitely superior weapons. The men of the estate would hold their ground until the very moment death overtook them but that might not take too long. More explosions sounded. A small army had made the house its target. Moshe grabbed Shaul's arm and pulled him toward the door.

"Where are we going?" the boy asked, too scared to cry.

"I have a place prepared to hide you until the danger passes." The giant lowered his huge eyes to meet the boy's. "You must hide, remain totally quiet, and not come out until you are absolutely sure no one is in the house."

The two figures crept into the hallway, the larger one using his body as a shield. Quickly they moved to a staircase at the end of the corridor and ascended it into the attic. A damp, murky smell filled their nostrils. Darkness was everywhere. Moshe led Shaul forward and pulled a flashlight from a shelf. The giant flipped the switch. The light hesitated for a second but then came on. The wide beam revealed dust-covered crates and furniture. Moshe moved to the rear wall of the attic and felt his way along its cracked panelling.

Outside the shots continued, more sporadically. The screams wailed, more often.

"What are you doing?" the boy asked.

The question was answered when Moshe found the spot he was looking for and pushed. A hidden door creaked open, its outline indistinguishable from the false wall that contained it. Moshe pushed Shaul inside and handed him the flashlight. The small room was full of dry goods and water cans, emergency supplies for an emergency like this.

"Now remember," the giant instructed, "do not leave this room until you are certain it is safe to."

"Can't you come back and get me?"

The giant hesitated before responding. "Perhaps, but it would not be wise to count on it. I said you were a man before. I meant it."

Shaul threw his arms around the big man's neck, squeezing hard, beginning to sob. "Please don't go."

Moshe moved Shaul gently away and smiled. "That grip of yours is getting strong. Soon you will be like your father, yes?" The boy acknowledged the statement with his eyes. "He would be proud of you."

A series of explosions shook the house. Shaul forced himself to remain silent. He would be brave and make no noise because that is what his father would want him to do. Then someday when he was more of a man he would find the men who were destroying his home and make them pay . . . if his father hadn't already.

The boy watched Moshe grab a pump action shotgun that had been propped up inside the small, well stocked room and move away.

"You will remember what I told you, yes?"

The boy nodded. Moshe closed the door, made sure the opening was again indistinguishable, and was gone.

Shaul was safe, the giant told himself. They will never find him here. Now, if he could only escape and get help from the farmers in the mountains. They were all men who had fought in Israel's wars and could mobilize a small army on a minute's notice.

The twelve-gauge shotgun felt like a toy in Moshe's powerful hands, as he moved quietly through the attic, using the instincts that had kept him alive for years in the mountains to steer his way clear of all objects and slice through the darkness. Finally, he stepped lightly down the staircase, braced his body against a wall, and slid forward. He had no concrete plan of escape yet. He would merely trust his feelings to save his life as they had countless times before when he was lost or endangered in the wilderness. They would get him out as they always had.

The giant neared the main staircase. Footsteps were pounding their way up. Moshe turned quickly and levelled the shotgun forward.

Two shapes appeared. Two shots were fired. Two bodies tumbled down the wood steps in bloody heaps.

Moshe moved to the window and peered out, keeping his body out of sight. The carnage outside sickened him. Bodies lay everywhere on the blood-soaked earth. He could still hear random firing from whatever token resistance remained. The enemy had won. He could see some of the invaders converging on the house, following the two dead men who now lay at the foot of the stairs.

Arabs, he realized, fucking Arabs. When Tel Aviv found out, reprisal parties would be sent all over the Mideast to deal with the perpetrators. For now, though, the giant could concern himself only with his own escape. He had one chance and one chance only: to sneak out one of the back doors and make his way out through an emergency escape cellar.

Pausing no longer, Moshe spun from the wall and rushed to the staircase. Taking three steps at a time, he was on the ground in just over two seconds.

An Arab who had been in ambush position fired from a prone posture in the hallway. The bullet merely grazed Moshe's shoulder and before the Arab could fire another the shotgun had blown his head off. The giant stepped over the body and blood, ignoring his own pain, and crept stealthily down the hall.

Behind him, the front door exploded and four more Arab guerillas rushed in. Moshe spun to his rear and fired. One man fell. The giant dived to the ground and turned, firing again. A second man was hurled backwards against what remained of the wall. The two others, shocked by the big man's quickness, jammed their fingers on their triggers without bothering to take aim. Their shots went wild, carving a jagged design in the walls above Moshe and floor around him. He rolled again and fired two more shots. Both for the chest. Both direct hits. Which was good because the shotgun was now empty.

The giant was on his feet in a single swift motion. His shoulder hurt and he could feel warm blood slipping down his arm. But he had to keep moving. Two more turns and the back door would be in sight. He snailed along until his progress was halted by the sound of boots grazing wood. Moshe propped himself up against a wall, out of the line of vision of whoever was approaching.

The soft, slow footsteps peaked in volume and then began to lower again. Moshe sprang. The Arab was two feet in front of him when the giant clasped a huge arm around his throat, swung a knee into his back and pulled violently. The crack was sharp, seeming as loud as a gunshot. The Arab's body went limp. Moshe eased him to the floor. The man landed on his rifle. It might have been useful but there was no time to waste prying it loose.

Moshe moved quickly around one corner, then another. The smell of cordite was everywhere, mixing with the scent of burning wood. Outside the firing had intensified again, the Arabs apparently converging on the last pockets of estate resistance. It was the break he needed. He sped for the back door, praying that Shaul would stay where he was until he could return with help from the men of the mountains. Moshe's huge hand closed around the knob and pulled.

He felt the coldness a split second before the door swung completely open.

Seif stood three feet away, blocking his path, grinning. Weaponless, the Butcher stood his ground, his bald head glistening with sweat. His full, lifeless eyes beckoned Moshe on.

In silence, the two giants approached each other.

TWENTY-NINE

"Mr. Rabanine, I've been instructed to escort you to your meeting with Dr. Schmidt."

The man facing David in the TWA terminal of the busy Geneva airport was tall enough to look him square in the eye. His appearance was punctuated by a thick mustache, bushy sideburns, and a bulge just under his left armpit.

"He must be a most thoughtful man, having someone meet me not ten feet past customs."

"He is a busy man who is taking an exceptional risk by meeting with you. Certain ground rules must be obeyed."

"It's his game."

"To begin with, you must understand that the doctor has built a new life for himself and that if his former identity was made known, he would be ruined."

"Of course."

"Then you must also understand that he can't take the chance that his rendezvous with you might reveal his past. Therefore, I will take you directly to him now and directly back here to the airport after the meeting is over. There will be no stops, no phone calls. I will be with you every minute until your plane leaves for America."

"It's been a long time since I've had a chaperone."

The man remained expressionless. "Please do not take our precautions lightly. This is Geneva, Mr. Rabanine. No phones are safe. All eyes are always open. Dr. Schmidt has gone through great pains forging a new life, a good life. There is too much at stake."

"Yet he initiated this meeting."

"Yes." The man checked his watch. "And we'd better be on

our way."

David hadn't been to Geneva in three years, though it had long been one of his favorite cities. Today, however, he found himself unable to enjoy its sights as the limousine motored through the downtown district because his mind was otherwise occupied with the problem of Dr. Walter Schmidt. Under what guise was he now living? How much did he know? Why had he made contact?

David didn't have much longer to wait for the answers.

The limousine pulled up outside a massive skyscraper sheeted with mirror windows in the center of Geneva's financial district. David had seen the building countless times before in magazines and on news programs—the headquarters of the International Peace Organization, a worldwide network of private citizens linked by an aversion to war and a penchant to help war's innocent victims. The organization was headed up by Franz Mueller, one of the world's greatest philanthropists.

"This way," said David's escort, climbing out of the limousine. "Dr. Schmidt will be waiting."

The escort led David through a private entrance in the building's side, down a narrow corridor, and into an elevator. There were only two buttons on its panel. The man pressed the top one. The machine began to move. Judging by the time lost before it came to a halt again, David guessed they had reached the top floor or very close to it. The doors slid open, revealing a spacious outer office.

"Dr. Schmidt is waiting for you inside there," the escort said, pointing to a double door. "Please go in. I'll be here when you come out."

David moved for the double door, hesitated, and then threw both sides open. The room revealed was massive, erected totally in wood and decorated with plants draped near plush leather furniture.

"Please come in, Mr. Rabanine."

The voice came from the far right corner. David hadn't even realized someone else was in the room. He turned slowly toward a mahogany desk, only half-surprised at the sight of the man behind it—a man familiar to him and anyone else who read magazines or watched television regularly. The man was Franz Mueller.

"Dr. Schmidt, I presume."

The man rose slowly from his chair. His hair was thick and white. His features and body were still well formed for a man of past seventy. But somehow his eyes dominated his appearance; tired eyes that seemed forever on the verge of shedding tears. David had noted that peculiar feature of Mueller's sometime in the past. Now he understood.

"Please make yourself comfortable, if that's possible." Mueller extended an open hand to an arm chair in front of his desk. He was wearing a custom tailored blue suit that fit him elegantly. David saw a jewelry chain of some kind around his neck, concealed by the collar, and couldn't help wondering what dangled on its end. "Your presumption is only half right," Mueller continued. "I *was* Dr. Walter Schmidt but he died; I killed him off forty years ago so that Franz Mueller could be born." A brief chuckle. "At the age of thirty-two, of course."

David sat down, gripping the chair's arms tightly. His eyes locked on the five pointed crest that was the symbol for the International Peace Organization, each point representing a letter of the word "peace." "And now Franz Mueller is president of an organization devoted to the elimination of war."

"Quite a switch, isn't it?" Mueller posed, searching for a humorous tone which escaped him. "Call it my personal penance. I escaped Nuremberg but I couldn't escape myself. I felt I owed the world something for what I did, for what all of us did."

"An old man in Washington said he owes you his life and that you saved countless Jews from Mengele in Auschwitz."

287

"Saved them from Mengele so they could be sent to the ovens . . . It's not much consolation, not even now." Mueller looked suddenly older, his gaze distant. "I was never a Nazi in belief, only in uniform and then it was only to save myself. Selfish? Yes, but a man will do almost anything when his own life is at stake. I had certain skills the Fatherland required. They were all too happy to put them to use."

"As a doctor?"

"More specifically, Mr. Rabanine, as a biologist." Mueller raised his hands just over the desk top and held his palms open. "That is the reason behind what you see around you." He held his eyes closed for an instant. "A noble venture to help right my own ignoble past. I've spent twenty years building the International Peace Organization up, dedicating my life to maintaining world stability so nothing like the Nazis can ever come to be again. But I understand my work may well go for naught."

"You know about the Shaitan Commandment?"

Mueller's white head went through the motions of a nod. "Once known as *der Teufels Befehl*. It's why I had you contacted."

"After having failed to kill me."

"That, I'm afraid, was the work of the fools of ODESSA. It was they, you know, who engineered my escape from Auschwitz. It was they who gave me a new identity and a great deal of money so I could continue the experiments started at Auschwitz and someday hand them the ultimate weapon so they could implement *der Teufels Befehl* and assure the ascendency of the Fourth Reich. But I fooled them. I used the money to start this organization and grew powerful enough to sever all links to them. They could expose me, I could expose a great number of them. A stalemate, so you say. Then they came to me a few weeks ago with news of what the Arabs had accomplished. Not that any advice I offered mattered because they had already made up their minds to execute all the Arabs responsible for the Shaitan Commandment before it became

288

operational. A man was sent."

"Cerberus?"

"Yes, but there were problems. The Arabs ODESSA wanted and needed to kill couldn't be found and other complications had sprung up. The Americans had learned of the Commandment's existence and sent for you. ODESSA's first strategy called for your elimination as well as the executions of the Arabs. But it was no use. Things had gone too far. Too many people knew. *Der Teufels Befehl* was finished and any hope for the Fourth Reich would be as well unless the Shaitan Commandment was destroyed. The men of ODESSA came back to me, this time to listen instead of talk. I convinced them to let me meet with you in order to provide you with all the information at my disposal." Mueller leaned back. "That is why I called you here. You must tell me what you know. That will give us a place to start."

"Basically that in the latter months of the war, Mengele, at Auschwitz, began work on the creation of a biological means to neutralize any nation—most likely America—that got in the way of the Nazi machine once Europe was . . ." David almost said "yours" but quickly smothered the word. ". . . theirs."

Mueller's eyebrows fluttered. "You are more or less correct. The research began after a direct order was handed down from the Führer. And not just to us at Auschwitz but to every scientist the Nazis had at their disposal. All the means they came up with were not biological. But Mengele's was by far the most unique, potentially successful, and was accepted almost immediately. There was little time left, though, to develop the operation coded 'The Devil's Command,' certainly not enough for Mengele's experiments to proceed with so much detail as they should have. I suppose the Führer and his high command knew this all along. I suppose *der Teufels Befehl* was always meant for the Fourth Reich and not the Third. It was the first step of a new order, not the final thrust of a dying one, a card they held in a game that hadn't even begun yet."

"But then the Arabs snatched it from them and came up

289

with the Shaitan Commandment."

"And I'm not sure precisely how or maybe I just don't want to. Mengele had another assistant working with him at Auschwitz, a man just as evil and cunning as he was."

"Johann Gessler."

Mueller showed surprise for the first time. "I'm impressed by your research. Yes, Gessler. He was always Mengele's favorite. I suppose the Angel of Death never really trusted me and if the war had gone on another six months, he probably would have had me killed himself. In any case, Gessler also escaped with the help of ODESSA at the war's close. Along with him went a black notebook that detailed all of Mengele's work, the doctor himself having already fled. Of course, they didn't trust me with it. Gessler was placed in France, given a first-rate identity because of his knowledge of the Devil's Command which was infinitely superior to my own. He was to have been one of the first recalled when the Nazi's day dawned again. But ten years ago he disappeared, vanished into thin air."

"Eluding the men of ODESSA?"

"It was a well run operation, they tell me. They weren't sure where Gessler went or why until just over a year ago. Then a German scientist placed in Cairo by ODESSA began to hear rumors of unusual medical experiments being conducted at three Arab research centers. He investigated. The results shocked him: It was *der Teufels Befehl* being made operational by Arab terrorists, undoubtedly with the help of Johann Gessler." Mueller hesitated. "That brings us up to the present. Now you must tell me everything else you've learned."

David did and Mueller's face grew progressively paler till it all but matched the color of his hair.

"You say there are 175 carriers in the primary force," Mueller noted when he had finished. "They are *die Bote des Todes*, the Deliverers of Death. The Arabs have made far greater strides than I had expected. I had hoped that Shaitan might fail on its own. Based on what you've told me, I know that now to be all but impossible."

"Why?"

"Let's begin with the carriers—*die Bote des Todes*. It must seem strange to you that men and women could carry a lethal organism within them and not be infected by it."

"Obviously."

"The problem was how to come up with carriers who would not be killed by the disease they held inside them. The plan of those who were coordinating the birth of the Fourth Reich was to infect America or any other troublesome country without infecting the rest of the world which meant that the Deliverers of Death couldn't be carriers until they reached the U.S. But for them to inject a shot of the serum for the first time at this stage would be worthless because they would be dead within hours and the infection would very likely die with them. It could not live in and spread from a corpse. The solution was to make the carriers immune to the pestilence they carried."

"And that's what Mengele accomplished?"

"Or came very close, at the very least laying the groundwork for Shaitan. Yes, he was a murderer and a butcher, a man who lived off death. But he was also brilliant in a twisted sense. Years before anyone else cared, he experimented with DNA and discovered how to create a virus which has the property of attaching itself to intracellular DNA and which could be increased gradually in its virulence, mutated that is, while it is made latent in the host by a series of injections."

"Vaccination?"

"Not really. In the beginning, *die Bote des Todes* would each be given an injection with an amount of the isolated virus so small that a minor subclinical infection is induced. Four weeks later, a slightly larger booster dose is given. Another subclinical infection ensues of the same level although the booster has been increased. This process would continue for a minimum of four years: forty-eight injections, one each month. This series of injections alters the viral organism lodged within the carriers' intracellular DNA. It doesn't infect

291

them, though, because at the same time the individuals in whom the organism is being developed are developing antibodies to the organism. But these antibodies don't act upon the organism because it lies latent within the DNA, not a threat to the body because the body has accepted it into its genetic structure. What you end up with is a force of individuals carrying a deadly disease dormant within them."

"Dormant?"

"Until the final injection, of course, which is the largest booster of all. The final injection releases the previously latent virus into the bloodstream and/or the respiratory secretions and therefore contagion begins. The antibodies that *die Bote* have built up for four years enable them to defeat the disease but it becomes an ongoing process, a chain reaction in which for the first time they become infectious carriers. You see, Mr. Rabanine, now there are sufficient numbers of microorganisms circulating in their bodies to allow them to expel disease particles from their nose and mouth. The latent virus is thus free to leave their body and find new hosts."

"And because the new hosts have not had the benefit of having the virus attached to their intracellular DNA, they have developed no antibodies for it and are accordingly helpless."

Schmidt nodded. "Every person from that point on who they come in close contact with, who shares the same breathing space, will become infected. The process multiplies from there. Before the infected person is laid up, he or she might conservatively come into contact with one hundred people. And each of these will come into contact with another hundred, and so on. . . . Do I need to make the picture any clearer?"

"Hardly." David felt something tremble inside him. "Tell me more about the experiments conducted at Auschwitz."

"The important breakthroughs were all listed in that black notebook which Gessler took out of Germany at the war's close."

"For instance . . ."

"The means by which, once the disease was isolated, the exact balance of booster shots could be ascertained for the carriers. This was most crucial, for if any of the preliminary injections was too large, the agent would die and all work done up until that point would be lost." Mueller looked away briefly. "That procedure and the theory behind it was the basis of almost everything we accomplished."

"What else did the notebook contain?"

"Primarily the means by which a mutant strain of a germ could be intracellularly attached to DNA and the methods by which it could be conditioned to resist all known disease fighting drugs as well as the natural bodily defenses. Of course, in those days there were few antibiotics and most were relatively ineffective which made that part of the work easy. But something else was missing which has made much of Mengele's work obsolete."

Rabanine eyed Mueller quizzically.

"Radiation, Mr. Rabanine. The use of radiation in creating new species of germs is now an accepted fact. It removes all the boundaries we originally faced. With proper equipment, there's no limit to what the Arabs have created. Their strain of germ could be conditioned to resist all bodily and chemotherapeutic measures that might be taken. Only one possible answer would remain."

Hope flashed in David's eyes. "I'm listening."

"The only people who are immune are the original force of *die Bote des Todes* because of their altered genetics. Antibodies drawn from their serum is the only possibility for a vaccine which would have to be distributed through mass innoculation centers all over the country."

"Then am I correct in assuming that until the final injection is taken, the Deliverers of Death are not true carriers?"

"Yes. Almost certainly each has in his or her possession a final vial of serum which they will inject at an opportune time. Until that time comes, though, they're no different than you or I."

"So we could end the threat they pose by finding and killing them before the final injection."

"Find them, yes. Kill them, no."

"Why?"

"You answered that question yourself earlier. Because of the test they are using to gauge the effectiveness of the organism before setting it loose on a national scale."

"Where would the most advantageous place be to carry it out?"

Mueller thought briefly. "Certainly not a largely populated area. I'd say a small town as isolated and as in the middle of nowhere as possible. That way, the least possible attention would be attracted. The element of surprise would still be in effect when the primary force arrived."

"That doesn't explain why killing *die Bote* won't solve our problems."

"I didn't mean it to." Mueller squirmed in his chair. "The point is that once the organism is freed in the test site, assuming everything works as planned, it would be only a matter of a few months before the disease had spread everywhere in the country. You might indeed be able to execute all the members of the larger Shaitan force but the advance force will remain alive in addition to the survivors in the test area who will have become carriers as well. It's impossible to estimate how far a small amount of afflicted persons can spread such a deadly organism if they aren't found and isolated. Conceivably, in fact, one person carrying an organism as deadly and infectious as Shaitan could be responsible for setting off a geometric reaction that would lead to infection of the entire country in little more than five months, if that long."

"One person . . . ?"

Mueller simply nodded.

"Is there any way the Commandment can fail on its own?"

Mueller interlaced his fingers beneath his chin. "Yes. The Arabs might have miscalculated the final dosage for the carriers and made it too small. In that case nothing would happen. The bodies of *die Bote* will successfully suppress the organism altogether and the virus will remain latent in their DNA as it has for the previous forty-eight shots. This, of course, explains the purpose of the test. An error could be found, adjustments made before the primary force enters the country."

"What about too large a dose?"

"If the final dosage is too large, the natural immunity the carriers have built up over four years might be worthless. Depending on the excess, they might very well die from their last shot as though it had been their first. The upshot would be a quick death for them and anyone else they had close contact with. Huge pockets of dead would begin to appear, or just one pocket if the error was made during the test stage. In this instance, the birth of a widescale epidemic would be obvious, the subtlety of the strike lost and a biological attack strongly suspected. You would hopefully be able to isolate the infected areas or area and buy time to find the answer. Millions and millions might still die but at least you would have a chance."

A chance . . .

The word echoed in David's head, smashing up against the walls of his reason.

A chance . . .

That was what the fate of America had been reduced to. Hope waned with each minute. The disease might be spreading already. People might be dying. Doctors might be raising questions for which no answers existed. A noose gradually tightening around the neck of America without anyone realizing it until their own breath had been choked away.

David stood up. "I must be going, Mr. Mueller."

Mueller rose also, extending a bony hand across the desk. "Thank you, Mr. Rabanine."

David took it, finding the grip feeble. "For what?"

"For not calling me Schmidt, for not reminding me of the person I have tried to convince myself was dead. If you have

295

any questions in the future, I'll give you a private number where I can be reached."

"I have one now. Why? Why have you risked everything to help me?"

"This is the International Peace Organization, Mr. Rabanine. If the Shaitan Commandment is successful, there will be no such thing as peace for years to come. Need I say more?"

"Only if it explains why you worked so hard at saving Jewish lives at Auschwitz."

A tremor passed over Mueller's lips giving way to the semblance of a smile as he reached under his collar for the chain that hung around his neck. "There were actually two Schmidts, Mr. Rabanine, and I guess both of them are dead, both by my own doing. But while I do my best to forget one, I'm careful not to forget the other," Mueller said, his fingers emerging with an ornament and holding it before him. "Nor will I ever."

It was a Star of David.

David's escort returned with him to the airport and stayed by his side till the very time he had boarded the plane back to America. In keeping with the rules of the bargain, no phone calls were made and no one spoken to.

David was in Washington a little after three AM Thursday morning and in his hotel room twenty minutes later ready to collapse. The exhaustion and hunger that tore through him were together almost unbearable. His stomach gurgled regularly to protest its emptiness and his head throbbed. But he was too tired to keep food down, perhaps even too tired to sleep which was good because sleep would be put off until he could reach Colonel Rossi.

That call, though, would have to wait because a red light was flashing on his phone. Nervously, David called the front desk and was told there were four urgent messages beginning six hours before from a Daniel Kaim in Tel Aviv. The operator gave David a number where he could be reached.

Daniel Kaim, the man whose troops had saved his life at the Temple of Amon-Ra. But what could be so urgent that the commander would violate security by calling him directly? Rabanine asked the operator to connect him with the overseas exchange Kaim had left.

"David, is that you?" Kaim had picked up the phone before the first ring had ended. His voice sounded frantic.

"What's wrong?"

"I have something I must tell you," Kaim said, his voice cracking, grim. "Something terrible has happened. I'm not sure how; it should never have . . ." David heard Kaim take a deep breath. "I'll say this as best I can. Sometime yesterday your house in Israel was attacked by a troop of an estimated fifty terrorists. I went down there myself as soon as the report came in. . . . All your men were dead, twenty-one in all."

David's insides sagged and knotted. "What about my son!" A cold blast began in the pit of his stomach and moved swiftly through the rest of his body. The unthinkable had happened. The fortress had been penetrated. "*What about my son!*" The answer dreaded.

"He's been kidnapped, David. They have him. . . . Al Fatah has him!"

THIRTY

More words were exchanged but the significance and meaning of them were lost. David hung up the phone clumsily, his thoughts far away. His weary mind fought to make sense of what Daniel Kaim had said, avoiding the truth.

His wife was dead because of him. And now his son seemed on the verge of joining her . . . because of him.

There was something else, though. The attack had been well planned, obviously meant to secure the boy alive. Otherwise his body would have been found with the others. Now Shaul was obviously going to be used as human barter. But what did Al Fatah seek in exchange?

The phone was ringing. Out of reflex, Rabanine picked it up, his eyes glassy and senses blurred.

"Hello," he mumbled.

"Good morning, Alabaster."

A sudden sharpening of thought. David had heard the voice a few select times in the past and never face-to-face. But he recognized it instantly.

"Salameh!"

"None other. I hope I'm not disturbing you. My man in the hotel informed me you had returned. I assume you have already returned Daniel Kaim's call and have learned about what happened in the town with no name."

"You *bastard!* Why must you involve the boy in this? He is—"

"—a part of you, Alabaster," the Red Prince completed. "Or should I say a part of Rabanine."

"How did you find out?"

"There are ways. . . . You know, it wasn't easy for my men

to capture the boy. He was exceptionally well hidden and your guards were quite proficient, especially the giant one. Even Seif had difficulty killing him."

Blood rushed to David's head. He felt faint. "Is the boy all right?"

"As well as can be expected. He's on his way to America."

"Where?"

"You will find out soon enough, providing you cooperate."

"Cooperate?"

"I know about your meeting with Schmidt and I'm sure the good doctor was helpful in putting things together for you."

"Not helpful enough."

"Still, you are now certainly aware of the true basis and structure of the Shaitan Commandment. Others have to be prevented from finding out as well. The information obtained in Geneva has to remain with you alone."

"I might have already relayed it."

"I don't think so. You were allowed to make no phone calls from Switzerland and the only call you've made since returning to your room was to Kaim in Tel Aviv."

"So you want my silence in exchange for the life of my son."

"In a bland way, I suppose that's a fair judgment," Salameh said complacently. "But I'm not going to take chances; I didn't four years ago and I don't intend to now. . . . Would you like to know how I escaped that day in Beirut?"

Rabanine remained silent.

"I'll tell you anyway. A brown station wagon carrying myself and four subordinates left the apartment house under the watchful eye of your people. As soon as our car turned onto Hamra Street, a bus began to edge its way forward a bit in front of us. The bus moved to the outside of our car when it stopped at a predetermined spot in front of a small parking garage. We pulled in and another car with operatives resembling us pulled out. It was that car your remote control device blew up." A pause. "It was necessary, I'm sure you understand, for me to disappear for the period of time needed to bring the

Commandment to completion. Then I stayed underground until it was ready to implement to make sure no one would catch on what we were planning. But a young boy with a camera ruined all the precautions I had taken. Other arrangements became mandated."

"The killing of a second boy?"

"That decision lies with you. Your son conveniently became my means to neutralize your effectiveness."

"He is an innocent."

"No more an innocent than my own wife and sons were."

David steadied the phone in his hand. Sweat from his palm had soaked the plastic receiver, making it difficult to grip. He tried to swallow. There'd be no reasoning with the Red Prince; that much was clear.

"What must I do to save my son?"

"Not all that much really," Salameh replied tauntingly. "To begin with, you will of course tell none of your men about this phone call or about the results of your meeting with Schmidt. We have assigned three of our best agents to watch the moves of Chevallier, Kowalski and Ben-David. If they make any attempt to contact Langley about what has happened, your son will die. If you make any attempt to contact them, your son will die. Yes, Alabaster, as of this moment we are watching you too. That's how I knew you had gotten back to your hotel room and returned the call from Kaim. Certainly you will be able to spot the tail but it doesn't matter. Elude him and the boy will die, by slow torture I might add. I suggest you cooperate fully and try nothing foolish. . . . We are everywhere."

"I'll do whatever you say," David muttered.

"Good. You are to be on the eight AM Eastern shuttle flight to Boston where you will arrive at approximately 9:45. At exactly 10:00 a phone will ring near the newsstand."

"It might be in use."

"It has an out of order sign on it."

"And then?"

"You'll be given further instructions."

"Which will lead me to my son . . ."

The Red Prince grunted an acknowledgement. "My offer to you is simple: The boy's life in exchange for delivering yours to me."

"You could just as easily kill both of us."

"Granted. But fail to comply with any of my *orders*, and there's no doubt that one of you will die. The wrong one, I might add."

"A life for a life?"

"So to speak."

Rabanine nodded to himself. "I'll do as you say."

"I thought so. Remember no modifications or tricks. They may work but then again they may not. You know the price of failure. We'll be watching your every move. We *are* everywhere. . . . Ten o'clock in Boston, Alabaster, or the boy dies."

The phone rang off.

David forced himself from the bed, his muscles and mind rebelling against the simple action. He began to pace nervously back and forth, contemplating the problem before him. The decision, if it could be called that, came swiftly. The only option available was the one in which a chance existed that Shaul would be spared. In all probability, the boy had watched in terror as the men protecting him had been slaughtered. The life of the father had become the life of the son. But the boy deserved a chance to live, free from the blood and horror the existence of the father had forced upon him.

The solution was painful in its clarity. He'd fly to Boston and submit totally to the Red Prince. He'd go as Rabanine and leave Alabaster to disappear into nothingness. He'd go as Rabanine to see Shaul one final time.

The decision finalized, David ceased pacing. But suddenly he began to tremble violently, as though conflicting forces had confronted each other within him.

What had he been thinking of? . . . What straw had he grasped at in desperation?

The Red Prince wouldn't let the son live any more than he would the father. The only question was which death would come first. Obeying the words of Salameh accomplished no more than denying them. Less when he considered that Schmidt's information had to be passed on to Rossi. Somewhere in America a town had been infected by the Shaitan organism. A small town, isolated and removed. The Agency had to be informed so it could take action. The town of death had to be found.

Wait! . . . There was a way, a chance. Salameh had said nothing about Leslie Kirkman. The Red Prince had placed all his other cards on the table. Why, then, not this one? Unless he didn't hold it, which meant David still did. He could still use Leslie as a go-between to Rossi!

David sped through the door toward the stairs; there was no time or patience available to wait for the elevator. Three floors passed and he was in a corridor, running toward room 1424 and pounding on the door until a voice inside acknowledged him.

"Who is it?" Leslie asked apprehensively.

"David. I have to speak with you. Hurry and open up."

Rabanine heard a chain rattle on the inside. The door swung open, revealing Leslie in a white nightgown, the dark curves of her face made all the lovelier by the glare of the slowly rising sun. David stepped inside, grasped both her hands, and drew her close to him until their bodies almost touched.

"Listen to me," he began, his voice soft but firm, "I need you, more than I've ever needed anyone before in my life."

She nodded, unsure of his meaning. David saw her son Jimmy stirring restfully in the room's second bed.

"Anything, David. You know that."

His eyes betrayed his anxiety. "Al Fatah has Shaul."

Leslie gasped. "Oh no. But—"

He silenced her with a tender hand on her lips. "There's no time to explain. They kidnapped him during a raid on my home yesterday. They've given me instructions I must follow if I ever want to see him alive again."

"You're not going to meet with them?"

David nodded. "It's the only way."

"They'll kill you! Both of you!"

"They'll kill Shaul for sure unless I try."

"You have a plan?"

"Only the beginnings of one."

"Am I a part of it?" The question posed without reluctance.

"Yes. I have to get my son back but there's far more at stake here. I've got to get word to Colonel Rossi about what Schmidt said and you're the only way I can do it."

"What about the others you're working with?"

"They're all being watched." He looked away briefly. "What I'm going to ask you to do will be dangerous. It will place your son in the same peril mine has been in since the day he was born. But when this is over, he'll never be in danger again because I'm finished. I'm going to put the last eleven years behind me."

Leslie almost smiled. "Just tell me what to do."

"By eight o'clock this morning you have to be in Langley, Virginia at the offices of the Central Intelligence Agency. I'm going to write down some information for you to pass on to Colonel Rossi and no one else."

"The Director? Why only him?"

"Because he's the only person I'm sure I can trust. There's a leak and I'm sure it's sprung at the Agency. You must get to Rossi with the message. There's very little time left, if any."

"But how can I convince the guards to let me in to see him?"

"Tell them you have a matter for the eyes of Uncle Demetrius."

"Uncle Demetrius?"

"It's a trigger phrase at the CIA for material of the highest intelligence level. It'll get you in to see Rossi."

Leslie started to speak, stopped, and then started again. "You said the others were being watched. How do you know I'm not?"

"I don't. But I think it's safe for you to act as go-between."

" 'Think'?"

"Certainty is a luxury we can no longer afford."

"How do you know the terrorists won't kill you before you reach Shaul?"

"Because the Red Prince wouldn't give up a chance to gloat in front of me before he killed me . . . and my son."

"So you have to come up with a plan to kill him instead."

"I need him alive. Salameh is the only man who can lead us to the 175 carriers of the Shaitan organism. Kill him and our chances of finding *die Bote des Todes* change from slim to none."

"Finding who?"

"Later," he told her. "Now we must work on the message." He moved toward the desk as the early morning sunlight began to sneak around the corners of the drawn blinds. "I'm just going to write notes, not a detailed explanation. I'll go over their significance with you as I write and rely on you to pass the information on in your own words to Colonel Rossi. He'll take it from there."

"You're asking a great deal of me, David."

"I know."

Crescent Falls stood empty in the hot Thursday morning sun, blind and unknowing, a barren shadow set against a still more barren horizon.

The sky was cloudless and the air was dry, the town itself parched and inert. It was the kind of hot spring day where people passing on Main Street would turn their faces in the direction of a cool breeze for relief. Today, though, Main Street sat in silent desolation. A cool breeze blew, scattering dust across the pavement, but there was no one to turn their face toward it. There was only a stray dog munching on garbage from an overturned trash can placed in front of the town hall the week before by the one member of the Public Works Department.

Inside the house that lay on the town's outskirts, televisions and radios blared. Phones rang unanswered. Electric alarm clocks buzzed and whined, unchecked by the tired fingers of their owners slapping at them with morning ire. No one was going to work.

Suddenly on Main Street, the drone of a motor penetrated the stillness. A red van marked "FARM FRESH PRODUCE" pulled to a halt across the street from the Bar & Grill. A door opened on the driver's side and a man with short-cropped gray hair, a hook nose, thick arms displayed in a tight short sleeve shirt, and beer belly climbed out.

Gus Dibner made this trip every Thursday morning just like clockwork. Crescent Falls was so isolated that few deliverymen felt it was worth their while to come all the way out on a regular basis. Dibner was one of the few which made him a welcome and popular face in the town. Kids would come up on the way to school and ask him to flex his bulging biceps. Men heading for work would say hello and wish him a good day. There was always someone friendly to talk to in Crescent Falls.

Except today.

The moment Gus' feet hit the pavement he knew something was wrong. There were no people, no noise, nothing in sight. Just an old dog nipping away at a pile of garbage. And there was a smell in the air, an acrid stench that his nostrils fought to close against. It was something like the one Gus remembered rising from body-laden battlefields in Korea—only worse.

A bit uneasily, Gus began to make his slow way for the Bar & Grill. Slow because his knees, torn up in football games played four decades before, buckled in protest over lying dormant in the van for so long. He turned the knob, somehow surprised that Norm's place was unlocked, and stepped inside.

The door had not even closed fully when it flew open again, allowing Gus Dibner—who had forgot all about his gimpy knees—to emerge into the street choking, gasping, and puking. He ran toward the van at a clip faster than any he had reached during his days as an all-conference fullback. Jamming the key into the ignition and turning it as he floored the pedal, Gus

-sped off screeching down Main Street and left behind him the scent of charred rubber to blend with the one already dominating the air.

One hour later he would be sitting in a Casper, Wyoming Highway Patrol station trying to convince the sergeant on duty that he had just come from hell. Three hours after that he'd begin to feel congested and queasy. The next morning he would be forced to take his first day out of work in six years.

Meanwhile, the sergeant who listened to his breathless story would be too tired to eat dinner that night and would go to bed before watching the ten o'clock news for the first time in almost eight months. And the two patrolmen he sent to check out the raving deliveryman's story would begin to feel severe headaches coming on right after they finished their shifts, forcing them to break dates with two of the prettiest girls in Casper, though it would have been hard to expect them to have had a good time anyway after what they had seen.

The patrolmen reported that . . . something . . . had killed *all* the inhabitants of Crescent Falls. Had they bothered to check the back room of the sheriff's office, however, they'd have found this not to be the case.

Sheriff Bugsy Tyler was still alive. Clinging to life by a slender thread increasingly unable to support his massive frame. But clinging to it nevertheless.

THIRTY-ONE

"You want to see *who?*"

The marine guard at the entrance to CIA headquarters in Langley, Virginia seemed considerably less than receptive to the request of the attractive woman toting a young boy by her side.

"Colonel Vernon Rossi. The Director," said Leslie Kirkman.

"Look, ma'am, I know who he is. But he's a pretty busy man. He can't see everyone who walks in off the street."

Leslie looked past the steel fence at the large expanse of interconnected buildings that collectively made up the Central Intelligence Agency. It was an awesome sight. The rectangular shaped complex seemed to stretch from one horizon to the other, its white exterior basking regally in the morning sun.

"I have a message for the Director," she told the guard.

"Send it to him in a letter."

"Oh, it's not for Colonel Rossi specifically." A slight pause. "It's for the eyes of Uncle Demetrius only."

The guard arched his eyebrows. "Hold on, ma'am." He picked up a phone located inside the small booth. "I've got a Red One here, Jim. . . . A woman, yeah. Wants to see the Director. . . . Okay." The guard turned back to Leslie. "A man will be here shortly to escort you to Colonel Rossi's office."

The escort appeared not two minutes later and led her through the gate, up a sidewalk, and into a mazelike extension of corridors made up of antiseptic white tile that led somehow to a door marked "Office of the Director."

"In here." The man opened the door and beckoned to Leslie to enter, glaring at the small boy now wide-eyed with fascination over the surroundings. Leslie found herself in what might have been a doctor's waiting room where she was met by a slight, bespectacled man with stooped shoulders and a long thin nose.

"My name's Kincannon, Mrs. Kirkman, Bob Kincannon. I'm Deputy Director here in charge of Intelligence."

"How did you know who I was?" Leslie asked.

"I know of no other woman who would come here with a matter for the eyes of Uncle Demetrius dragging a boy alongside her. You've been sent by Alabaster obviously."

"He couldn't come himself."

"We're curious about his visit with Walter Schmidt."

"There were complications."

"Complications?"

Leslie nodded. "I'll explain them to the Director."

Kincannon shrugged. "I'm afraid we have a problem there. The Director suffered a collapse brought on by nervous exhaustion last night. He's an old man, Mrs. Kirkman, and his health has been failing for some time now. As Deputy Director in charge of Intelligence, I've been appointed to fill in for him, well, indefinitely. I'm afraid the Colonel is never expected to return."

"I'm sorry," Leslie said, considering what her next step should be.

"It would be a tragic loss for the Agency as well as the country. For now, though, I suggest we concern ourselves with the matter at hand meant for the eyes of Uncle Demetrius."

A contradiction surfaced in Leslie's mind. She was supposed to speak only to Colonel Rossi *and* she was supposed to pass on the information David had given her as quickly as possible. Now it was impossible to accomplish both. To follow one order was to disregard the other. There was no Colonel Rossi and likewise there was no time.

"Mrs. Kirkman, is something wrong?"

"What? . . . Ah, no. No." The slight man before her seemed

a competent enough sort, albeit an unimpressive one. Still he was the next best thing to Colonel Rossi and time, she thought, was a more crucial factor at this point. "Where can we talk privately?"

"The Director's office, presently mine. Your son will be safe out here . . ."

Bob Kincannon sat behind the Director's desk in his own chair he had moved into the office that morning. His face had grown progressively paler as Leslie had gotten further and further into the message for Uncle Demetrius. She spoke well, if not eloquently, putting David's thoughts and notes into her own words. The Deputy Director remained silent after she had finished, his stare trancelike. At once, the large desk seemed much too big for him.

"Mr. Kincannon, are you all right?"

"I'm just scared, Mrs. Kirkman, damn scared," Kincannon said, removing his glasses.

"David felt the same way."

"Why couldn't he deliver the message himself?"

"He had something else to attend to."

"Which is?"

"I'm not really sure," Leslie lied.

"I think you are. You're not a good liar, Mrs. Kirkman."

"I haven't had much practice."

"In this business that's refreshing to hear. But if Alabaster is involved in something to do with Shaitan without informing us, complications might result. For his sake and yours, please tell me where he is. . . . I might be able to help."

"It's a personal matter, Mr. Kincannon. There's nothing you can do to help; there's nothing anyone can do."

"This is the CIA, Mrs. Kirkman. We're tied in on this operation directly with the FBI and a dozen other organizations. Put any three letters of the alphabet together and you're bound to come up with one. At least let us *try* and help."

"He needs to work alone," Leslie said simply, fighting against the temptation to give in and tell Kincannon everything.

Kincannon stretched his small mouth sideways into a frown. "Well, if you change your mind, please call me. For now I want you to go back to your hotel and lock yourself in your room. I'll have men assigned to guard you and your son at all times."

"And what are you going to do?"

"To start with, I'm going to find that town where the experiment is taking place. If it's in this country, we'll lock onto it. How many possibilities can there be?"

"Enough, Mr. Kincannon. Enough."

The phone in the Eastern Airlines' terminal booth rang precisely at 10:00. Rabanine picked it up after the first ring.

"Is that you, Alabaster?" The Red Prince's voice.

"Yes."

"You are to take the 10:30 flight on Delta Airlines from Boston to Portland, Maine. At the terminal in Portland, you will proceed to a row of phone booths outside the snack bar and stand in the third from the right. It will ring at 11:15 sharp. If you aren't there at that time, the boy will die."

The phone clicked off.

David left the booth and ran from the terminal building. He hailed a cab. It was only a short distance to the Delta terminal but he didn't have the time to walk it. The driver scowled at him, balking at the instructions until Rabanine flipped him a ten dollar bill.

He'd had no trouble spotting the tails the Red Prince had assigned him. He guessed he had been supposed to, the men being placed there as reminders more than anything else. There had been two on the plane to Boston, one of which seemed to be watching him openly at all times without even bothering to disguise the fact.

Neither had been with him in the small lavatory, though, when he removed his shirt and carefully rolled a fresh bandage

310

around the upper part of his right arm. The wound from the terrorist's bullet in Fort Dupont Park had all but totally healed and, even if it hadn't, Rabanine put far more gauze around it than would have been necessary.

Because it was something other than the wound that had to be protected.

The third phone from the right in the row of booths inside the Portland, Maine terminal building rang exactly at 11:15.

"Yes," said David anxiously.

"You have done well today, Alabaster. My orders have been obeyed to the letter. I am quite pleased with you," said the Red Prince.

"Just tell me how I can see my son."

"Patience, patience. There is plenty of time. The boy is fine. A bit frightened perhaps, but alive for now. He is like you, Alabaster. Foolish and full of false ideals. It is fitting that you are the only one who can save him."

"How?"

"There's a car in your name, Rabanine's name that is, waiting for you at the Avis desk inside the airport. Drive it directly down route 302 through the towns of Westbrook, Windham, Raymond, Naples, Bridgeton; down the Kangamangis Highway into New Hampshire until you come to Attitash Mountain in Bartlett just past North Conway. Our men will be waiting for you in the lodge. And remember, you will be followed the whole way. Do one thing that looks the slightest bit suspicious and the torture of your son begins. Understand?"

David bit his lip in frustration. "Yes."

"See you soon, Alabaster."

David returned the receiver to its hook and left the booth. Slowly he walked toward the Avis counter directly before him and was in a green Grand Prix five minutes later.

Once on the road, he began to work out the final details of the only plan he had available. For it to work, the Arabs would have to behave exactly as he expected them to. There was simply no margin for error.

Mt. Attitash is a busy place virtually the entire year. In the winter it is a favorite spot of skiers searching for a variety of slopes on perfectly landscaped trails that tilt at exactly the right angles through forests of trees and nests of shrubbery. And during the summer it is a favorite attraction of tourists and natives wishing to ride on the first Alpine slide ever constructed in America.

The slide is actually a white surfaced track made of asbestos asphalt that winds and bends through the center of the mountain between two ski slopes. Summer ticket holders take the ski lift to a point two-thirds up the mountain, climb onto a plastic sled with wheels on its bottom, and proceed to glide down the asphalt at their own regulated speed; safely aware that the sled is almost certain to be contained within the sides of the slide which has been tailored to its precise specifications.

But this was April, the in-between time for the proprietors of Attitash. The onset of an early spring had shut down the skiing business two weeks before and the Alpine slide did not open for another four. Outside of a few passing tourists wishing to get a closer look at the slide, no one came by. And today even these are warded away by two well dressed men standing subserviently in the parking lot, politely informing all those who pull in that they are trespassing. The people leave a bit angered but still they leave.

There had been only four cars in the parking lot for nearly two hours when a green Grand Prix pulled up. A tall man with broad shoulders got out and was quickly led into the ski lodge by one of the two guards, the other maintaining his vigil while reaching for a walkie-talkie.

"This is Abiz. Come in, sir."

"Yes, Abiz," snapped the voice of the Red Prince.

"Alabaster has arrived, sir, and has been taken into the lodge to be searched by Hamal. I will remain at my post."

312

"Good work, Abiz. . . . Come in, Hamal. Come in."

Inside the lodge a large Arab interrupted his search of Alabaster to pick up his walkie-talkie.

"Theese is Hamal," he said in barely perceptible English only because the Red Prince required his men to speak the language of whatever country they were in. "I was joost about to call you, sir."

"Just about isn't good enough, Hamal," roared Salameh. "You were supposed to call as soon as he came in."

"I am soory, sir."

"Just finish the search and call me again when you're ready to bring him up."

The Red Prince released the button on his walkie-talkie and glanced around him on the platform the lift carrying Alabaster would stop on. It was little more than a wooden shed, open on all sides to allow the lift seats to pass freely through. The plank floor, perhaps ten by fifteen feet in size, was coated with white lines to signal riders when to get off and move away in order to avoid being struck in the head by the seat they had rode up in as it passed over them. It was a small area that would allow Alabaster little maneuverability should he elect to try something. And, more importantly, it was ideally isolated. A perfect place to deposit two bodies that you didn't want found for a week at least.

Besides Salameh, no less than ten Al Fatah agents were present on the platform. They were among the best available in America; all killers, good at their professions and well experienced. In their hands lay an arsenal of weapons ranging from a submachine gun to a twelve-gauge to a .44 magnum pistol.

The Red Prince was taking no chances. Alabaster had to die. Still he missed Seif. This was his type of work. But his presence had been required elsewhere to complete another part of the plan, as had al-Kahir's.

Between the two largest Arabs on the platform stood a young boy, his face dirty, one eye puffy and bruised. His straight brown hair had been curled at the ends by perspiration and dust. The boy's lips were pressed together determinedly, fighting against fear, trying not to let themselves tremble. But his chin pulsated slightly nonetheless, teeth clapping lightly together again and again. The boy's eyes swung around him, wide with terror.

Looking at the boy, the Red Prince could do nothing but smile. He had decided long ago that Rabanine's son would die. The only questions were when and how. Both now answered themselves. When Alabaster arrived in the lift, Salameh resolved, he would personally slit the boy's throat as his father watched. That way, he would allow the great Jew a final moment of ultimate agony before the guns of the Al Fatah agents, assembled early that morning, cut him down in a blaze of bullets. Until the instant when his knife pierced the boy's throat, the Red Prince expected Alabaster to cling to the hope that his son might be allowed to live. After all, what else did the Israeli have now but hope? Certainly there was nothing he could do.

Salameh realized minutes had passed since he had spoke with Hamal in the lodge. He pushed the button on his walkie-talkie down furiously. "Hamal! Hamal! Come in! Come in! . . . Is something wrong?"

Crackling followed by a click.

"It eese all right now, sir," Hamal said, breathing hard. "Dee Jew he try to keel us wit a knife heeden in his sleeve. But dee two of us, we fight eem off good. He passed out. What shood we do, sir?"

"You didn't kill him?"

"No, he still alive."

"Then turn on the lift and bring him up. I'll stop it from this end when you get here."

"Very good, sir. We be on our way."

So the great Alabaster had tried something after all, thought Salameh. A final futile blow struck out in desperation. The end of the circle had finally arrived. All was as it had been long ago.

The man who had chased him underground three-and-a-half years before was about to be blasted into oblivion.

The lift began to move. Through his binoculars, the Red Prince saw the Israeli's body slumped down between his two agents, head on chest, face down. Both of the men, the strongest he had, held a shoulder tightly on either side. Their grasp was tight, especially Hamal's, a man trained by Seif himself. Salameh focused the binoculars a bit and a large Arab appeared clearly before him dressed in a blue navy jacket and black porkpie hat, tilted as always over his forehead. Hamal was a good man. He'd be rewarded for this.

The end of Alabaster had come. Finally.

The lift was well past the halfway point now. The Red Prince ran his tongue over his lips in anticipation, lowering the binoculars. He edged forward across the wooden planks, stealing a glance at the boy behind him whose young life was about to come to a bloody end. Salameh was quivering now with eagerness. The lift was twenty yards away. His eyes searched for those of the man in the center of the seat, a man he had taken on and bested. A worthy opponent for awhile but in the end not really up to the challenge.

Ten yards . . .

The death of Alabaster, sealing the success of Shaitan. The lift was over the platform now.

"Stop the machine!" the Red Prince commanded, eyes bulging and features taut.

A man flipped a switch in a junction box behind him. The lift sputtered to a halt. Salameh watched Hamal shake Alabaster's still body.

"He dooze not move," Hamal said, facing the Israeli. "I tink maybe we heet him too hard. Maybe he ees dead."

The Red Prince stormed forward, furious.

"If that man is dead," he howled, almost upon the lift seat, "you will have seen the last of—"

The next few moments were suspended in a surreal blur. Salameh wasn't sure which came first, nor did the precise

315

order concern him. He was aware for a fleeting second that something was very wrong, even before the Arab on the left side of the Israeli slumped forward to the wooden platform.

In this instant came the realization of the trick and the effectiveness of it, but not before the man dressed as Hamal had let the body of the man dressed as Alabaster tumble as he sprung forward, a blade flashing in the sun and seeming a part of his hand. The black porkpie hat flew off the man's head and revealed thick brown hair. Salameh, though, saw the hair for only a second before he felt himself being spun violently around at the same time a razor sharp edge was pressed against the soft flesh near his jugular.

The man holding him jerked backwards so that the force of ten levelled their weapons straight for his heart. Their fingers rested on the triggers of their guns uneasily, unsure of what their next move should be and mesmerized by the sudden turn of events.

As the blur gave way to the gradual sharpening of clarity, the boy who stood between two of the Arabs broke away and shot forward out of their reach, finding sanctuary behind the tall man whose knife remained locked on the Red Prince's throat. He threw his arms around the man gently, not wanting to disrupt him, and buried his softly sobbing face in the dark coat between the shoulder blades.

"If any of you gentlemen move one inch," Alabaster warned, breaking the tense silence, "I'll slit the throat of your leader. We wouldn't want that now, would we?"

THIRTY-TWO

"Shaul, move slowly to my right so I can see you."

The son obeyed the words of the father. Alabaster studied him out of the corner of his eye. Besides the bruise on the right side of his face, he looked the same as he had in Israel before the explosion. Even his clothes, American levis and blue shirt, were almost identical. Except now they were dirty.

"Now, gentlemen," Alabaster said to the terrorist force before him, "you will all kindly drop your weapons and lie face down on the platform."

The men hesitated. Alabaster yanked the Red Prince's head backwards so that his eyes faced the sky, the sharp blade pressed firmly against his flesh.

"Do as he says," gasped Salameh. The men dropped their weapons and slowly laid their bodies down on the wood beneath them.

The easiest strategy for Alabaster to use would be to kill all the Arabs including the Red Prince here and now but two factors prevented him from carrying it out. First, he could not bring himself to force Shaul to bear witness to yet another massacre. And second, more importantly, he needed Salameh alive. His death would postpone Shaitan, not destroy it. The carrier force would remain in the shadows, the threat they posed looming indefinitely over the world. The identities of *die Bote des Todes* had to be learned and a means found to prevent the disease from spreading beyond the test site.

"Now, Shaul, I want you to pick up all the weapons lying on the ground and toss them down the mountain as far as you can."

The boy smiled, brushing the hair from his eyebrows with a

dirty hand. "You bet."

"Except for that pistol over there," Alabaster said with his eyes fixed on the .44 magnum. "Bring that one to me."

The boy followed this instruction first, sticking the powerful pistol into his father's belt. Then, somewhat unsurely, he began to systematically gather and toss the other weapons down the steep incline that led up to the platform. They fell forty feet down, retrievable but not easily so.

"What are you going to do with me?" the Red Prince asked, his voice muted by the pressure on his throat.

"I haven't decided yet. But you can be sure it won't be pleasant."

Shaul had finished tossing the weapons over the side. He stood beside his father now, proud and erect, trying to look older than he was. Alabaster addressed himself to the prone Arabs.

"We, the three of us that is, are going to walk down this mountain and none of you are going to make any attempt to follow us. If you do, I will kill your leader in the same fashion he would've killed me. Don't bother thinking you can sneak up on me from behind because countless others have tried and have all failed. Besides, I don't think anyone of you wants to be responsible for the death of the leader of the movement you so humbly subscribe to, so I suggest you stay right where you are for twenty minutes at least." Alabaster tightened his grip around the Red Prince's throat. "Right, Salameh?"

The Red Prince's eyes swam in their sockets. "Do as he says."

The men remained spread over the wooden platform, making no effort to change their positions, as Alabaster led Salameh off the platform and down a horizontal plane of land toward the forest that lay between the two main ski slopes. Shaul stayed closely by his side. Alabaster stopped when they reached the beginning of the trees that angled downward toward the lodge, his knife still jammed against Salameh's throat, and turned back to his son.

"I am proud of you, Shaul. You are a brave . . . man."

The boy's expression gleamed. "I want to be like you."

"You will be better, much better."

"When they kidnapped me I wasn't scared because I knew you'd come and save me." The boy's fingers clenched themselves into fists. "They killed all our men at home, even Moshe."

"I know."

"You'll make them pay for it, won't you?"

"We both will. We both are. ! . ." Alabaster turned toward the trees. "Come, we must move quickly before the men on the platform grow restless." He pressed the blade's release, allowing it to snap back into its handle, and put it in his jacket pocket. He had wrapped it within the bandage around his shoulder to hide it from the cursory frisk he expected would come in the parking lot, leaving him with a weapon once he entered the lodge.

The Red Prince ran his fingers over the back of his cramped neck, free to move again but not relieved in the slightest. "You will not escape, Alabaster. You and your son will both be killed before you leave this mountain."

Alabaster drew the magnum from his belt. "Then you will die with us," he said, his resolve strengthened by the lack of fear on his son's face. "And now, Salameh, you will set a fast pace down this mountain you seem so sure I will never reach the bottom of. Try to escape or make one move against either of us and I will be more than happy to succeed where I failed four years ago." He thrust the magnum forward. "At much closer range."

Salameh turned his eyes to the woods, shrugging. "As you wish." He entered the forest and began to walk, choosing his steps discreetly.

"Faster!" Alabaster commanded.

"You wouldn't want me to sprain an ankle would you. I would be quite a load to carry."

"Then again, it would also make you as big a target for your

319

men's bullets as I am, should they be foolish enough to come after you."

"You have nothing to fear from them. They would not endanger my life by trying anything."

"For awhile anyway. But before too long they will realize that it makes no sense *not* to try and get you back. Obviously, if I decided to let you live, it would be only as my prisoner. If they are good men, they cannot allow that any more than they can allow me to escape."

"They *are* good men." Salameh chuckled. "And you're right, they have their orders. They will kill you *and* me, if necessary."

Alabaster prodded Salameh in the kidney with the magnum's barrel, urging him to move faster through the underbrush. "Not if we make it down the mountain before they have sufficiently recovered their weapons as well as their sense of reason."

The Red Prince kept moving. "Then why bother to keep that gun pointed at me? I know you won't kill me. I am worthless to you dead. You need information I alone possess."

"Yes, but I might decide to get selfish and blow your brains out anyway."

Salameh was silenced.

Shaul was leading the way now, his eyes focused keenly in front of him. His father, meanwhile, kept the .44 lodged in the Red Prince's lower back, coaxing him on. The incline became steeper and suddenly the ski slopes came clearly into view on both sides of them. Alabaster saw the wires of the lift stretching above him and, in the rapidly approaching distance, made out the brown outline of the lodge.

"Step up the pace, Shaul."

The boy nodded and did as he was told, moving in a slow trot, parting branches and bushes which were again parted by Salameh and Alabaster. The closer they drew to ground level, the taller the trees became and thus the thicker their cover. The slight forest around them, though, was thinning out with every foot. Another 250 yards and it would have disappeared completely, leaving them with a good seventy-five to cover in the open field without benefit of any camouflage before they reached the safety of the lodge.

Fifty feet to his right, across the open path beneath the tram line, Alabaster heard something move. The sound of soles crushing pine needles was unmistakable. There was someone watching them. They were exposed on that side, vulnerable to an attack. Alabaster cocked the magnum, feeling Salameh's muscles tense under the click.

Crackle, crackle, crackle . . . A walkie-talkie was sputtering in the distance, men talking to each other.

"Keep moving," the Israeli ordered.

Up ahead, Shaul was four feet in front of them, his eyes searching for holes in the ground. Alabaster was about to yell to him to hit the ground when a creaky scratching sound filled the air. The cables of the lift had begun to move!

"Shaul—"

It was the only word Alabaster could get out before a blast roared through the woods, greeted by a scream from the boy as he fell forward with blood running down the back of his leg through his jeans. Alabaster tossed the Red Prince hard to the ground, spinning in the direction the shot had come from. Another bullet, poorly aimed, struck a tree five feet to his right as the shape of the Arab named Aziz who had searched him in the parking lot ran for cover. But he did not run fast or far enough to avoid the first shot that exploded from the magnum's barrel, striking him in the side of the head and hurling him backwards.

"Help me! Help me! *It hurts!* . . ."

Shaul rolled back and forth on the ground, his face a mask of twisted pain, his eyes fading in and out of darkness. His father flew toward him, cupped a powerful hand under the boy's neck, and lifted him up to a sitting position to better examine the wound.

The boy's body was trembling all over. His eyes were

growing glassy, a sign he was going into shock. Alabaster laid him down again easily. He grasped for Shaul's hand and felt the youthful grip tighten around it to quell the awful fear that raced through his body.

"Bastards! . . . The dirty bastards!"

Alabaster turned to the rear and steadied the magnum's barrel in line with the dazed body of the Red Prince which had just lifted itself from the ground. The Arab backed away, hands stretched before him in a plea, his high-set cheekbones and angular nose merging in fear. The dark features of his face paled.

"No!" he screamed.

"Yes!"

Alabaster was about to shoot when automatic rifle fire ricocheted around him, coughing up dirt and pebbles into his face. He shifted his body weight and forced it downward so that his frame covered that of his son. The scent of the boy's young flesh burned his nostrils.

The shots came again in a louder burst this time, the angle improving. The man with the weapon was firing from a seat in the lift which had come to a halt. From his prone position, Alabaster could see two other seats were occupied as well by two more of the Arabs he had left alive on the platform. In trying to save Shaul from witnessing a massacre, he had very probably made him the victim of one.

Above him, up the incline, Alabaster heard the rustling of feet and the sound of raging voices drawing closer. He tried to shift his body in that direction but found his motion stopped by another series of bullets which tore up the earth around him. He turned enough, though, to see the Red Prince disappear into a thick nest of trees, escaping.

Another spurt exploded and Alabaster tightened his grip on the wounded boy beneath him. This, though, was no strategy for escape, only a guarantee of certain death. The position he held now was at an angle too sharp for the bullets of the men on the lift to hit him. If he dared rise, however, he would become a

322

clear target. The strategy of the Arabs was obvious: those in the lift would keep him pinned down, while those on the mountain closed for the kill. The Red Prince would have won. But the battle was not over yet.

"Shaul, I'm going to move away from you now," he said softly into the boy's ear. "But you can't move, not even an inch."

The boy remained silent but Alabaster sensed he would obey. The bullet, he guessed, was lodged in the fleshy part of the upper leg, dangerously close to a major artery that if ruptured would result in a quick and certain death which might come anyway from a combination of shock and blood loss. Alabaster knew he had to move and move fast. Shaul had to be taken to a doctor within a half hour or he would . . .

The shuffling feet in the woods above him drew closer. The automatic fire surged again, effectively sealing him within the small space he occupied just beyond the angle of its range. Once again it stopped, the men reloading. It was the moment to move, to turn disadvantage into advantage.

Five bullets remained in the magnum's chambers.

Each would have to find its mark.

The men on the lift were suspended forty feet off the ground, perhaps sixty more away from him. Their bullets had to dodge trees to reach him. The trees held the answer. The bullets exploded at him once more.

Alabaster spun off Shaul's trembling body and rolled forward in line with a large tree ten feet away that had cut off the angle of fire. In seconds he was behind it, breathing hard, the magnum steady in his hand. He rose slowly, aware the men could only guess his actual position. They had plenty of firepower but their uncomfortable perch in the sky afforded them a minimum of mobility. Quick turns in the small seats while holding bulky weapons were out of the question. Theirs was strictly an offensive position. Defense had not even been considered.

More bullets spit around him, chewing up tree bark and

spraying it everywhere. The lift seats swayed under the pressure, squealing in the cool air. The firing had stopped again.

Alabaster sprung from the tree and moved away from the Arabs, trying to shift his position to behind them. He darted behind one pine and then another, the men with the rifles unable to change their positions fast enough to catch him with their bullets. Finally he was twenty feet behind the lowest man on the lift, well out of sight in the woods. The idea was to make it appear as though he was fleeing, leaving the boy behind for dead. The men on the lift would let themselves relax and in that moment would come his chance.

Alabaster watched the lowest man's eyes swing to his rear, searching for his target, attentive but detached. Alabaster tightened his grip on the magnum. It was time.

As the man's eyes swept unseeingly past him, the Israeli dashed out and ran almost directly under the path of the lift seats. Their target's cover gone, the stunned men fought to swing their weapons around to stop his charge. The confinement of the tram, though, made it impossible for them to shift their positions before Alabaster drew directly beneath them.

The Israeli watched the barrel of the lowest placed Arab's machine gun smash into the side of his seat. He raised the magnum to an angle approaching ninety degrees and pulled the trigger. The bullet found its way into the first man's spine at the same time Alabaster was lurching forward in line with the second. He fired again and hit this one in the head.

Still moving beneath the progression of seats on the lift, Alabaster saw the barrel of the third Arab's rifle poke itself over the rear of his seat. The Israeli dove to the ground and fired an errant shot upwards, hoping to distract the man and make him hesitate for the briefest of seconds before depressing the trigger. The strategy worked, though in a different way. The man fired immediately without bothering to aim in the hope that the random blasts would catch their target. They didn't. Alabaster vaulted back to his feet and pulled the magnum's trigger one final time. The bullet tore into the raised shoulder the Arab had used to steady his gun, disabling him. The rifle tumbled from his hands.

Alabaster tossed the magnum aside and sped back into the woods. He reached Shaul and was about to speak to him when he realized the boy had slipped into shock. Above him, heavy footsteps thrashed through the underbrush. The Red Prince's force would be on him any moment. Pausing no longer, the Israeli lifted his son off the ground, supporting him under the knees and neck in an attempt to use his body as a shock absorber against possible rupturing of the artery in the boy's leg. There was no time for a tourniquet. There was time only for escape.

Alabaster was running now toward the brown shape of the lodge that grew larger and larger. He could not risk a fall and yet neither could he risk a slower pace. Salameh's men were gaining, almost within firing range now. Certainly within sight, though he didn't dare disrupt his rhythm by turning to the rear.

Instead, he continued to hurdle through the brush, avoiding holes and drawing his son closer to him when especially difficult obstacles rose to be passed. Finally he was in the open, running faster than his legs knew how to carry him even without the excess weight in his arms. He raced across a grass path and saw the final stretch of the white asphalt slide on his right. The parking lot was not far away.

Behind the Israeli orders were being shouted, guns raised and fired. But the bullets missed their marks when Alabaster ducked behind a dark building that housed the mechanical workings of the lift. He then spun through a break in a rail fence marked with a weathered sign announcing "THE LINE STARTS HERE." He was in the gravel parking lot now, his son's arms flapping freely like those of a doll. Just a little further . . . The Grand Prix was in view, not a hundred feet away.

But what if they had tampered with the engine as a precaution?

The possibility could not be considered. He had no contingencies left. If the car didn't start, he was finished. It was as simple as that.

The Arabs converged behind him, firing as they approached but not stopping to steady their aim. Alabaster threw open the door on the driver's side of the green car with a hand temporarily detached from his son. He climbed in slowly, placing Shaul's head on his lap and laying the boy's legs across the seat.

The men of Al Fatah were almost upon him, their guns shattering glass and spraying it on his body as well as his son's. The key turned in the ignition. The car roared to a start.

Alabaster shoved the transmission into reverse, spewing dirt as he tore backwards spinning the wheel so that the front of the Grand Prix faced the exit. He braked and jammed the handle into drive. The transmission rattled in protest but responded just as the windshield was disintegrated by a shotgun blast. The projectiles missed the driver's head only because he had forced it down level with the top of the dashboard to avoid them.

Alabaster spun the wheel with one hand and floored the pedal. The Grand Prix shook under the pressure, its back tires pouring a cloud of dirt to the rear as the car surged forward. His other hand was wrapped around Shaul's midsection near his waist to cushion the boy's limp body against the rapid thrusts of the car. The Grand Prix lurched on, gaining speed, leaving the Red Prince and his men in the brown cloud behind it. Above the dashboard, Alabaster saw the dark pavement of route 302 appear and felt the car leap onto it, tires rejoicing atop its smooth surface.

The speedometer quickly climbed beyond seventy and held there. The car fought to hold its ground on the winding road. But the excess speed was necessary. A few miles up ahead, Alabaster remembered noticing a doctor's office in a restored old house between a vegetable stand and a cemetery. He *had* to get there.

His son was dying.

THIRTY-THREE

The doctor approached slowly, his face blank and solemn.

"He's lost a lot of blood, Mr. Rabanine. But I've removed the bullet and closed the wound and generally done everything I can do for him here. I recommend we move him to a hospital as soon as it is safe for him to travel."

"Will he live?"

Dr. Ben Macaphee shrugged his tired shoulders. He was a man of not more than forty who looked considerably older. His hair had gone prematurely gray and his features were long and ashen. "It's hard to say at this point," the doctor responded. "He's lapsed into a coma which is to be expected. But he's young and strong and, so long as there are no further complications in the form of internal hemorrhaging, his chances are no worse than fifty-fifty, also no better. The bullet was lodged a half inch away from a major artery in the thigh. Any closer and it would have taken a far more skilled surgeon than I to remove it."

David rose from the couch in the waiting room to face Macaphee, whose white lab coat was stained with blood. "What about the aftereffects, assuming he lives?"

"Will he regain full use of the limb, you mean? Also very hard to say. The muscle was severely damaged, though not irreparably. Barring complications, the odds are good that he will achieve a one hundred percent recovery."

"Can I see him?"

Macaphee nodded and led David into the adjacent examination room that had served as the operating chamber, colored sterile white and smelling of alcohol. The walls were bare, the monotony broken occasionally by a shelf of books or instruments. Somehow a glass jar of lollipops stood out. Shaul laid on a table in the middle of the room. A youthful nurse huddled over him setting up an IV. She, too, had blood on her uniform. The boy's face was peaceful, seeming at rest. His breathing was soft but regular. David grasped Shaul's arm for a moment before turning back toward Macaphee.

"Doctor, I want to thank you."

"For saving your son's life or not asking questions?"

"Both."

"I usually don't keep office hours on Wednesday. You caught me in a lucky week. The next doctor's office is another ten miles down the road."

David glanced down at the blood drying on his shirt. "I don't think we would have made it."

"I'm sure you wouldn't have." Macaphee led David back into the waiting room where the two men faced each other, the doctor's weary expression becoming stern. "I'm curious, Mr. Rabanine, as to what it was that led to a rather large bullet finding its way into a thirteen-year-old boy's leg."

"I could say it was a hunting accident."

"And that's the way it will go down on the books. But it's not the truth. The bullet came from a pistol, not a hunting rifle."

"You want the truth?"

"I'm not sure it matters especially. I just don't want to be used."

"You already have been—to save an innocent boy's life, a task you have performed admirably."

"Toward whose end?"

"The boy's, no one else's."

"And what is your end, Mr. Rabanine? I know by your slight accent that you are a foreigner and I know by your wallet that you are carrying a fair sum of cash you intend to pay me with. You show up on my doorstep carrying a boy you say is your son and ask me to take a bullet out of his leg. Excuse my curiosity."

David stepped forward. "Doctor, I ask you to trust me."

"I already have more than I should. Proper procedure

328

indicates that I must inform the police."

"They would ask questions I can't answer and take time I can't spare."

Macaphee's sagging jowls rose into a scowl. "That sounds very mysterious but it shouldn't surprise me coming from a man who removed my shingle from the post outside and brought it in with him."

"That was for your safety, as well as my son's."

"Who are you protecting us against?"

"The people who shot the boy."

"And blew out the windows of your car? My nurse saw the damage when you pulled it inside the garage." A pause. "What have you done, Mr. Rabanine? Why are these men chasing you?"

"Actually, it's me who's chasing them."

"And who are they?"

"Killers, Doctor, killers who are after me because they're afraid I might be able to stop them."

"From doing what?"

"Giving the American medical community more business than it can possibly handle."

"You talk in riddles."

"There's no time to explain further."

Macaphee folded his arms. "You sound desperate."

"We all are."

The doctor nodded. "I see."

"If only you did. . . . I must use your phone."

"To call Washington, I assume."

"No. Langley."

"The CIA? You work for them?"

"Through them. But there's little time. I've got to get us some help. The men tracking me will be here soon. They might be outside already. Do you have a gun in this house?"

Macaphee swallowed hard. "Just an old hunting rifle upstairs."

"Load it and bring it down here."

"Why don't we call the—"

"Do as I say," David cut in. "There's no time for anything else."

The doctor disappeared up a staircase in the foyer next to the waiting room. Rabanine walked into the reception area and picked up the phone usually manned by a secretary who was on her day off. He dialed a number long since committed to memory. The Agency had to be informed so that a reconnaissance team could be sent.

"Service department," a male voice announced.

"I've had a breakdown. I need to be brought home."

"What is the nature?"

"All tires blown. I'm in for repairs in a house in North Conway."

The voice hesitated. "A . . . *domestic* breakdown?"

"It's fucking New Hampshire, isn't it?"

"Who is the vehicle registered to?"

"Alabaster. Clearance A-1000. Security code Blue." Silence. "I have a passenger with me. He's a poor traveller." More silence. "What the hell's wrong, goddammit! I said we need to be brought home!"

"I'm sorry, sir, your ticket is no longer valid."

The phone rang off.

David slammed the receiver back down, nearly cracking the plastic. Rage surged within him, confused rage that sought a vent just as his mind craved an explanation.

. . . your ticket is no longer valid.

The Agency's way of telling him to fuck off. No reconnaissance team was going to come. What in God's name had happened down there? What kind of game was Colonel Rossi playing? He'd find out from Rossi himself. He picked up the receiver and dialed the Director's private number in Langley, changed on a weekly basis for security reasons. Screw procedure.

"Office of the Director," answered a secretary.

"I need to speak to Colonel Rossi immediately."

"I'm afraid that's impossible."

The rage swelled further. "Listen, miss, my name is Alabaster. My clearance is A-1000 and I've got a triple X security rating. Do you know what that means?"

"Certainly, but I still can't reach him. He's ill, severely so I'm told. I have no idea of where to reach him even if I wanted to and I've been ordered not to try."

"Ordered by who?"

"I don't know."

"What?"

"Standard procedure in such matters."

"Who's in charge now?"

"Mr. Kincannon."

"Let me speak to him, then."

"He left for the field two hours ago."

"Where in the field?"

"I don't know. He left no forwarding."

"That's impossible! Your bloody 'standard procedure' requires that the position of the Director or his substitute be known at all times."

"There *are* exceptions."

"There are rules, goddammit! What the hell is going on down there?"

"I believe you have the wrong number," the woman said, snidely and then hung up.

Macaphee walked into the room holding his hunting rifle. "I heard you shouting. What's the matter?"

David swung toward him, his face wooden. "Everything. Look I've got to get you and my son out of here. Do you have a private line upstairs?"

"Of course."

"Then call the nearest hospital and arrange for a room and all necessary facilities. Get an ambulance here as soon as possible to transport Shaul there."

The doctor's lips curled upwards in indecision. "It's not safe to move him."

"It's not safe for him to stay here."

"The wall of the artery has weakened under pressure from the clotting. If he's moved, it could rupture. He might die."

"He'll die for sure if he remains where he is. Now just do as I say."

Macaphee shrugged and moved back toward the stairs. "I hope you know what you're doing."

"We'll see."

Something had gone wrong in Langley, very wrong. But David could not waste precious seconds dwelling on what it might be. They had isolated him, left him out in the cold; that was all he knew, all he needed to know. He would call his task force headquarters in the suite at the Ambassador. Isser, Jacques and Stanislaw would know what to do. They would find out what was happening at the Agency and arrange for help to be sent, if not for him at least for Shaul once the boy had reached the hospital.

The phone was ringing.

"Come on, come on," he pleaded into the receiver but the phone on the other end went unanswered.

Impossible! The line was manned twenty-four hours a day. Rabanine hung up and dialed again, hoping that in his anxiety he may have dialed the wrong number. He hadn't; the results the second time were identical with the first. He dialed the manager's office, a man named Lapoint who was used to people like David staying in his hotel. The Ambassador had not been a random choice of lodging.

"Mr. Lapoint's office."

"Mr. Lapoint, please. David Rabanine calling."

David tapped the desk beneath him with his free hand, trying to stem the tension that raced through him.

"Mr. Rabanine," said Lapoint coming on the line, "I'm glad you called. I'm afraid I have some rather bad news for you."

The manager's voice was laced by a false calm that could not hide the breathlessness of his distraught.

"What?"

"Two of your associates, Mr. Ben-David and Mr. Kowalski, were found murdered not two hours ago."

Something empty erupted in David's stomach, giving a weightless sensation to his body and a numb feeling to his head. The receiver began to shake in his hand. The room swung in and out of darkness, his mind swirling toward collapse. He forced himself steady. The dark periods ended.

"Mr. Rabanine, are you still there?"

"How were they killed?"

"Their spines appear to have been snapped, although I can't be sure."

"What about the third man—Chevallier?"

"The man in the white suits with the mustache?"

"Yes."

"He left the hotel early this morning and hasn't returned since. Of course, I have men posted in the lobby waiting for him to come back in order to warn him." A pause. "There's something else, Mr. Rabanine. I called the number in Langley for the disposal unit, only no one has shown up yet. I'm worried. Such incidents have occurred before in the hotel—not often, you understand—but never has it taken so long for the Agency to respond. I fear something is wrong."

"So do I."

David hung up the phone as Lapoint started to speak again. He felt his grip on reason trying to desert him, using fatigue to its advantage. He fought to hold on, to contemplate what had happened.

More madness!

His son lay in the next room, suspended between life and death. The people that had so wanted his services had left him isolated to face the animals of Al Fatah by himself. Two of the only men he had ever trusted, men he could call true friends, had been murdered by the one man capable of killing with his bare hands in such a manner—Seif the Butcher. Because he had called them for help ten days before. . . .

We are everywhere.

By now, Al Fatah would surely be closing in. Yes, he had hidden the Grand Prix in the garage next to Macaphee's station wagon and removed all advertisement of the fact that a doctor's office was contained within the house. How long, though, would it be before the Arabs sought out the other physicians in the area and realized they had missed one? David sprung away from the desk and grabbed the rifle that was leaning on the wall, placed there by Macaphee. He checked it, balancing its awkward weight in his hands, certain now he would have to use it. Or would he? . . .

"The ambulance is on its way," the doctor announced coming back down the stairs. "I've reserved a room at Mount Washington Medical Center but I still strongly suggest that the boy not be moved."

David thought for a moment, a plan forming. "Where is your nurse, Doctor?"

"With your son."

"We will need her."

"For what?"

"Later. How well do you know the police in this town?"

"Well enough."

"Call them. Get them over here as soon as possible, sirens blasting. As many men and cars as they can spare."

"They will want to know why."

"Tell them a motorcycle gang is converging outside your house for your failure to treat one of its wounded members. Tell them you suspect the gang has recently been involved in some sort of violent crime."

"The lie will not last long."

"It will last long enough. We'll tell them a part of the truth when they arrive. How long before the ambulance gets here?"

"Another eight minutes or so."

334

"And how far away are the police?"

"I'd say about five minutes, a little less maybe."

"Then wait three minutes before you call them. Try to time it so the ambulance and the police cars arrive at the same time. We must create a diversion."

"A diversion for what?"

"Our escape."

THIRTY-FOUR

Bob Kincannon, interim Director of the CIA, entered the front of the restaurant and emerged immediately from the back. A black limousine, its engine idling, sat in the alley. Kincannon opened the rear door on the driver's side and climbed in nervously.

"I've done it," he told the man seated next to him. "Alabaster's been isolated. He's finished."

Mohammed al-Kahir's eyelids fluttered. "Do not be so sure about that, Mr. Kincannon."

"Why? Because he already escaped one of your traps today?"

"*Our* trap," al-Kahir corrected mildly. "But his son was shot in the process which will slow him down considerably."

"All the more reason why he should be dead soon."

In the front seat sat the driver and a huge man with a bald head. Neither spoke nor turned. Kincannon paid no attention to them.

"And what of the hotel?" al-Kahir asked.

"The order for a cleanup crew was countermanded."

"Good. We can't have the Ambassador swarming with CIA men when Seif returns to finish his work this afternoon." The Arab smiled. "You have done your job well, Mr. Kincannon."

"From the Director's chair, none of the tasks were difficult to accomplish. No one questioned me. The orders were followed out by men who have spent their careers doing what they are told and no more." Kincannon took off his glasses and began to clean the lenses with his handkerchief.

"Then it was convenient that the Director suffered his collapse when he did."

336

"Yes," smiled Kincannon, "very convenient."

"Arranged by you, no doubt."

Kincannon replaced his glasses on the bridge of his nose. "A slight change of medication, nothing more. As of this moment, Rossi should be feeling quite sick. He's do for another dosage of what he thinks are his painkillers in two hours. By morning, the great Colonel will be dead of an apparent heart attack."

"The Red Prince will be most pleased."

"He should be. It was, after all, his plan that worked so well today. He knew Alabaster would try to get word to the CIA somehow so he set Leslie Kirkman up as the only possible messenger. Thus, Alabaster was put at ease, while the person whose help he enlisted wasn't about to challenge me in the least or press things any farther. She was a perfect dupe."

"All the same, you deserve a reward for your loyalty."

"A place for me when all this is over would more than suffice."

"It is over for you now, I'm afraid."

In the front seat the bald man had turned fully around, revealing his scarred face. Slowly he began to lean his torso into the back, reaching out with a massive hand.

"It's been good working with you, Mr. Kincannon," al-Kahir said.

Kincannon tensed his body backwards, unable to speak, fear pouring from his eyes. He groped for the door latch but found it locked in place at the same instant Seif's fingers closed around his throat. The Butcher lifted him effortlessly from the seat and mashed his face hard enough against the top to make the roof buckle outwards and turn his features to bloody pulp.

Kincannon was nearly unconscious when Seif tightened his fingers into a final death grip. A sound like that of crinkling paper except much louder filled the limousine and air began to bottleneck in his throat. The CIA man's eyes dimmed, as though a curtain was closing before his glasses. The last thing he saw was Seif smiling at him.

"Well done, my friend," al-Kahir told the Butcher.

*   *   *

The men of Al Fatah stood silently in the woods across from the old house that served as Dr. Macaphee's office, concealed behind trees or bushes, there and yet not there at the same time. There were seven in all, waiting for a signal from the one appointed by the Red Prince as the leader to rush the house and kill all of its occupants.

The garage had been checked, a green car with shattered widows found within. This was surely the place.

The leader, a large man with a thick scar running across the dark flesh of his chin, lowered his binoculars and spoke to the man on his right behind the thick bush.

"It is time, Azazz."

He raised his right hand into the air, preparing to signal the small force to launch its attack. But the sound of sirens wailing close by and drawing closer made him reconsider his decision and shrink back behind the bush.

Various stages of disgust and disappointment appeared on all the Arabs' faces in the ensuing minutes. First, a parade of police cars—four in all, two men in each—screeched to a stop in front of the old house. The officers leaped from their seats, pistols drawn and ready. They had barely reached their positions in the front yard when another siren whined to a halt, announcing the arrival of an ambulance. Three men in white suits emerged from the vehicle and carted a stretcher quickly toward the front door. In this period of frenzy, a tall man appeared in the doorway.

"Alabaster," noted the leader.

The Arabs watched silently as the ambulance attendants carried the stretcher out of the house. A body lay on top of it, covered everywhere except the face by a white sheet. At that exact moment, Alabaster emerged from the doorway and the Arabs' eyes moved to him. Then the man they guessed to be Dr. Benjamin Macaphee moved swiftly toward Alabaster's son holding an IV bottle in the air, issuing instructions. The stretcher was placed carefully in the rear of the red and white mbulance, its top lights still turning and flashing.

Macaphee slammed the ambulance's rear doors and approached Alabaster. Together the two men hurried into a police car which sped off in line with the ambulance, both sirens screaming. A few seconds later, the rest of the police officers climbed back into their cars, still scrutinizing the area. Satisfied, they gunned their engines and took off after the two vehicles already on their way.

The Arab leader moved quickly toward the grove where the van was parked and signalled his men to follow.

"The nearest hospital is twenty minutes away in North Conway," he told Azazz. "I know the route they will take. We should have no trouble catching them."

"They might spot us."

"Our driver will see that they don't. We will follow them to the hospital and ambush them while the boy is being wheeled in."

The eight Arabs piled into the van and took off in pursuit of the flashing lights now temporarily out of sight. The skilled Al 'atah driver drew to within seventy feet five minutes later, the leader electing to remain at that distance until the very last moment when he would close the gap so quickly that the police, bungling old men anyway, would be powerless to react in time.

The leader smiled tightly. It would be a massacre. They would all be killed, Alabaster included, as they approached the doors of the hospital emergency room. He relished this thought, keeping the flashing dome of the ambulance clearly in his sights.

Not bothering to notice that the caravan of police cars behind it now numbered only three.

Ten minutes later the fourth police car pulled up back outside Macaphee's office, depositing its two passengers in the driveway. David dismissed the officers' offer to stay and help politely but firmly.

339

The plan did not include them.

Rabanine and Macaphee moved swiftly inside and headed for the room in which Shaul was lying. Both breathed a sigh of relief. All was just as they had left it. The boy was safe.

"I still say you took quite a chance by leaving him here all alone," the doctor said, checking his patient.

"It was our only chance because it was something the terrorists never would've expected."

"All the same, if they had bothered to check . . ."

"And risk not being able to catch us at the hospital? . . . No that isn't Al Fatah's style. They deal strictly with the realm of confrontation and attack. The best weapon against them is subtlety. They don't know how to respond to it." David studied the boy's features which looked serene and at ease. "How is he doing, Doctor?"

"Stable and holding his own under the circumstances. But wish we didn't have to move him."

"That is a foregone conclusion. By the way, you did a fine job of dressing up your nurse's face to look like Shaul's."

"As you said, the men across the street wouldn't be looking for him so much as you. But they will undoubtedly find out where he really is before long," Macaphee pronounced grimly "They may try again after we reach the other hospital."

"I'll arrange for protection."

"From who?"

"I'm not sure yet."

Macaphee hesitated. "Get the station wagon out of the garage, David. I'll get your son ready to travel."

David leaned back in the recovery room of the hospital allowing his eyes to close but forcing his mind to remain awake This day had been as long as any he could remember, beginning in turmoil and ending in chaos.

He had given Leslie Kirkman a message to deliver to Colonel Rossi. Rossi's health, though, had failed and he had not been at the Agency. Who, then, had she spoken to? Better yet, why had the forces of Langley turned against him? He wanted to find out but doing so now would mean Shaul would have to be left alone which was of course impossible.

A thought struck him. What about Chevallier? So far as David knew, the Frenchman was alive as of the time Isser and Stanislaw were killed. Conceivably, he had gone underground after learning of the murders. Chevallier's men were everywhere, a small army constantly at his disposal. But how to reach him? There was only one chance.

David walked to the pay phone on the wall in the sterile waiting room and charged a Paris number to his American credit card.

"*Bonjour. C'est le numero de Jacques Chevallier.*"

"*Où est Chevallier?*"

"*Je ne sais pas, monsieur. Il n'est pas ici.*"

"*Parlez-vous Anglais?*"

"*Oui, monsieur.* What can I do for you?"

"This is Alabaster. You have heard the Frenchman speak of me?"

"I have heard him speak of Alabaster many times, monsieur," the male voice said suspiciously, its accent thick. "But not necessarily of you."

"You have heard the phrase, Quoth the Raven, 'Nevermore.'"

"*D'accord. . . .* You need say no more to convince me. Monsieur Chevallier warned me I might hear from you someday. I am at your service."

"You know that Chevallier was in America working with me and several others on a certain operation?"

"I was aware only that he was in America."

"In any event, the others were killed this morning. The Frenchman escaped death only because he was not in the hotel at the time of the killer's arrival. I'm sure he has learned that his life is in danger and has gone underground. I must find him. It is imperative."

The man on the other end sighed. "A man in Washington

called this afternoon and gave me a number where Monsieur Chevallier could be reached in an emergency. He has gone more than underground, he has buried himself."

"But you *can* reach him."

"I can try. It might take time. Precautions have been taken. Many channels must be crossed."

"Cross them. Get word to Chevallier that I must speak with him. I can be reached here at . . ." David read the man the number printed on the pay phone.

"For how long, monsieur?"

"As long as it takes."

David hung up the phone and sat down in a chair three feet from it, staring at the black plastic as though his eyes would induce it to chime. His mind strayed to Leslie Kirkman, thoughts clashing. He wanted to let himself love her and yet he didn't. Too many of those he had loved in the past had been hurt by that love. His was a world of bullets not embraces and, so long as Alabaster existed, no change was possible. Always there would be men seeking to destroy him. And when they failed, they would turn their attentions to those he loved.

Leslie Kirkman . . .

Was she next in line to be hurt or killed by his loving hand? *Oh God* . . .

Seif was in Washington. The man who had killed the first woman he had loved was in ready position to kill the last he might. Protection for Leslie had to be secured, a safe hiding place found. The Frenchman had to call. If not . . .

The phone began to ring.

"Hello," he said anxiously.

"David, what's been happening?" demanded the frantic voice of Jacques Chevallier. "Isser and Stanislaw are dead. I would have been too, had it not been for—"

"I know. We've been crossed somewhere. A leak, a spy—I don't know. There's no time to figure it out. I need your help. Where are you?"

"Very well hidden, *mon ami*, rest assured, in a house outside of Washington that resembles a fortress. I have ten men watching the windows alone."

"I thought your men did no more than wear glasses and pass information."

"Some, not all. But you must tell me what happened? We knew you had returned last night but you were gone again before any of us woke up. I was out asking some questions when the others were murdered. . . . *Qu'est-ce qui se passe?*"

"My son was kidnapped."

"Shaul? . . . By Salameh? . . . *Mon dieu!*"

"I have him back but he's been shot rather seriously in the leg. I've managed to get him to a hospital but it won't be long before Al Fatah tracks us down. An assault on the entire intensive care ward is not beyond them."

"You've seen the Red Prince, then."

"And had a knife at his throat but failed to slit it."

"He has nine lives."

"We must hope he has used all of them up. For now, Jacques, I need you to send men up here to guard Shaul, as many as you can round up."

"Where exactly are you?" David gave him the particulars of his location. "*Mon ami,* I don't have that many operatives in New England. I will have to send them in from New York. But they will be good men, the best available on such short notice."

"As long as they can handle a gun as well as they can a message."

"If nothing else, they can hold one which should discourage Al Fatah from launching an assault. *Surtout,* the Red Prince is after you, not the boy."

"He is after me *through* the boy."

"*Je comprends.* . . . I'll have a dozen men there within two hours. They will be quite an imposing sight even before they draw their guns."

Rabanine's taut features relaxed a bit. "And there's something else, Jacques. The Kirkman woman's life is in danger again. I sent her to Langley to deliver a message to the

343

Director this morning but he wasn't there and now the whole goddamned CIA is running off track. I'm not sure what's going on but I know she's in trouble. She may even be—"

The Frenchman cut him off. "I suspected as much so I checked on her. As of one hour ago, she and her son were safe in their hotel room."

"She needs more lasting sanctuary."

Chevallier thought for a few moments. "Call her as soon as we are off the phone and tell her that fifteen minutes from now a black limousine will appear outside the Ambassador. She will know it by a flag of France hanging from the antenna. The car will transport her to a locale where she will be relatively safe."

"'Relatively,' Jacques?"

"*Oui*. Everything is relative now."

THIRTY-FIVE

David reached Leslie Kirkman seconds later.

"Are you all right? What happened?" she asked rapidly, her voice hoarse with concern.

"Everything's fine," he answered, trying to keep her calm as well as himself.

"I was so worried. I never thought I'd hear your voice . . . But what about Shaul?"

"He's alive, slightly wounded but resting comfortably."

"I would like to meet him someday."

"You will . . . soon. For now we have other matters to concern ourselves with. You went to Langley?"

"Yes, but I spoke to a man named Kincannon because the Director had suffered some kind of collapse. I told him everything you asked me to. Did I do the right thing?"

"It doesn't matter. You have to get out of the hotel quickly. Al Fatah has sent men to kill you."

Leslie's stomach sank. "But I was promised protection. Agents are supposed to be—"

"You're alone. They've isolated you just like they've isolated me. They're trying to make this the end game. You've got to escape. I've found a place for you to stay." David checked his watch. "Be downstairs near the entrance in twelve minutes. A black limousine with a French flag strung to its radio antenna will be waiting to transport you to a house occupied by Jacques Chevallier and his men. You and Jimmy will both be very well protected."

"I'm scared," she said, glancing at her son who was glued to the TV screen.

"Just don't delay. Get downstairs as quickly as you can and

be careful."

Leslie was about to respond when she realized the phone had clicked off.

"We've got to leave," she told Jimmy firmly, already moving for her suitcase.

"Where we going?" the boy asked.

"To a friend's house."

"Can I watch the end of the show first?"

Before Leslie could reply, the phone rang again.

"Hello," she said anxiously, hoping to hear David's voice on the other end.

"Mrs. Kirkman, this is the front desk. We've had a complaint about the maid service on your floor and we were wondering if you feel that your service has been adequate during the course of your stay with us."

"Quite."

"Thank you."

Leslie returned the receiver to its hook and began tossing hers and Jimmy's clothes into one medium sized suitcase.

In the lobby, meanwhile, a stocky old man nodded to Seif the Butcher. Seif's shoulders were poorly contained within the brown suit that left no room for movement. It was tight, restrictive, and made an already uneasy Seif all the more uncomfortable. After all, he had already killed two men in this very hotel just hours before. Coming back was a chance he preferred not to take. But orders were orders.

The Butcher moved into the elevator and pressed 14.

At that moment, Leslie Kirkman was walking swiftly down the long corridor toting the suitcase in one hand and her son in the other. She was anxious to leave the hotel. David's words had frightened her. His voice had sounded nervous . . .

Voice! . . . The phone call from the front desk!

The man had addressed her as "Mrs. Kirkman." But she was registered under a different name. He could not have known and yet he seemed to. The implications were obvious.

Someone wanted to see if she was inside. That person would almost certainly be on their way up now. She grabbed Jimmy's arm, stopping him in his tracks.

"Are we going back to watch the end of the show?" he asked hopefully.

"No, we're going to take the stairs down."

"I want to take the elevator," Jimmy protested. "It goes real fast."

"It'll be more fun this way."

"All right," the boy agreed reluctantly.

"And we've got to run, like in a race."

Jimmy finished studying her lips and took off back down the corridor.

Seif felt for the knife as the elevator came to a halt and the doors slid open. The Butcher's feet met the soft carpet of the hallway. The kill would be quick, easy, and above all silent; the knife would see to that, in addition to providing a sense of variety. Seif had killed many with his hands lately. He wanted a change.

Fifty yards away, mother was straining to keep up with child, afraid to glance behind her. They passed the room that had been theirs and turned onto another corridor, heading for a door marked "Emergency Exit."

Leslie reached the door a second after her son, tossed aside the suitcase, and thrust the side of her body against the steel crash bar that should have given under the pressure. But it didn't.

Seif turned the master key in the lock and surged into the room expecting the chain to be in his way. It wasn't. The door simply gave. The Butcher whirled forward and slammed it behind him, knife in hand. The room was empty.

Leslie crashed her shoulder into the steel bar for the fourth time. Finally it budged and then gave altogether on the next impact to reveal linoleum steps that smelled of ammonia. Fourteen flights separated her from the lobby. Leslie grabbed her son's hand.

"Come on!"

"Can't we take the elevator?"

Leslie's answer was to pull him alongside her and begin the descent, mother and child keeping the same furious pace.

The condition of the room told Seif that his two targets had left in a hurry. The phone call, he surmised, had made the woman suspicious so she had fled. But not toward the elevator; he would have seen her. Where then? He stepped back into the hallway and bolted for what he knew was their only other possible route of escape.

The tan suitcase that lay at the entrance to the emergency stairwell confirmed his conclusion. He crashed into the steel bar, sending the heavy door smashing against the wall. About four flights below him, the Butcher heard the monotonous echo of soles churning against the hard surface. His targets had quite a headstart. There was much space to make up.

Leslie's breath was already gone. She was spurred on only by the boy whose hand she held tightly, as if to shut off the circulation. Fear had all but choked off her remaining wind when footsteps began to pound above her. Someone was closing fast, taking two steps to her one.

"Faster, Jimmy! Faster!" she screamed breathlessly.

The boy sensed his mother's terror and tensed his muscles in confusion. Leslie tugged at his hand, forcing him to increase his speed to match hers. The steps became a blur before her eyes. She was conscious of sudden turns and temporary flat areas, signifying a new flight was beginning and that the lobby was coming nearer. But she was equally conscious of the maddening rhythm of the footsteps above her, closing the gap with each second.

Leslie had lost track of how many flights had passed and how many remained. Her legs continued to turn, muscles cramping under her slacks. Icy needles of agony plunged in and out of her thighs. Her calves locked out to protest the strain.

Closer . . . Closer . . . The footsteps were almost directly above her now. Two flights, no more, separated hunter from hunted.

Leslie's free hand dug into the handrail for support and guidance. The insides of her stomach stitched themselves together. A blast of hot pain erupted in her left shoulder, throbbing in rhythm with her heart.

Closer still . . . One flight now . . .

Another steel crash bar appeared before her, the door not yet distinguishable from the wall around it. But it was there, signalling she had reached the lobby. Her grasp tightened involuntarily around Jimmy's hand.

Seif took the final flight in two steps, catching his first fleeting glimpse of his quarries. He had drawn the long, shiny knife from its sheath at the precise moment Leslie had lunged into the crash bar, the door this time giving immediately under the pressure. Mother and son dashed into the crowded lobby, both panting, breaking stride, oblivious to the hulking man who had drawn almost directly behind them. Their actions drew angered looks from several hotel patrons who were offended by the disruption. Such displays were not supposed to occur in the Ambassador.

Jimmy stumbled and nearly fell. Leslie reached down to help him regain his balance, her eyes swinging to the rear. A huge man filled her line of vision, his bald head glowing in the bright light of the lobby. I'm going to die, she thought, shoving Jimmy safely away from her as she closed her eyes and began a scream that was swallowed by her windless panic. She lifted her lids again, surprised pain had not poured into her body through a hole made by gun or knife. Perhaps with death there was no pain. But for now there would be no death. The huge man had disappeared.

Leslie scooped her son up and pulled him through the electronic sliding doors at the front of the hotel. She moved her eyes around the circular drive, wondering if the bald figure was moving for her again. A French flag flapped in the early evening breeze. It was attached to the antenna of a long, black limousine. She sped toward the car, her right leg locked out and her left one dragging. Her hand still grasped that of her son. The boy followed along like a machine incapable of independent thought or action.

From the lobby, Seif watched one of the limousine's rear doors open and a man emerge to help the writhing woman and her son inside. The knife was back in the sheath cleverly strapped around his calf. While Leslie was making her reckless way through the lobby, the Butcher had closed to within three feet. Not that he intended to kill her—chancing an attack within the crowded lobby would have been foolish. But it was important for him to know that he could have killed both the woman and child in under four seconds had he wished to. He had decided to let them go . . . for now.

They weren't his prime targets anyway.

Art Bartose wheeled Colonel Vernon Rossi down the long corridors of the CIA's Langley headquarters.

"When was Kincannon last seen?" the Director asked.

"Two o'clock this afternoon," Bartose answered. "He was dropped off by his driver outside a restaurant for what was supposed to have been a quick lunch and meeting. Twenty minutes later the driver entered and found no trace of him."

"Perhaps we should ask our friends at Black September what's become of our illustrious Deputy Director," Rossi remarked dryly.

Workers; the men clad in finely cut suits, the women in neatly pleaded skirts; passed Rossi and Bartose regularly and issued perfunctory greetings. The Agency seemed just as bustling at ten o'clock at night as it had twelve hours earlier.

"I can't understand why he turned," Bartose said, finding a better hold on the handgrips atop the Director's wheelchair.

"The why is inconsequential now, Art. What matters is learning exactly how much damage has been done. We know about the isolation of Alabaster and the scratching of a cleanup

350

crew that should have been sent to the Ambassador. According to the tape made of his conversation with Mrs. Kirkman, you also say that valuable information was not relayed to the proper channels." Rossi glanced up at the man pushing his chair. "Does it surprise you, Art, that I bugged my own office?"

"It surprises me more that you knew your medication had been tampered with."

"I didn't know, I only suspected. You see, Art, I have this rule, call it a doctrine to live by. Whenever I feel suddenly sick for no apparent reason, I don't take more medication, I take less if any. Too many people in positions like mine have died too conveniently over the years. I don't wish to join them." Rossi took a labored breath. "Did you call Herb Weinberg? I want him to hear this tape too."

"I got hold of him just after I spoke to you. He should be waiting for us inside your office."

"And Alabaster?"

"No word at all. He appears to have dropped out of sight."

"More likely, he was pushed there by our own blasted stupidity. But that's beside the point. Right now we've got to get word to him that it's safe to come in, perhaps through that man Chevallier."

"He's disappeared as well."

"Then we'll have to find another means. But first I've got to hear that tape."

They had reached the Director's office. Herb Weinberg rose from the vinyl couch in the outer room as Bartose closed the door behind Colonel Rossi. Dark circles had formed beneath the FBI man's eyes that had fought so long to stay open. His cheeks sagged and his graying hair hung unkemptly over his scalp. He had been reached at the hospital where his wife had slipped into a coma she was never expected to come out of.

"Let's go inside," said Rossi.

The Director pushed a button on his wheelchair and the knobless door swung open. One of the lights was on in his office and its dim rays struck the face of a tall man standing in the far right corner looking out at the moonlit woods that bordered the compound. The man didn't bother to turn around.

"You have some explaining to do, Colonel Rossi," Rabanine said after Rossi had wheeled himself in flanked by Weinberg and Bartose.

"I'm glad to see you, David," the Director said uneasily. "We weren't sure what happened."

"Is that part of your explanation?" Rabanine turned to face the three men for the first time. His eyes were cold. A set of clothes borrowed from Ben Macaphee fit him too tightly.

"We had a security problem."

"Kincannon?"

"Kincannon. He's disappeared, more than likely executed, but not before doing considerable damage." The Director's gravel voice was uneven, broken by strain and sickness.

"Did you know, Colonel, that that damage includes the right thigh of my son? He was shot this morning. He'll live. He just may not ever be able to use his leg fully again."

The Director's mouth dropped, his hands grasping the arms of his wheelchair. "I didn't know. . . . I'm sorry."

"It would seem there's much you don't know."

"I'd like to remind you, David, that we're still fighting the same enemy."

"Except that I haven't had much help lately."

"So you're going to punish the world by not accepting any more because of one old man's incompetence."

Rabanine's cheeks relaxed and his eyes warmed, singed by heartfelt compassion for the crippled man before him. "It's been a long day . . . for both of us."

"Its length didn't prevent you from finding a way to get inside my office. There are men who'd pay millions to learn how."

"A good magician never reveals his tricks."

"And a bad one can't make them work anyway. . . . You

knew I was coming. From Chevallier, of course."

"Of course."

"Tell the little bastard I've got something planned for him for the next twenty years."

"A prison term?"

"This job when I finally die—I guess you could call it that." A pause. "I'd like to hear about your meeting with Dr. Schmidt." Colonel Rossi wheeled his chair behind the large desk, at once seeming more comfortable.

David sat down in the chair immediately in front of him. His exhaustion and pain, both inside and out, were clearly evident to the other men in the room. Weinberg and Bartose remained standing as he began to speak.

"So the primary point," David concluded, "is that the Deliverers of Death have to be taken alive because a vaccine drawn from their blood is the only thing that can stop the advance team of carriers from spreading the disease beyond the test site and accomplishing the purpose of Shaitan even if none of the 175 primary agents ever entered the country."

Here, Herb Weinberg's expression went white and his knees buckled. He brought his hands up to meet his drooping face and steadied himself on the side of his chair before slowly sinking into it. His fingers then left his flesh to reveal a gray tint etched over a ghostly pallor.

"I had it in my hands," he muttered, eyes locked mindlessly on his open palms. "I had it and I let it go. . . ."

"Had what?" Rossi asked.

"I didn't know; how could I have? There were so many. I had to make decisions, set priorities. And my wife, I couldn't stop thinking about her. Now it's too late."

"What are you talking about?"

Weinberg swung his eyes about the room in aimless anxiety before finally finding the Director's.

"Crescent Falls, Wyoming."

PART FIVE

THIRTY-SIX

The soldiers at the roadblock on route 59 leading into
Crescent Falls watched the helicopter slice its way through the
thick morning air just past dawn on Friday. They did not know
why the area twenty-five miles in every direction of the town
had been cut off from the rest of civilization. Or why they had
been summoned at midnight from their barracks in Sheridan to
stand a vigil that was now stretching into its eighth hour. Or
what it was precisely that they were supposed to be looking for.

They hadn't asked questions, except among each other. And
here answers were sorely lacking while speculation was
running high. Perhaps the Russians had finally landed—in
Wyoming. It seemed as conceivable as anything else.

Twenty-five miles away, the helicopter set down right on
Main Street, its whirling propeller catching the sun's rays and
shooting them upward as it swung to a halt. Both men inside
were wearing protective suits flown in with them the night
before on a special military jet. The white material looked like
cloth, felt like vinyl, and was topped by a helmet that fit snugly
in place. The men had secured their helmets and begun to
breathe oxygen from tanks slung across their shoulders just as
the chopper began its descent. A small, short-range transmitter
built into their headgear would provide their means of
communication once they left the chopper.

Both men had been flown into Wyoming from the Center for
Disease Control in Atlanta, Georgia. They had been briefed
over the phone by the Director of the CIA personally, chosen
for this assignment because they were experts in the field of
biological disasters.

They had been told simply that an extremely contagious and

deadly germ was believed to have been released in Crescent Falls sometime within the last five days. They were warned that some of those infected would already be dead and several others would be very close to it. Most would probably be in the developmental stages, exhibiting symptoms similar to flu. And approximately half of the town's population would not be infected at all.

This information, though, had been passed on before all attempts to reach anyone in Crescent Falls had failed. If half of the town was alive, why was no one answering their phones?

The task of the two men, named Marks and Kilcoyne, was to find the answer. They were to survey the entire radius of Crecent Falls and report their findings to Washington as soon as possible. Any residents found alive were to be placed in isolation areas on the main strip of the town which would be equipped with all necessary instruments and machines, presently contained on the chopper.

Inside the helicopter, Kilcoyne flashed a thumbs-up sign to Marks. The two men climbed out looking like astronauts about to explore a distant planet. The search for life had begun.

"Marks," Kilcoyne said into the invisible mike when he reached the residential outskirts of the town, "I'm at the north end. I've just come out of a house. Four occupants: man, woman, two children. All dead. Whatever it was came on quick. They all died in their sleep. Severe vomiting and internal hemorrhaging. Blood vessels along throat and nasal cavity ruptured resulting in major blood loss through all venting areas."

"I've got a ditto of that in the southeast with a family of three," Marks reported, "only the father seems to have made it into the bathroom for all the good it did him."

"How long you estimate they've been dead?"

"Between seventy-two and ninety-six hours. Ever seen anything like this before?"

Kilcoyne swallowed hard inside his helmet. "Only in classrooms. I'm proceeding back toward the center of town.

Check in with you then."

"Roger."

Ten minutes passed.

"Marks," Kilcoyne began, "I'm in the local sheriff's office. It looks like something out of . . . Hey, wait a minute. . . ."

Silence. For the first time, Sam Marks was scared.

"Marks to Kilcoyne. Marks to Kilcoyne. Come in Kilcoyne."

"I read you Marks," came the breathless reply. "I've found someone alive in here. Not by much but alive just the same."

"What have you got for vitals?"

"Not promising. Low blood pressure and barely perceptible pulse. Sever comatose condition worsened by malnutrition."

"Man or woman?"

"Man, and a big one. It's probably the only thing that's kept him alive this long. He should be dead. Seems like he hasn't eaten or drank anything for a minimum of four days."

"Since the disease hit."

Kilcoyne nodded to himself. "Yeah, but he *is* alive. Whatever killed the rest of the town spared him. Let's rendezvous back at the chopper. We've got to prepare an isolation unit to transport him to Atlanta . . . and fast."

"What are we going to tell Washington?"

Kilcoyne hesitated for the briefest of seconds. "That we've got a plague on our hands but we're bringing in a survivor."

"I don't like your explanation, David. I don't like it one bit." Colonel Rossi's tight-lipped countenance was wedged somewhere between terror and disbelief.

"Neither do I but we've got to face the fact that it's accurate. Everything adds up to it."

"Mind doing the addition again for me?"

Rabanine moved his eyes to the window and then back to the director. "All the information we have states that only fifty percent of the town's population should have been killed by the disease and that it should more than likely have taken a

359

minimum of seven days to enter its fatal stage. Yet the entire population of Crescent Falls, save one, has been wiped out. According to Schmidt, this could happen only if the final dosage taken by the carriers was too large. Now Herb Weinberg recently received a telegram from the sheriff of Crescent Falls, coincidently the lone survivor, requesting information about five strangers who had shown up in town. Let's assume that these five strangers made up the advance carrier force and that they knew the sheriff was onto them. In that situation they took it on themselves to increase the final dosage and speed up the infection process so they would be able to leave the town with their task completed before the sheriff had an opportunity to deal with them."

"And they ended up killing themselves in the process."

"Exactly. Four years of injections couldn't protect them against the potency of the organism released by the excessive final dose. In essence, they took their own lives in addition to the lives of the town's residents."

Herb Weinberg sighed. "I'm having trouble believing that one disease could cause so much destruction so rapidly."

"You shouldn't be." The speaker was Dr. Tanner Lewiston, an epidemiologist who had arrived from the Center for Disease Control (CDC) just hours before as the ranking member of the Biological Disaster Unit. He was a man much younger in appearance than his various titles and degrees indicated. He was just over forty and had wavy brown hair that stretched over his ears. His glasses were the kind that darkened when exposed to the sun. "Such diseases have existed for well over a generation, or should I say man's ability to *control* these diseases. Near the end of World War II, for example, the allies lost sleep worrying that the Germans were planning to fill their V-1 rockets with biological warheads equipped with botulinus toxin, eight ounces of which could kill the entire world's population if properly dispersed."

"But," noted Herb Weinberg, "there aren't any rockets involved here. *People* are carrying the organisms."

"It's still biological warfare," Lewiston explained, "actually in its most advanced and deadly state. For years we've always thought of biological attack in terms of overt military delivery through missiles designed to create an aerosol cloud of a fatal, infectious agent. I submit that the Arabs have discovered a far more elaborate and covert means that could wipe out an entire country with no evidence of strategic biological warfare. The idea of using human carriers is as brilliant as it is deadly."

"Then we *are* dealing with a germ here," advanced Rossi.

"Most certainly, though an extremely sophisticated one."

"But if it's a germ, you should still be able to come up with a way to kill it," suggested Art Bartose.

"I'll have to find it first and that promises to be no easier than finding a contact lens on a football field," said Lewiston. "You must realize that we live in a world of germs, of microorganisms. The precise number stretches into the hundreds of trillions and beyond. We take them into our lungs when we breathe, our stomachs when we eat, and our skin when we touch. But disease is brought on only by those germs capable of becoming parasites and using the human body as a host. A parasite like Shaitan is able to form hundreds of thousands of colonies which spread toxins throughout the body. The body, of course, will try to defend itself through the production of antibodies. Since it has never been exposed to this particular disease before, however, it will be unable to come up with the proper defenses for fighting it."

Rossi hedged nervously in his chair. "What about *our* defenses?"

"Not much better off I'm afraid. To begin with, Crescent Falls must be totally isolated from the rest of the country. We then must make a concerted effort to track down as many people as we can who've been in the town since Monday and those that they, in turn, have come into contact with."

"We'd never find them all," grumbled Art Bartose.

"But we have to find as many as possible."

"Do you have any idea how many people one man can pass

361

by in five days, Tanner?" challenged Rossi.

"Half as many as he will have in ten, which is why we must act fast while the number is still relatively manageable. No, we won't be able to get all of them. But at least we might be able to slow down the geometric spreading of the disease." Lewiston took a deep breath. "And toward that end I would also suggest sealing off the entire state of Wyoming."

"That would set off a national panic," protested Rossi.

"As opposed to a national disaster? I believe the alternative is a favorable one."

"It won't work," said Rabanine. He shook his head slowly, features squinted. The four other men looked at him quizzically. "Isolating Wyoming is not in our best interests. It'll hurt us more than help us."

"On the contrary—"

David cut Tanner Lewiston off. "How long could we keep up the farce of trying to keep an entire state under quarantine? How long would it be, *could it be,* before some infected person got out of the state if one hasn't already?"

"That's irrelevant," protested the man from Atlanta. "The fact remains that we've got to try. We've got to buy ourselves some time."

"But the price might be too high." David rose and walked to the office's one window. "The only hope we have right now is to capture the 175 Deliverers of Death. But if the Red Prince knew that the disease had already spread beyond Crescent Falls, he might delay their entrance or not send them in at all. He might even kill them and our chances of coming up with a vaccine at the same time."

"So?" From Rossi.

"So we put all our attention on Crescent Falls and act as though the disease has been confined there. Salameh knows that something must have gone wrong in the town. The element of surprise has been lost. We now know the weapon as well as the means of attack. Salameh will have to move fast. But everyone in the town is dead which means, as far as he can see,

362

that there's nobody left alive to spread the disease. He'll have to depend on *die Bote* more than ever. And since he knows we're onto him, he'll want them in the country even sooner than was originally planned. That will give us the opportunity we need to capture them before it's too late to matter."

"And in the meantime we just open the floodgate and let the disease pour out of Wyoming unchecked," noted Rossi skeptically.

"It's probably too late to close them anyway."

"You're talking about a bluff, David. What if the Red Prince calls it?"

"He'll have no reason to. So long as we focus our attention on Crescent Falls, Salameh will too. He'll have no reason to suspect that Shaitan has spread to other parts of the state and the country because it will appear as though we've successfully isolated it in the town."

Lewiston frowned. "Letting people pass freely in and out of Wyoming is like playing Russian roulette with only one chamber empty."

"Isolate Wyoming and you load the sixth bullet. We might as well send Salameh a telegram telling him that the disease is already spreading and that his plan has worked. A bluff is actually the safest way to play the game because it's the best way to insure that the carriers—and our vaccine—will enter the country."

Colonel Rossi leaned back and pondered the words. He sighed loudly. "I'll have to get an okay from the White House but let's tentatively accept David's plan."

"I'll still need living subjects for testing in Atlanta," Lewiston reminded, obviously displeased with the decision.

"Besides the sheriff?"

Lewiston nodded. "People whose bodies manifest the disease in various stages."

Rossi swung toward Weinberg. "Herb, how many have we found so far who've had direct contact with Crescent Falls since Shaitan invaded?"

"Three: a deliveryman and two highway patrolmen. Of course their families have to be included in the isolation along with the people they've had extensive contact with. . . ."

"The contact doesn't have to be extensive," broke in Lewiston.

"In any case," Weinberg resumed, "the deliveryman was the first, we gather, to enter the town after the disease took effect. He brought his story to the Highway Patrol."

"What have you done about him and the patrolmen?"

"Nothing yet. They're all incapacitated, in bed with what they think is the flu."

"We've got to get them out of there," interjected Lewiston, "and into isolation units in Atlanta."

"But we'll never be able to transport all those they've come into contact with," Rossi pointed out dolefully.

"As many as we can, then."

"And the rest?"

"We're going to set up a field office in Wyoming, the facilities of which will be virtually identical to our home base in Atlanta."

"How, though, can we gather up and transport even the most severe cases to CDC without infecting others?" From Bartose.

"A specially sealed truck will pick them up at their homes. The men in the cab section will be outfitted with space suits and oxygen supplies as well as . . . weapons."

"Weapons?"

"Those who don't want to go will be taken anyway, one way or another."

"Where's the nearest truck of this kind now?" From Rossi.

"On its way to Wyoming by military transport. I took the liberty of sending it out after our phone conversation this morning as a precautionary measure. I've also ordered a team of men into Crescent Falls with six personnel carrying helicopters to collect all the bodies for transport back to Atlanta. Afterwards, we have to be sure that no one comes within twenty miles of the town."

"Why not just blow it up as it stands?" Bartose asked.

"That might come later. At this point, though, the only lead we have to finding a cure for the Shaitan disease—outside of capturing the 175 carriers—is discovering what made that sheriff different from the rest of the residents. Something in the town might hold the answer."

"Dr. Lewiston," said David, "tell the team going into Crescent Falls to bring out all the personal effects belonging to those corpses found inside hotel rooms or boardinghouses."

"Why?"

"Because those people are almost certainly the members of the advance force. Their passports, identifications, maybe even their clothing might give us some clue to determine the identities of *die Bote.*" Rabanine turned to face the Director. "And, Colonel Rossi, there is one man who might be able to help us: Mengele's other assistant at Auschwitz, a doctor named Johann Gessler. ODESSA got him out of Germany after the war and then lost track of him in 1972. They spotted him some years later in Syria and now believe it was Gessler who developed Shaitan for the PLO. If so, he might be able to help us find a way to destroy it." David paused. "I also suggest we contact Yassir Arafat."

The other men in the room stared at David dumbfounded.

"Arafat . . . ?"

"Why not? He's become more and more of a moderate these past few years. The revolutionary leanings he maintains, some say, are merely to appease the less moderate factions of the PLO. He still supports terrorist actions, but more as a distraction now than anything else. He agreed to the development of the Shaitan Commandment in the aftermath of Munich ten years ago when it appeared that terrorist warfare was the only means the PLO could use to achieve its ends. Much of that has changed, perhaps even enough. I'm not even sure Arafat knows that the Commandment exists in its present form."

"What do you mean?" Rossi asked, intrigued.

"That the Red Prince may have told him one thing and done another. Salameh might well be one of the emerging leaders of the splinter faction of the PLO that has grown steadily in numbers and power as the diplomatic preachings of the moderates have been repeated again and again without success. The conflict is kept out of the open for the better of the Organization. But if Arafat was told the truth about what was happening, he might take steps to stop Shaitan by handing over the 175 Deliverers of Death to us. He is probably the only person left who can reach Salameh on a reasonable level."

"Assuming, of course, that he does not *condone* the actions of the Red Prince," advanced Weinberg.

"And that he believes *us*," added Bartose.

"We'd have no reason to lie about something like this and Arafat knows it."

"All the same," sighed Rossi, "he wouldn't help us without charging an awful price."

"Could it be any greater than the one we're about to pay? He'll listen to reason. . . . This is his world too."

"Speaking of which, Tanner," the Director began in a more normal tone, "what is there to stop Shaitan from spreading beyond our borders?"

Lewiston thought for a few moments. "I'd say something about the germ's chemical structure. But I won't be able to even venture a guess as to what until I've done thorough examinations of the corpses as well as the infected living bodies that will very likely be joining them before long."

"And if you don't find anything?"

"Just pray that I do."

THIRTY-SEVEN

"What went wrong there, Mohammed?"

The Red Prince's eyes stared blankly before him, uncertain in their derision. He stood in the living room of a Syracuse home which was another in a long chain of houses owned by the PLO and used in America as reference or refuge points. The living room was plainly furnished with furniture of cheap fabric and poor design, the individual pieces clashing. Most would have found its many sun-spilling windows a welcome feature. Ali Hassan Salameh did not. His strong, handsome face was creased and worn. His eyes were dull and listless, his hair rumpled. His movements had lost their surety and confidence. His fingers twitched uncontrollably.

"Something very serious, Ali," al-Kahir replied, looking up at the Red Prince from a couch that creaked every time he shifted his position. "The agents we sent to investigate were turned back at a roadblock. All routes leading into Crescent Falls have been sealed off. Helicopters buzz the skies, heading off anyone who strays in the town's direction over the land. Rumors are flying everywhere that the town's entire population has been wiped out. They are denied vehemently by the authorities. But we have reason to know otherwise."

"None of that answers my original question."

"I don't have an answer, Ali." Al-Kahir rose in frustration, the couch squealing beneath him. "The men had strict orders as to what they were supposed to have done. They would not have disregarded them, at least not knowingly."

"They would not have disregarded them at all!" Salameh roared. "I handpicked them myself. They were well trained; no, superbly trained. They could *not* have failed."

"In that case," al-Kahir began unevenly, "the only answer is that something has gone wrong with the formula in which case everything has changed."

"*Nothing has changed!*" The dark features of the Red Prince's face flared with rage. "In some ways, the experiment can be considered a success," he said with forced calm, maneuvering the cigarette from one hand to the other. "Yes, the disease might very well carry a one hundred percent mortality rate instead of only fifty—a one hundred percent mortality rate in the most sensitive areas of the United States once the larger Shaitan force arrives. Yes. . . . The 175 carriers must be brought into the country, only sooner than planned in order to maintain the advantage we now possess."

"Arafat might disagree. It would be easy for him to conclude that we have *lost* the advantage, Ali. The Americans know what we intend to do, in point of fact *have already done*. The element of surprise has been lost. They will retaliate against us before the Commandment is complete. Our plan has failed. We'd be wise to pull out while there is still a chance to salvage something through blackmail."

"Pull out? After all these years? . . ." Salameh's expression was trapped somewhere between determination and disappointment. The cigarette began to twirl faster in his hands. "Ten years, Mohammed, ten years of work, of research, of planning for the day when we would be masters of our destiny instead of prisoners of it. Now that day is almost upon us and you would have me abandon it."

"What happened in Crescent Falls forces us to reconsider our strategy."

"On the contrary, what happened in the town merely confirms its effectiveness." Salameh turned toward the large bay window, suddenly not minding the sun. "We're too close to stop, too far not to continue. The carriers and the residents of Crescent Falls are dead. The Americans have sealed the town off. The disease cannot spread further unless we bring the Shaitan force in and bring them in we will."

"Arafat might think otherwise."

"Arafat is a fool! He has tried to barter and reason with the governments of the free world and where has it got him—and us?" Salameh paused, his eyes blazing. "Nowhere, Mohammed, nowhere at all. We are no better off now than we were ten years ago, only worse. The time of the moderates has passed, ours is arriving. *My* time, at least. What about yours, Mohammed?"

"My time as well, Ali," al-Kahir conceded, fearful of the consequences the truth would bring.

"I'm glad to hear that, Mohammed, because I need you to complete the plan. The Shaitan force must have no trouble securing entry into the country."

"They won't. Their identities and positions are secure."

"Good." The Red Prince broadened his small grin into a large one that stretched from cheek to cheek. "The Commandment will bring on worldwide revolution and anarchy. Everywhere the oppressed people of the globe will rise up against those who have used them for so long. These people will look to someone who can unite them in their quest and bring them the power they so richly deserve. That person, Mohammed, will be me. Arafat and his stinking moderates have what they want and seek no more. They are finished. I, on the other hand, have just begun, Mohammed. *Just begun! . . .*"

Friday evening was descending on Langley, Virginia as the four men met in a private room in the cafeteria. Only Tanner Lewiston was missing from the same group that had been present in the Director's office that morning.

"Lewiston just called in from Atlanta," Colonel Rossi began after their orders had been taken for dinner. "The bodies have all been collected and are on their way to Atlanta and a deep isolation ward at the Center for Disease Control at this very moment." Rossi checked his watch. "In fact, they've probably arrived already."

"What about the personal effects of all occupants of any

rooming houses or motels?" David asked.

"There's only one such location in the town and only five men were registered—obviously the Al Fatah agents. All their bodies have been recovered. Their wallets, passports and other possessions are being forwarded here by special messenger. They should be arriving any time now."

"That'll give us a place to start."

"I wish I could say the same for Tanner. He's already examined the sheriff from Crescent Falls, Bugsy Tyler, and preliminarily has found nothing. The fact that whatever kept the disease from killing him is not obvious makes finding it a longshot. The only hope we have now is that the man will wake up and provide the answer himself."

"What's his condition?"

"Deteriorating. But Tanner says that's to be expected at this point, a reaction to being given nutrition again."

"And what about Arafat?"

"The President spoke to him at length this afternoon, briefing him on the particulars of what we're facing without dwelling on the politics involved. Arafat, I'm told, promised to make contact with Salameh at the earliest possible time to find out what he can. But he gave no assurances. And, as we suspected, there is a price involved."

"What do you mean?" asked Weinberg.

"Did you really expect Arafat to help us without guaranteeing something for himself? Hardly. I'm afraid the President was forced to make a deal. If Arafat is successful in aborting Shaitan and in delivering *die Bote* to us, then America will support Palestinian autonomy openly before the world."

"The bastard," mumbled Weinberg.

"The President or Arafat?"

"Take your pick."

"And what would you suggest we do, Mr. Weinberg?" Rossi challenged. "Sit back quietly and watch our country die?"

"It might be preferable to turning our backs on the only ally we have in the Mediterranean." Weinberg turned toward

Rabanine, as though to look for support.

"I don't think it will come to that," David said simply.

"Why?" Rossi asked.

"Because I'm not convinced that Arafat will be able to order Salameh to abort Shaitan."

"I disagree," argued Art Bartose. "No Arab terrorist would dare swat a fly without Arafat's approval. What's more, Salameh's file is full of information about how close he and Arafat have been since 1968."

"And that conclusion is based on a file that presumed Salameh to be dead in 1979. Three-and-a-half years have passed. The Red Prince's family has been murdered. You yourself admit he may be mad. The issue comes down to how far Salameh has taken his Al Fatah guerilla group away from the mainstream of the PLO movement. Conceivably, he could be beyond even Arafat's control."

"Incidently," Rossi broke in, wishing to change the subject, "the information on Johann Gessler, Mengele's other assistant came through. A few major holes have been filled in but nothing that promises to help us at this point." The Colonel removed a pair of bifocals from the breast pocket of his pinstripe suit, resting them uncomfortably on the bridge of his nose. He then opened a manilla folder, staring at its contents in the dim light of the private dining room as he continued. "With the help of ODESSA; Johann Gessler, scientist; became Karl Woering, engineer. He was one of ODESSA's most select prizes and remained active in that movement until 1972 when he went to work at an industrial plant one day and never came home. No one knew anything about his whereabouts, including ODESSA. It made no sense until a man matching Gessler's description was seen in Damascus two years later by one of Wiesenthal's operatives. His report stressed that the man believed to be Gessler was now named Abdul Yarmak and that he made daily trips to and from the Akhdar medical facility in Damascus. The same Abdul Yarmak was listed as a staff member at the Al Khozama facility in Amman, Jordan; and the

Achra facility in Tripoli. All three facilities were built with Saudi Arabian money as fronts for PLO activities, although they also served partially as legitimate medical centers."

"So assuming Yarmak is Gessler," David picked up, "it's quite possible he carried on the work of Mengele for Al Fatah in these centers."

"More than possible. A study of Gessler's, then Woering's, family bank accounts revealed that huge sums of money were deposited through a bank in Damascus five months *before* he disappeared."

"Then the only thing we don't know is whether Gessler contacted the Arabs or the Arabs contacted him."

The Director nodded. "But we do know that he completed his work for them six months ago because in the space of two weeks this past November all three medical facilities at which he was registered were blown up. Sabotage was the cause in each. The Mossad was blamed, falsely of course."

"I vaguely recall the allegations."

Rossi's face stiffened. "Al Fatah blew up their own buildings in order to cover up all traces of what had been going on inside. The last one to go was the Damascus center. Twenty-one people were killed. Twenty were Arabs; one was pretending to be."

"Abdul Yarmak?"

"None other."

"He's come out of the coma, David. He's going to live."

The words of Dr. Ben Macaphee surged through Rabanine, raising goose bumps to his skin's surface. He sat down on the bed in his room in the well guarded CIA safe house, feeling his tense muscles, strung into sinewy strands of iron, relax. He smiled.

"Ben, I can't tell you how much I want to thank you! How is he? Can I talk to him?"

"I'd rather you wait until tomorrow. He's a bit groggy and weak and it would be better not to excite him. He's still got a long road ahead of him."

"But, thanks to you, at least he'll be able to travel it." An uneasy pause. "On both legs?"

"The leg's initial healing process is proceeding at an excellent clip. It'll take time and patience but I don't see why not."

"Remind me to send all of my friends to you."

"I'm just an old country doctor. Your kind of business I can do without. A man can remove only so many bullets."

"What about Chevallier's men?"

"They're with the boy all the time, bulls every one of them. They frighten the doctors by checking the medication and the nurses by testing the food."

"To check the medication, one of them would have to be a physician."

"One of them is and a damn good one. The men from the CIA have arrived to give them some relief. But, David, I hardly think two guards for me is necessary."

"I thought otherwise."

"I suppose I couldn't persuade you to change your mind?"

"You could try, but I warn you that I can be a very stubborn man."

"Yes, I got that impression. . . . Call tomorrow morning. You can speak to Shaul then."

"So long, Ben."

Rabanine replaced the receiver. He had never before felt the kind of relief which now poured through his body. So many things had been taken from him, never to be given back. But Shaul had been returned to him, never to be taken again.

David reclined on the bed, his thoughts leaving Shaul for Leslie Kirkman. It was a natural progression. The return of a love he had feared gone forever allowed him to admit the possibility of a love he had up till now refused to acknowledge. He had called her at Chevallier's the night before after his meeting in Langley, relieved to find her safe and taking pleasure in just hearing her soft, soothing voice. . . .

The thoughts came as cleansers for his soiled emotions, leaving him with a refreshed feeling of self-understanding and acceptance. The conviction to avoid pain had led to him only finding more. He saw that now.

The lessons had been learned. And yet the lessons were incomplete, unconsummated.

He would go to her now.

The love they made that night was soft and gentle, consuming each other with passion tempered by a mature awareness of the beginning.

"I've heard women reach their sexual peak at thirty-five," David said as they lay against each other in exhaustion. "But this is the first time I've seen it proven."

He felt her smile. "And I've heard men reach theirs at eighteen. You seem to have disproved that theory."

"Just making up for lost time. I'm a little rusty but hopefully I'll have plenty of opportunities to sharpen things up."

Leslie started to smile again but a frown quickly smothered it. "What about Alabaster? Is he gone from our lives?"

"I don't know what you mean." The cheerfulness out of his voice.

"Killing, David. Are you going to kill again?"

Rabanine swallowed hard. "I must go after the Red Prince."

"And after that?"

Silence.

"Don't lie to me, David. I want to know what's going to happen if you're successful. I want to know what's going to happen to us if you kill the Red Prince."

"I don't know," David said, his voice flat and empty. "I love you, Leslie. Eleven years ago, I didn't think I'd ever be able to say that to a woman again. Eleven days ago, I felt the same way. But I won't promise you there will be no more killing, I won't promise you that Alabaster will disappear from my—our— lives because I'm not sure he'll agree to those terms. I tried to phase him out once but I couldn't. I fear he's more a part of me

374

than I know."

"And what about me?"

"It's . . . different."

"I don't understand," Leslie said, near tears.

"Neither do I."

"When Shaul was kidnapped and you came to my room at the hotel, you said when this was over, you were going to give up this kind of life."

"I know what I said but I can't promise I'll be able to do it. And that's what you want, a promise. You said it yourself, though: someone else will pick up where the Red Prince leaves off. There will always be bombs planted in buses or restaurants or synagogues."

"And won't there be other people to catch the perpetrators?"

"I don't think I could live without doing something about it myself. Hearing and reading about the work of others would gnaw at me until there was nothing left. I *have* to take action."

"Shaul needs a father."

"He'll have one 95% of the time."

"What about the other five?"

Again David was silent. The choice had finally confronted him. He could not have it both ways. It was either Leslie or Alabaster. If only he could have them both . . .

"Leslie, we could make some arrangements," he said, holding her. "I'm not saying that I'll go back into the field; I just can't promise that I won't."

The warmth was gone from her embrace. "They're one in the same. And one day you wouldn't come back and some well dressed man from Tel Aviv would show up at our front door with the news that Shaul was an orphan and I was a widow again. I couldn't live with that shadow over us just as you couldn't without it. . . . You've got to promise me that you're finished."

"I can't," he said painfully, feeling something swell in his throat and a knife tear into his stomach as his breath became

375

short. Because he knew he was very likely refusing the love of the only woman who had meant anything to him for so long. And once he let it go this time, it would be gone forever.

"I just can't," David repeated and Leslie knew she had lost him.

At that moment, 500 miles away in Atlanta, Dr. Tanner Lewiston lifted his eyes from the lens of the microscope and rubbed them gently. Fatigue was making the images of the small cells isolated on the slide swirl in his mind. Colors merged and became one. Motion was impossible to chart. His head was pounding. He needed sleep.

His eyes, though, would not close. The inconsistencies tore at his brain. Along with his assistants he had performed a dozen autopsies on corpses lifted from Crescent Falls and had compared the results to those of an examination he had conducted of Sheriff Bugsy Tyler. The comparison yielded nothing. And yet Tyler was alive. Why? What had set him apart? Why was the disease lying dormant within him? If only the sole survivor of Crescent Falls could furnish the answer himself . . .

Lewiston lowered his tired eyes back to the microscope, hoping he would see a clue he had somehow been missing for the past three hours. Relaxed by the hypnotic movements enlarged 10,000 times before him, Lewiston felt himself dozing off when the door to his lab burst open and one of his assistants rushed in, breathless.

"Sheriff Tyler just came out of the coma!"

Lewiston rose, recharged. "Can he talk?"

"Talk? He's already threatened to level this entire building unless we let him go. Boy, has he got questions. . . ."

"So do I."

THIRTY-EIGHT

"Shaitan has been terminated, Ali. You will report to me immediately in Amman for further assignment."

The voice of Yassir Arafat was assertive, leaving no room for the Red Prince to see his words as anything but a direct order. A gleam filled his eyes and a narrow smile crossed his lips. It was always that way when he spoke. He was a man used to having his orders obeyed. Challenge on the part of his subordinates did not exist and wouldn't have been tolerated if it had. Arafat had risen to his present stature by giving little and taking much. Today would be no exception.

Salameh twirled an American cigarette around in his fingers, having run out of the Turkish variety. "You'll have to speak louder, Yassir. The connection is bad."

"You heard me. I am aborting Shaitan."

"Ah, but it is too late."

"I disagree."

"You have yet to explain to me why," Salameh said coolly.

"I don't owe you any explanations. I merely have to issue instructions, one of which I just have. I strongly suggest you obey it."

The Red Prince's eyes bulged. His fingers closed around the cigarette. "'Obey,' Yassir? You have never used such a word with me before."

"It was never necessary before. Times have changed. . . . You lied to me about Shaitan."

"I merely left out part of the truth."

"Then you admit it!"

"I have no reason to deny it. You have obviously been in conference with the Americans. You know what my true

377

intention is—the destruction of their country."

"There are other ways, Ali, other channels."

"Not for us. They have branded us with the mark of savages, barbarians. We will never be given what we need and deserve, so we must take it."

"By killing hundreds of millions of people? Proving that we really are the murderers they have always insisted we were?"

The cigarette began to twirl faster. "It's the only alternative we have left."

"And I order you not to use it."

"And I remind you it is too late."

"This is treason, Ali."

"On your part, not mine. You are faithful only to yourself now, Yassir. You have betrayed the Movement."

"The Shaitan Commandment holds the seeds for the Movement's destruction."

"It will destroy only America. And then not until the 175 carriers enter the country."

Arafat raised his eyebrows. "I know about the town, Ali."

Salameh hesitated. "It is better forgotten. The advance team failed. The ones who follow them will not. They will spread the disease everywhere and destroy this country you suddenly seem so fond of."

Arafat started to speak, then stopped. Salameh's words contradicted those of the President who had told him the disease was *already spreading* and fast. Obviously, the Red Prince was unaware of the truth. The Americans' ploy was working.

"Well, Yassir, does your silence mean you have come to see my side of things again?"

His trance broken, Arafat spoke. "I never saw your side of things; I saw only what you let me. You recruited that scientist who worked with Mengele after hearing mention of some obscure plan Hitler had had devised which would allow the Nazis to control the world. That was ten years ago and times were different. I agreed with you on the principle that the *threat* of such a weapon would help us achieve what we wanted and eliminate our dependence on the Russians. The carrier force was recruited and the initial injections begun after years of experiments. That injection process concluded with only the final shot withheld. It was never meant to be given, Ali. And even if it had been, on my orders only. The carrier force was released to start new lives all over the world, waiting to be called—by me and me alone."

"You never would have called them, Yassir, so I took the liberty myself."

"You exceeded my authority."

"My authority is now supreme! It is you who exceeds yours!" Agitated, the Red Prince reached for another cigarette on the table beneath him but tipped the pack over onto the floor and stamped at it with his foot in anger. Sweat poured from his face. He was breathing heavily, a narrow grin stretching across his lips. "It wasn't hard to arrange all this without you knowing, Yassir," Salameh resumed. "The members of the force had no reason to question any orders they received from me. They readily accepted the fact that they were being mobilized for action in various parts of the United States. Al-Kahir made all the arrangements with little trouble. All was done so that you would never notice a thing."

"And the 200 black cases that were placed in my vaults six months ago?"

"Contained vials of alcohol, not the final dosage of the serum. They were decoys to make you believe you held the power of Shaitan when in reality I did. I kept all 200 to be used when *I* directed that they should be."

"Which obviously you have."

"180 boxes were sent out one month ago. They all arrived on schedule. The force is ready, waiting for the appointed day to arrive."

"Of course that day has already been decided."

"Everything has been arranged, all contingencies worked out. We can't be stopped."

379

"If you stay in America, you will be infected too."

Salameh's grin grew into a hideous laugh. "I am immune."

"There is an . . . antidote?"

"A vaccine, a small batch made up by Gessler before it became necessary to eliminate him." He laughed again. "It was my final ace over you, Yassir. If I wanted, I could dispatch one of the carriers to your doorstep and have him leave the infection in your home. So you see, my authority *is* the supreme one now."

Arafat could hold himself back no longer. "You must be stopped, Ali," he said firmly into the phone. "And if necessary I will be the one to stop you."

"You can't . . . not anymore."

"You forget, perhaps, that I have all the names and addresses of the 175 carriers. I will arrange for their immediate execution," he lied, knowing the Americans needed them alive. "With America's help, it—"

"Don't bother, Yassir," the Red Prince broke in. "Al-Kahir has provided them with new identities. And all of them have moved. By the time you tracked them down, they will not be there any longer."

"But I have knowledge of the precise agenda of the travel procedures that will bring them into the U.S. Al-Kahir sent me a—"

"Another decoy to draw you further off the track. You see, I always assumed you would turn on me eventually. And as final insurance, I intend to move the timetable up. You will have less than a week now to learn the revised agenda, hardly enough time. . . . Give up the attempt to stop me, Yassir, while you still can. Your time is past. You have been corrupted by your own power."

"And are you really any different, Ali? Has not this project of yours corrupted you in the slightest?"

"Not so much as the murder of my family did. The Americans were responsible. I must have my revenge."

Arafat took a deep breath. He had prayed his next words

would not be necessary. "It was not the Americans, Ali."

"What are you . . . Of course it was!"

Arafat continued as though he hadn't heard him. "I was with Khomeni at a secret meeting. I couldn't be reached. A report came in that your family was travelling to America. You had taught them to love the good life as you did. They wanted it permanently and since they thought you to be dead nothing seemed to stand in their way. A defection was arranged. One of my lieutenants stopped it the only way he knew how."

"No! No! It can't be! . . . *It can't be!*" The Red Prince might have cried if he remembered how.

"It was a terrible accident, Ali. I wasn't consulted. I can't tell you how much I cried when word reached me. I didn't know how to tell you the truth, so I lied."

Salameh opened his mouth but nothing emerged, not even air. Everything he had always believed in had just been ripped away. Nothing seemed to matter. He thought of putting his pistol against his temple and pulling the trigger to end the anguish now. But there was still work to be done. People would have to pay.

"So you see, Ali," Arafat was saying, "there is no reason to kill the Americans. It was our hands that took the lives of your wife and sons. A horrible mistake and I assure you that the man who made it paid a most severe price. I had him tortured for hours before he was killed."

"Is that supposed to console me?"

Arafat forced a sigh. "I guess not."

Salameh felt something rush through him, a wave of prickly needles passing through his bloodstream. His eyes gleamed. He found himself smiling and then chuckling and then laughing hysterically.

"Allah has chosen my path well," he told Arafat with firm, quiet resolve after the fit had ended. "I am his instrument of fate and I will not fail him. My family died because the great world that America promised was too much of a temptation for them. And, so long as America is allowed to live, that world will

381

remain only a dream for Palestinians and other oppressed peoples. We have passed the point of no return, Yassir. Shaitan will continue and the world as it is presently known will be no more. But then I will emerge as the leader of a new and better world."

"You are mad, Ali."

"Aren't we all, Yassir?"

The line went dead.

In Syracuse, the Red Prince immediately summoned Mohammed al-Kahir to the upstairs study he had been talking from.

"It is over, Mohammed," he said flatly when the planner appeared.

Al-Kahir's face beamed. "The Commandment?"

"No, the resistance to it." A smile filled Salameh's face. "Can you believe the Americans and Arafat struck a bargain aimed at stopping us? How naive, how ignorant they must be. You cannot change fate, Mohammed."

"They will still try."

"Let them. They will find nothing. They will follow our tracks and discover that we have led them around in circles." The Red Prince's expression became rigid. "We are leaving, Mohammed. Now."

"I thought we were safe here."

"Not any longer. There is nowhere we can be safe for the time being. Even our closest friends and allies have become our enemies. Tell Seif I want him by my side at all times. Our strategy will have to be changed accordingly."

"Changed?"

"Stepped up. We must remodel Shaitan as follows . . ."

Meanwhile, at PLO headquarters in Amman, Yassir Arafat had hesitated for a full minute before returning the receiver to its hook. The dome of his balding head was wet with perspiration, cold and dripping, beneath his flowing turban. The Red Prince had betrayed the PLO. He was a certifiable lunatic who possessed a weapon that could wipe out the entire world. Correction, Arafat thought, *was wiping out* the entire world. And now the 175 Deliverers of Death, as the Americans called them, were going to enter the U.S. to speed up the process, though on a schedule vastly different than the one planned originally.

Arafat sat down to think for a few minutes before editing the tape and calling Langley. It had been a long, hard climb for his people, with more valleys than peaks. Now all was about to be lost because a man he had once trusted and loved had broken away from his hold. Arafat interlaced his fingers, trying to quell their trembling.

And it was all his fault. One way or another it was all his fault.

Sixteen months ago, when he had learned that Salameh was leaning toward a dramatic reemergence into the world and return to his westernized life style, Arafat had taken the only action he could think of to keep the Red Prince under his control. But the action had succeeded only to push Salameh past the brink of clear reason into the twilight zone of irrational thought. And as a result the PLO leader knew a hefty measure of the blame for the horror that was soon to be lay on his desk along with unfinished dreams and unfulfilled promises.

Because it had been he who ordered the execution of Salameh's family in America. He had set them up. There had been no accident, no mistake on the part of a subordinate. No defection had ever been arranged.

What other choice did he have?

In a vacant office down the hall from the Director's, David had been going over the personal papers of the five Al Fatah men found in Crescent Falls for nearly two hours. Airplane tickets, passports, social security cards, driver's licenses. Everything was perfect. Such was the way of Mohammed al-Kahir. Outside of the late Isser Ben-David, he was the most meticulous planner there was. The pieces always fit where they should have. Nothing was ever out of place or left to chance.

No weaknesses. No flaws.

David could find no hint anywhere in the five sets of documents laid out neatly before him on the desk that might lead him to the identities of *die Bote des Todes*. But he felt there was something he saw and yet did not see. Something that stood out in its mundaneness. Something . . .

Al-Kahir had done a magnificent job. The covers of the men were perfect, holding no link to each other, no less to their 175 counterparts. Somewhere, though, there was a common denominator. Rabanine felt it; he just couldn't see it.

He was about to begin the process again when there was a knock on the door followed by the appearance of Art Bartose; his tired, unnerved expression giving him even more the look of a frustrated academic than usual.

"Arafat's on the phone with the Director." Bartose's silver-tipped brown hair hung wildly about his face. "The Colonel would like you to hear what he has to say."

Thankful for the break in routine, David left his desk and accompanied Bartose down the hall into Rossi's office.

"Come in, gentlemen. Pull up a chair," the Colonel offered. "He's just about to start the tape of his talk with the Red Prince."

Bartose and Rabanine took seats in front of Rossi's massive desk, as the words of Yassir Arafat filled the room through an amplifier on the Director's desk; a bit garbled by the taped transmission but discernible nonetheless. Arafat had held the conversation in English and then had had the tape carefully edited to provide him with a halo of purely just intentions. Now the four men in Langley listened to the accented words and phrases that told them Ali Hassan Salameh was beyond the reach of even his own superior.

"I'm sorry, Colonel Rossi, that my first direct alliance with your country has not achieved the results we had hoped for," Arafat said after he ejected the tape in Amman. His voice still filled the room through the amplifier. "I regret to report that other means must be found to stop the Red Prince. He and his

384

people are no doubt in the process of switching locations right now. All the steps of the Commandment are being changed."

"But the carrier force will still be entering the country, which means we still have a chance to capture them and develop a vaccine."

"Yes. Mercifully the Red Prince does not seem to be aware that the Shaitan organism is already spreading. He believes it was stymied with the death of Crescent Falls."

"Then our gamble is paying off."

"It may not last much longer," Arafat cautioned. "Soon Salameh will realize the truth. All our coffins will be sealed."

"Don't count your nails yet," Rossi said plainly.

"I fear the Red Prince has already raised the hammer. I have just played you a tape revealing that all my authority has been subverted. I, Yassir Arafat, must watch as a subordinate wreaks havoc everywhere. . . . It is a black day for us both, Colonel Rossi, a black day for the world."

Rabanine sprang from his chair, his arms grasping the front of the Director's desk, startling the old man.

"This is Alabaster, President Arafat. I must ask you a question." Something was clicking in his head.

"And the two hundred black cases that were placed in my vault six months ago?"

A question posed by Arafat to the Red Prince.

"You spoke of black cases that contained the final dosage of the infection in addition to a syringe," David said abruptly. "Describe them."

"Black leather with a zipper that ended with a key lock."

"What size were they?"

"Small enough to fit into a man's jacket pocket or a woman's pocketbook."

"Why?"

"Because once the carriers left for their destinations, the cases were never to leave their persons. They were to have them within arm's reach at all times."

"Then they would have had to carry them on their bodies

when on planes." David's face was red, his lips curling together with building intensity.

"I suppose, though I don't—"

Rabanine cut him off. "We have the answer. I know what to look for—a link that will identify the Deliverers of Death."

Colonel Rossi leaned forward. "A link?"

David nodded. "The black cases would have to be examined by customs officials before *die Bote* could enter this country. Therefore, the 175 men and women would have to have a legitimate reason for toting them on their persons."

"So?"

"A legitimate *medical* reason for possessing syringes and sterile medicines and carrying them into the country. The reason showed up on the five men's ticket vouchers in Crescent Falls. They all ate special meals aboard the planes that brought them to America. Al-Kahir covered his tracks but he covered them so well that they became obvious."

The Director's face was twisted in bewilderment. "David, what are you talking about?"

"We checked the airlines before but we didn't know what to look for. Now we do."

"Special . . . *meals?*"

David nodded again, slower this time. "Diabetics, Colonel Rossi. The Deliverers of Death have been given the covers of diabetics."

THIRTY-NINE

"Look, Doc, holdin' me here 'gainst my will is a clear violation of my constitutional rights. I'm a lawman. *I* know."

"Sheriff Tyler," Lewiston said from behind the thick glass window of the isolation room, his voice piped in through a nearby microphone, "I promise you'll be released in good time."

"Good time? What the hell's that supposed to mean?" Tyler glanced around him at the flashing lights and video displays that continually monitored all of his vital signs, some of which he didn't know he had. "I go to sleep in my office in Crescent Falls and wake up in the Outer Limits. Nurses in space suits come and take enough of my blood to keep the Red Cross supplied for a year. Doctors from Mars keep stickin' needles in my arms and ce-pos-a-tories up my ass. Christ, the last one was so damn big I thought I was gettin' buttfucked by a Clydesdale."

Lewiston looked at the hulk of a man propped up on the small bed complete with handrails. Only constant sedation, he knew, had prevented Bugsy Tyler from trying to break out. Not that even a healthy Tyler could escape. But Tanner wasn't looking forward to his attempts.

"I promise it won't be much longer," he said as calmly as he could. "Right now I want to ask you a few more questions."

"Again! . . . Doc, you sure must've had a helluva hard time in medical school, 'cause things don't seem to sink into your head too quick at all. I think I better do the askin' and you better do the answerin' for awhile."

"I've told you everything I can."

"Like hell. You haven't even told me what I'm doing here."

The clipboard suddenly felt very heavy in Lewiston's hand. His shoulders struggled for comfort inside his tight lab coat. "There was an accident in your town. Some sort of disease got loose and you survived it, you and nobody else."

"That crap *again!*"

"It's the truth."

"Then why am I still alive?"

"That's what I'm trying to find out."

"Well, Doc, for my money you're doin' your job no better than a whore with a chastity belt. I got a good mind to get out of this bed and bust this place up a mite. You know what? I think all you people are full of sweet shit. All that crap 'bout monster germs wipin' out towns. . . . Maybe you just been watchin' too many of those 'Jap-o-neese' horror movies."

Lewiston moved closer to the glass until his face was almost right up against it. Before him, red lines darted up and down on a dozen monitor screens in rhythm with Tyler's building rage. The isolation room was soundproof and air locked. The walls were three feet thick and insulated with solid lead. A fifty caliber shell couldn't penetrate the chemically bonded glass. It took three keys to open the single white door.

"Sheriff Tyler," he said finally, "whatever happened in Crescent Falls isn't going to end in two hours after fifteen commercial breaks. Your town was destroyed by some kind of plague and you're the only one who survived for a reason we have yet to uncover. The disease is spreading, Sheriff, and you are the only man who can help us stop it."

The red lines began to flutter less spasmatically, as Tyler relaxed under the reassurance of his own importance. He sat up slowly, two closed circuit television cameras shifting their positions on the wall to chart his movement.

"I can't do a whole helluva lot stuck in this here bed."

"You can answer some questions."

"The same ones as before?"

"A few. We might have missed something. We can't take chances."

388

"You're takin' a mighty big one by keepin' me locked up in here. I don't care how thick these goddamn walls are, they won't hold me if I don't get a chew soon."

Lewiston's attention was riveted on his clipboard. "All right if I begin?"

"Shoot."

"When was the last medical checkup you had?"

"The county requires one every September."

"What were the results of yours?"

"Healthy as a thoroughbred on a stud farm."

"Do you take any regular medications?"

"Not unless you consider Jack Daniels medicinal."

"Does your diet consist of anything out of the ordinary?"

"It didn't until I came here."

"Have you ever been exposed to radiation?"

"Not that I know of."

"Have you ever had any serious diseases such as small pox, malaria, or the swine flu?"

"Nope."

"Do you live or have you ever lived near a chemical plant?"

"Nope."

"Are you parents still living?"

"See 'em every Christmas."

Lewiston remained silent and sighed in frustration.

"Is that it, Doc?"

"It may well be."

"Don't worry yourself, Doc, the world's been in some pretty tough scrapes before and she's always been able to pull out of 'em just as cleanly as a stud from a virgin's hole. You got any more questions?"

Lewiston's eyes met Tyler's through the thick glass. "Not for now."

"Then how 'bout doin' me a little favor?"

"If I can."

"Hell, if you know how to read all these goddamn gizmos, I'm sure you can. All I want is you to get me some chew."

"Chew?"

"Skoal preferably. But I'd settle for Copenhagen, even Happy Days under the circumstances."

"You chew . . . tobacco?"

"Wouldn't ask for it if I didn't. Some people calls it snuff. On a bad day, I go through a whole can." Lewiston's face had gone white. "Hey Doc, you all right?"

"Oh my God . . ."

Twenty-four hours later, a meeting began in a conference room located down the hall from Colonel Rossi's office in Langley.

"Okay, Tanner," the Director opened, "what have you got for us?"

"As you all know by now, we finally got a break," Lewiston said tiredly. "Sheriff Bugsy Tyler is alive because of chewing tobacco. It's the one thing that sets him apart from everyone else in the town. A few others did chew but not regularly and not in the quantities that Bugsy does."

"Then you're close to finding the answer," Rossi suggested.

Lewiston shrugged. "Not really."

The four other men glanced at each other.

"I don't understand," said Art Bartose. "If the tobacco saved Tyler, then it should lead us to a cure."

"That's a simplistic solution to a complex problem." Lewiston paused, searching for layman's terms with which to phrase his explanation. "You see, something in the chewing tobacco became chemically bonded with the mucous membrane lining along his throat, mouth, and nasal cavity. Since we have already established rather certainly that the Shaitan organism is an airborne infection contracted by inhalation, it's equally certain that the new chemical makeup of Tyler's mucous lining was able to trap and kill a majority of the invading cells before they passed into his respiratory system."

"But he *did* suffer from the disease," Herb Weinberg interjected.

"Though with far less virulence." Lewiston ran his hands through his hair and then held them before him, gesturing as he spoke. "It's fairly obvious that the simple breathing of anyone who has contracted Shaitan is enough to expel large amounts of microorganisms into the air to be carried into the lungs of anyone who comes close enough, say within a yard. Keeping this in mind, in Bugsy Tyler's case only a small percentage of these microorganisms ever took hold in his system. The rest were neutralized and killed off by his mucous membrane."

"Still," offered Colonel Rossi, "his antibodies were able to subdue the less active Shaitan. Why can't they be used as the basis for an antidote or vaccine?"

"Mainly, because, as I said before, the severity of the disease he suffered from was not nearly so great as that which killed the rest of the community. In essence, we're talking about two entirely different clinical states. . . . And there's more working against us—the Shaitan organism itself. Everything I'm about to say is theoretical but computer analysis assures us it's pretty damn close to the mark. To start with, the truly great strength of Shaitan lies in the ability of the disease's microbes to destabilize the white blood cells which should kill them. The germs then use the defensive cells' subparticles as shelter and multiply rapidly inside them. In a matter of days, the germ will increase 100,000,000-fold, thereby overwhelming the antibody manufacture entirely and throwing the defensive mechanisms of the body into total disarray, as well as making conventional antibiotics all but worthless."

"Then what are you doing to keep the infected patients you have in isolation alive?" from Rossi.

"Half are being treated with every possible therapy in the book and some that aren't, while the other half are just being made comfortable and fed placebos."

"That seems callous."

"But totally necessary. The millions of people about to be exposed to the organism won't have the benefits of the

Center's laboratories, will they? So we've got to find out just how long the infection takes to enter its incubatory and lethal stages. We have to monitor the progression of the disease unchecked in enough test subjects to determine our chances of isolating the disease and developing a vaccine in time."

"It's all very confusing," moaned Rossi, lightly massaging his eyelids to relieve the pressure that was splitting his head apart.

"From a scientific standpoint, the best is yet to come," Lewiston continued. "Originally I had suspected that nothing could stop Shaitan from spreading throughout the entire world. I was wrong, or, at least, I think I was. It seems the organism in its current state can survive and flourish only in the environmental conditions present in the northern hemisphere."

"Why?"

"Ionizing radiation. The Arabs, and maybe even the Germans before them, must have discovered a way to program environmental needs into the organism that can be found only in a given target area. Once the organism leaves the target area, it's deactivated by the ionizing radiation it was not preconditioned to survive in." Lewiston's front teeth crawled briefly over his lower lip. "And the upshot of this is that it's conceivable the Arabs have developed several variations of the organism which survive only under different environmental conditions, different angles of ionizing radiation. Unfortunately, though, all of America is contained within the same angle grid."

"Then can you give us an estimate of our expected casualties?"

"Between fifty and sixty-five percent."

"*One hundred twenty million people? . . .*"

"Roughly. The deaths will begin slowly and sporadically, say within the next three weeks, and then rise geometrically until they reach a peak four weeks after that. The process will then begin to wind down as the disease periodically loses a minute

392

portion of its virulency and will continue to do so for upwards of six weeks at which point the disease as we now know it will have mutated into something else entirely. And the only chance we have to reverse the process or at least stagnate it is to come up with a vaccine that contains both active and passive immune agents, combining attenuated Shaitan organisms with successful antibodies. We can use the attenuated cells lying dormant in Sheriff Tyler. But the useful antibodies can be found only in the blood of the Deliverers of Death."

"And what kind of timetable are we looking at?" asked Rossi.

"I'd say we must begin distribution of the vaccine a *minimum* of four weeks before Shaitan reaches its peak under present circumstances *without* the additional 175 carriers entering the country unnoticed; say twenty one days from now. It won't be long after that all our emergency systems designed to cope with such a disaster break down totally. Then it won't matter whether we find the vaccine or not because we'll have no way of getting it to the people."

"So we're talking about three weeks until doomsday."

"Generously."

Rossi brought his tired hands up to his face and dragged his fingers over the sides of his nose. He tilted his glance toward Rabanine. "Well, David, in view of this, I hope you've already gathered the Deliverers of Death at the Airport Hilton."

Rabanine managed a smile. "Not exactly, but we're getting closer. First off, our bluff has achieved its purpose as we learned through Arafat's conversation with Salameh. The Red Prince has speeded up his timetable considerably which gave me something to focus in on." David withdrew a stapled series of papers from his jacket pocket. "I gathered information from airline computer systems all over the world concerning tickets booked for persons requiring special meals due to medical ailments. There were 1,600 possibilities listed in the next six weeks. Next, I ran a check on how those 1,600 had booked and arranged payment for their tickets. The usual regularities came

393

up with one glaring exception: seven European travel services through which exactly twenty-five each had been reserved."

"So we should know exactly when the Shaitan force will be entering the country," advanced Weinberg.

"Not exactly. Remember, Salameh warned Arafat that all the arrangements, the entire agenda, were going to be stepped up. But al-Kahir knows that the men and women can pass through customs only with the identities they now possess. There's no time to issue new ones. And yet he can't book new reservations under the same names because we'd be able to turn up the discrepancies through the computers. He wouldn't do anything to give himself away but he would know that a means must be found to make new international arrangements without cancelling the old ones; seats secured by number instead of specific names."

"A charter?"

"Yes, a charter. *Die Bote des Todes* will be gathered in one city from which they will depart in mass to America where they will move on to their precise destinations at a later time."

"You've checked the possibilities, of course."

David nodded. "There are six charters that have been booked within the last two days originating from Paris, Madrid, Frankfurt, Vienna, and two from London. Each has a legitimate cover; it could conceivably be any one of them. But I think we should focus our attentions on Paris, Madrid and Vienna because each is scheduled for next week beginning on Thursday and special meals have been requested on all three. Even on a charter, *die Bote* will have to pass through customs and they can't take the chance that their cases will be examined or confiscated."

"Then we'll have a team watching each airport at the time the flights are scheduled to leave," said Colonel Rossi.

"Why not take them before they get on the plane?" posed Weinberg.

"Because it'll only compound our problems," answered Rossi. "We won't have full freedom to act on foreign soil, not to mention the fact that transporting 175 captured agents overseas from a neutral country will create a political stink that'll smell all the way to the Kremlin." A pause. "Now, Herb, will you please summarize the information that came in this morning to the Bureau."

Weinberg leaned forward in his chair. "In a period of eighteen hours beginning yesterday at six AM, ten reputed Arab terrorists stationed in this country eluded their constant survellance and vanished from six different cities across the nation."

"Your conclusion?"

"That the ten are representative of a much larger force massing somewhere in the U.S. to lend support to the Red Prince."

Art Bartose took a deep breath and let it out slowly. "There's one thing about all this that bothers me. It doesn't seem right that Salameh would take a chartered plane right smack into a major airport. Granted, flights to other cities from the destination point might have been conveniently arranged. And he as no way of knowing that we've caught on to his diabetic cover. But allowing the entire Shaitan force to be in a major city in a confined space at this stage of the game? . . . It just isn't consistent."

"No," agreed David, "it isn't."

David couldn't sleep. After succumbing for hours to the inevitable tossing and turning he had given up, coiled his arms beneath a pillow and stared into the darkness before him.

Something was nagging at him. Why would Salameh have told Arafat that all the arrangements were being changed if Arafat didn't know the correct agenda in the first place? A better and more logical strategy would have been to let Arafat believe he knew the true agenda and proceed to waste his time trying to destroy it.

Unless . . .

David sprang to a sitting position, his heart pumping

furiously. The Red Prince had told him to look for something he would have anyway, like a magician holding up one hand to distract you from the other where the true action was occurring. The idea of a charter was right but when had it been booked? Salameh had made him think it was a recent move when perhaps it had been an option from the beginning.

Misdirection . . .

Salameh had led him into sending Leslie Kirkman straight to Al Fatah's man at the CIA and now he was trying to lead him astray again. How did the saying go?

Fool me once, shame on you. Fool me twice, shame on me.

David was out of bed now, his hand moving for the lamp and then the phone, pressing out an emergency number in Langley, Virginia.

"Patch me through to the Director."

"Do you know what time it is?" The voice of a bureaucrat.

"Later than we think. . . . Now do as I say!"

FORTY

The human traffic hurried itself along the endless floors of Paris' Orly Airport. It was near nine o'clock on a Tuesday morning and the pace set was indecently fast, impatience etched on the faces of eager travellers with places to go and people to meet. There was no time for a smile, a chat, or even a passing wave. There was no time at all.

The large group of distinguished looking men and women in the middle of the mass allowed themselves to be swept up in its movements, flowing forward in perfect step and rhythm. Assimilated. Invisible. Moving as one while appearing as many. They were right on schedule. There was no reason to rush but neither was there call to lag. All was going as planned. It had to stay that way.

Years before they had become other people. And now, as they moved quickly through the airport, they wondered seriously whether those they had once been had ever existed at all. They had become Americans, on paper but not in heart. Their methods of speech and life style had been changed. They had been placed strategically all over the world, a silent army posed to strike at a moment's notice.

The notice had been given. The moment had come.

The large group continued to walk until it reached the gate beyond which the chartered plane waited. Here the man at the head of the procession with the strong angular features swung toward a departure lounge with two hundred red cushioned chairs and a bar that was presently unmanned and unstocked contained inside. The delay in the area would be brief. It was almost time.

To the curious viewer, even the casual one, the diversity of the group's members was striking. Not age, nor appearance, nor dress linked any with more than a handful of his or her fellows. Outwardly there was no common denominator between them at all. Concealed in the pockets of their jackets or tucked carefully away in their handbags, though, was a small black leather case, the contents of which would not be utilized until they reached their designated areas in America.

Where? . . . When?

The specific answers were not known to them . . . yet.

As the Deliverers of Death began to file into a passageway that would lead them onto the chartered 747, a short man with one day's beard growth painted over his face stepped into a phone booth.

"I'd like to place a long-distance call to Langley, Virginia please. . . ."

It was just past three AM in Langley when the call came through.

"They're on their way, David," Colonel Rossi said, returning the receiver to its hook. "Our agent identified Salameh, al-Kahir, and a giant between them who the man said was the biggest 'thing' he'd ever seen. That's his word, not mine."

"Seif, of course."

"Know anyone else who fits that description?"

"In any case, I trust *die Bote* got off safe and sound."

"We had fifteen agents in Orly to make sure." The Director checked his watch. "They should be arriving at Stapleton Airport in Denver at 2:45 this afternoon, Denver time."

Rabanine leaned back in his chair and ran his hands over his tired face. He had realized Sunday night that the charter contingency was a product of weeks of planning, not days. The Red Prince had cleverly maneuvered him into thinking it was a desperate move when in reality it had been a calculated one. The Paris to Denver charter, with all passengers on board requesting special meals, had been booked nearly a month before.

"You and Mr. Bartose will be leaving from Dulles International for Stapleton at 9:00 this morning," Rossi went on. He glanced briefly at his wheelchair. "I'd come along myself but I'm not much of a traveller. Might I suggest that you get some sleep beforehand?"

"There'll be plenty of time for sleep when all this is over."

"We need you in top condition or it may never be."

"I'll be all right."

"Not if you keep berating yourself for not realizing the truth earlier. If it hadn't been for your call Sunday night, we would have spent the latter part of this week chasing red herrings while the Shaitan force made itself at home on our front doorstep."

"What about Gamma Group?" David asked, referring to the code name for a select force of American anti-terrorist commandoes.

"Fifty of them will be on route from their training center in Texas to Stapleton at seven this morning. There's nothing to worry about on their accounts. They have been trained by the best anti-terrorist commando leaders in the world, including some from Israel. I understand their leader is one tough son of a bitch. . . . What's your plan?"

"Gamma Group will move in as soon as the jet is on the ground, placing themselves between it and the terminal before docking takes place. I'm going on the theory that those Al Fatah agents that the FBI lost track of have been recruited by Salameh to serve as added protection. My plan is to have the commandoes seal off the plane from them. That way in the event of a battle none of the carriers will be caught in the fire. They'll be trapped on the plane until we take them out."

"The people at Stapleton are prepared to give you any assistance you request."

"Just tell them to stay out of my way. What about the helicopters?"

"Five military personnel carrying choppers have been cleared mechanically and will soon be arriving in Denver. They're the newest kind, equipped with jet-assisted engines, nearly three times faster than ordinary ones. You think you'll have to use them?"

"If the Red Prince still has one card left to play, they'll be our ace in the hole."

"Stapleton Control, this is Transworld 16 Heavy, requesting approach clearance."

Crackle . . . crackle . . . crackle . . .

"16 Heavy, this is Stapleton Control. We have you on our screen. You are cleared at 20,000 feet heading two-zero-niner, five hundred miles southeast. Change course to two-one-five and begin descent."

"Roger, Control, two-one-five."

There was a knock on the cockpit door. "Captain Delaney, it's Lisa. I've got to talk to you." The voice of the head stewardess.

Delaney nodded to the navigator who swung the cockpit door open. Two men pushed their way in, the stewardess named Lisa being held by the larger one—a bald colossus with an ear lobe missing.

"There's been a change in plans, gentlemen. This plane is not going to land in Denver," the Red Prince announced, pistol in hand.

"Mister, I don't know who you are or where you come from but I'm taking this plane down in Stapleton," Delaney said firmly, feeling for the emergency Mayday button.

"It's my charter, Captain. I suggest you change your course as I direct. You can push that button if you like, but . . ."

Here, Seif jerked the stewardess' head further back, allowing the Red Prince to shove the end of the silencer into her mouth.

"Where do you want to go?" Delaney asked.

"When was the last time you had contact with it?" David asked a much distraught air traffic controller.

The man buried his face in his hands, looking up after a number of seconds. "400 miles out of Denver just after it

400

began its descent."

"And then it just . . . vanished?"

"First it dipped off course, as though something had gone wrong. I tried to raise the pilot but got nothing other than static. This kind of thing has never happened to me before. Fifteen years without a . . . I guess it must have gone down."

"Why?"

"Because it left my screen. No pilot in his right mind would take a jet down that low unless he was in trouble."

"But a good one could fly even a 747 below radar range if he had to." A statement.

"I suppose," the controller said hopefully.

Rabanine glanced out the window over the airfield. He could see the dark uniforms of the Gamma Group commando force protruding from several areas of cover out of sight of the terminal, waiting for the signal to move in. They were good men, he thought. He could tell by their eyes after he had met them all briefly two hours before. They were also formidable in appearance, even without the M-16 each held in his hands. For now, though, their prowess was not going to be put to use. The enemy had disappeared.

"Is there an abandoned military facility somewhere in this area, say within a 300 mile radius?" David asked Art Bartose who was standing nervously beside him.

"No, the nearest one is just outside of Salt Lake City, say approximately . . . Wait, there is one closer—Melrose Airforce Base, about 300 miles from here right over the Utah border. It hasn't been operational for two years."

"And it's right in the middle of nowhere."

"To say the least. How did you know?"

"Because Salameh did, and well before me." Rabanine pulled a walkie-talkie from the pocket of his windbreaker. "Captain Ferguson, assemble your men in the airport briefing room. There's been a change in plans."

Captain Bob Delaney swung the 747 upwards, clearing the

401

mountain peaks that stretch across the Colorado-Utah border with little room to spare. The giant machine lurched a bit, buckling against the suddenness of the command issued it.

"That was too close, Captain," said Salameh, his gun held less than a foot from Delaney's head.

The pilot wiped the sweat from his brow. "These jets aren't built for this kind of maneuvering."

"I suggest you take measures to compensate for their construction."

"If you'd let me climb higher—"

"—they'd know where we were, wouldn't they? We can't have that, can we?"

"Then we're stuck riding in a sluggish bird. Maintaining this altitude much longer will cause the engines to overheat."

"In which case my bald friend will break one of your fingers for every minute we fall behind schedule." The Red Prince moved the pistol still closer.

"Will there be men in the tower at Melrose?" Delaney asked.

"Whose reports can be heard all the way back to Denver? . . . Hardly. You'll be on your own."

"The runway?"

"It's been checked and has passed a rather vigorous inspection. Believe me, Captain, no one wants this plane to land safely more than I do."

"What about other craft? Will there be any on the ground that might be in our way? This baby isn't going to be all that easy to set down coming over that mountain range."

"The only other craft present will be thirty Lear jets well away from the landing strip."

Delaney turned to his rear. "Lear jets?"

"Keep your eyes on the road, Captain."

Rabanine downed a cup of coffee, oblivious to the burning sensation that tore at his insides. Before him, in chairs laid out like they might have been in a classroom, sat fifty of the toughest men he had ever set eyes on; all garbed in dark green with black berets resting on their laps. Next to him stood the bulky frame of Commander "Tut" Ferguson, leader of the force imported from Texas six hours before and the toughest of them all.

"Our target is Melrose Airforce base," David said, pointing to a scale drawing outlined in chalk on a blackboard. Two runways swirled side by side each other, bordered on the right flank by three hangars. Fifty yards behind them sat a sizable barracks in line with a large building that served once as the base headquarters. These buildings were indicated on the scale drawing, in addition to a series of private quarters and equipment sheds that lay scattered in a grassy area between the hangars and the main building, all but obscuring the barracks from view at ground level. Melrose was a small SAC base emptied by budget cuts two years before. Today it sat still and ghostlike against the horizon, its equipment mothballed in case an emergency forced an unexpected reopening in the future. The chalk outline, which emphasized the position of the barracks in the camp's rear, was akin to an architect's blueprint. A plan for construction instead of attack.

"Once there," David continued, "we will in all probability encounter a force similar in number and weaponry to our own with the distinct advantage of being on the ground while we must plunge toward it. For a time, we're all going to be sitting ducks."

"We'll be taking helicopters in, right?" asked a muscle-bound commando seated in the front.

"Yes."

"Then we won't be sitting ducks for long." The room broke out into nervous laughter.

Rabanine forced a smile. "The real catch is that the people coming in on the 747 have to be taken alive. Shoot them and we subvert the purpose of our mission."

"How will we be able to tell the difference between them and the terrorists?" From another commando.

"The ones we want alive will be ushered to positions of safety before the first shots are fired, most likely into the barracks." David pointed at the rectangular shape on the top of the diagram. "We will isolate them there as soon as possible after we land in the area of the runways."

"Why don't we just bring the choppers down in that vicinity?"

"Because in all the confusion, the people we must take alive might get caught in the cross fire. We can't afford to lose any."

"But we've still got to isolate them from the rest of the base," reminded a commando in the rear. "Prevent them from running off on their own."

"That's right."

"Christ, it's hard enough to rescue hostages that want to be rescued, never mind ones that don't."

"And," began the commando sitting next to the one in the rear, "the barracks is fifty yards behind the line the terrorist force will undoubtedly set up along the runway. That means we'll have to move right through the middle of their defenses to isolate our targets, *without* drawing fire in the targets' direction."

"There's a way," David promised.

The 747 struck the field harder than Bob Delaney would have preferred even under the circumstances, shaking all and everything inside violently before settling back as the pilot applied the brakes to ease the giant bird to a halt.

The Red Prince, meanwhile, picked up the microphone and began to speak to the passengers at the precise time an alert stewardess on a commercial flight would have.

"Ladies and gentlemen, after we disembark you can recover your luggage inside the barracks located in the rear of the base. After that, we will have a meeting in which your revised assignments will be given out. All of you will be in the air again on route to your destinations within two hours by Lear jet."

404

Salameh paused reflectively. "Our destiny is about to be fulfilled."

The five helicopters sliced their way through the bright sky, huge green hornets in a two-one-two attack formation. Their pace was consistent, unchanging. Five moving as one. The distance between each never appearing to vary. Barring mechanical failure, it would take them an estimated two hours to reach Melrose Airforce base. Fifty men now wordlessly wondered what would be waiting for them when they got there.

Each chopper held ten commandoes inside it, all of the occupants dressed in dark green combat fatigues, intently studying their weapons with eyes that occasionally met those of a fellow.

In the middle helicopter, David Rabanine rubbed a light brown paste into his face and arms, giving his skin a darker, richer look. He was dressed in civilian clothes that were intentionally mundane. The pants were baggy, the soiled white shirt worn outside of them. He had combed the curls out of his hair and applied enough oil to allow him to brush it straight back. Still more oil would add a shiny glaze to it. This, though, would not be applied until the very last moment.

David knew that Melrose was only a stopover point from which the Deliverers of Death would be distributed all over the country, probably by small, six-passenger jets. Once they left the abandoned base, the path of the carriers would be untraceable. Or, at least, not traceable within the limited time span currently in effect. The Shaitan Commandment had to be stopped now if it was ever to be stopped at all.

The 175 carriers had to be trapped. The threat of fire could be used but the triggers never pulled in their direction. Yet the terrorist force recruited to protect them at the base had to be overcome by pulling those same triggers. . . .

David leaned back against the wall of the chopper, closing his eyes to shut out the madness.

*   *   *

". . . I wish you luck, my friends," the Red Prince was saying on the rostrum of the stage in the conference room of Melrose. Every seat in the hall was taken and there were people standing in the rear. "You are about to embark on a mission that is now unstoppable. Once you are settled in the hotel rooms, apartments, or houses we have secured for you, the final injection must be taken under the precise specifications. Then all you must do is mix with people, pass closely by them. Each will then carry the infection to others, and they—others. The process will multiply. The organism will spread. America, in a matter of a few short months, will be helpless." Salameh paused and swung his head slowly from one side of the room to the other, trying to look all the 175 men and women seated on various levels above him in the eyes. "It is the will of Shaitan finally come to pass. You have your assignments on the jets that will begin taking off in twenty minutes time. Load your belongings. In an hour you will all be gone." A smile flashed across Salameh's lips. *"Salaam alehkum."*

Quietly the men and women rose from their seats and filed into the aisles, while on the dias the Red Prince turned to Mohammed al-Kahir. "You did your job superbly, Mohammed. The pilots, the planes, the guards; everything was secured just as it was supposed to be."

"We have done it, Ali," the planner said without enthusiasm.

"Yes . . . we have," Salameh agreed, savoring each word.

Al-Kahir frowned slightly. "I would feel better, though, if the original assignments were still in effect. The proportions are off now, geographically as well as by importance. We no longer have carriers placed in the Pentagon, Senate, or anywhere else where a swift neutralization was called for."

"The results will be the same; it will just take more time."

"And us?"

"You, myself, and Seif will journey to Palm Springs where we will watch the Commandment unfold and America collapse.

406

At the proper time, we will leave for Beirut where I will assume command of the Movement. Before long, my voice shall be heard, my instructions obeyed by nations everywhere."

Outside, a few of the Deliverers of Death, suitcases in hand, had begun to make their way for the Lears they were assigned to. In thirteen minutes the long white line of jets would begin to pour down the runway and climb toward the sky in a steady procession until Melrose Airforce Base was deserted once more.

FORTY-ONE

The helicopters cleared the final range of mountains, appearing as distant specs in the sky. Their propellers dipped downward slightly, the slow swoon beginning.

"This is Green leader," said Commander Tut Ferguson into his headset in the middle chopper. "Target area approaching. Assume attack formation."

In unison, as in the steps of a complex dance routine, the choppers shifted positions and angled toward Melrose in a straight line, each machine equidistant from the one in front and behind it. The choppers banked, seeming to drop out of the sky.

"Prepare to dispense cover gas on my signal," Ferguson continued. "Door guards ready all nylon ropes."

The men and women on the ground at Melrose weren't sure which came first: the swirling sounds or the sight of the growing blotches over the horizon. They had all almost reached their designated jets by this point and there was an initial impulse felt by each to ignore the iron insects descending upon them and continue everything as planned. The impulse was fleeting.

"Get into the barracks! Get into the barracks!" The Red Prince's words exploded over the public address system seconds after he had seen the shapes swelling in the sky. "Get into the barracks until the danger has passed!"

Still toting their luggage, the Deliverers of Death began scurrying back toward the rear of the base, their eyes frozen on the sharpening forms in the shrinking distance.

Inside the base headquarters, the Red Prince turned to al-Kahir. "Who are they, Mohammed?"

"It doesn't matter. We are finished."

"Finished? What are you talking about? We have fifty men ourselves. Assemble them in positions of cover immediately. We will shoot the soldiers as they leave their helicopters. It will be simple. . . . But how could they have known?"

"Alabaster."

"Of course! The Jew haunts me one last time. Seif is outside. Tell him Alabaster is among those in the helicopters. *I want the bastard killed!*"

Outside all was chaos. The terrorists recruited for a situation such as this had never worked together before and as a result were unsure of themselves. They moved as individuals rather than as a group, seeking cover behind the equipment shacks and personnel quarters that lay between the hangars and the headquarters. They checked the ammunition in their automatic rifles or machine guns and slid back the bolts. Their dress ranged from PLO combat fatigues to blue jeans. There was nothing to indicate that the men resembled a unit.

The helicopters roared overhead, assuming a two column formation. Rows of metal canisters dropped down from all five. At impact with the cement below, the canisters erupted into a bank of green, red, or gray smoke that provided a thick cover. It spilled out everywhere, maintaining a heavy blanket over the runway and stinging the eyes of the terrorists who fought to follow the path of the helicopters.

For several seconds the choppers surged beyond the smoke-filled area, then turned sharply and headed back in a straight line. Thick nylon rope of custom construction fell from each, the men inside readying their gloved hands for the drop.

The helicopters came to almost a dead stop. Doors slid open and the members of Gamma Group began to float rapidly downward in the blanketed air as bullets wailed around them. Their feet reached the asphalt in less than three seconds, M-16s grasped tightly in their hands.

Then the commandoes were on the ground rolling, spinning, diving for cover on the side of the runway opposite from the terrorists. They perched themselves behind the Lear jets or scampered against the line of fire for positions closer to the terrorists in the vicinity of the base headquarters. Their barrels blazed red, the fire returned accordingly by those across from them, not more than thirty yards away. Neither side gained the edge initially. Both held their ground without buckle or lapse.

The terrorists saw one of their own run toward them dressed in baggy blue pants and white shirt, a Thompson machine gun erupting in his hands. Several turned in his direction and sprayed bullets to cover his endangered approach. For what seemed like a minute, he stood suspended between the two rival forces, wedged in the cross fire. Suddenly his body was pressed against the asphalt, rotating toward the position of two of his fellows who helped him to his feet when he had safely reached them.

The brave terrorist watched the man on his right pitch backwards, the right side of his face torn off by a raging bullet. Another body dropped beside the first, blood belching from its stomach as it shook violently with the pain of approaching death. Gamma Group had secured positions in semicircular cover around the terrorists. The advantage clearly belonged to them. The Arabs were dropping at regular intervals. This, though, didn't faze the brave terrorist in the least.

Alabaster tossed the machine gun loaded with blanks away and drew his standard army issue .45 from the belt that held his baggy pants up. His white shirt was stained with the blood of the two Arabs who had fell around him. Unbothered by its presence seeping toward his skin, the Israeli moved out of the line of action and scrambled behind the fire in the direction of the barracks set off in the rear of the compound. A machine gun toting terrorist was poised at the front door.

"They've broken through our lines!" Alabaster screamed. "They're heading for the people inside the barracks!"

By the time the terrorist realized that the man approaching was a stranger, Alabaster had lunged at him, the .45 spitting fire which sent him crashing backwards against the front entrance of the barracks. The Israeli shoved his dead body out of the way and threw open the door.

"Stay down, all of you! The Americans are outside! Get under the beds and don't lift your heads to the windows! *Do not leave* this barracks!"

The 175 frightened faces stared in silence at Alabaster, trusting his words because they had no reason not to. The Israeli's eyes swung around the room, amazed at the heterogeneity of the people facing him.

"We will defeat them soon. But all of you must stay inside. Do not attempt to help us!"

Alabaster backed slowly out the door and slammed it behind him. It wasn't good enough. Sooner or later the carriers might panic and leave the barracks for the line of fire that still roared behind him. He had to make fleeing the building impossible. The doors posed the only problem, the windows being too small to crawl through. He had to secure them. A heavy hasp was screwed into the hard frame, joining it to the door. He had nothing to jam through it, though, in order to lock the Deliverers of Death inside.

Alabaster recalled the diagram of Melrose that had been drawn for him in Denver. There was an equipment shack thirty yards to the left near the base headquarters. Tools might still be contained inside, something he could use to wedge through the hasps in front and back. It was a chance. He sped toward the shed.

Suddenly the cement beneath him exploded, sending chips flying everywhere. Dust filled his eyes. The Israeli dove to the ground and rolled onto his stomach, the .45 gripped firmly in his hand. A terrorist with a submachine gun darted before him toward the cover of a pump house. Alabaster fired twice, the first shot striking the man in the side, spinning him furiously. The second struck the heart dead center just as the Arab was about to fire at him again. The man collapsed in a heap on the cement.

411

Footsteps pounding behind him . . .

Still perched on the asphalt, Alabaster whirled to the right and angled his body toward the rear. Two terrorists surged at him, their guns levelled and ready to fire. But their fingers never pressed the triggers. Alabaster halted their charge with a bullet in each head. The bodies lurched backwards, suspended for a drawn out moment in midair before plummeting to the ground, faces a mass of exploded flesh and bone.

The Israeli was on his feet again, gliding forward. His eyes shifted wildly about him, searching for more who sought to stand in his way. There were none. He began to move for the equipment shack, his pace deliberate.

The sound of heavy boots striking cement met his ears at the same time his eyes found the terrorist wearing them spinning around the corner with a Russian Kalashnikov AK-47 automatic rifle in his hands. The man stopped in his tracks, frozen by shock. Alabaster sunk to the cement and fired the .45 for a certain and easy kill.

Nothing happened. . . . The gun had jammed!

Relief replaced fear in the terrorist's expression. Shock and indecision vanished from his eyes. His finger found the trigger and pulled it. Alabaster rolled forward. Once, twice, three times as the AK-47 stitched a path of torn cement around him. He could feel its bullets closing in. Their ricocheting stung his ears. Still rolling, his right hand unsheathed the knife he wore on his hip and flung it in the same motion. It whisked through the air as the AK-47 coughed more dust into his eyes, blinding him.

The firing stopped.

The knife had lodged itself just under the terrorist's solar plexus. A suspended second followed in which the rifle fell and his hands moved to his chest. His eyes bulged. He looked puzzled. Then he moved his reddened fingers outward as though to grope for something. But there was only air before him and his fingers closed around it as he thudded to the ground.

Alabaster rose, steadied himself and again vaulted for the equipment shed. No more Arabs were in sight which meant that Gamma Group would have the field secured in a matter of minutes. Nothing could be allowed to happen to the carrier force before then. Alabaster saw what he recognized to be the shack and sprung toward it.

Inside the headquarters, twenty yards away, the Red Prince was breathing heavily, thoughts of escape interrupted by the apparent error taking place before his eyes.

"Mohammed, the Americans' strategy is wrong. Why are they not attacking the barracks? Why do they not launch their forces at those inside, the real threats to them? Why did they not land back there to begin with? Their first objective should have been to kill the carriers."

"Does it matter, Ali?" al-Kahir asked hysterically. "We are beaten, finished. They have won."

Salameh seemed not to hear him. His fingers were webbed around his temples, trembling. "Unless . . . Unless . . . They want the carriers alive. I failed to see it. . . . We had already won and I didn't see it."

"Enough, Ali! We must make our escape! We're running out of time."

"It's the Americans who are running out of time. Yes, they have precious little time left and we can take even that away from them."

"We have lost. Let us save ourselves before it is too late," al-Kahir said rapidly.

"*We have won!*" The Red Prince clenched his fingers into tight fists that pounded the air in front of his face. "Don't you see, Mohammed? Shaitan is spreading even now. It didn't die with the people of Crescent Falls. The Americans tricked us! They tricked us! . . ."

"Such a conclusion contradicts everything we know about the organism. You have gone mad, Ali. We must get out of here *now!* Soon it will be too late."

413

"It is already too late, for us as well as America. But we have one final task to perform. The Americans are here to capture the carriers in an attempt to save themselves. It's their last chance; *we* can make it fail. *We must kill the Shaitan force!*"

Al-Kahir's face was contorted in disbelief. "Arafat was right: You *have* lost your mind. You refuse to realize that it's over."

"Because it won't be until we destroy the carriers. And then it will be over only for America." Salameh shuffled quickly toward the door. "I will get the plastic explosives. You must help me, Mohammed. We must blow up the barracks."

Al-Kahir shook his head. "I am staying here, Ali. This is the end of the road for me."

Salameh smiled. "As you wish."

With that, he reached inside his jacket and withdrew a Browning automatic, pointing it at al-Kahir's chest. The planner's eyes exploded with shock, his face scarlet. But only for a moment.

The Red Prince fired.

In the equipment shack, Alabaster had stuffed the unjammed .45 into his pants while he searched for something that would serve the purpose of a lock. The carriers could not be expected to remain inside much longer. They were professionals, but not of a sort used to the overwhelming possibility of imminent death. Panic would soon overtake them. He had considered staying inside the barracks to restrict their movement but there were other matters to attend to. The Red Prince was here and he wanted the pleasure of killing him.

The Israeli was in the rear of the fifteen-by-fifteen foot cinder block shed, filled with boxes of mothballed tools and equipment that were placed on storage shelves that had small aisles between them. He had just caught sight of some garden tools when the heavy door of the small building opened and closed again. His back was turned but the feeling that entered the small perimeter was unmistakable. Alabaster whirled to the rear, his hand on the .45's grip.

As he drew the pistol, his eyes locked on the figure standing in the half-light, a bald head glinting atop a massive frame. A slight smile etched on the scarred, twisted features of the face.

Seif!

Without taking his eyes from the monstrous man before him, Alabaster squared the .45 forward. But the Butcher was more than equal to the task, dodging with lightning quickness to his left and hurling a shiny object in the direction of the Israeli's midsection. But Alabaster too had spun, thankfully away from the glimmering blade so that it sped away from his body, though not his hand. The knife crashed into the .45's barrel before he had a chance to fire it, stunning his wrist and sending the gun flying to his rear.

The two adversaries met stares, their eyes seething and sure. Simultaneously, they began to move forward.

Outside at the barracks, the Red Prince had placed padlocks through the hasps in both front and rear, sealing the carriers inside. He then set a pound of plastic explosives in four strategic areas against the outer walls of the building, sticking a timing device into the largest mound of the puttylike substance. The impact of this blast would set off the rest of the explosives. Only one timer was necessary. He set it for just over seven minutes, enough time for him to make his way around the battlefield toward the first Lear jet lined up on the runway in which he would make his escape.

The Red Prince smiled. The Shaitan force, once the means for destroying America, was now the only means that could save it. But not for much longer.

Seven minutes to be exact.

Seif made the first move, lunging at Alabaster with a huge outstretched hand that grasped for the throat. But Alabaster moved under it at the last possible second, slamming his left elbow into the Butcher's ribs as he passed by. Not waiting to gauge the effect of the blow, he pummelled his right forearm

415

into Seif's kidney from a position now behind the killer. Any normal man would have been rendered helpless by the strike. Seif, though, barely grimaced. He backed away grinning.

Alabaster was totally relaxed, his body free of tension, his mind in touch with its center. He moved closer to the giant, baiting him to make the next move. Seif snatched the bait. The Butcher sprang forward and tried to catch Alabaster off guard by sending a swirling kick toward his groin. The Israeli, though, sidestepped, caught the massive leg, and spun Seif backwards crashing into the wall with a thud that sent boxes of equipment tumbling from their raised perch onto the hard floor.

As the Butcher regained his balance, Alabaster was on him with a violent punch to the solar plexus and a crushing knee to the groin. Seif gasped only marginally before smashing the Israeli in the stomach with the heel of his hand, propelling him into a backward spin. The Butcher, sensing the advantage, lunged but found only air when Alabaster whirled to avoid the attack. He tried to regain his balance, failed, and careened into a six-foot station of shelves. Equipment toppled everywhere. Boxes split and emptied their contents on the floor.

A chain saw landed by Seif's feet.

Alabaster was moving toward him for what he hoped would be the kill when he saw the Butcher grasp it from his half-sitting position and tug at the machine's starter chord. It sputtered but then roared to a deafening start, rising and fading in regular intervals. The eighteen inch blade turned furiously around as the Butcher climbed back to his feet. Alabaster could only partially make out the swirling blur of promised death as he backpedaled, considering his options and finding none.

Seif levelled the rotating monster before him and edged forward, forcing the Israeli to retreat further. His huge fingers were draped around the handle, one on the control regulating the speed of the chain with which he continually revved the small engine and made the blur swing in and out of clarity. Suddenly the Butcher lurched, the saw an extension of his upper body heading directly for its target's stomach.

But Alabaster avoided the surge by stepping away so that Seif was at once behind him. He lashed out with a powerful strike that found the rear of the huge head. The Butcher wavered but did not fall. He turned to face Alabaster once more at the same time the Israeli reached for a pitchfork on the floor.

Seif lunged, the steel of the chain met by the teeth of the pitchfork. The killer backed off and revved the engine. Without hesitating further, he lashed out, the saw's surge again stopped by the impact of the pitchfork upon it. A twisted clanging sound echoed in the small shack.

At this moment, Alabaster tried to turn his defensive weapon into an offensive one by thrusting the pitchfork under the saw at the Butcher's legs. Seif, though, responded immediately and deflected the weapon toward the cement floor with his saw and then brought the rotating blade up for Alabaster's chest. The kill seemed near.

And it would have come to pass had not Alabaster seen the action unfold quickly enough to grasp the pitchfork's handle with both hands spaced far apart and bring the tool upwards in an arc that lifted the chain away from him. But the blade sliced through the wooden handle like it was paper and roared at him again, swinging death downward. Alabaster ducked under the saw then maneuvered to the Butcher's rear. The saw gave Seif power but cut down his mobility. Once behind him, the Israeli would be able to strike a hard, fast blow to the small of the back.

Such was the plan. But the Butcher anticipated it perfectly. He recoiled and used a powerful leg to trip Alabaster up, sending him reeling to the surface below. Dazed, the Israeli looked up to see the chain saw descending on line with his throat and jerked his body to the side just in time to avoid death.

The saw, though, sliced into the muscular flesh across his left shoulder. Blood spurted, coating the steel blade, and Alabaster felt the seething agony pour through him. He thought he screamed but wasn't sure because the noise was

417

buried by the swirling grind above him. The cut was deep and jagged. Alabaster first smelled his own blood and then tasted it on his lips. He felt himself weaken and knew his left arm would be virtually useless.

The world darkened for an instant but light returned in time for the Israeli to see the chain saw descending toward his midsection. Instinctively he thrust his hands forward and locked his fingers on the shaft just above the blade. Hot slivers of pain soared through his left arm into his head. His blood was everywhere around him. His strength couldn't hold out much longer. For the moment, though, the machine's motion toward him had been stopped. The blade twirled six inches from his torso, the smell of gasoline heavy on his nostrils. He pushed up with all his strength.

Seif revved the engine and tried to force the blade downward, succeeding to cut the distance from his target's stomach in half to three inches. Alabaster's head and shoulders lay suspended in the air, pulsating with agonized tension. Beneath him the asphalt continued to redden. The muscles of his large arms strained and flexed, glowing with sweat and blood. They shook violently as his hands tightened their grasp on the shaft to better maintain the stalemate against the Butcher's concerted effort to push the blade into his flesh. His mangled arm was almost numb now. The circulation had begun to leave his hand. Shredded ligaments and tendons had been exposed beneath his shirt. But the Israeli didn't see them because his fading eyes remained frozen on the killer above him and the churning weapon about to rip into his abdomen.

Alabaster pushed his drained body further, straining to force his shoulders up to better his position. His momentum, though, had stopped. He had gone as far as he could go. The best he could hope for now was an eternal draw, two mortal foes locked in this position for an infinity or until Commander Ferguson's troops came to the rescue.

Which was too much to hope for, because Seif was summoning all the reserves of his vast strength. Muscles cracked and popped beneath his tattered jacket. The swirling blade began to descend again. Almost unnoticeable in its gradual motion, but descending all the same. The grinding sound ripped into the Israeli's eardrums.

Two-and-a-half inches . . . Two . . .

The flesh of Alabaster's midsection tightened in a violent spasm of anticipated penetration. He pushed his muscles past the breaking point, feeling ligaments stretch and pull in his shoulders from the strain. The pain was staggering, hot needles jabbing in and out of his arms as he tried to resist the killer's force. The blade was little more than an inch above him. Would it be better to submit? Was a quick death—

No! No!

Other thoughts tore through his mind, confronting the one that had somehow snuck in. Above him was the man who had killed Rivkah, Isser, Stanislaw and Moshe. It could not end for him here, not this way. There was one chance, born in desperation, to be executed with such perfect motion that success seemed impossible. He grasped for it because it was all he had.

His strategy set, Alabaster allowed the blade to descend until he could feel its heat above his skin and his shirt began to tear. Bits of smoke rose as chain met fabric. At that moment, that *precise* moment, the Israeli jerked his body to the right and his arms to the left, burying the chain saw in the cement suddenly beneath it. The gears howled in protest, spitting steel, tearing themselves apart. The engine died. The chain snapped. Seif lost his balance.

Still perched on the cement, resting half on his side and half on his back, Alabaster shot his right foot upwards and caught the Butcher with a glancing blow to the temple. Already dazed, Seif felt his bearings totally betray him when a second kick surged savagely into his neck near the windpipe, hurling him backwards in a massive heap.

More angered than injured, the Butcher allowed his calm to desert him, leaping forward at the enemy still propped up on

419

the floor. Seif's fingers poised themselves to dig into the flesh around Alabaster's neck and he pounced. Before they reached the throat, though, the fingers tensed outward in a violent spasm. Seif's eyes went glassy. He gasped, feeling something tear in and through him, conscious for a fleeting second that the contents of his stomach and torso were spilling out below him.

The sharp end of the broken pitchfork had totally imbedded itself in the body above it. Alabaster released the pressure on its shaft and moved his now red hand away, allowing the huge frame to plunge downward in its final death throes. A gurgling sound emerged from the blood-soaked mouth. The Butcher's fingers fought to grope for something that no longer existed. Seif collapsed in a final spasm, his abdomen held over the red stained cement by the iron teeth still wedged deeply through him. His huge eyes lost whatever color they might have possessed and locked in a death stare.

But Alabaster had no time to rejoice. He sprang to his feet, the hot shots of pain pouring through his entire upper body. His torn shoulder was numb. Still he brought his right hand up to comfort it, perhaps to reassure himself it remained attached to the rest of his body. The blood, he found, had stopped pouring from the wound. He ran out the door of the equipment shed and realized that the regular wailing of bullets had stopped. Only an occasional spurt sounded, signalling that Gamma Group had closed in on another terrorist. The Deliverers of Death were safe. The Israeli moved toward the barracks.

The timing device ticked past the final minute. . . . Forty-five seconds now . . .

Alabaster heard the pounding on the doors and windows of the building before him. Screams shouted something that barely reached his ears in their desperate pitch, bellowed through windows broken with bare hands.

"There's a bomb! Help us! Help us!"

Thirty seconds . . .

Alabaster sped forward. In the end, the Red Prince had recognized the truth and had taken steps to eliminate the only means America had to avoid 120 million fatalities. He reached the barracks breathless with fear, guessing a minimum of three charges would have been planted. In one of them would lie a timing mechanism that, if not disarmed, would cause the building to go up in a torrent of fury that would spray scarlet vapor into the air.

Twenty seconds . . .

The first mound of plastic, wedged on the right side of the building, contained no fuse or timer. Another mound was stuck against the peeling paint twenty-five feet away. He ran for it.

Fifteen seconds . . .

Again nothing. Almost losing his balance and panting heavily, Alabaster turned the corner. Another white mound appeared before him. This one, too, lacked a timer.

Ten seconds . . .

He was at the final mound now. A black shape glimmered before his eyes, stuck firmly into the thick explosives. He tugged at the small device and fought to remove it without setting the blast off. His body trembled inside, as though to anticipate the explosion that would cast it into a thoughtless vacuum.

Eight . . . seven . . . six . . .

Finally it was free, resting in his hands, its rhythmical ticking stripping away what remained of his sanity. Alabaster lifted the device over his shoulder and threw it like a baseball with all the force his torn muscles could muster.

The black box exploded with a soft pop in midair. The Shaitan force was safe. The Deliverers of Death would become the sustainers of life.

David saw Captain Tut Ferguson's bulky frame running toward him.

"You look like hell," the commander said with a wry smile.

"You don't look so great yourself."

The smile vanished. "I lost nine men."

"But you got the terrorists."

"Captured fourteen. Killed the rest. We haven't done a body count yet. All the Lear pilots surrendered. Claimed they didn't know what the hell they'd been hired for."

"What about Salameh?"

"Haven't had time to think about him."

Both men heard the soft sputter of a jet engine revving up, readying the machine for takeoff.

"That's one of the Lears," Ferguson said, turning toward the airstrip. "But who the hell's in it?"

"Give me your rifle!" the Israeli commanded.

"What?"

Alabaster felt a blazing bolt of pain shoot through his mangled shoulder as he grabbed the M-16 from Ferguson's arms and headed toward the helicopters.

The Lear jet that had been first in the long progression pulled onto the runway and began to edge its way forward. It was quickly past the helicopters, headed for the open sky and freedom. The widely scattered Gamma Group commandoes lit out after it. With the end of the battle, though, had come a letdown so that their speed and enthusiasm were drained, their feet not going far or fast enough. Bullets fired from their rifles struck the white bird in non-vital areas, ricocheting off in the approaching dusk. Only one spurt did any significant damage at all, that to the left fuel line.

So when the Red Prince shoved the throttle forward in search of more power, the small jet rebelled. It furthered the distance between itself and the soldiers but the controls felt heavy and sluggish in the hands of its pilot. He tried to coax the Lear to move faster in order to lift it from the ground. The wheels struggled to rise, reached the air for a few seconds, and then bobbed back to earth. The Red Prince tried again. The jet hung in the air longer this time and still longer the time after. Just a bit more power was all he needed. . . .

The absence of an explosion had told Salameh that his

422

device had been found which meant his only hope now was to escape. He had been beaten . . . this time. But there were countless other groups similar in form and purpose to the PLO that would welcome his particular brand of expertise. He still had his copy of the black notebook that detailed the Shaitan procedure. The Commandment could be started all over again. Another time. Another place. Another disease. He would learn from his mistakes and be sure not to repeat them. It was not the end. Hardly.

Salameh pushed the throttle forward again. The engines roared. The Lear shuddered, gliding down the surface of the runway unsure of whether to leave or to stay. Finally the wheels parted from the asphalt. The jet buckled and whined but rose all the same. That was it; he had done it!

The helicopter appeared before him just when the Lear had begun to climb upwards in what was for it pitifully slow fashion. Alabaster had taken the jet-powered chopper on a direct route meant to intercept Salameh which is exactly what had happened. The Red Prince flinched for a moment before turning the wheel a hair to the right, darting past the helicopter but losing precious altitude in the process.

Not this time, Alabaster, not this time, he thought.

Alabaster steadied his hand on the chopper control knob and circled for another pass. His left shoulder was still numb but there was feeling in his hand which would have to stay if he was going to stop the Red Prince here and now. He watched the Lear's nose rise and fall. Once, twice, three times. The machine was struggling to maintain its present height, no less climb further. Then he was in front of it again, hovering, daring Salameh to charge him. Again the Red Prince altered his path, this time to the left, and once more the steel bird lost a measure of the altitude it would need to roar upwards to freedom.

Inside the Lear, Salameh pressed buttons and turned knobs frantically. Finally he found the right combination. The machine lurched in the air with sudden power, bursting forward. He smiled and angled the jet for its climb for the clouds where it would be safe from Alabaster.

But there was the Jew again, whirling forward directly in line with the Lear, forcing him to change course. The engine sputtered. The steel bird aborted its attempt to climb and hung limbolike at an unvarying altitude.

Inside the chopper, Alabaster wiped the sweat from his face as the jet tore past him. He pushed the control knob to its furthest limits and began to gain gradually on the Lear, knowing he would have only one more chance. Then, even though the jet's fuel line was leaking, the Red Prince would be able to make another escape. His flying range would be greatly reduced but Salameh would still find his way to another airport and then flee to another country. That couldn't be allowed to happen.

Alabaster moved his right hand from the controls to the M-16 on the seat beside him. The distance between the high-powered chopper and the injured jet had been cut in half when his finger reached the trigger and he raised the gun toward the open window, resting the tip of its barrel on the metal frame. The control knob shook in his throbbing left hand.

The two flying machines were almost even now but overtaking the jet was still a long shot. Alabaster knew that Salameh wasn't much of a pilot but even a poor one would locate the necessary power to compensate for the jet's handicap and lead it into the heavens before long. Only fifteen yards separated the chopper from the Lear's right wing, and Alabaster thought for a moment about ramming the jet and sending both machines—and pilots—into a flaming inferno. The moment was brief.

For the Red Prince had been responsible for the loss of enough life. There could be no more, not even indirectly.

Alabaster tensed his finger on the M-16's trigger and readied the chopper for the final assault.

The Red Prince shoved the throttle arm forward once more, his eyes locked on the helicopter just off his right wing. The nose of the Lear turned upward. The jet was finally climbing, charging into the wind, refusing to be denied. Coinciding with that moment of ascent, though, was a temporary loss of speed. Not much but enough to allow Alabaster to slice by, rising above the jet and planting himself right in its path.

Alabaster spun the controls one last time so that the M-16 faced the approaching Lear. He took the best aim he could as the white bird roared toward him. For a fleeting second he thought his eyes had met the Red Prince's.

He pulled the trigger and held it.

The long bullets spit forward, shattering the glass of the cockpit. Salameh had seen the assault coming in time to push his body down so that none of the bullets found it. But as he ducked his shoulder struck the steering mechanism, angling the Lear's wings at a level that forced it to bank downward. So the next series of M-16 bullets tore into its already damaged fuel tank and ruptured it totally. The jet skipped forward, skirting the air, its engines gone. Its left wing grazed one of the helicopter's landing nodules, a blow that sent the chopper whirling wildly out of control and out of range of the blast that followed.

The Lear exploded in a thunderous flash, the body of the small craft nearly ripped in two. Fire roared from its carcass, charring the silvery metal black and crinkling it under the strain of the heat as a series of secondary eruptions sounded. The carcass crackled a final orange epitaph, then began to fall. The flames clawed and scratched at the blue sky, attempting to maintain their grasp. But the grasp slipped. The jet had been reduced to metallic cinders before it even reached the ground.

Alabaster, though, had seen none of this because he was trying desperately and futilely to regain control of the helicopter. The chopper swirled and banked, its propeller angled downwards, the machine's equilibrium grossly out of whack. The control knob vibrated madly in the Israeli's hands. His teeth chattered in rhythm with the convulsions his body was forced to endure. His stomach mounted a frantic charge for his throat. He closed his eyes and waited for the final impact as the plunge continued.

It came seconds later.

Alabaster's head seemed to explode. A kaleidscope of colors filled his eyes, fading in and out. He had a surreal vision of a huge green mattress breaking his fall. Spongy and resilient. It felt as though the chopper was still in the air and would remain there suspended in time and space forever.

Then he was drifting, drifting . . .

EPILOGUE

"Another cup of coffee, Vern?" The President grasped the handle on the pot before him centered on the neatly set breakfast table in the Rose Garden. He was a vigorous looking man with carefully colored hair that disguised his years.

"No thanks, Mr. President," Colonel Rossi replied. "My doctor recommends against a second cup in the morning."

"A new diet, I suppose."

"One that will hopefully keep me alive a bit longer."

"And what about the rest of America?"

It had been fourteen days since the Gamma Group commandoes had escorted the 175 Shaitan carriers from Melrose Airforce Base to Atlanta via the same jet they had entered the country in.

"Dr. Lewiston wasted no time in isolating a vaccine. Production began immediately and distribution soon after that," Rossi explained. "By now almost one half of the country has been innoculated. The process is proceeding smoothly with a minimum of panic. We've come up with a cover story dealing with a new strain of lethal flu virus that hit the U.S. without warning. And Lewiston is communicating the formula for the vaccine to similar centers all over the world to prevent further outbreaks of Shaitan."

"I trust we are getting something in exchange for our services."

"Sir?"

"It just seems to me that the countries of the world owe us quite a debt for providing them with the formula. I'd like to be able to call it in someday, Vern."

"That may not be wise, sir. Shaitan is better laid to rest. The

427

less anybody remembers about it the better."

"At least we still have those 175 vials," the President rejoiced, taking a hearty sip of his coffee.

"Not anymore."

"What do you mean?"

"I had them destroyed."

"Who the hell authorized that?"

"I did."

"You may have overstepped yourself this time, Vern."

Rossi glanced at his wheelchair. "In this contraption, that's quite an accomplishment."

The President backed off. "So where do we stand?"

"Hospitals all over the country still have patients packed like sardines in the aisles. Clinics have been set up in town halls and gymnasiums. People are still getting sick and will be for some time."

"How many do we stand to lose?"

"It's difficult to say. Lewiston estimates somewhere in the vicinity of half a million."

The President sighed. "So many people . . ."

"It could've been a lot more, the whole country even."

"I guess we should be grateful."

"The credit belongs with Rabanine—Alabaster, that is, sir."

"Ah, yes. How is he?"

"Pretty well banged up, I'm afraid. His helicopter's fall was broken by a grove of trees. That's the only thing that saved his life. He had a broken leg, a concussion, a helluva lot of contusions and a shoulder that may never work right again. They used enough sutures on him to keep an emergency room stocked for a month."

"But he *will* live."

"For sure."

"And after he recuperates?"

"He may never recuperate fully, sir. And if he does, that decision lies with him."

The President drained the rest of his coffee. "Where is he now?"

"We've secured some property for him and his son under twenty-four hour guard in one of our safe towns."

"Which one?"

"US 16."

The President leaned forward. "Let's not quibble, Vern. You know as well as I do that safe towns are nothing more than elaborate retirement communities and I hardly think Alabaster is ready for retirement."

"The point is that he might. He's done a helluva lot for us. We owe him this much."

"Whatever you say, Vern. It's your department. What about Crescent Falls?"

"Dr. Lewiston says that Shaitan particles are still dangerously thick in the air around the town in a radius that's gradually widening. He recommends seal off. Code Omega X."

"*Total* neutralization."

"That's the size of it."

"I see." The President brought his right hand up to meet his chin. "A tactical Capricorn should do the job. I'll arrange for clearance this afternoon."

"Good. And I've left some papers with your secretary for you to sign pertaining to the appointment of James 'Bugsy' Tyler as a federal marshall."

"My signature should cut through the red tape."

"That's the idea."

"Couldn't agree with you more, Vern. I just as soon get everyone connected with this mess out of the way, speaking of which whatever happened to that woman from Rhode Island who got herself tangled up in this affair?"

"I personally decided that her involvement will place her life in perpetual danger for an indefinite period into the future. Since I feel personally responsible for her well-being, I took the liberty of arranging a stay for her in one of our safe towns as well."

"Which one?"

"US 16."

"Interesting coincidence," the President noted.

Rossi merely smiled.

Ground Zero . . .

The sun came up slowly over the barren wasteland that had once been the town of Crescent Falls. It was a cool, slightly overcast morning, the hot spell long since ended. The temperature was seasonable, perhaps a little below. The breeze picked up, turning into a stiff wind that spread dust and small rocks over Main Street. This day had begun just as yesterday had and the day before that. Time seemed frozen. Or maybe there had never been any such thing at all.

On the horizon, a small shape appeared and grew steadily as it swept across the sky closer to town. Behind it a trail of white exhaust stained the air, slowly dissipating into nothingness. The jet engines were roaring at an even, unfaltering pitch when the streamline steel bird angled its wings and banked downward for the pass.

One pass. One pass only.

The jet fighter was over Main Street now, a mile up, slicing through a dawn sky that squealed in protest. A cylindrical object had been released. The jet tore upwards, climbing fast, quickly out of sight though its roar could still be heard if there had been anyone around to hear it.

The object was falling . . . falling . . . falling . . .

The explosion came with the impact, shattering the stillness of the dawn, the blinding light brighter than any the sun could muster. Buildings shook violently and then disappeared. The pavement on Main Street melted under the heat and sunk into the ground. For an instant, the entire town blazed angry red. Then the color was swallowed by a mushroom-shaped white cloud that enveloped the town and stretched for the sky.

When the cloud finally receded, all color was gone. Everything was gone. There was . . . nothing. As though there had been nothing to start with .

Crescent Falls had vanished into oblivion.

THE CONTINUING MERCENARY SERIES
BY AXEL KILGORE

#8: ASSASSIN'S EXPRESS (955, $2.50)

Intrigue at every curve. That's what Frost finds while driving a sultry undercover agent from Los Angeles to Washington, D.C. But someone wants them off the road, and Frost has to find out why!

#9: THE TERROR CONTRACT (985, $2.50)

Frost follows a bloody trail of killings and kidnappings when he infiltrates a global terror network. His aim: to seek revenge on the gang that killed his woman!

#10: BUSH WARFARE (1023, $2.50)

Hijacked in Africa, Frost awakens in a jungle and finds himself poisoned by a deadly woman. After he gets the antidote—he plans to give her a taste of her own medicine!

#11: DEATH LUST! (1056, $2.50)

Frost is trailing the treacherous Eva Chapman, a munitions runner who has enough weapons to field an army. He vows to killer her—before she plunges the world into nuclear war!

#12: HEADSHOT! (1129, $2.50)

As Frost fights against Castro death squads, M-19 guerillas, and professional hitmen, it's hard for him to figure if the fiery beauty who hired him wants him more as a lover—or as a target!

#13: NAKED BLADE, NAKED GUN (1162, $2.50)

When the merc runs into an old adversary—who blew away his C.O. back in 'Nam—he's on a trail that leads to the murderously eager arms of a group of religious fanatics—being run from Moscow!

Available wherever paperbacks are sold, or order direct from the Publisher. Send cover price plus 50¢ per copy for mailing and handling to Zebra Books, 475 Park Avenue South, New York, N.Y. 10016. DO NOT SEND CASH.

COMING SOON!